P9-DFK-756

These twelve engrossing adventures involve the famous detective and his loyal friend with:

- A young man who irrationally smashes clocks
- A distressed parson with a hotheaded nephew who might be accused of murder
- The grievous domestic tragedy that occurs in a locked room
- A dealer in jewels who is obsessively fond of his umbrella
- The innocent victim of a trap fashioned 400 years before

And seven more unusual and exciting cases, all faithfully recorded by the inimitable Dr. Watson.

THE EXPLOITS OF SHERLOCK HOLMES

*by Adrian Conan Doyle
and John Dickson Carr*

PUBLISHED BY POCKET BOOKS NEW YORK

THE EXPLOITS OF SHERLOCK HOLMES

Random House edition published 1952

POCKET BOOK edition published July, 1976

4th printing.....................October, 1976

The Exploits of Sherlock Holmes—with the exception
of one story, which was published in *Life* Magazine
—appeared in *Collier's* Magazine, which originally
published some of the Holmes stories by Sir Arthur
Conan Doyle.

This POCKET BOOK edition includes every word contained in
the original, higher-priced edition. It is printed from brand-
new plates made from completely reset, clear, easy-to-read type.
POCKET BOOK editions are published by
POCKET BOOKS,
a division of Simon & Schuster, Inc.,
A GULF+WESTERN COMPANY
630 Fifth Avenue,
New York, N.Y. 10020.
Trademarks registered in the United States
and other countries.

ISBN: 0-671-80604-1.
Library of Congress Catalog Card Number: 54-5387.

Cover art by Roger Kastel.

Printed in the U.S.A.

CONTENTS

ALWAYS HOLMES

It is fairly certain that no reader of the *Strand Magazine* in 1887 could have guessed that Sherlock Holmes and Dr. Watson, then making their debut in that British magazine, would soon become the world's most famous characters of fiction. It is, however, quite certain that their creator, Sir Arthur Conan Doyle, had no inkling of it at that time nor many years later when he decided to do away with Holmes by having him pushed off a cliff at the Reichenbach Falls. This incident created such repercussions that public clamor forced Conan Doyle to bring his hero right back to life and to the familiar surroundings of his lodgings at 221 B Baker Street.

In view of Holmes's immense popularity it is not surprising that in the hearts and minds of hundreds of millions his name has not only become a household word, but also that of a man thought to have lived. Actually, the invention of Holmes is much less an invention than some people think. The chivalry of Holmes, his penetrating mind, his erudition, his physical feats and his entire character are really and truly those of the genius who created him. Sir Arthur in real life, as Holmes in fiction, came to the rescue of people convicted for crimes they did not commit and he used the very logic and deductive reasoning that enabled Holmes to solve the problems of his clients. Sir Arthur, like Holmes, was a man of unusual physical strength who would undoubtedly have been a great boxer had he pursued that endeavor rather than being first a doctor, then a writer.

Even Holmes's background, to a certain extent, parallels that of the man who created him.

Though his ancestors were of the Irish landed gentry, Sir Arthur's grandmother, like Holmes's was of French extraction. His grandfather, John Doyle, was the most brilliant political cartoonist of the early 1800's. His uncle Richard ("Dicky") Doyle drew the cover for *Punch* which is still used. His uncle Henry Doyle was the director of the National Gallery of Ireland. His uncle James the compiler of *The Chronicle of England.* Sir Arthur Conan Doyle and his immediate forbears are the only family in Great Britain to have given in the space of three generations five separate members to the record of achievement, *The National Biography*.

And yet, despite his distinguished ancestry, despite his celebrated historical novels, and despite his glorious Boer War record, Conan Doyle is best known to the world for having created Sherlock Holmes.

Since 1887, books of Sherlock Holmes have been translated into every known language and have never been out of print. Holmes has been the hero of fifteen different legitimate stage plays, more than one thousand radio dramatizations, and he is now making his television debut in America, having already appeared on television in England.

Some of the investigative methods created for Holmes by Sir Arthur were shortly thereafter adopted by Scotland Yard, the French Sûreté and police forces of many other nations. Holmes has even become the cult of many societies and the object of many imitations all of which have failed to catch the spirit of the man about whom Somerset Maugham says, in his recent book, *The Vagrant Mood:* "No detective stories have had the popularity of Conan Doyle's and because of the invention of Sherlock Holmes I think it may be admitted that none has so well deserved it."

It is fortunate for the millions of Holmes's admirers that this new series of stories, *The Exploits of Sherlock Holmes,* comes from the pen of Sir Arthur's youngest son, Adrian Conan Doyle, in collaboration with John Dickson Carr, who is the author of the widely acclaimed

Life of Sir Arthur Conan Doyle, and has also written many of probably the best contemporary mystery novels.

Adrian Conan Doyle, the author of *Heaven Has Claws*, a personal-experience book about his deep-sea fishing expeditions, was brought up in the tradition of the Victorian era and in close contact with his father. The son, like the father, has a lust for adventure, cherishes relics of the past, and above all has the same sense of chivalry that so completely characterized his father—or should we say Holmes?

Adrian Conan Doyle uses the very desk on which his father wrote. He is surrounded by the same objects that his father handled, and he has in every way endeavored to recreate each particle of atmosphere that formed Sir Arthur's environment.

The Exploits of Sherlock Holmes are based on the unsolved cases to which Watson refers in the original fifty-six short stories and four novels. Sherlockians will find added interest in the quotations which appear at the end of each story. Here are the references to the unsolved cases of Sherlock Holmes as they appeared in the original stories by Arthur Conan Doyle and which the present authors used as their points of departure for the twelve cases which follow. The plots are new, but the stories are painstaking reproductions of the originals, in construction as well as in texture. Conan Doyle and Carr wrote together "The Adventure of the Seven Clocks" and "The Adventure of the Gold Hunter." "The Adventure of the Wax Gamblers" and "The Adventure of the Highgate Miracle" were written almost entirely by Carr. "The Adventure of the Black Baronet" and "The Adventure of the Sealed Room" were written almost entirely by Conan Doyle. The last six stories were conceived and written by Adrian Conan Doyle after John Dickson Carr suffered a brief illness.

The *Exploits* were inspired by the single desire of producing stories of the "old vintage"; of recreating those moments of true delight when the approaching step of a new client tells us that "the game's afoot," or when Holmes unravels his solutions to the astonished questioning of his colleagues, as in these celebrated four lines from "Silver Blaze," when the inspector asks Holmes:

"Is there any point to which you wish to draw my attention?"

"To the curious incident of the dog in the night-time."

"The dog did nothing in the night-time."

"That was the curious incident," remarked Holmes.

—THE PUBLISHERS

THE EXPLOITS OF
SHERLOCK HOLMES

1

The Adventure of the Seven Clocks

I find recorded in my notebook that it was on the afternoon of Wednesday, the 16th of November, 1887, when the attention of my friend Mr. Sherlock Holmes was first drawn to the singular affair of the man who hated clocks.

I have written elsewhere that I had heard only a vague account of this matter, since it occurred shortly after my marriage. Indeed, I have gone so far as to state that my first post-nuptial call on Holmes was in March of the following year. But the case in question was a matter of such extreme delicacy that I trust my readers will forgive its suppression by one whose pen has ever been guided by discretion rather than by sensationalism.

A few weeks following my marriage, then, my wife was obliged to leave London on a matter which concerned Thaddeus Sholto and vitally affected our future fortunes. Finding our new home insupportable without her presence, for eight days I returned to the old rooms in Baker Street. Sherlock Holmes made me welcome without question or comment. Yet I must confess that the next day, the 16th of November, began inauspiciously.

It was bitter, frosty weather. All morning the yellow-brown fog pressed against the windows. Lamps and gas-jets were burning, as well as a good fire, and their light shone on a breakfast-table uncleared at past midday.

Sherlock Holmes was moody and distraught. Curled up in his arm-chair in the old mouse-coloured dressing-gown and with a cherry-wood pipe in his mouth, he scanned the morning newspapers, now and again uttering some derisive comment.

"You find little of interest?" I asked.

"My dear Watson," said he, "I begin to fear that life has become one flat and monotonous plain ever since the affair of the notorious Blessington."

"And yet," I remonstrated, "surely this has been a year of memorable cases? You are over-stimulated, my dear fellow."

" 'Pon my word, Watson, you are scarcely the man to preach on that subject. Last night, after I had ventured to offer you a bottle of Beaune at dinner, you held forth so interminably on the joys of wedlock that I feared you would never have done."

"My dear fellow! You imply that I was over-stimulated with wine!" My friend regarded me in his singular fashion.

"Not with wine, perhaps," said he. "However!" And he indicated the newspapers. "Have you glanced over the balderdash with which the press have seen fit to regale us!"

"I fear not. This copy of the *British Medical Journal*—"

"Well, well!" said he. "Here we find column upon column devoted to next year's racing season. For some reason it seems perpetually to astonish the British public that one horse can run faster than another. Again, for the dozenth time, we have the Nihilists hatching some dark plot against the Grand Duke Alexei at Odessa. One entire leading article is devoted to the doubtless trenchant question, 'Should Shop-Assistants Marry?' "

I forbore to interrupt him, lest his bitterness increase.

"Where is crime, Watson? Where is the *weird,* where that touch of the *outré* without which a problem in itself is as sand and dry grass? Have we lost them forever?"

"Hark!" said I. "Surely that was the bell?"

"And someone in a hurry, if we may judge from its clamour."

With one accord we stepped to the window, and looked down into Baker Street. The fog had partly lifted. At the kerb before our door stood a handsome closed carriage. A top-hatted coachman in livery was just closing the carriage-door, whose panel bore the letter "M." From below came the murmur of voices followed by light, quick footsteps on the stairs, and the door of our sitting-room was flung open.

Both of us were surprised, I think, to perceive that our caller was a young lady: a girl, rather, since she could hardly have been as much as eighteen, and seldom in a young face have I seen such beauty and refinement as well as sensitiveness. Her large blue eyes regarded us with agitated appeal. Her abundant auburn hair was confined in a small hat; and over her travelling-dress she wore a dark-red jacket trimmed with strips of astrakhan. In one gloved hand she held a travelling-case with the letters "C.F." over some sort of label. Her other hand was pressed to her heart.

"Oh, please, please forgive this intrusion!" she pleaded, in a breathless but low and melodious voice. "Which of you, I beg, is Mr. Sherlock Holmes?"

My companion inclined his head.

"I am Mr. Holmes. This is my friend and colleague, Dr. Watson."

"Thank heaven I have found you at home! My errand—"

But our visitor could go no further than "My errand." She stammered, a deep blush spread up over her face, and she lowered her eyes. Gently Sherlock Holmes took the travelling-case from her hand, and pushed an arm-chair towards the fire.

"Pray be seated, madam, and compose yourself," said he, laying aside his cherry-wood pipe.

"I thank you, Mr. Holmes," replied the young lady, shrinking into the chair and giving him a grateful look. "They say, sir, that you can read the human heart."

"H'm! For poetry, I fear, you must address yourself to Watson."

"That you can read the secrets of your clients, and even the—the errands upon which they come, when they have said not a single word!"

"They over-estimate my powers," he answered, smiling. "Beyond the obvious facts that you are a lady's companion, that you seldom travel yet have recently returned from a journey to Switzerland, and that your errand here concerns a man who has engaged your affections, I can deduce nothing."

The young lady gave a violent start, and I myself was taken aback.

"Holmes," cried I, "this is too much. How could you possibly know this?"

"How, indeed?" echoed the young lady.

"I see it, I observe it. The travelling-case, though far from new, is neither worn nor battered by travel. Yet I need not insult your intelligence by calling attention to the paper label of the Hotel Splendide, at Grindelwald in Switzerland, which has been affixed with gum to the side of the case."

"But the other point?" I insisted.

"The lady's attire, though in impeccable taste, is neither new nor costly. Yet she has stayed at the best hotel in Grindelwald, and she arrives in a carriage of the well-to-do. Since her own initials, 'C.F.,' do not match the 'M.' on the carriage-panel, we may assume her to occupy a position of equality in some well-to-do family. Her youth precludes the position of governess, and we are left with a lady's companion. As for the man who has engaged her affections, her blushes and lowered eyelids proclaim as much. Absurd, is it not?"

"But it is true, Mr. Holmes!" cried our visitor, clasping her hands together in even deeper agitation. "My name is Celia Forsythe, and for over a year I have been companion to Lady Mayo, of Groxton Low Hall, in Surrey. Charles—"

"Charles? That is the name of the gentleman in question?"

Miss Forsythe nodded her head without looking up.

"If I hesitate to speak of him," she continued, "it is because I fear you may laugh at me. I fear you may think me mad; or, worse still, that poor Charles himself is mad."

"And why should I think so, Miss Forsythe?"

"Mr. Holmes, he cannot endure the sight of a clock!"

"Of a clock?"

"In the past fortnight, sir, and for no explicable reason, he has destroyed seven clocks. Two of them he smashed in public, and before my own eyes!"

Sherlock Holmes rubbed his long, thin fingers together.

"Come," said he, "this is most satis—most curious. Pray continue your narrative."

"I despair of doing so, Mr. Holmes. Yet I will try. For the past year I have been very happy in the employ of Lady Mayo. I must tell you that both my parents are dead, but I received a good education and such references as I could obtain were fortunately satisfactory. Lady Mayo, I must acknowledge, is of somewhat forbidding appearance. She is of the old school, stately and austere. Yet to me she has been kindness itself. In fact, it was she who suggested that we take the holiday in Switzerland, fearing that the isolation of Groxton Low Hall might depress my spirits. In the train between Paris and Grindelwald we met—met Charles. I should say Mr. Charles Hendon."

Holmes had relapsed into the arm-chair, putting his finger-tips together as was his wont when he was in a judicial mood.

"Then this was the first time you had met the gentleman?" he asked.

"Oh, yes!"

"I see. And how did the acquaintanceship come about?"

"A trifling matter, Mr. Holmes. We three were alone in a first-class carriage. Charles's manners are so beautiful, his voice so fine, his smile so captivating—"

"No doubt. But pray be precise as to details."

Miss Forsythe opened wide her large blue eyes.

"I believe it was the window," said she. "Charles (I may tell you that he has remarkable eyes and a heavy brown moustache) bowed and requested Lady Mayo's permission to lower the window. She assented, and in a few moments they were chatting together like old friends."

"H'm! I see."

"Lady Mayo, in turn, presented me to Charles. The journey to Grindelwald passed quickly and happily. And yet, no sooner had we entered the foyer of the Hotel

Splendide, than there occurred the first of the horrible
shocks which have since made my life wretched.

"Despite its name, the hotel proved to be rather small
and charming. Even then, I knew Mr. Hendon for a man
of some importance, though he had described himself
modestly as a single gentleman travelling with only one
manservant. The manager of the hotel, M. Branger, approached and bowed deeply both to Lady Mayo and to
Mr. Hendon. With M. Branger he exchanged some words
in a low voice and the manager bowed deeply again.
Whereupon Charles turned round, smiling, and then quite
suddenly his whole demeanour altered.

"I can still see him standing there, in his long coat and
top hat, with a heavy malacca walking-stick under his
arm. His back was turned towards an ornamental half-
circle of ferns and evergreens surrounding a fireplace with
a low mantelshelf on which stood a Swiss clock of ex-
quisite design.

"Up to this time I had not even observed the clock.
But Charles, uttering a stifled cry, rushed towards the
fireplace. Lifting the heavy walking-stick, he brought it
crashing down on the hood of the clock, and rained
blow after blow until the clock fell in tinkling ruins on
the hearth.

"Then he turned round and walked slowly back. Without a word of explanation he took out a pocketbook,
gave to M. Branger a bank-note which would ten times
over have paid for the clock, and began lightly to speak
of other matters.

"You may well imagine, Mr. Holmes, that we stood as
though stunned. My impression was that Lady Mayo,
for all her dignity, was frightened. Yet I swear Charles
had not been frightened; he had been merely furious
and determined. At this point I caught sight of Charles's
manservant, who was standing in the background amid
luggage. He is a small, spare man with mutton-chop
whiskers; and upon his face there was an expression only
of embarrassment and, though it hurts me to breathe the
word, of deep shame.

"No word was spoken at the time, and the incident was

forgotten. For two days Charles was his usual serene self. On the third morning, when we met him in the dining-room for breakfast, it happened again.

"The windows of the dining-room had their heavy curtains partly drawn against the dazzle of sun on the first snow. The room was fairly well filled with other guests taking breakfast. Only then did I remark that Charles, who had just returned from a morning walk, still carried the malacca stick in his hand.

" 'Breathe this air, madame!' he was saying gaily to Lady Mayo. 'You will find it as invigorating as any food or drink!'

"At this he paused, and glanced towards one of the windows. Plunging past us, he struck heavily at the curtain and then tore it aside to disclose the ruins of a large clock shaped like a smiling sun-face. I think I should have fainted if Lady Mayo had not grasped my arm."

Miss Forsythe, who had removed her gloves, now pressed her hands against her cheeks.

"But not only does Charles smash clocks," she went on. "He buries them in the snow, and even hides them in the cupboard of his own room."

Sherlock Holmes had been leaning back in his chair with his eyes closed, and his head sunk into a cushion, but he now half opened his lids.

"In the cupboard?" exclaimed he, frowning. "This is even more singular! How did you become aware of the circumstance?"

"To my shame, Mr. Holmes, I was reduced to questioning his servant."

"To your shame?"

"I had no right to do so. In my humble position, Charles would never—that is, I could mean nothing to him! I had no right!"

"You had every right, Miss Forsythe," answered Holmes kindly. "Then you questioned the servant, whom you describe as a small, spare man with muttonchop whiskers. His name?"

"His name is Trepley, I believe. More than once I have heard Charles address him as 'Trep.' And I vow,

Mr. Holmes, he is the faithfullest creature alive. Even the sight of his dogged English face was a comfort to me. He knew, he felt, he sensed my—my interest, and he told me that his master had buried or concealed five other clocks. Though he refused to say so, I could tell he shared my fears. Yet Charles is not mad! He is not! You yourself must admit that, because of the final incident."

"Yes?"

"It took place only four days ago. You must know that Lady Mayo's suite included a small drawing-room containing a piano. I am passionately devoted to music, and it was my habit to play to Lady Mayo and Charles after tea. On this occasion I had scarcely begun to play when a hotel servant entered with a letter for Charles."

"One moment. Did you observe the postmark?"

"Yes; it was foreign." Miss Forsythe spoke in some surprise. "But surely it was of no importance, since you—"

"Since I—what?"

A sudden touch of bewilderment was manifest in our client's expression, and then, as though to drive away some perplexity, she hurried on with her narrative.

"Charles tore open the letter, read it, and turned deathly pale. With an incoherent exclamation he rushed from the room. When we descended half an hour later, it was only to discover that he and Trepley had departed with all his luggage. He left no message. He sent no word. I have not seen him since."

Celia Forsythe lowered her head, and tears glimmered in her eyes.

"Now, Mr. Holmes, I have been frank with you. I beg that you will be equally frank with me. What did you write in that letter?"

The question was so startling that I, for one, leaned back in my chair. Sherlock Holmes's face was without expression. His long, nervous fingers reached out for the tobacco in the Persian slipper, and began to fill a clay pipe.

"In the letter, you say," he stated rather than asked.

"Yes! You wrote that letter. I saw your signature. That is why I am here!"

"Dear me!" remarked Holmes. He was silent for several minutes, the blue smoke curling about him, and his eyes fixed vacantly upon the clock on the mantelshelf.

"There are times, Miss Forsythe," he said at last, "when one must be guarded in one's replies. I have only one more question to ask you."

"Well, Mr. Holmes?"

"Did Lady Mayo still preserve her friendliness for Mr. Charles Hendon?"

"Oh, yes! She became quite attached to him. More than once I heard her address him as Alec, apparently her nickname for him." Miss Forsythe paused, with an air of doubt, and even suspicion. "But what can you mean by such a question?"

Holmes rose to his feet.

"Only, madam, that I shall be happy to look into this matter for you. You return to Groxton Low Hall this evening?"

"Yes. But surely you have more to say to me than this? You have answered not one of my questions!"

"Well, well! I have my methods, as Watson here can tell you. But if you could find it convenient to come here, say a week from this day, at nine o'clock in the evening? Thank you. Then I shall hope to have some news for you."

Palpably it was a dismissal. Miss Forsythe rose to her feet, and looked at him so forlornly that I felt the need to interpose some word of comfort.

"Be of good cheer, madam!" I cried, gently taking her hand. "You may have every confidence in my friend Mr. Holmes; and, if I may say so, in myself as well."

I was rewarded by a gracious and grateful smile. When the door had closed behind our fair visitor, I turned to my companion with some asperity.

"I do feel, Holmes, that you might have treated the young lady with more sympathy."

"Oh? Sets the wind in that quarter?"

"Holmes, for shame!" said I, flinging myself into my

chair. "The affair is trivial, no doubt. But why you should have written a letter to this clock-breaking madman I cannot conjecture."

Holmes leaned across and laid his long, thin forefinger upon my knee.

"Watson, I wrote no such letter."

"What?" I exclaimed.

"Tut, it is not the first time my name has been borrowed by others! There is devilry here, Watson, else I am much mistaken."

"You take it seriously, then?"

"So seriously that I leave for the Continent tonight."

"For the Continent? For Switzerland?"

"No, no; what have we to do with Switzerland? Our trail lies further afield."

"Then where do you go?"

"Surely that is obvious?"

"My dear Holmes!"

"Yet nearly all the data are before you, and, as I informed Miss Forsythe, you know my methods. Use them, Watson! Use them!"

Already the first lamps were glimmering through the fog in Baker Street, when my friend's simple preparations were completed. He stood at the doorway of our sitting-room, tall and gaunt in his ear-flapped travelling-cap and long Inverness cape, his Gladstone bag at his feet, and regarded me with singular fixity.

"One last word, Watson, since you still appear to see no light. I would remind you that Mr. Charles Hendon cannot endure the s——"

"But that is clear enough! He cannot bear the sight of a clock."

Holmes shook his head.

"Not necessarily," said he. "I would further draw your attention to the other five clocks, as described by the servant."

"Mr. Charles Hendon did not smash those clocks!"

"That is why I draw your attention to them. Until nine o'clock this day week, Watson!"

A moment more, and I was alone.

During the dreary week which followed, I occupied myself as best I might. I played billiards with Thurston. I smoked many pipes of Ship's, and I pondered over the notes in the case of Mr. Charles Hendon. One does not associate for some years with Sherlock Holmes without becoming more observant than most. It seemed to me that some dark and sinister peril hung over that poor young lady, Miss Forsythe, nor did I trust either the too-handsome Charles Hendon or the enigmatic Lady Mayo.

On Wednesday, November 23rd, my wife returned with the welcome news that our fortunes were in better order and that I should soon be able to buy a small practice. Her home-coming was a joyous one. That night, as we sat hand in hand before the fire in our lodgings, I told her something of the strange problem before me. I spoke of Miss Forsythe, touching on her parlous plight, and on her youth and beauty and refinement. My wife did not reply, but sat looking thoughtfully at the fire.

It was the distant chime of Big Ben striking the half hour after eight, which roused me.

"By Jove, Mary!" cried I. "I had all but forgotten!"

"Forgotten?" repeated my wife, with a slight start.

"I have promised to be in Baker Street at nine o'clock tonight. Miss Forsythe is to be there."

My wife drew back her hand.

"Then you had best be off at once," said she, with a coldness which astonished me. "You are always so interested in Mr. Sherlock Holmes's cases."

Puzzled and somewhat hurt, I took my hat and my departure. It was a bitter-cold night, with no breath of fog, but with the roads ice-blocked in mud. Within the half hour a hansom set me down in Baker Street. With a thrill of excitement I observed that Sherlock Holmes had returned from his mission. The upper windows were lighted, and several times I saw his gaunt shadow pass and repass on the blinds.

Letting myself in with a latch-key, I went softly up the stairs and opened the door of the sitting-room. Clearly Holmes had only just returned, for his cape, his cloth cap, and his old Gladstone bag were scattered about the room in his customary untidy fashion.

He stood at his desk, his back towards me, and the light of the green-shaded desk-lamp falling over him as he ripped open envelopes in a small pile of correspondence. At the opening of the door he turned round, but his face fell.

"Ah, Watson, it is you. I had hoped to see Miss Forsythe. She is late."

"By heaven, Holmes! If those scoundrels have harmed the young lady, I swear they shall answer to me!'

"Scoundrels?"

"I refer to Mr. Charles Hendon, and, though it grieves me to say as much about a woman, to Lady Mayo as well."

The harsh, eager lines of his face softened.

"Good old Watson!" said he. "Always hurrying to the rescue of beauty in distress. And a pretty hash you have made of it, upon occasion."

"Then I trust," I replied with dignity, "that your own mission on the Continent was a success?"

"A touch, Watson! Pray forgive my outburst of nerves. No, my mission was not a success. It seemed to me that I had a direct summons to a certain European city whose name you will readily infer. I went there, and returned in what I fancy is record time."

"Well?"

"The—Mr. Hendon, Watson, is a badly frightened man. Yet he is not without wit. No sooner had he left Switzerland, than he must have divined that the false letter was a decoy to trap him. But I lost him. Where is he now? And be good enough to explain why you should call him a scoundrel."

"I spoke, perhaps, in the heat of the moment. Yet I cannot help disliking the fellow."

"Why?"

"In one of doubtless exalted position, a certain elaborateness of manner is permissible. But he bows too much! He makes scenes in public. He affects the Continental habit of addressing an English lady as 'madame,' instead of an honest 'madam.' Holmes, it is all confoundedly un-English!"

My friend regarded me strangely, as though taken aback, and was about to reply when we heard the clatter of a four-wheeler drawing up outside our street-door. Less than a minute later Celia Forsythe was in the room, followed by a small, hard-looking, dogged man in a bowler hat with a curly brim. From his mutton-chop whiskers I deduced him to be Trepley, the man-servant.

Miss Forsythe's face was aglow with the cold. She wore a short fur jacket, and carried a dainty muff.

"Mr. Holmes," she burst out without preamble, "Charles is in England!"

"So I had already supposed. And where is he?"

"At Groxton Low Hall. I should have sent a telegram yesterday, save that Lady Mayo forbade me to do so."

"Fool that I am!" said Holmes, striking his fist upon the desk. "You spoke of its isolation, I think. Watson! Will you oblige me with the large-scale map of Surrey? Thank you." His voice grew more harsh. "What's this, what's this?"

"My dear fellow," I expostulated, "can you read villainy in a map?"

"Open country, Watson! Fields. Woods. The nearest railway station fully three miles from Groxton Low Hall!" Holmes groaned. "Miss Forsythe, Miss Forsythe, you have much to answer for!"

The young lady fell back a step in amazement.

"*I* have much to answer for?" she cried. "Can you credit me, sir, when I tell you that so much continued mystery has all but driven the wits from my head? Neither Charles nor Lady Mayo will speak a word."

"Of explanation?"

"Precisely!" She nodded her head towards the servant. "Charles has sent Trepley to London with a letter, to be delivered by hand, and I am not even suffered to know its contents."

"Sorry, miss," observed the little man, gruffly but deferentially. "That's orders."

For the first time I noted that Trepley, who was

dressed more like a groom than a manservant, jealously pressed an envelope flat between his hands as though he feared someone might snatch it away. His pale eyes, framed in the mutton-chop whiskers, moved slowly round the room. Sherlock Holmes advanced towards him.

"You will be good enough to show me that envelope, my man," he said.

I have often remarked that a stupid person is the most doggedly loyal. Trepley's eyes were almost those of a fanatic.

"Begging your pardon, sir, but I will not. I will do as I have been ordered, come what may!"

"I tell you, man, this is no time to hesitate. I don't wish to read the letter. I wish merely to see the address on the front and the seal on the back. Quickly, now! It may mean your master's life!"

Trepley hesitated and moistened his lips. Gingerly, still gripping one corner of the envelope, he held it out without releasing it. Holmes whistled.

"Come!" said he. "It is addressed to no less a personage than Sir Charles Warren, the Commissioner of Metropolitan Police. And the seal? Ah! Just as I thought. You are engaged to deliver this letter at once?"

"Yes, Mr. Holmes."

"Then off with you! But detain the four-wheeler, for the rest of us will want it presently."

He did not speak until Trepley had clattered down the stairs. But the old feverishness was again upon him.

"And now, Watson, you might just look up the trains in Bradshaw. Are you armed?"

"My stick."

"For once, I fear, it may prove inadequate." And he opened the left-hand drawer of the desk-table. "Oblige me by slipping this into your greatcoat pocket. A .320 Webley, with Eley's No. 2 cartridges—"

As the light gleamed on the barrel of the revolver, Celia Forsythe uttered a cry and put one hand on the mantelpiece to steady herself.

"Mr. Holmes!" she began, and then seemed to change her mind. "There are frequent trains to Groxton station, which, as you say, is three miles from the Hall. Indeed, there is one in twenty minutes."

"Excellent!"

"But we must not take it."

"Must not take it, madam?"

"I have had no time to tell you, but Lady Mayo herself now appeals to you for help. Only this afternoon I persuaded her. Lady Mayo requests that we three take the 10:25, which is the last train. She will meet us at Groxton station with the carriage." Miss Forsythe bit her lip. "Lady Mayo, despite her kindness, is—imperious. We must not miss that last train!"

And yet we very nearly missed it. Having forgotten streets of frozen mud, and the crush of vehicles under blue, sputtering arc-lamps, we arrived at Waterloo only just in time.

Presently, as the train emerged into open country, our dim-lit compartment took on a greater quality of eeriness with each click of the wheels. Holmes sat silent, bending slightly forward. I could see his hawk-like profile, under the fore and aft cap, clear-cut against the cold radiance of a full moon. It was nearly half-past eleven when we alighted at a wayside station whose village had long been lightless and asleep.

Nothing stirred there. No dog barked. Near the station stood an open landau, without a clink of harness from the horses. Bolt upright sat the coachman, as motionless as the squat elderly lady who sat in the back of the landau, watching us stonily as we approached.

Miss Forsythe eagerly began to speak, but the elderly lady, who was wrapped in grey furs and had a good deal of nose, raised a hand to forestall her.

"Mr. Sherlock Holmes?" she said, in a singularly deep and musical voice, "and this other gentleman, I take it, is Dr. Watson. I am Lady Mayo."

She scrutinized us for a moment with a pair of singularly sharp and penetrating eyes.

"Pray enter the landau," she continued. "You will find quite a number of carriage-rugs. Though I deplore the necessity of offering an open conveyance on so cold a night, my coachman's fondness for fast driving," and she indicated the driver, who hunched up his shoulders, "has contrived to break the axle of the closed carriage. To the Hall, Billings! Make haste!"

The whip cracked. With an uneasy swing of the rear wheels, our landau was off at a smart pace along a narrow road bordered with spiky hedgerows and skeleton trees.

"But I did not mind," said Lady Mayo. "Lackaday, Mr. Holmes! I am a very old woman. My youth was a time of fast driving; ay, and of fast living too."

"Was it also a time of fast dying!" asked my friend. "Such a death, for instance, as may overtake our young friend tonight?"

The hoof-beats rang on the icy road.

"I think, Mr. Sherlock Holmes," said she quietly, "that you and I understand each other."

"I am sure of it, Lady Mayo. But you have not answered my question."

"Have no fear, Mr. Holmes. He is safe now."

"You are certain?"

"I tell you, he is quite safe! The park at Groxton Low Hall is patrolled, and the house is guarded. They cannot attack him."

Whether my own outburst was caused by the smart clip of the landau, the rushing wind past our ears, or the maddening nature of the problem itself, to this day I cannot say.

"Forgive the bluntness of an old campaigner," cried I, "who has no answer for anything. But at least take pity on the poor young lady beside you! Who is Mr. Charles Hendon? Why does he smash clocks? For what reason should his life be in danger?"

"Tut, Watson," said Holmes, with a touch of tartness. "You yourself staggered me by enumerating the points in which Mr. Charles Hendon, as you put it, is confoundedly un-English."

"Well? And why does that assist us?"

"Because the so-called 'Charles Hendon' is assuredly not English."

"Not English?" said Celia Forsythe, stretching out her hand. "But he speaks English perfectly!" The breath died in her throat. "Too perfectly!" she whispered.

"This young man," I exclaimed, "is not, then, of exalted station?"

"On the contrary, my dear fellow. Your shrewdness never fails. He is of very exalted station indeed. Now name for me the one Imperial Court in Europe—ay, Watson, Imperial Court!—at which the speaking of English has all but superseded its own native language."

"I cannot think. I don't know."

"Then endeavour to remember what you do know. Shortly before Miss Forsythe first called upon us, I read aloud certain items from the daily press which at the time seemed tediously unimportant. One item stated that the Nihilists, that dangerous band of anarchists who would crush Imperial Russia to nothingness, were suspected of plotting against the life of the Grand Duke Alexei at Odessa. The Grand Duke Alexei, you perceive. Now Lady Mayo's nickname for 'Mr. Charles Hendon' was—"

"Alec!" cried I.

"It might have been the merest coincidence," observed Holmes, shrugging his shoulders. "However, when we reflect upon recent history, we recall that in an earlier attempt on the life of the late Tsar of all the Russias—who was blown to pieces in '81, by the explosion of a dynamite bomb—the ticking of the bomb was drowned beneath the playing of a piano. Dynamite bombs, Watson, are of two kinds. One, iron-sheathed and fairly light, may be ignited on a short fuse and thrown. The other, also of iron, is exploded by means of a clockwork mechanism whose loud ticking alone betrays its presence."

Crack went the coachman's whip, and the hedgerows seemed to unreel as in a dream. Holmes and I sat with our backs to the driver, *vis-à-vis* the moon-whitened faces of Lady Mayo and Celia Forsythe.

"Holmes, all this is becoming as clear as crystal! That is why the young man cannot bear the sight of a clock!"

"No, Watson. No! The sound of a clock!"

"The sound?"

"Precisely. When I attempted to tell you as much, your native impatience cut me short at the first letter. On the two occasions when he destroyed a clock in public, bear in mind that in neither case could he actually see the clock. In one instance, as Miss Forsythe informed us, it was hidden inside a screen of greenery; in the other, it was behind a curtain. Hearing only that significant ticking, he struck before he had time to take thought. His purpose, of course, was to smash the clockwork and draw the fangs of what he believed to be a bomb."

"But surely," I protested, "those blows of a stick might well have ignited and exploded a bomb?"

Again Holmes shrugged his shoulders.

"Had it been a real bomb, who can tell? Yet, against an iron casing, I think the matter doubtful. In either event, we deal with a very courageous gentleman, haunted and hounded, who rushed and struck blindly. It is not unnatural that the memory of his father's death and the knowledge that the same organization was on his own trail should tend toward hasty action."

"And then?"

Yet Sherlock Holmes remained uneasy. I noticed that he glanced round more than once at the lonely sweep of the grey rolling country-side.

"Well," said he, "having determined so much in my first interview with Miss Forsythe, it seemed clear that the forged letter was bait to draw the Grand Duke to Odessa, urging on him the pluck to face these implacable men. But, as I have told you, he must have suspected. Therefore he would go—where?"

"To England," said I. "Nay, more! To Groxton Low Hall, with the added inducement of an attractive young lady whom I urge to leave off weeping and dry her tears."

Holmes looked exasperated.

"At least I could say," replied he, "that the balance of probability lay in that direction. Surely it was obvious from the beginning that one in the position of Lady Mayo would never have entered so casually into railway-carriage conversation with a young man unless they had been, in Miss Forsythe's unwitting but illuminating phrase, 'old friends.' "

"I underestimated your powers, Mr. Sherlock Holmes." Lady Mayo, who had been patting Celia's hand, spoke harshly. "Yes, I knew Alexei when he was a little boy in a sailor-suit at St. Petersburg."

"Where your husband, I discovered, was First Secretary at the British Embassy. In Odessa I learned another fact of great interest."

"Eh? What was that?"

"The name of the Nihilists' chief agent, a daring, mad, and fanatical spirit who has been very close to the Grand Duke for some time."

"Impossible!"

"Yet true."

For a moment Lady Mayo sat looking at him, her countenance far less stony, while the carriage bumped over a rut and veered.

"Attend to me, Mr. Holmes. My own dear Alec has already written to the police, in the person of Sir Charles Warren, the Commissioner."

"Thank you; I have seen the letter. I have also seen the Imperial Russian Arms on the seal."

"Meanwhile," she continued, "I repeat that the park is patrolled, the house guarded—"

"Yet a fox may escape the hounds none the less."

"It is not only a question of guards! At this minute, Mr. Holmes, poor Alec sits in an old, thick-walled room, with its door double-locked on the inside. The windows are so closely barred that none could so much as stretch a hand inside. The chimney-piece is ancient and hooded, yet with so narrow an aperture that no man could climb down; and a fire burns there. How could an enemy attack him?"

"How?" muttered Holmes, biting his lip and tapping his fingers on his knee. "It is true he may be safe for one night, since—"

Lady Mayo made a slight gesture of triumph.

"No precaution has been neglected," said she. "Even the roof is safeguarded. Alec's manservant, Trepley, after delivering the letter in London with commendable quickness, returned by an earlier train than yours, and borrowed a horse at the village. At this moment he is on the roof of the Hall, faithfully guarding his master."

The effect of this speech was extraordinary. Sherlock Holmes leaped to his feet in the carriage, his cape rising in grotesque black silhouette as he clutched at the box-rail for balance.

"On the roof?" he echoed. "On the roof?"

Then he turned round, seizing the shoulders of the coachman.

"Whip up the horses!" he shouted. "For God's sake, whip up the horses! We have not a second to lose!"

Crack! Crack! went the whip over the ears of the leader. The horses, snorting, settled down to a gallop and plunged away. In the confusion, as we were all thrown together, rose Lady Mayo's angry voice.

"Mr. Holmes, have you taken leave of your senses?"

"You shall see whether I have. Miss Forsythe! Did you ever actually hear the Grand Duke address his man as Trepley?"

"I—no!" faltered Celia Forsythe, shocked to alertness. "As I informed you, Char—oh, heaven help me!—the Grand Duke called him 'Trep.' I assumed—"

"Exactly! You assumed. But his true name is Trepoff. From your first description I knew him to be a liar and a traitor."

The hedgerows flashed past; bit and harness jingled; we flew with the wind.

"You may recall," pursued Holmes, "the[1] man's consummate hypocrisy when his master smashed the first clock? It was a heavy look of embarrassment and shame, was it not? He would have you think Mr. Charles Hendon insane. How came you to know of the other five clocks, which were purely imaginary? Because Trepoff told you. To hide a clock or a live bomb in a cupboard would really have been madness, if in fact the Grand Duke Alexei had ever done so."

"But, Holmes," I protested. "Since Trepoff is his personal servant—"

"Faster, coachman! Faster! Yes, Watson!"

"Surely Trepoff must have had a hundred opportunities to kill his master, by knife or poison perhaps, without this spectacular addition of a bomb?"

"This spectacular addition, as you call it, is the revolutionaries' stock-in-trade. They will not act without it. Their victim must be blown up in one fiery crash of ruin, else the world may not notice them or their power."

"But the letter to Sir Charles Warren?" cried Lady Mayo.

"Doubtless it was dropped down the nearest street drain. Ha! I think that must be Groxton Low Hall just ahead."

The ensuing events of that night are somewhat confused in my mind. I recall a long, low-built Jacobean house, of mellow red brick with mullioned windows and a flat roof, which seemed to rush at us up a gravel drive. Carriage-rugs flew wide. Lady Mayo, thoroughly roused, called sharp instructions to a group of nervous servants.

Then Holmes and I were hurrying after Miss Forsythe up a series of staircases, from a broad and carpeted oak stairway in the hall to a set of narrow steps which were little more than a ladder to the roof. At the foot of these, Holmes paused for a moment to lay his fingers on Miss Forsythe's arm.

"You will stay here," he said quietly.

There was a metallic click as he put his hand into his pocket, and for the first time I knew that Holmes was armed too.

"Come, Watson," said he.

I followed him up the narrow steps while he softly lifted the trap-door to the roof.

"Not a sound, on your life!" he whispered. "Fire if you catch sight of him."

"But how are we to find him?"

The cold air again blew in our faces. We crept cautiously forward across the flat roof. All about us were chimneys, tall ghostly stacks and clusters of squat smoke-blackened pots, surrounding a great leaden cupola shining like silver under the moon. At the far end, where the roof-tree of an old gable rose against the sky, a dark shape seemed to crouch above a single moon-washed chimney.

A sulphur-match flared blue, then burned with a cedar yellow glow and, an instant later, came the hissing of an ignited fuse followed by a clattering sound in the chimney. Holmes ran forward, twisting and turning through the maze of stacks and parapets, toward the hunched figure now hastily clawing away.

"Fire, Watson! Fire!"

Our pistols rang out together. I saw Trepoff's pale face jerk round toward us, and then in the same instant the whole chimney-stack rose straight up into the air in a solid pillar of white fire. The roof heaved beneath my feet, and I was dimly conscious of rolling over and over along the leads, while shards and splinters of broken brickwork whizzed overhead or clanged against the metal dome of the cupola.

Holmes rose unsteadily to his feet. "Are you hurt, Watson?" he gasped.

"Only a trifle winded," I replied. "But it was fortunate we were thrown on our faces. Otherwise—" I gestured toward the slashed and scarred stacks that rose about us.

We had advanced only a few yards through a mist of gritty dust when we came upon the man whom we were seeking.

"He must now answer to a greater tribunal," said Holmes, looking down at the dreadful object sprawled on the leads. "Our shots made him hesitate for that fatal second, and he took the full blast of the bomb up the chimney." My friend turned away. "Come," he added, and his voice was bitter with self-reproach. "We have been both too slow to save our client, and too late to avenge him through the machinery of human justice."

Suddenly his expression altered, and he clutched my arm.

"By Jove, Watson! A single chimney-stack saved our lives!" he cried. "What was the word the woman used!

Hooded! That was it, hooded! Quickly; there's not a moment to lose!"

We raced through the trap-door, and down the stairway to the main landing. At the far end, through a haze of acrid smoke, we could discern the ruins of a splintered door. An instant later we had rushed into the bedroom of the Grand Duke. Holmes groaned aloud at the scene which met our eyes.

What was once a stately fireplace now yawned in a great jagged hole beneath the remnants of a heavy stone hood. The fire from the grate had been blasted into the room, and the air was foul with the stench of the carpet smouldering under its powder of red-hot ashes. Holmes darted forward through the smoke, and a moment later I saw him stoop behind the wreckage of a piano.

"Quick, Watson!" he cried. "There is life in him yet! This is where I can do nothing, and you can do everything."

But it was touch and go. For the remainder of the night the young Duke hovered between life and death in the old wainscotted bedroom to which we had carried him. Yet, as the sun rose above the trees in the park, I noted with satisfaction that the coma induced by shock was already passing into a natural sleep.

"His wounds are superficial," I said. "But the shock alone could have proved fatal. Now that he is asleep, he will live, and I have no doubt that the presence of Miss Celia Forsythe will speed his recovery."

"Should you record the facts of this little case," remarked Holmes a few minutes later, as we strolled across the dew-laden grass of the deer-park, all glittering and sparkling in the fresh beauty of the dawn, "then you must have the honesty to lay the credit where it is due."

"But does not the credit lie with you?"

"No, Watson. That the outcome was successful is owing entirely to the fact that our ancestors understood the art of building. The strength of a fireplace-hood two hundred years old saved that young man's head from being blown off his shoulders. It is fortunate for the Grand Duke Alexei of Russia, and for the reputation of Mr. Sherlock

Holmes of Baker Street, that in the days of the good King James the householder never failed to allow for the violent predilections of his neighbour."

—:—

From time to time I heard some vague account of his doings: of his summons to Odessa in the case of the Trepoff murder.
FROM "A SCANDAL IN BOHEMIA."

2

The Adventure of the
Gold Hunter

"Mr. Holmes, it was death by the visitation of God!"

We have heard many singular statements in our rooms at Baker Street, but few more startling than this pronouncement of the Rev. Mr. James Appley.

I need no reference to my note-book to recall that it was a fine summer day in the year 1887. A telegram had arrived at the breakfast-table. Mr. Sherlock Holmes, with an exclamation of impatience, threw it across to me. The telegram stated merely that the Rev. James Appley requested the favour of waiting upon him that morning, to consult him in a matter of church affairs.

"Really, Watson," Holmes had commented with some asperity, as he lighted his after-breakfast pipe, "matters have indeed come to a pretty pass when clergymen seek my advice as to the length of their sermons or the conduct of the Harvest Festival. I am flattered but out of my depth. What does Crockford say of this strange client?"

Endeavouring to anticipate my friend's methods, I had already taken down the clerical directory. I could find only that the gentleman in question was the vicar of a small parish in Somerset, and had written a monograph on Byzantine medicine.

"An unusual pursuit for a country clergyman," Holmes remarked. "But here, unless I am much mistaken, is the man himself."

As he spoke, there had arisen from below an excited pealing of the door-bell, and, before Mrs. Hudson could announce him, our visitor had burst into the room. He was a tall, thin, high-shouldered man in rustic clerical dress with a benevolent, scholarly face framed in antiquated side-whiskers of the sort once known as Dundreary weepers.

"My dear sirs," he cried, peering at us myopically from behind oval spectacles, "pray accept my assurance that it is only the pressure of events that prompts my invasion of your privacy."

"Come, come," said Sherlock Holmes good-humouredly, waving him to the basket-chair before the empty fireplace. "I am a consulting detective, and therefore my privacy is of no more consequence than that of a doctor."

The clergyman had hardly seated himself when he blurted out the extraordinary words with which I have begun this narrative.

"Death by the visitation of God," repeated Sherlock Holmes. Though his voice was subdued, yet it seemed to me that there was a roll and thrill in the words. "Then surely, my dear sir, the matter lies rather within your province than within mine?"

"I ask your pardon," said the vicar, hastily. "My words were perhaps over-emphatic and even irreverent. But you will understand that this horrible event, this—" his voice sank almost to a whisper as he leaned forward in his chair. "Mr. Holmes, it is villainy: cold-blooded, deliberate villainy!"

"Believe me, sir, I am all attention."

"Mr. John Trelawney—Squire Trelawney, we called him—was the richest landowner for miles about. Four nights ago, when only three months short of his seventieth birthday, he died in his bed."

"Hum! That is not so uncommon."

"No, sir. But hear me!" cried the vicar, raising a long forefinger curiously smudged on the very tip. "John Trelawney was a hale and hearty man, suffering from no organic disease, and good for at least a dozen more years in this mundane sphere. Dr. Paul Griffin, our local medical practitioner and incidentally my nephew, flatly refused to issue a death-certificate. There was a most dreadful business called a post-mortem."

Holmes, who had not yet doffed his mouse-coloured dressing-gown, had been leaning back languidly in his arm-chair. Now he half opened his eyes.

"A post-mortem!" said he. "Performed by your nephew?"

Mr. Appley hesitated. "No, Mr. Holmes. It was performed by Sir Leopold Harper, our foremost living authority on medical jurisprudence. I may tell you, here and now, that poor Trelawney did not die a natural death. Not only the police but Scotland Yard have been called in."

"Ah!"

"On the other hand," continued Mr. Appley agitatedly, "Trelawney was not murdered, and he could not possibly have been murdered. The greatest medical skill has been used to pronounce that he could not have died from any cause whatsoever."

For a moment there was a silence in our sitting-room, where the blinds had been half drawn against the summer sun.

"My dear Watson," said Holmes cordially, "will you be good enough to fetch me a clay pipe from the rack over the sofa? Thank you. I find, Mr. Appley, that a clay is most conducive to meditation. Come, where is the coal-scuttle? May I venture to offer you a cigar?"

"Cras ingens iterabimus aequor," said the vicar, running his curiously mottled fingers over his side-whiskers. "At the moment, thank you, no. I cannot smoke. I dare not smoke! It would choke me. I am aware that I must tell you the facts in precise detail. But it is difficult. You may have remarked that I am considered somewhat absent-minded?"

"Indeed."

"Yes, sir. In youth, before my call to the Church, I once desired to study medicine. But my late father forbade it, due to this absent-mindedness. Were I to become a doctor, said my father, I should instantly chloroform the patient and remove his gall-stones when he had merely come to enquire about a slight cough."

"Well, well," said Holmes, with a touch of impatience. "But you were disturbed in your mind this morning," he continued, regarding our client with his keen glance. "That, no doubt, was why you consulted several books in your study before catching the train to London this morning?"

"Yes, sir. They were medical works."

"Do you not find it inconvenient to have the bookshelves in your study built so high?"

"Dear me, no. Can any room be too high or too large for one's books?"

Abruptly the vicar paused. His long face, framed in the Dundreary weepers, grew even longer as his mouth fell open.

"Now I am positive, I am quite positive," said he, "that I mentioned neither my books nor the height of the shelves in my study! How could you have known these things?"

"Tut, a trifle! How do I know, for instance, that you are either a bachelor or a widower, and that you have a most slovenly housekeeper?"

"Really, Holmes," cried I, "there is another besides Mr. Appley who would like to know how you deduced it!"

"The dust, Watson! The dust!"

"What dust?"

"Kindly observe the index finger of Mr. Appley's right hand. You will note, on its tip, smudges of that dark-grey dust which accumulates on the top of books. The smudges, somewhat faded, were made no later than this morning. Since Mr. Appley is a tall man with long arms, surely it is obvious that he plucked down books from a high shelf. When to this accumulation of dust we add an unbrushed top hat, it requires small shrewdness to determine that he has no wife, but an appalling housekeeper."

"Remarkable!" said I.

"Meretricious," said he. "And I apologize to our guest for interrupting his narrative."

"This death was incomprehensible beyond all measure! But you have not yet heard the worst," continued our visitor. "I must tell you that Trelawney has one surviving relative: a niece, aged twenty-one. Her name is Miss Dolores Dale, the daughter of the late Mrs. Copley Dale, of Glastonbury. For several years the young lady has kept house for Trelawney in his great whitewashed home, called Goodman's Rest. It has always been understood that Dolores, who is engaged to be married to a fine young man named Jeffrey Ainsworth, would inherit her uncle's fortune. When I tell you that a sweeter or kinder spirit never existed, that her hair is darker than Homer's wine-dark sea and that upon occasion she can be all flash and fire suggestive of Southern blood—"

"Yes, yes," said Holmes, closing his eyes. "But you stated that I had not heard the worst?"

"True. Here are the facts. Shortly before his death, Trelawney changed his will. Disinheriting his niece, whom the stern-minded old man considered to be too frivolous, he left his entire fortune to my nephew, Dr. Paul Griffin. Sir, it was the scandal of the country-side! Two weeks later, Trelawney was dead in his bed and my unhappy nephew is now under suspicion of murder."

"Pray be particular in your details," said Holmes.

"In the first place," continued the vicar, "I should describe the late Squire Trelawney as a man of stern and implacable habit. I seem always to see him, tall and big-boned, with his great head and his grizzled silver beard, against the brown of a ploughed field or a line of heavy green trees.

"Each evening, in his bedroom, he would read a chapter of the Bible. Afterwards he would wind up his watch, which had almost run down at that hour. Then he would retire to bed at ten o'clock precisely, and rise at five each morning."

"One moment!" interposed Holmes. "Did these habits of his ever vary?"

"Well, should he become absorbed in the Bible, he

might read until very late. But this happened so seldom, Mr. Holmes, that I think you may disregard it."

"Thank you; that is quite clear."

"In the second place, I am sorry to say that he was never on the best of terms with his niece. He was stern to a point of brutality. On one occasion, two years ago, he thrashed poor Dolores with a razor-strop, and confined her to her room on bread and water, because she had gone to Bristol to witness a performance of Gilbert and Sullivan's comic opera, *Patience*. I can still see her, with the tears running down her warm-blooded cheeks. You must forgive the intemperance of her language. 'Old devil,' she sobbed. 'Old devil!' "

"Am I to understand," interposed Holmes, "that the young lady's future welfare depends on the inheritance of this money?"

"Far from it. Her fiancé, Mr. Ainsworth, is a rising young solicitor who is already making his way in the world. Trelawney himself was among his clients."

"I seemed to detect a certain apprehension when you mentioned your nephew," said Holmes. "Since Dr. Griffin inherits this fortune, he was presumably on friendly terms with Trelawney?"

The vicar shifted uncomfortably in his chair. "On the friendliest possible terms," he replied with some haste. "Indeed, on one occasion he saved the squire's life. At the same time, I must confess that he has always been a wild, hot-headed man. His intemperate behaviour has gone a long way towards creating the strong local prejudice which has now risen against him. If the police could show how Trelawney died, my nephew might be under arrest at this moment."

The vicar paused and looked round. There had come an authoritative rap at the door. An instant later, as it was flung open, we had a glimpse of Mrs. Hudson over the shoulder of a short, thin, rat-faced man, clad in a check suit and bowler hat. As his hard blue eyes fell on Mr. Appley, he paused on the threshold with a growl of surprise.

"You have a certain gift, Lestrade, for timing your

appearances with a pleasant touch of the dramatic," observed Holmes languidly.

"And very awkward for some folk," remarked the detective, depositing his hat beside the gasogene. "Well, from the presence of this reverend gentleman I take it that you are up to date with this cosy little murder in Somerset. The facts are pretty obvious and all point one way as clear as signposts, eh, Mr. Holmes!"

"Unfortunately, signposts are so easily turned in the opposite direction," said Holmes; "a truism of which I have given you one or two small demonstrations in the past, Lestrade."

The Scotland Yard man flushed angrily.

"Well, well, Mr. Holmes, that's as may be. But there is no doubt this time. There are both the motive and the opportunity. We know the man and it only remains to find the means."

"I tell you that my unfortunate nephew—!" broke in the clergyman distractedly.

"I have named no names."

"But you have made it obvious from the moment you heard he was Trelawney's doctor! Admittedly he stands to benefit under that deplorable will."

"You have forgotten to mention his personal reputation, Mr. Appley," said Lestrade grimly.

"Wild, yes; romantic, hot-headed if you like! But a cold-blooded murderer—never! I have known him from his cradle."

"Well, we shall see. Mr. Holmes, I would value a word with you."

During this interchange between our unhappy client and Lestrade, Holmes had been staring at the ceiling with that far-away, dreamy look upon his face which I had noted only on those occasions when his mind whispered that some subtle thread of evidence was already there to hand, but buried as yet in the maze of obvious facts and no less obvious suspicions. He rose abruptly and turned to the vicar.

"I take it that you return to Somerset this afternoon?"

"By the 2:30 from Paddington." There was a tinge

of colour in his face as he leapt to his feet. "Am I then to understand, my dear Mr. Holmes——?"

"Dr. Watson and I will accompany you. If you will have the kindness to ask Mrs. Hudson to whistle a cab, Mr. Appley?"

Our client clattered down the stairs.

"This is a somewhat curious affair," said Holmes, filling his travelling-pouch with shag from the Persian slipper.

"I am glad that at last you see it in that light, my dear fellow," I remarked, "for it did seem to me that you were a little impatient from the first with the worthy vicar, especially when he strayed into his early medical ambitions and the probability that he would absent-mindedly have removed a patient's gall-stones."

The effect of this casual remark was extraordinary. After looking fixedly into space, Holmes sprang to his feet.

"By Jove!" he exclaimed. "By Jove!"

There was a touch of colour in his high cheekbones and that sudden gleam in his eyes that I knew of old.

"As usual, Watson, your help has been invaluable," he went on warmly. "Though not yourself luminous, you are a conductor of light."

"I have helped you? By mentioning the vicar's gall-stones?"

"Precisely."

"Really, Holmes!"

"At the moment, I must find a certain surname. Yes, unquestionably I must find a certain surname. Will you hand me the commonplace book under the letter 'B'?".

I had given him the bulky volume, one of many in which he pasted press-cuttings of any incidents arresting his attention, before I had time to reflect.

"But, Holmes, there is no one in this affair whose surname begins with a 'B'!"

"Quite so. I was aware of it. B-a, Ba-r, Bartlett! H'm! Ha! Good old index."

After a short perusal, turning over the pages eagerly, Holmes closed the book with a bang and sat tapping its cover with his long, nervous fingers. Behind him, the tubes and beakers and retorts of the chemical table glittered in the sunlight.

"I had not all the data, of course," he added musingly. "Even now they are not complete."

Lestrade caught my eye and winked.

"They are complete enough for me!" he said with a grin. "They can't deceive me. That red-bearded doctor is a murdering devil. We know the man, and we know the motive."

"Then why are you here?"

"Because there is one thing lacking. We know he did it, right enough! But *how* did he do it?"

No less than a dozen times did Lestrade ask the same question during the course of our journey, until it seemed to throb and echo in my head with the very click of the train wheels.

It was a long, hot day and the afterglow of sunset lay on the crests of the softly rounded Somersetshire hills when we alighted at last at the little wayside station. On the hillside beyond the half-timbered gables of the village and set amid noble elm trees from whence, even at that distance, the clear evening air carried the cawing of the homing rooks, there shone a great white house.

"We have a mile before us," said Lestrade sourly.

"I should prefer not to go to the house at first," said Holmes. "Does this village run to an inn?"

"There is the Camberwell Arms."

"Then let us go there. I prefer to commence on neutral ground."

"Really, Holmes!" cried Lestrade. "I cannot imagine—"

"Precisely," remarked Holmes, and not another word would he utter until we were all ensconced in the private parlour of the ancient hostelry. Holmes scribbled a few lines in his note-book and tore out two leaves.

"Now, Mr. Appley, if I might take the liberty of sending your groom with this note to Goodman's Rest and the other to Mr. Ainsworth?"

"By all means."

"Excellent. Then we have time for a pipe before Miss Dolores and her fiancé join us."

For some time we sat in silence, each busy with his own thoughts. As for myself, I had too much confidence in my friend to accept the obvious at its face value so long as he appeared to be perplexed in his own mind.

"Well, Mr. Holmes," said Lestrade sternly, at last. "You have been sufficiently mysterious to satisfy even Dr. Watson here. Let us have your theory."

"I have no theory. I am merely sounding my facts."

"Your facts have overlooked the criminal."

"That remains to be seen. By the way, Vicar, what are the relations between Miss Dolores and your nephew?"

"It is strange that you should mention this," replied Mr. Appley. "Their relationship has been a source of pain to me for some time past. But in justice I must add that the fault lies with the young lady. For no reason, she is gratuitously offensive to him. Worst of all, she shows her dislike in public."

"Ah! And Mr. Ainsworth?"

"Ainsworth is too good a fellow not to deplore his fiancée's behaviour to my nephew. He takes it almost as a personal affront."

"Indeed. Most praiseworthy. But here, unless I am much mistaken, are our visitors."

The old door creaked open and a tall, graceful girl swept into the room. Her dark eyes, glowing with an unnatural brilliance, turned from one to the other of us with a long, searching glance that had in it a glint of animosity and something more of despair. A slim, fair-haired young man with a fresh complexion and a pair of singularly clear, shrewd blue eyes followed behind her and greeted Appley with a friendly word.

"Which of you is Mr. Sherlock Holmes?" cried the young lady. "Ah, yes. You have uncovered fresh evidence, I imagine?"

"I have come to hear it, Miss Dale. Indeed, I have heard everything except what actually happened on the night your uncle—died."

"You stress the word 'died,' Mr. Holmes."

"But hang it all, my dear, what else could he say?" asked young Ainsworth, with an attempt at a laugh. "You have probably got a lot of superstitious nonsense in your head because the thunder-storm on Tuesday night upset your uncle. But it was over before he was dead."

"How do you know that?"

"Dr. Griffin said that he didn't die until about three o'clock in the morning. Anyway, he was all right in the early hours!"

"You seem very sure."

The young man looked at Holmes in obvious perplexity. "Of course I am. As Mr. Lestrade can tell you, I was in that room three times during the night. The squire asked me to go there."

"Then be good enough to let me have the facts from the beginning. Perhaps, Miss Dale—?"

"Very well, Mr. Holmes. On Tuesday night, my uncle asked my fiancé and Dr. Griffin to dine with us at Goodman's Rest. From the first, he was uneasy. I put it down to the far-off muttering of thunder; he loathed and feared storms. But now I am wondering whether his uneasiness lay in his mind or his conscience. Be that as it may, our nerves grew more and more tense as the evening went on, nor did Dr. Griffin's sense of humor improve matters when lightning struck a tree in the copse. 'I've got to drive home tonight,' he said, 'and I hope nothing happens to me in this storm.' Dr. Griffin is positively insufferable!

" 'Well, I'm glad that I'm staying,' laughed Jeffrey; 'we are snug enough with the good old lightning-conductors.'

"My uncle leaped from his chair.

" 'You young fool!' he cried. 'Don't you know that there are none on this house?' And my uncle stood there shivering like a man out of his wits."

"I couldn't imagine what I'd said," interrupted Ainsworth naïvely. "Then, when he flew off about his nightmares—"

"Nightmares?" said Holmes.

"Yes. He screeched out that he suffered from nightmares, and that this was no night for the human soul to be alone."

"He grew calmer," continued Miss Dale, "when Jeffrey offered to look in once or twice during the night. It was really rather pitiful. My fiancé went in—when was it, Jeffrey?"

"Once at ten-thirty; once at midnight and finally at one in the morning."

"Did you speak with him?" asked Sherlock Holmes.

"No, he was asleep."

"Then, how do you know that he was alive?"

"Well, like many elderly people, the squire kept a night-light. It was a kind of rushlight burning blue in a bowl on the hearth. I couldn't see much, but I could hear his heavy breathing under the howl of the storm."

"It was just after five on the following morning—" said Miss Dale, "when—I can't go on!" she burst out. "I can't!"

"Gently, my dear," said Ainsworth, who was looking at her steadily. "Mr. Holmes, this has been a great strain on my fiancée."

"Perhaps *I* may be permitted to continue," suggested the vicar. "Dawn was just breaking when I was roused by a heavy pounding on the vicarage door. A stableboy had been dispatched post-haste from Goodman's Rest with horrible news. It appears that the housemaid carried up the squire's morning tea as usual. On drawing the curtains, she screamed out in horror at beholding her master dead in the bed. Huddling in my clothes, I rushed to Goodman's Rest. When I entered the bedroom, followed by Dolores and Jeffrey, Dr. Griffin—who had been summoned first—had concluded his examination.

" 'He has been dead for about two hours,' said the doctor. 'But for the life of me I can't understand how he died.'

"I had moved round to the other side of the bed, composing myself to pray, when I caught sight of Trelawney's gold watch, gleaming in a ray of morning sunlight. The watch was a stem-winder, without a key. It lay on a small marble-topped table, amid a litter of patent-medicine bottles and liniment-bottles which diffused a strong odour in the stuffy room.

"We are told that in times of crisis our minds will

occupy themselves with trifles. This is so, else I cannot account for my own behaviour.

"Fancying that the watch was not ticking, I lifted it to my ear. But it was ticking. I gave the stem two full turns until it was stopped by the spring; but, in any case, I should not have proceeded. The winding caused a harsh noise, *cr-r-ack,* which drew from Dolores an unnerving scream. I recall her exact words.

" 'Vicar! Put it down! It is like—like a death-rattle.' "

For a moment we sat in silence. Miss Dale turned away her head.

"Mr. Holmes," said Ainsworth earnestly, "these wounds are too recent. May I beg that you will excuse Miss Dale from any further questions tonight?"

Holmes rose to his feet.

"Fears are groundless things without proof, Miss Dale," he observed. Taking out his watch, he looked at it thoughtfully.

"The hour grows late, eh, Mr. Holmes," remarked Lestrade.

"That did not occur to me. But you are right. And now, to Goodman's Rest."

A short journey in the vicar's carriage brought us to a pair of lodge gates opening into a narrow drive. The moon had risen and the long, glimmering avenue stretched away before us, all mottled and barred with the shadows of the great elm trees. As we swung round the final curve, the golden cones of light from the carriage-lamps gleamed faintly on the face of a gaunt, ugly mansion. All the drab-painted window-shutters were closed against the casements, and the front door was shrouded in black crepe.

"It's a house of gloom, all right," said Lestrade in a subdued voice as he tugged at the bell-pull. "Hullo! How's this! What are you doing here, Dr. Griffin?"

The door had swung open and a tall, red-bearded man, clad in a loose-fitting Norfolk jacket and knickerbockers, stood in the entrance. As he glared fiercely from one to the other of us, I noted the clenched hands and heaving chest that told of some fearsome inner tension.

"Must I get your permission to walk a mile, Mr. Lestrade?" he cried. "Isn't it enough that your cursed suspicions have roused the whole country-side against me?" His great hand shot out and siezed my friend by the shoulder. "You're Holmes!" he said passionately. "I got your note, and here I am. Please God that you live up to your repute. So far as I can see, you are all that stands between me and the hangman. There, now, what a brute I am! I've frightened her."

With a low moan, Miss Dale had buried her face in her hands.

"It's the strain, it's—it's everything!" she sobbed. "Oh, horror unthinkable!"

I was really very annoyed with Holmes; for, while we gathered round the weeping girl with words of comfort, he merely observed to Lestrade that presumably the dead man's body was inside. Turning his back on us, he strode into the house, whipping out a pocket lens as he did so.

After a decent interval, I hurried after him with Lestrade on my heels. Through a door on the left of a great dark hall, we caught a glimpse of a candle-lit room piled high with half-withered flowers and of Holmes's long, thin figure stooping over a white-shrouded form in the open coffin. The candlelight twinkled on his lens as he bent down until his face was only a few inches above that of the dead man. There was a period of absolute stillness while he scrutinized the placid features beneath him. Then gently he pulled up the sheet and turned away.

I would have spoken, but he hurried past us swiftly and silently with no more than a curt gesture towards the stairs. On the upper landing, Lestrade led the way into a bedroom with massive dark furniture that loomed up gloomily in the light of a shaded lamp burning on a table beside a great open Bible. The sickly stuffiness of funeral flowers, as well as the dampness of the house, followed me everywhere.

Holmes, his brows drawn into two hard black lines, was crawling on all fours under the windows, examining every inch of the floor with his lens. At my stern word of injunction he rose to his feet.

"No, Watson! These windows were not opened three nights ago. Had they been opened during so heavy a storm, I must have found traces." He sniffed the air. "But it was not necessary to open the windows."

"Listen!" said I. "What is that strange noise?"

I looked over towards the bed, with its curtains and high dark canopy. At the head of the bed my gaze fastened on a marble-topped table littered with dusty medicine-bottles.

"Holmes, it is the dead man's gold watch! It lies upon that little table there, and it is still ticking."

"Does that astonish you?"

"Surely, after three days, they would have allowed it to run down?"

"So they did. But I wound it up. I came up here before I examined the dead man downstairs. In fact, I made this whole journey from the village to wind up Squire Trelawney's watch at precisely ten o'clock."

"Upon my word, Holmes—!"

"And see," he continued, hastening to the small table in question, "what a treasure-trove we have here! Look at this, Lestrade! Look at it!"

"But, Holmes, it is only a small pot of vaseline such as you may buy at any chemist's!"

"On the contrary, it is a hangman's rope. And yet," he finished thoughtfully, "there remains that one point which continues to puzzle me. How was it that you were able to avail yourself of Sir Leopold Harper?" he asked suddenly, turning to Lestrade. "Does he live here?"

"No, he is staying with some friends in the neighbourhood. When the post-mortem was decided on, the local police looked upon it as a bit of luck that the best-known expert in England on medical jurisprudence should be within reach, so they sent for him. And a fine time they had to get him to do it," he added with a sly grin.

"Why?"

"Because he was in bed with a hot-water bottle, a glass of hot toddy, and a cold in his head."

Holmes threw his arms in the air.

"My case is complete," he cried.

Lestrade and I looked at each other in amazement.

"I have only one more instruction to give," said Holmes. "Lestrade, nobody must leave this house to-night. The diplomacy of detaining everyone here I leave to you. Watson and I will compose ourselves in this room until five o'clock tomorrow morning."

It was in vain, considering his masterful nature, to ask why we must do this. While he settled into the only rocking-chair, it was in vain to protest that I could not even sit down on the dead man's bed, much less take a brief nap there. I objected for some time. I objected until—

"Watson!"

Cleaving through my dreams, that voice roused me from slumber. I sat bolt upright on the quilt, feeling much dishevelled, with the morning sun in my eyes and the dead man's watch still ticking near my ear.

Sherlock Holmes, with his customary catlike neatness of appearance, stood watching me.

"It is ten minutes past five," said he, "and I felt I had best awaken you. Ah, Lestrade," he continued, as there came a knock at the door. "I trust that the others are with you. Pray come in."

I bounded off the bed as Miss Dale entered the room followed by Dr. Griffin, young Ainsworth and, to my astonishment, the vicar.

"Really, Mr. Holmes," cried Dolores Dale, her eyes sparkling with anger. "It is intolerable that a mere whim should keep us here all night—even poor Mr. Appley."

"It was no whim, believe me. I wish to explain how the late Mr. Trelawney was cold-bloodedly murdered."

"Murdered, eh!" blurted out Dr. Griffin. "Then Inspector Lestrade wants to hear you. But the method—?"

"Was diabolical in its simplicity. Dr. Watson here was shrewd enough to call my attention to it. No, Watson, not a word! Mr. Appley gave us the clue when he said that if he had practiced medicine he might absent-mindedly have removed a patient's gall-stones. But that was not all he said. He stated that first he would have chloroformed the patient. The suggestive word was *chloroform*."

"Chloroform!" echoed Dr. Griffin, rather wildly.

"Exactly. It might well suggest itself to a murderer, since only last year, in a famous murder-trial at the Old Bailey, Mrs. Adelaide Bartlett was acquitted from a charge of poisoning her husband by pouring liquid chloroform down his throat as he lay asleep."

"But, deuce take it! Trelawney swallowed no chloroform!"

"Of course not. But suppose, Dr. Griffin, I were to take a large pad of cotton-wool saturated in chloroform, and press it over the mouth and nostrils of an old man —a heavily sleeping man—for some twenty minutes. What would happen?"

"He would die. Yet you could not do that without leaving traces!"

"Ah, excellent! What traces?"

"Chloroform tends to burn or blister the skin. There would be burns, at least very small burns."

Holmes shot out a long arm towards the marble-topped table.

"Now suppose, Dr. Griffin," said he, holding up the tiny pot of vaseline, "I were first softly to spread on the face of the victim a thin film of such ointment as this. Would there be burns afterwards?"

"No, there wouldn't!"

"I perceive that your medical knowledge leaps ahead and anticipates me. Chloroform is volatile; it evaporates and quickly vanishes from the blood. Delay a post-mortem examination for nearly two days, as this was delayed, and no trace will be left."

"Not so fast, Mr. Sherlock Holmes! There is—"

"There is a slight, a very slight possibility, that an odour of chloroform may be detected either in the room of death or at the post-mortem. But here it would have been hidden by the thick pungency of medicine and liniment. At the post-mortem it would have been hidden by that bad cold in the head from which Sir Leopold Harper suffered."

Dr. Griffin's face seemed to stand out white against his red beard.

"By God, that's true!"

"Now we ask ourselves, as the vicar might, *cui bono?* Who profits from this dastardly crime?"

I noticed that Lestrade moved a step closer to the doctor.

"Take care, curse you!" snarled Griffin.

Holmes put down the ointment and took up the dead man's heavy gold watch, which seemed to tick even more loudly.

"I would draw your attention to this watch, of the sort known as a gold hunter. Last night I wound it up fully at ten o'clock. It is now, as you see, twenty minutes past five."

"And what of that?" cried Miss Dale.

"It is the exact time, if you recall, when the vicar wound up this same watch on the morning you found your uncle dead. Though the performance may distress you now, I beg of you to listen."

Cr-r—r-ack went the harsh, rasping noise as Holmes began slowly to wind it up. On and on it seemed to go, while the stem still turned.

"Hold hard!" said Dr. Griffin. "There's something wrong!"

"Again excellent! And what is wrong?"

"Deuce take it, the vicar made only two full turns of that stem, and it was fully wound up! You've made seven or eight turns, but it still is not wound!"

"Precisely so," returned Holmes, "but I do not emphasize this particular watch. Any watch, if it be wound up at ten o'clock in the evening, cannot possibly be fully wound on the following morning with only two turns."

"My God!" muttered the doctor, staring at Holmes.

"Hence the late Mr. Trelawney did not go to bed at ten o'clock. Surely, considering his badly disturbed nerves and the continued thunder-storm, it is far more likely that he sat up reading his Bible until an unearthly hour, as the vicar said he sometimes did. Though he wound up his watch as usual, he did not retire until three o'clock. The murderer caught him in a heavy sleep."

"And therefore?" almost screamed Dolores.

"Therefore—since one person tells us he saw Trelawney asleep at ten-thirty, at midnight, and again at one o'clock—that person has told us a provable and damning falsehood."

"Holmes," cried I, "at last I see the direction in which all this points. The culprit is—"

Jeffrey Ainsworth sprang for the door.

"Ah, would you!" shouted Lestrade. He hurled himself on the young man, and there was a snap of closing handcuffs.

Miss Dolores Dale ran sobbing forward. She did not run towards Ainsworth. Instead she rushed into the outstretched arms of Dr. Paul Griffin.

"You see, Watson," concluded Mr. Sherlock Holmes, as that night we sat once more in Baker Street, refreshing ourselves with whisky and soda, "the probable guilt of young Ainsworth, who fervently desired to marry the young lady for her money, was at least indicated without even the evidence of the watch."

"Surely not!" I objected.

"My dear fellow, consider Trelawney's will."

"Then, after all, Trelawney did not make that unjust will?"

"Indeed, he did. He let it be known that such was his intention and he carried out that intention. But there was only one person who was aware of the final outcome; namely, that he never actually signed it."

"You mean Trelawney himself?"

"I mean Ainsworth, the solicitor who drew the will. He has admitted as much in his confession."

Holmes leaned back in his chair and placed his fingertips together.

"Chloroform is easily obtainable, as the British public knows from the Bartlett case. In such a small community, a friend of the family, like Ainsworth, would have easy access to the medical works in the vicar's library. He evolved rather a clever plan at his leisure. In my little analysis last night, I should have been less confident had not examination of the dead man's face with a lens revealed jury-proof evidence in the form of minute burns and traces of vaseline in the skin-pores."

"But Miss Dale and Dr. Griffin!"

"Their conduct puzzled you?"

"Well, women are strange."

"My dear Watson, when I hear of a young woman, all fire and temperament, who is thrown into the company of a man of exactly similar characteristics—in sharp contrast to a cold-minded solicitor who watches her carefully —my suspicions are aroused, especially when she expresses unprovoked dislike on all public occasions."

"Then why did she not simply break her engagement!"

"You overlook the fact that her uncle always upbraided her for fickleness. Had she revoked her pledge, she would have lost dignity in her own eyes. But why on earth, Watson, are you chuckling now?"

"Merely a sense of incongruity. I was thinking of the singular name of that village in Somerset."

"The village of Camberwell?" said Holmes, smiling. "Yes, it is indeed different from our London district of Camberwell. You must give the chronicle a different title, Watson, lest readers be confused as to the true locale of the Camberwell poisoning case."

—:—

The year '87 furnished us with a long series of cases of greater or less interest, of which I retain the records. Among my headings under this one twelve months I find . . . the Camberwell poisoning case.

FROM "THE FIVE ORANGE PIPS."

3

The Adventure of the Wax Gamblers

When my friend Mr. Sherlock Holmes sprained his ankle, irony followed upon irony. Within a matter of hours he was presented with a problem whose singular nature seemed to make imperative a visit to that sinister, underground room so well known to the public.

My friend's accident had been an unlucky one. Purely for the sport of it, he had consented to an impromptu glove-match with Bully Boy Rasher, the well-known professional middle-weight, at the old Cribb Sporting Club in Panton Street. To the amazement of the spectators, Holmes knocked out the Bully Boy before the latter could settle down to a long, hard mill.

Having broken Rasher's hanging guard and survived his right hand, my friend was leaving the sparring-saloon when he tripped on those ill-lighted, rickety stairs which I trust the Honorary Secretary of the club his since caused to be mended.

The intelligence of this mishap reached me as my wife and I finished our midday meal one cold season of rain and screaming winds. Though I have not my note-book at hand, I believe it was the first week in March, 1890. Uttering an exclamation as I read the telegram from Mrs. Hudson, I handed the message to my wife.

"You must go at once and see to the comfort of Mr. Sherlock Holmes for a day or two," said she. "Anstruther will always do your work for you."

Since at that time my house was in the Paddington area, it took me no great time to be in Baker Street.

Holmes was, as I expected, seated upon the sofa with his back to the wall, wearing a purple dressing-gown and with his bandaged right ankle upon a heap of cushions. A low-power microscope stood on a small table at his left hand, while on the sofa at his right lay a perfect drift of discarded newspapers.

Despite the weary, heavy-lidded expression which veiled his keen and eager nature, I could see that the misfortune had not sweetened his temper. Since Mrs. Hudson's telegram had mentioned only a fall on some stairs, I asked for an explanation and received that with which I have prefaced this chronicle.

"I was proud of myself, Watson," he added bitterly, "and careless of my step. The more fool I!"

"Yet surely some modest degree of pride was permissible! The Bully Boy is no mean opponent."

"On the contrary, I found him much overrated and half drunk. But I see, Watson, that you yourself are troubled about your health."

"Good heavens, Holmes! It is true that I suspect the advent of a cold. But, since there is as yet no sign in my appearance or voice, it is astonishing that you can have known it!"

"Astonishing? It is elementary. You have been taking your own pulse. A minute trace of the silver nitrate upon your right forefinger has been transferred to a significant spot on your left wrist. But what on earth are you doing now?"

Heedless of his protests, I examined and re-bandaged his ankle.

"And yet, my dear fellow," I went on, endeavouring to raise his spirits as I might cheer any patient, "in one sense it gives me great pleasure to see you thus incapacitated."

Holmes looked at me fixedly, but did not speak.

"Yes," said I, continuing to cheer him, "we must curb our impatience while we are confined to our sofa for a fortnight or perhaps more. But do not misunderstand me. When last summer I had the privilege of meeting your brother, Mycroft, you stated that he was your superior in observation and deduction."

"I spoke the truth. If the art of detection began and ended in reasoning from an arm-chair, my brother would be the greatest criminal agent that ever lived."

"A proposition which I take the liberty of doubting. Now behold! Here are you enforced to the seated position. It will delight me to see you demonstrate your superiority when you are presented with some case—"

"Case? I have no case!"

"Be of good cheer. A case will come."

"The agony column of *The Times*," said he, nodding towards the drift of newspapers, "is quite featureless. And even the joys of studying a new disease germ are not inexhaustible. As between you and another comforter, Watson, I really prefer Job's."

The entrance of Mrs. Hudson, bearing a letter which had been delivered by hand, momentarily cut him short. Though I had not actually expected my prophecy to be fulfilled with such promptness, I could not but remark that the note-paper bore a crest and must have cost fully half a crown a packet. Nevertheless, I was doomed to disappointment. After tearing open the letter eagerly, Holmes uttered a snort of vexation.

"So much for your soothsaying!" said he, scribbling a reply for our landlady to give to a district messenger. "It is merely an ill-spelt note from Sir Gervase Darlington, asking for an appointment at eleven tomorrow morning, and requesting that it be confirmed by hand to the Hercules Club."

"Darlington!" remarked I. "Surely you have mentioned that name before?"

"Yes, so I have. But upon that occasion I referred to Darlington the art-dealer, whose substitution of a false Leonardo painting for a real one caused such a scandal at the Grosvenor Galleries. Sir Gervase is a different and more exalted Darlington, though no less associated with scandal."

"Who is he?"

"Sir Gervase Darlington, Watson, is the bold, bad

baronet of fiction, addicted to pugilism and profligate
ladies. But he is by no means a swaggering figure of
the imagination; too many such men lived in our grand-
fathers' time." My friend looked thoughtful. "At the
moment, he had best mind his step."

"You interest me. Why so?"

"Well, I am no racing man. Yet I recall that Sir Gervase won a fortune during last year's Derby. Ill-disposed
persons whispered that he did so by bribery and secret
information. Be good enough, Watson, to remove this
microscope."

I did so. There remained upon the little table only the
sheet of crested note-paper which Holmes had flung down
there. From the pocket of his dressing-gown he took out
the snuff box of old gold, with a great amethyst in the
centre of the lid, which had been a present from the King
of Bohemia.

"However," he added, "every move made by Sir
Gervase Darlington is now carefully watched. Should he
so much as attempt to communicate with any suspicious
person, he will be warned off the turf even if he does not
land in gaol. I cannot recall the name of the horse on
which he wagered—"

"Lord Hove's Bengal Lady," cried I. "By Indian Rajah
out of Countess. She finished three furlongs ahead of the
field. Though, of course," I added, "I know little more
of racing matters than yourself."

"Indeed, Watson?"

"Holmes, such suspicions as you appear to entertain
are base and unworthy! I am a married man with a
depleted bank balance. Besides, what race is run in such
wild weather as this?"

"Well, the Grand National cannot be too far off."

"By Jove, yes! Lord Hove has two entries for the
Grand National. Many fancy Thunder Lad, though not
much is expected of Sheerness. But to me," I added, "a
scandal attached to the sport of kings is incredible. Lord
Hove is an honourable man."

"Precisely. Being an honourable man, he is no friend
to Sir Gervase Darlington."

"But why are you sure Sir Gervase can bring you nothing of interest?"

"If you were acquainted with the gentleman, Watson, you would acquit him of being concerned in anything whatever of interest, save that he is a really formidable heavy-weight boxer——" Holmes whistled. "Come! Sir Gervase was among those who witnessed my own trifling encounter with the Bully Boy this morning."

"Then what can he want of you?"

"Even if the question were of any moment, I have no data. A pinch of snuff, Watson? Well, well, I am not enamoured of it myself, though it represents an occasional variation from too much self-poisoning by nicotine."

I could not help laughing.

"My dear Holmes, your case is typical. Every medical man knows that a patient with an injury like yours, though the injury is slight and even of a humorous character, becomes as unreasonable as a child."

Holmes snapped shut the snuff-box and put it into his pocket.

"Watson," said he, "grateful though I am for your presence, I shall be obliged if you do not utter one word more for at least the next six hours, lest I say something which I may regret."

Thus, remaining silent even at supper, we sat very late in the snug room. Holmes moodily cross-indexed his records of crime, and I was deep in the pages of the *British Medical Journal.* Save for the tick of the clock and the crackle of the fire, there was no sound but the shrieking of the March gale, which drove the rain against the windows like handfuls of small shot, and growled and whooped in the chimney.

"No, no," my friend said querulously, at long last. "Optimism is stupidity. Certainly no case will come to my——Hark! Was that not the bell?"

"Yes. I heard it clearly in spite of the wind. But who can it be?"

"If a client," said Holmes, craning his long neck for a glimpse of the clock, "it must be a matter of deep

seriousness to bring someone out at two in the morning
and in such a gale."

After some delay, during which it took Mrs. Hudson
an interminable time to rise from her bed and open the
street door, no less than two clients were ushered into our
room. Both of them had been speaking at once, but their
conversation became distinct as they approached the
door-way.

"Grandfather, you mustn't!" came a young woman's
voice. "For the last time, please! You don't want Mr.
Holmes to think you are," here she lowered her voice to
a whisper, *"simple."*

"I'm not simple!" cried her companion. "Drat it, Nellie,
I see what I see! I should have come to tell the gentleman
yesterday morning, only you wouldn't hear of it."

"But, Grandfather, that Room of Horrors is a fear-
fully frightening place. You imagined it, dear."

"I'm seventy-six years old. But I've got no more
imagination," said the old man, proudly, "than one of
them wax figures. Me imagine it? Me, that's been night-
watchman since long before the museum was took where
it is now, and was still here in Baker Street?"

The newcomers paused. The ancient visitor, squat and
stubborn-looking in his rain-sodden brown greatcoat and
shepherd's check trousers, was a solid man of the people
with fine white hair. The girl was different. Graceful and
lissom, with fair hair and grey eyes encircled by black
lashes, she wore a simple costume of blue with narrow
white frills at the wrists and throat. There was grace as
well as timidity in her gestures.

Yet her delicate hands trembled. Very prettily she
identified Holmes and myself, apologizing for this late
call.

"My—my name is Eleanor Baxter," she added; "and,
as you may have gathered, my poor grandfather is the
night attendant at Madame Taupin's exhibition of wax
figures in the Marylebone Road." She broke off. "Oh!
Your poor ankle!"

"My injury is nothing, Miss Baxter," said Holmes.
"You are both very welcome. Watson, our guests' coats,

the umbrella; so. Now, you may be seated here in front of me. Though I have a crutch of sorts here, I am sure you will forgive me if I remain where I am. You were saying?"

Miss Baxter, who had been looking fixedly at the little table in evident distress at her grandfather's words, now gave a start and changed colour as she found Holmes's keen eye upon her.

"Sir, are you acquainted with Madame Taupin's wax-works?"

"It is justly famous."

"Do forgive me!" Eleanor Baxter blushed. "My meaning was, have you ever visited it?"

"Hum! I fear I am too much like our countrymen. Let some place be remote or inaccessible, and the Englishman will lose his life to find it. But he will not even look at it when it lies within a few hundred yards of his own front door. Have you visited Madame Taupin's, Watson?"

"No, I am afraid not," I replied. "Though I have heard much of the underground Room of Horrors. It is said that the management offers a large sum of money to anyone who will spend a night there."

The stubborn-looking old man, who to a medical eye showed symptoms of strong physical pain, nevertheless chuckled hoarsely as he sat down.

"Lord bless you, sir, don't you believe a word of that nonsense."

"It is not true, then?"

"Not a bit, sir. They wouldn't even let you do it. 'Cos a sporting gentleman might light a cigar or what not, and they're feared to death of fire."

"Then I take it," said Holmes, "that you are not unduly troubled by the Room of Horrors?"

"No, sir; never in general. The' even got old Charlie Peace there. He's with Marwood, too, the hangman what turned Charlie off not eleven years ago—but they're friendly like." His voice went higher. "But fair's fair, sir; and I don't like it a bit when those blessed wax figures begin to play a hand of cards!"

A drive of rain rattled against the windows. Holmes leaned forward.

"The wax figures, you say, have been playing at cards?"

"Yes, sir. Word of Sam Baxter!"

"Are all the wax figures engaged in this card game, or only some of them?"

"Only two, sir."

"How do you know this, Mr. Baxter? Did you see them?"

"Lord, sir, I should hope not! But what am I to think, when one of 'em has discarded from his hand, or taken a trick, and the cards are all mucked up on the table? Maybe I ought to explain, sir?"

"Pray do," invited Holmes, with some satisfaction.

"You see, sir, in the course of a night I make only one or two rounds down in the Room of Horrors. It's one big room, with dim lights. The reason I don't make more rounds is 'cos of my rheumatics. Folks don't know how cruel you can suffer from rheumatics! Double you up, they do."

"Dear me!" murmured Holmes sympathetically, pushing the tin of shag toward the old man.

"Anyway, sir! My Nellie there is a good girl, in spite of her eddication and the fine work she does. Whenever my rheumatics are bad, and they've been bad all this week, she gets up every blessed morning and comes to fetch me at seven o'clock—that's when I go off duty—so she can help me to a omnibus.

"Now tonight, being worried about me—which she oughtn't to be—well, Nellie turned up only an hour ago, with young Bob Parsnip. Bob took over my duty from me, so I said, 'I've read all about this Mr. Holmes, only a step away; let's go and tell him.' And that's why we're here."

Holmes inclined his head.

"I see, Mr. Baxter. But you were speaking of last night?"

"Ah! Well, about the Room of Horrors. On one side there's a series of tabloos. Which I mean: there's separate compartments, each of 'em behind an iron railing so nobody can step in, and wax figures in each compartment. The tabloos tell a story that's called 'The History of a Crime.'

"This history of a crime is about a young gentleman—and a pleasant young gentleman he is, too, only weak—who falls into bad company. He gambles and loses his money; then he kills the wicked older man; and at last he's hanged as fast as Charlie Peace. It's meant to be a—a—"

"A moral lesson, yes. Take warning, Watson. Well, Mr. Baxter?"

"Well, sir! It's that wretched gambling tabloo. There's only two of 'em in it, the young gentleman and the wicked wrong 'un. They're sitting in a lovely room, at a table with gold coins on it; only not real gold, of course. It's not a-happening today, you see, but in old times when they had stockings and britches."

"Eighteenth-century costume, perhaps?"

"That's it, sir. The young gentleman is sitting on the other side of the table, so he faces towards you straight. But the old wrong 'un is sitting with his back turned, holding up his cards as if he was laughing, and you can see the cards in his hand.

"Now last night! When I say last night, sir, course I mean two nights ago, because it's towards morning now. I walked straight past that blessed tabloo without seeing nothing. Then, about a hour later, all of a sudden I thinks, 'What's wrong with that tabloo?' There wasn't much wrong, and I'm so used to it that I'm the only one who'd have noticed. 'What's wrong?' I thinks. So I goes down and has another look.

"Sir, so help me! The wicked older man—the one whose hand you can see—was holding less cards than he ought. He'd discarded, or played a trick maybe, and they'd been messing up the cards on the table.

"I've got no 'magination, I tell you. Don't want none. But when Nellie here came to fetch me at seven in the morning, I felt cruel, what with rheumatics and this too. I wouldn't tell her what was wrong—well, just in case

I might-a seen things. Today I thought perhaps I dreamed it. But I didn't! It was there again tonight.

"Now, sir, I'm not daft. I see what I see! You might say, maybe, somebody did that for fun—changed the cards, and messed 'em up, and all. But nobody couldn't do it in the daytime, or they'd be seen. It might be done at night, 'cos there's one side door that won't lock properly. But it's not like one of the public's practical jokes, where they stick a false beard on Queen Anne or maybe a sun-bonnet on Napoleon's head. This is so little that nobody'd notice it. But if somebody's been playing a hand of cards for those two blessed dummies, then who did it and why?"

For some moments, Sherlock Holmes remained silent.

"Mr. Baxter," he said gravely, and glanced at his own bandaged ankle, "your patience shames me in my foolish petulance. I shall be happy to look into this matter."

"But, Mr. Holmes," cried Eleanor Baxter, in stark bewilderment, "surely you cannot take the affair seriously?"

"Forgive me, madam. Mr. Baxter, what particular game of cards are the two wax figures playing?"

"Dunno, sir. Used to wonder that myself, long ago when I was new to the place. Nap or whist, maybe? But I dunno."

"You say that the figure with his back turned is holding fewer cards than he should. How many cards have been played from his hand?"

"Sir?"

"You did not observe? Tcha, that is most unfortunate! Then I beg of you carefully to consider a vital question. Have these figures been gambling?"

"My dear Holmes—" I began, but my friend's look gave me a pause.

"You tell me, Mr. Baxter, that the cards upon the table have been moved or at least disturbed. Have the gold coins been moved as well?"

"Come to think of it," replied Mr. Samuel Baxter, after a pause, "no, sir, they haven't! Funny, too."

Holmes's eyes were glittering, and he rubbed his hands together.

"I fancied as much," said he. "Well, fortunately I may devote my energies to the problem, since I have nothing on hand at the moment save a future dull matter which seems to concern Sir Gervase Darlington and possibly Lord Hove as well. Lord Hove—Dear me, Miss Baxter, is anything wrong?"

Eleanor Baxter, who had risen to her feet, now contemplated Holmes with startled eyes.

"Did you say Lord Hove?" asked she.

"Yes. How should the name be familiar to you, may I ask?"

"Merely that he is my employer."

"Indeed?" said Holmes, raising his eyebrows. "Ah, yes. You do type-writing, I perceive. The double line in the plush costume a little above your wrist, where the type-writist presses against the table, proclaims as much. You are acquainted with Lord Hove, then?"

"No, I have never so much as seen him, though I do much type-writing at his town house in Park Lane. So humble a person as I—!"

"Tcha, this is even more unfortunate! However, we must do what we can. Watson, have you any objection to going out into such a tempestuous night?"

"Not in the least," said I, much astonished. "But why?"

"This confounded sofa, my boy! Since I am confined to it as to a sick-bed, you must be my eyes. It troubles me to trespass upon your pain, Mr. Baxter, but would it be possible for you to escort Dr. Watson for a brief visit to the Room of Horrors? Thank you; excellent."

"But what am I to do?" asked I.

"In the upper drawer of my desk, Watson, you will find some envelopes."

"Well, Holmes?"

"Oblige me by counting the number of cards in the hand of each wax figure. Then, carefully keeping them in their present order from left to right, place each set in a separate envelope which you will mark accordingly. Do the same with the cards upon the table, and bring them back to me as quickly as you may accomplish it."

"Sir——" began the ancient man in excitement.

"No, no, Mr. Baxter, I should prefer not to speak now. I have only a working hypothesis, and there seems one almost insuperable difficulty to it." Holmes frowned. "But it is of the first importance to discover, in all senses of the word, what game is being played at that wax exhibition."

Together with Samuel Baxter and his grand-daughter, I ventured forth into the rain-whipped blackness. Despite Miss Baxter's protests, within ten minutes we were all three standing before the gambling tableau in the Room of Horrors.

A not ill-looking young man named Robert Parsnip, clearly much smitten with the charms of Eleanor Baxter, turned up the blue sparks of gas in dusty globes. But even so the gloomy room remained in a semi-darkness in which the ranks of grim wax figures seemed imbued with a horrible spider-like repose, as though waiting only until a visitor turned away, before reaching out to touch him.

Madame Taupin's exhibition is too well known to need any general description. But I was unpleasantly impressed by the tableau called "The History of a Crime." The scenes were most lifelike in both effect and colour, with the wigs and small-swords of the eighteenth century. Had I in fact been guilty of those mythical gambling lapses charged upon me by Holmes's ill-timed sense of humour, the display might well have harassed my conscience.

This was especially so when we lowered our heads under the iron railing, and approached the two gamblers in the mimic room.

"Drat it, Nellie, don't touch them cards!" cried Mr. Baxter, much more testy and irascible in his own domain. But his tone changed as he spoke to me. "Look there, sir! There's," he counted slowly, "there's nine cards in the wicked wrong 'un's hand. And sixteen in the young gentleman's."

"Listen!" whispered the young lady. "Isn't someone walking about upstairs?"

"Drat it, Nellie, it's only Bob Parsnip. Who else would it be?"

"As you said, the cards on the table are not much disarranged," I remarked. "Indeed, the small pile in front of your 'young gentleman' is not disarranged at all. Twelve cards lie at his elbow——"

"Ah, and nineteen by the wrong 'un. Funny card game, sir!"

I agreed and, curiously repulsed by the touch of waxen fingers against my own, I put the various sets of playing-cards into four marked envelopes, and hastened up from the stuffy den. Miss Baxter and her grandfather, despite the latter's horrified protest, I insisted on sending home in a stray cab whose driver had just deposited some hopelessly intoxicated gentleman against his own door.

I was not sorry to return to the snug warmth of my friend's sitting-room. To my dismay, however, Holmes had risen from the couch. He was standing by his desk with the green-shaded lamp, eagerly studying an open atlas and supported by a crutch under his right arm.

"Enough, Watson!" he silenced my protests. "You have the envelopes? Good, good! Give them to me. Thank you. In the hand of the older gambler, the wax figure with his back turned, were there not nine cards?"

"Holmes, this is amazing! How could you have known that?"

"Logic, my dear fellow. Now let us see."

"One moment," I said firmly. "You spoke earlier of a crutch, but where could you have obtained one at such short notice? That is an extraordinary crutch. It seems to be constructed of some light-weight metal, and shines where the rays of the lamp——"

"Yes, yes, I already had it in my possession."

"Already had it?"

"It is made of aluminum, and is the relic of a case before my biographer came to glorify me. I have already mentioned it to you, but you have forgotten. Now be good enough to forget the crutch while you examine these cards. Oh, beautiful, beautiful!"

Were all the jewels of Golconda spread out before him, he could not have been more ecstatic. He even rejoiced when I told him what I had seen and heard.

"What, you are still in the dark? Then do you take these nine cards, Watson. Put them upon the desk in their order, and announce the name of each as you do so."

"Knave of diamonds," said I, placing the cards under the lamp, "seven of hearts, ace of clubs—Good heavens, Holmes!"

"Do you see anything, then?"

"Yes. There are two aces of clubs, one following the other!"

"Did I not call it beautiful? But you have counted only four cards. Proceed with the remaining five."

"Deuce of spades," said I, "ten of hearts—merciful powers, here is a third ace of clubs, and two more knaves of diamonds!"

"And what do you deduce from that?"

"Holmes, I think I see light. Madame Taupin's is famous for its real-life effects. The older wax figure is a brazen gambler, who is depicted as cheating the young man. By a subtle effect, they have shown him as holding false cards for his winning hand."

"Hardly subtle, I fancy. Even so brazen a gambler as yourself, Watson, would surely feel some embarrassment at putting down a winning hand which contained no less than three knaves of diamonds and three aces of clubs?"

"Yes, there are difficulties."

"Further. If you count all the cards, both those in the hands and upon the table, you will observe that their total number is fifty-six: which is four more than I, at least, am accustomed to use in one pack."

"But what can it mean? What is the answer to our problem?"

The atlas lay upon the desk where Holmes had thrown it down when I gave him the envelopes. Snatching up the book, groaning as he staggered and all but fell on that curious crutch, he eagerly opened the book again.

" 'At the mouth of the Thames,' " he read, " 'on the island of—' "

"Holmes, my question concerned the answer to our problem!"

"This is the answer to our problem."

Though I am the most long-suffering of men, I protested strongly when he packed me off upstairs to my old room. I believed that I should get no sleep upon the rack of this mystery, yet I slept heavily, and it was nearly eleven o'clock when I descended to breakfast.

Sherlock Holmes, who had already breakfasted, again sat upon the sofa. I was glad of my clean, fresh shave when I found him deep in conversation with Miss Eleanor, whose timidity was lessened by his easy manner.

Yet something in the gravity of his face arrested my hand as I rang the bell for rashers and eggs.

"Miss Baxter," said he, "though there still remains an objection to my hypothesis, the time has come to tell you something of great importance. But what the devil—!"

Our door had been suddenly dashed open. To be precise, it was kicked open with a crash. But this had been done only as a jest by the man who kicked it, for his loud, overfed burst of laughter rang like a brazen trumpet.

In the aperture stood a burly, red-faced gentleman with a shining hat, a costly frock-coat open over a white waistcoat to show the diamonds on his watch-guard, and the single flaming ruby in his cravat.

Though not so tall as Holmes, he was far broader and heavier; indeed, with a figure not unlike my own. His loud laugh rang out again, and his cunning little eyes flashed, as he held up a leather bag and shook it.

"Here you are, cully!" cried he. "You're the Scotland Yard man, ain't you? A thousand gold sovereigns, and all yours for the askin'!"

Sherlock Holmes, though astonished, regarded him with the utmost composure.

"Sir Gervase Darlington, I think?"

Without paying the slightest notice of either Miss Baxter or myself, the newcomer strode across and rattled the bag of coins under Holmes's nose.

"That's me, Mister Detective!" said he. "Saw you fight yesterday. You could be better, but you'll do. One day, my man, they may make prize-fightin' legal. Till they do, a gentleman's got to arrange a neat little mill in secret. Stop a bit, though!"

Suddenly, cat-footed despite his weight, he went to the window and peered down into the street.

"Curse old Phileas Belch! He's had a man following me for months. Ay, and two blasted manservants in succession to steam open my letters. Broke the back for one of 'em, though." Sir Gervase's shattering laugh rang again. "Never mind!"

Holmes's face seemed to change; but an instant later he was his cool, imperturbable self as Sir Gervase Darlington turned back, flinging the bag of money on the sofa.

"Keep the dibs, Scotland Yarder. *I* don't need 'em. Now, then. In three months we'll match you with Jem Garlick, the Bristol Smasher. Fight a cross, and I'll skin you; do me proud, and I can be a good patron. With an unknown feller like you, I can get eight to one odds."

"Do I understand, Sir Gervase," said Holmes, "that you wish me to box professionally in the ring?"

"You're the Scotland Yarder, ain't you? You comprey English, don't you?"

"When I hear it spoken, yes."

"That's a joke, hey? Well, so is this!"

Playfully, deliberately, his heavy left fist whipped out a round-arm which passed—as it was meant to pass— just an inch in front of my friend's nose. Holmes did not even blink. Again Sir Gervase roared with laughter.

"Mind your manners, Mister Detective, when you speak to a gentleman. I could break you in two even if you didn't have a bad ankle, by God!"

Miss Eleanor Baxter, white-faced, uttered a little moaning cry and seemed to be trying to efface herself against the wall.

"Sir Gervase," cried I, "you will kindly refrain from using offensive language in the presence of a lady."

Instantly our guest turned round, and looked me up and down in a most insolent manner.

"Who's this? Watson? Sawbones feller? Oh." Suddenly he thrust his beefy red face into mine. "Know anything about boxin'?"

"No," said I. "That is—not much."

"Then see you don't get a lesson," retorted Sir Gervase playfully, and roared with mirth again. "Lady? What lady?" Seeing Miss Baxter, he looked a little disconcerted, but directed a killing ogle. "No lady, Sawbones. But a fetchin' little piece, by God!"

"Sir Gervase," said I, "you are now warned for the last time."

"One moment, Watson," interposed the calm voice of Sherlock Holmes. "You must forgive Sir Gervase Darlington. No doubt Sir Gervase has not yet recovered from the visit he paid three days ago to the wax exhibition of Madame Taupin."

In the brief silence that followed, we could hear a coal rattle in the grate and the eternal rain on the windows. But our guest could not be dismayed.

"The Scotland Yarder, eh?" he sneered. "Who told you I was at Madame Taupin's three days ago?"

"No one. But, from certain facts in my possession, the inference was obvious. Such a visit looked innocent, did it not? It would arouse no suspicion on the part of anyone who might be following—some follower, for instance, employed by the eminent sportsman Sir Phileas Belch, who wished to make certain you did not win another fortune by secret information as you did on last year's Derby."

"You don't interest me, my man!"

"Indeed? And yet, with your sporting proclivities, I feel sure you must be interested in cards."

"Cards?"

"Playing-cards," said Holmes blandly, taking some from his dressing-gown pocket and holding them up fan-wise. "In fact, these nine cards."

"What the devil's all this?"

"It is a singular fact, Sir Gervase, that a casual visitor

to the Room of Horrors—on passing the gambling tableau
—can see the cards in the hand of a certain wax figure
without even giving them more than an innocent-appear-
ing glance.

"Now some strage tampering was done one night with
these cards. The cards in the hand of the other player,
the 'young gentleman,' had not even been touched, as
was shown by their dusty and gritty condition. But some
person, a certain person, had removed a number of cards
from the hand of the so-called 'wrong 'un,' throwing
them down on the table, and, further, had added four
cards from no less than two extra packs.

"Why was this done? It was not because someone
wished to play a practical joke, in creating the illusion
that wax dummies were occupied in reckless gambling.
Had that been the culprit's motive, he would have moved
the imitation gold coins as well as the cards. But the coins
were not moved.

"The true answer is simple and indeed obvious. There
are twenty-six letters in our alphabet; and twenty-six,
twice multiplied, gives us fifty-two; the number of cards
in a pack. Supposing that we were arbitrarily to choose
one card for each letter, we could easily make a childish,
elementary form of substitution-cipher—"

Sir Gervase Darlington's metal laugh blared shrilly.

"Substitution-cipher," jeered he, with his red hand
at the ruby in his cravat. "What's that, hey? What's the
fool talkin' about?"

"—which would be betrayed, however," said Holmes,
"should a message of only nine letters contain a double
'e' or a double 's.' Let us imagine, therefore, that the
knave of diamonds stands for the letter 's' and the ace
of clubs for the letter 'e.' "

"Holmes," interposed I, "this may be inspiration. But
it is not logic! Why should you think a message must contain those letters?"

"Because already I knew the message itself. You told
it to me."

"I told you?"

"Tut, Watson. If these cards represent the letters indicated, we have a double 'e' towards the beginning of the word and a double 's' at the end of it. The first letter of the word, we perceive, must be 'S,' and there is an 'e' before the double 's' at the end. No cunning is required to give us the word Sheerness.' "

"But what in the world has Sheerness—" I began.

"Geographically, you will find it towards the mouth of the Thames," interrupted Holmes. "But it is also, you informed me, the name of a horse owned by Lord Hove. Though this horse has been entered for the Grand National, you told me that little is expected of it. But if the horse has been trained with the utmost secrecy as another smashing winner like Bengal Lady—"

"There would be a tremendous killing," said I, "for any gambler who could learn that well-guarded secret and back the horse!"

Sherlock Holmes held up the fan of cards in his left hand.

"My dear Miss Eleanor Baxter," cried he, with a sorrowful sternness, "why did you let Sir Gervase Darlington persuade you? Your grandfather would not like to hear that you used the wax exhibition to leave this message—telling Sir Gervase what he wished to know without even speaking to him, writing to him, or approaching within a mile of him."

If previously Miss Baxter had turned pale and uttered a moan at seeing Sir Gervase, it was as nothing to the piteous look now in her stricken grey eyes. Swaying on her feet, she began to falter out a denial.

"No, no!" said Holmes, gently. "It really will not do. Within a few moments of the time you entered this room last night, I was aware of your—your acquaintanceship with Sir Gervase here."

"Mr. Holmes, you cannot have known it!"

"I fear so. Kindly observe the small table at my left as I sit upon the sofa. When you approached me, there was nothing upon the table save a sheet of note-paper emblazoned with the somewhat conspicuous crest of Sir Gervase Darlington."

"Oh, heaven help me!" cried the wretched young lady.

"Yet you were strangely affected. You looked fixedly at the table, as though in recognition. When you saw my eye upon you, you gave a start and changed colour. By apparently casual remarks, I elicited the fact that your employer is Lord Hove, the owner of Sheerness—"

"No! No! No!"

"It would have been easy for you to have substituted the new cards for those already in the wax figure's hand. As your grandfather said, there is a side door at Madame Taupin's which cannot properly be locked. You could have made the substitution secretly at night, before you called formally to escort your grandfather home in the morning.

"You might have destroyed the evidence before too late, if on the first night your grandfather had told you what was amiss in the museum. But he did not tell you until the following night, when both he and Robert Parsnip were there, and you could not be alone. However, I do not wonder you protested when he wished to see me. Later, as Dr. Watson quite unconsciously told me, you tried to seize and scatter the cards in the wax figure's hand."

"Holmes," cried I, "enough of such torture! The true culprit is not Miss Baxter, but this ruffian who stands and laughs at us!"

"Believe me, Miss Baxter, I would not distress you," said Holmes. "I have no doubt you learned by accident of Sheerness' powers. Sporting peers will speak quite carelessly when they hear only the harmless clicking of a type-writer from an adjoining room. But Sir Gervase, long before he was so carefully watched, must have urged you to keep your ears open and communicate with him in this ingenious way should you acquire information of value.

"At first the method seemed almost too ingenious. Indeed, I could not understand why you did not merely write to him, until when *he* arrived here I learned that even his letters are steamed open. The cards were the only possible way. But we have the evidence now—"

"No, by God!" said Sir Gervase Darlington. "You've got no evidence at all!"

His left hand, quick as a striking snake, snatched the cards from Holmes's grasp. As my friend instinctively stood up, the pain in his swollen ankle making him bite back a cry, Sir Gervase's open right hand drove into Holmes's neck and sent him sprawling back on the sofa.

Again the triumphant laugh rang out.

"Gervase!" pleaded Miss Baxter, wringing her hands. "Please! Don't look at me so! I meant no harm!"

"Oh, no!" said he, with a sneer on his brutal face.

"N-no-o-o! Come here and betray me, would you? Make me jump when I see you, hey? You're no better than you should be, and I'll tell that to anybody who asks. Now stand aside, damn you!"

"Sir Gervase," said I, "already I have warned you for the last time."

"Sawbones interfering, eh? I'll—"

Now, I am the first to admit that it was luck rather than judgment, though perhaps I may add that I am quicker on my feet than my friends suppose. Suffice to say Miss Baxter screamed.

Despite the pain of his ankle, Sherlock Holmes again leaped from the sofa.

"By Jove, Watson! A finer left on the mark and right to the head I never witnessed! You've grassed him so hard he will be unconscious for ten minutes!"

"Yet I trust," said I, blowing upon cracked knuckles, "that poor Miss Baxter has not been unduly distressed by the crash with which he struck the floor? It would also grieve me to alarm Mrs. Hudson, whom I hear approaching with bacon and eggs."

"Good old Watson!"

"Why do you smile, Holmes? Have I said something of a humorous character?"

"No, no. Heaven forbid! Yet sometimes I suspect that I may be much shallower, and you far more deep, than customarily I am wont to believe."

"Your satire is beyond me. However, there is the evidence. But you must not publicly betray even Sir Gervase Darlington, lest you betray Miss Baxter as well!"

"Humph! I have a score to settle with that gentleman, Watson. His offer to open for me a career as a professional boxer I could not in honesty resent. In its way, it is a great compliment. But to confuse me with a Scotland Yard detective! That was an insult, I fear, which I can neither forget nor forgive."

"Holmes, how many favours have I ever asked of you?"

"Well, well, have it as you please. We shall keep the cards only as a last resort, should that sleeping beauty again misbehave. As for Miss Baxter—"

"I loved him!" cried the poor young lady passionately. "Or—well, at least, I thought I did."

"In any event, Miss Baxter, Watson shall remain silent as long as you like. He must not speak until some long, long distant date when you, perhaps as an ancient great-grandam, shall smile and give your leave. Half a century ere that, you will have forgotten all about Sir Gervase Darlington."

"Never! Never! Never!"

"Oh, I fancy so," smiled Sherlock Holmes. *"On s'enlace; puis, un jour, on se lasse; c'est l'amour.* There is more wisdom in that French epigram than in the whole works of Henrik Ibsen."

—:—

4

The Adventure of the Highgate Miracle

Though we were accustomed to receiving strange telegrams at our rooms in Baker Street, there was one which served to introduce an affair unique even in the annals of Mr. Sherlock Holmes.

I had met Holmes for a stroll in the Regent's Park one dark, drizzling, but not too cold afternoon in December, during which we discussed certain personal affairs of mine with which I need not burden the reader. When we returned to the snug sitting-room at four o'clock, Mrs. Hudson brought up the telegram along with a substantial tea-tray. It was addressed to Holmes, and ran thus:

"Can you imagine man worshipping umbrella? Husbands are irrational. Suspect chicanery with diamonds. Will call upon you tea-time.—Mrs. Gloria Cabpleasure."

I rejoiced to see a gleam of interest flash in Sherlock Holmes's deep-set eyes.

"What's this, what's this?" said he, as with unusual appetite he attacked the hot buttered scones and jam.

"Highgate postmark, hardly a fashionable area, and dispatched at three-seventeen. Study it, Watson!"

At this time—to be more precise, it was late December of the year 1896—I was not living in Baker Street, but I had come for a few days to visit old haunts. Under the heading for this year, my note-book records few cases. Of these only one, the affair of Mrs. Ronder, the veiled lodger, have I seen fit so far to set down; and Mrs. Ronder's problem afforded little scope for my friend's great powers.

Thus Holmes entered a brief period of stagnation and desperation. As I saw his gaunt countenance in the shaded light of the table-lamp, I could not but rebuke myself. Of what moment were my trivial affairs against the thirst for abstruse problems raging in that extraordinary intellect?

"It is possible," continued Holmes, snatching back the telegram to read it again, "that there may be in London two women with the singular and even striking name of Gloria Cabpleasure. But I doubt it."

"You are acquainted with the lady, then?"

"No, no, I have never even seen her. Still, I fancy she must be a certain beauty-specialist who—in any event, what do you make of this?"

"Well, it presents that feature of the bizarre which is so dear to you. 'Can you imagine man worshipping umbrella?' But it is a little difficult."

"True, Watson. A woman, however extravagant she may be in large matters, is usually economical in small. Mrs. Cabpleasure has been so thrifty of her 'an's' and 'the's' that I am not at all sure of her meaning."

"Nor I."

"Does it mean that a certain man worships a certain umbrella? Or is man in the abstract, Englishmen perhaps, desired to bow down to the umbrella as his tribal deity and shield against the climate? At least, what can we deduce from it?"

"Deduce? From the telegram?"

"Of course."

I was glad to laugh, since for that same brief time I had been feeling rheumatic and less than young.

"Holmes, we cannot possibly deduce. We can only guess."

"Tut, how often must I tell you that I never guess? It is a shocking habit, destructive of the logical faculty."

"And yet, were I to adopt your own somewhat didactic manner, I should say that nothing affords less opportunity to the reasoner than a telegram, because it is so brief and impersonal."

"Then I fear you would be wrong."

"Confound it, Holmes—"

"Yet, consider. When a man writes me a letter of a dozen pages, he may conceal his true nature in a cloud of words. When he is obliged to be terse, however, I know him at once. You may have remarked a similar thing in public speakers."

"But this is a woman."

"Yes, Watson, no doubt the fact makes a difference. But let me have your views. Come! Apply to a study of this telegram your own natural shrewdness."

Thus challenged, and flattering myself that in the past I had not been altogether unhelpful to him, I did as I was requested.

"Well," said I, "Mrs. Cabpleasure is surely very inconsiderate, since she makes an appointment without confirming it, and seems to think your time is her own."

"Capital, Watson. You improve with the years. What else?"

Inspiration rushed upon me.

"Holmes, the word, 'Mrs.,' in so compressed a message, is totally unnecessary! I think I see it all!"

"Better still, my dear fellow," said Sherlock Holmes, throwing down his napkin and clapping his hands together without noise. "I shall be happy to hear your analysis."

"Mrs. Gloria Cabpleasure, Holmes, is a young bride. Being still in the proud flush of her newly wedded name, she is so insistent upon it that she uses it even in this message. What could be more natural? Especially when we think of a happy, perhaps beautiful young woman—"

"Yes, yes. But be good enough, Watson, to omit the descriptive passages and come to the point."

"By Jove, I am sure of it!" said I. "It supports my first modest deduction too. The poor girl is inconsiderate, let us say, merely because she is pampered by an affectionate young husband."

But my friend shook his head.

"I think not, Watson. If she were in the first strong pride of so-called wedded bliss, she would have signed herself 'Mrs. Henry Cabpleasure,' or 'Mrs. George Cabpleasure,' or whatever the name of her husband chanced to be. But in one respect, at least, you are correct. There is something odd—even disturbing—about that word 'Mrs.' She insists upon it too much."

"My dear fellow!"

Abruptly Holmes rose to his feet and wandered towards his arm-chair. Our gas was lit, and there was a cheery fire against the dark, bleak drizzle which we could hear dripping outside the window.

But he did not sit down. Deep in concentration, his brows knitted, he slowly stretched out his hand towards the right side angle of the chimney-piece. A genuine thrill of emotion shot through my being as he picked up his violin, the old and beloved Stradivarius which, in his moodiness and black humor, he told me he had not touched for weeks.

The light ran along satiny wood as he tucked the violin under his chin, and whisked up the bow. None the less, my friend hesitated. He lowered both violin and bow with something like a snarl.

"No, I have not yet enough data," said he, "and it is a cardinal error to theorize without data."

"Then at least," said I, "it is a pleasure to think that I have deduced from the telegram as much as you have deduced yourself."

"Oh, the telegram?" said Holmes, as though he had never heard of it.

"Yes. Is there any point which I have overlooked?"

"Well, Watson, I fear you were wrong in almost every particular. The woman who dispatched that telegram has been married for some years, and is no longer in her first youth. She is of either Scottish or American origin, well educated and well-to-do, but unhappily married and of a domineering disposition. On the other hand, it is probable that she is quite handsome. Though these are only trifling and obvious deductions, perhaps they may do."

A few moments ago I had hoped to see Sherlock Holmes in such a mood, vigorous and alert, with the old mocking light in his eyes. Yet the bright-patterned china rattled upon the snowy napery as I smote the table a blow with my fist.

"Holmes, this time you have carried a jest too far!"

"My dear Watson, I do really beg your pardon. I had no idea you would take the matter so seri—"

"For shame! In popular esteem, at least, only the vulgar live at Hampstead and Highgate, which are usually pronounced without the aspirate. You may be making sport of some wretched, ill-educated female who is on the point of starving!"

"Hardly, Watson. Though an ill-educated woman might attempt such words as 'irrational' and "chicanery,' she would be unlikely to spell them correctly. Similarly, since Mrs. Cabpleasure tells us that she suspects false dealing in a matter of diamonds, we may assume she does not scavenge her bread from dustbins."

"She has been married for some years? And unhappily?"

"We live in an age of propriety, Watson; and I confess I prefer it so."

"What on earth has that to do with the matter?"

"Only a woman who has been married for years, and hence past her first youth, will so candidly write in a telegram—under the eye of a post-office clerk—her belief that all husbands are irrational. You must perceive some sign of unhappiness, together with a domineering nature? Secondary inference: since the charge of chicanery appears to relate to her husband, this marriage must be even more unhappy than are most."

"But her origin?"

"Pray re-peruse the last sentence of the telegram. Only a Scot or an American says, 'Will call upon you,' when he, or in this case she, means the 'shall' of simple futurity, which would be used as a matter of course by any Englishwoman educated or uneducated. Are you answered?"

"I—I—stay a moment! You stated, not as fancy but as fact, that she must be handsome!"

"Ah, I can say only that it is probable. And the hypothesis comes not from the telegram."

"Then from where?"

"Come, did I not tell you I believe her to have been a beauty-specialist? Such ladies are seldom actually hideous-looking, else they are no strong advertisement for their own wares. But this, if I mistake not, is our client now."

While he had been speaking, we heard a loud and decisive ring of the bell from below. There was some delay, during which the caller presumably expected our landlady to escort her formally to our sitting-room. Sherlock Holmes, putting away the violin and its bow, waited expectantly until Mrs. Gloria Cabpleasure entered the room.

She was certainly handsome—tall, stately, of almost queenly bearing, though perhaps too haughty, with an abundance of rather brassy fair hair and cold, blue eyes. Clad in sables over a costly gown of dark-blue velvet, she wore a beige hat ornamented with a large white bird.

Disdaining my offer to remove her outer coat, while Holmes performed introductions with easy courtesy, Mrs. Cabpleasure cast round one glance which seemed to sum up unfavourably our humble room, with its worn bear-skin hearth-rug and acid-stained chemical table. Yet she consented to be seated in my arm-chair, clasping her white-gloved hands in her lap.

"One moment, Mr. Holmes!" said she, politely, but in a hard, brisk voice. "Before I commit myself to anything, I must ask you to state the fee for your professional services."

There was a slight pause before my friend answered.

"My fees never vary, save when I remit them altogether."

"Come, Mr. Holmes, I fear you think to take advantage of a poor weak woman! But in this case it will not do."

"Indeed, madam?"

"No, sir. Before I employ what you will forgive me for terming a professional spy, and risk being overcharged, I must again ask you to state your exact fee."

Sherlock Holmes rose from his chair.

"I am afraid, Mrs. Cabpleasure," said he, smiling, "that such small talents as I possess might be unavailing to assist you in your problem, and I regret exceedingly that you have been troubled by this call. Good-day, madam. Watson, will you kindly escort our guest downstairs?"

"Stop!" cried Mrs. Cabpleasure, biting hard at her handsome lip.

Holmes shrugged his shoulders and sank back again into the easy-chair.

"You drive a hard bargain, Mr. Holmes. But it would be worth ten shillings or even a guinea to know why on earth my husband cherishes, worships, idolizes that pestilent shabby umbrella, and will never allow it away from his presence even at night!"

Whatever Holmes might have felt, it was gone in his sense of starvation for a fresh problem.

"Ah! Then your husband worships the umbrella in a literal sense?"

"Did I not say so?"

"No doubt the umbrella has some great financial or sentimental value?"

"Stuff and nonsense! I was with him when he bought it two and a half years ago. He paid seven-and-six-pence for it at a shop in the Tottenham Court Road."

"Yet perhaps some idiosyncrasy—?"

Mrs. Gloria Cabpleasure looked shrewdly calculating.

"No, Mr. Holmes. My husband is selfish, inhuman, and soulless. It is true, since my maternal great-grandfather was The McRea of McRea, in Aberdeenshire, I take good care to keep the man in his place. But Mr. Cabpleasure, aside from his vicious nature, has never done anything without very good reasons."

Holmes looked grave.

" 'Inhuman?' 'Vicious nature?' These are very serious terms indeed. Does he use you cruelly, then?"

Our visitor raised even haughtier eyebrows.

"No, but I have no doubt he would wish to do so. James is an abnormally strong brute, though he is only of middle height and has no more of what is called figure than a hop-pole. Pah, the vanity of men! His features are quite nondescript, but he is inordinately proud of a very heavy, very glossy brown moustache, which curves round his mouth like a horseshoe. He has worn it for years; and, indeed, next to that umbrella—"

"Umbrella!" muttered Holmes. "Umbrella! Forgive

the interruption, madam, but I should desire more details of your husband's nature."

"It makes him look only like a police-constable."

"I beg your pardon?"

"The moustache, I mean."

"But does your husband drink? Interest himself in other women? Gamble? Keep you short of money? What, none of these things?"

"I presume, sir," retorted Mrs. Cabpleasure loftily, "that you are desirous of hearing merely the relevant facts? It is for you to provide an explanation. I *wish* to hear this elucidation. I will tell you whether it satisfies me. Would it not demonstrate better breeding on your part were you to permit me to state the facts?"

Holmes's thin lips closed tightly. "Pray do so."

"My husband is the senior partner of the firm of Cabpleasure & Brown, the well-known diamond-brokers of Hatton Garden. Throughout the fifteen years of our wedlock—ugh!—we have seldom been separated for more than a fortnight's time, save on the latest and most sinister occasion."

"The latest occasion?"

"Yes, sir. Only yesterday afternoon James returned home from a protracted six months' business journey to Amsterdam and Paris, as idolatrous of that umbrella as ever. Never has he been more idolatrous, throughout the full year during which he has worshipped it."

Sherlock Holmes, who had been sitting with his fingertips pressed together and his long legs stretched out, gave a slight start.

"The full year, madam?" demanded he. "Yet a moment ago you remarked that Mr. Cabpleasure had bought the umbrella two and a half years ago. Am I to understand that his—his worship dates from just a year ago?"

"You may certainly so understand it, yes."

"That is suggestive! That is most suggestive!" My friend looked thoughtful. "But of what? We—yes, yes, Watson? What is it? You appear to have become impatient."

Thought it was not often that I ventured to vouchsafe

my own suggestion before Holmes had asked for one, upon this occasion I could not forbear.

"Holmes," cried I, "surely this problem is not too difficult? It is an umbrella: it has a curved handle, which is probably thick. In a hollow handle, or perhaps some other part of the umbrella, it would be easy to hide diamonds or other valuable objects."

Our guest did not even deign to look at me.

"Do you imagine that I would have stooped to visit you, Mr. Holmes, if the answer were as simple as all that?"

"You are sure it is not the true explanation?" Holmes asked quickly.

"Quite sure. I am sharp, Mr. Holmes," said the lady, whose handsome profile did in truth appear to have a knife-edge; "I am very sharp. Let me illustrate. For years after my marriage I consented to preside over the Madame Dubarry Salon de Beauté in Bond Street. Why do you think that a McRea of McRea would condescend to use such a cognomen as Cabpleasure, open as it is to comment from a primitive sense of humour?"

"Well, madam?"

"Clients or prospective clients might stare at such a name. But they would remember it."

"Yes, yes, I confess to having seen the name upon the window. But you spoke of the umbrella?"

"One night some eight months ago, while my husband lay in slumber, I went privily into his sleeping-chamber from my own, removed the umbrella from beside his bed, and took it downstairs to an artisan."

"An artisan?"

"A rough person, employed in the manufacture of umbrellas, whom I had summoned to Happiness Villa, The Arbour, Highgate, for that purpose. This person took the umbrella to pieces and restored it so ingeniously that my husband was never aware it had been examined. Nothing was concealed inside; nothing is concealed inside; nothing could be concealed inside. It is a shabby umbrella, and no more."

"None the less, madam, he may set great store by

the umbrella only as some men cherish a good-luck charm."

"On the contrary, Mr. Holmes, he hates it. 'Mrs. Cab-pleasure,' he has said to me on more than one occasion, 'that umbrella will be the death of me; yet I must not relinquish it!' "

"H'm! He made no further explanation?"

"None. And even suppose he keeps the umbrella as a good-luck charm, which he does not! When in a moment of abstraction he leaves it behind for only a few seconds, in house or office, why does he utter a cry of dread and hasten back for it? If you are not stupid, Mr. Holmes, you must have some notion. But I see the matter is beyond you."

Holmes was grey with anger and mortification.

"It is a very pretty little problem," said he. "At the same time, I fail to see what action I can take. So far I have heard no facts to indicate that your husband is a criminal or even in the least vicious."

"Then it was not a crime, I dare say, when yesterday he stole a large number of diamonds from a safe be-longing jointly to himself and to his business partner, Mr. Mortimer Brown?"

Holmes raised his eyebrows.

"H'm. This becomes more interesting."

"Oh, yes," said our fair visitor, coolly. "Yesterday, before returning home, my husband paid a visit to his office. Subsequently there arrived at our home a telegram sent to him by Mr. Mortimer Brown. It read as follows:

"Did you remove from our safe twenty-six diamonds belonging to the Cowles-Derningham lot?"

"H'm. Your husband showed you the telegram, then?"

"No. I merely exercised a perfect right to open it."

"But you questioned him as to its contents?"

"Naturally not, since I preferred to bide my time. Late last night, though little he suspects I followed him, my husband crept downstairs in his night-g—crept downstairs, and held a whispered conversation in the mist with some unseen person just outside a ground-floor window. I could overhear only two sentences. *'Be outside the gate before eight-thirty on Thursday morning,*' said my husband. '*Don't fail me!*' "

"And what did you take to be the meaning of it?"

"Outside the gate of our house, of course! My husband always leaves for his office punctually at eight-thirty. And Thursday, Mr. Holmes: that is tomorrow morning! Whatever criminal scheme the wretch has prepared, it will reach fruition tomorrow. But you must be there to intervene."

Holmes's long, thin fingers crept out towards the mantelshelf as though in search of a pipe, but he drew his hand back.

"At eight-thirty tomorrow morning, Mrs. Cabpleasure, there will be scarcely a gleam of daylight."

"Surely that is no concern of yours! You are paid to spy in all weathers. I must insist that you be there promptly and in a sober condition."

"Now by heaven, madam—!"

"And that, I fear, is all the time I can afford to spare you now. Should your fee be more than nominal or what I consider reasonable, it will not be paid. Good day, sir. *Good* day!"

The door closed behind her.

"Do you know, Watson," remarked Holmes, with a bitter flush in his thin cheeks, "that if I did not crave such a problem as this, actually crave it—"

Though he did not complete the sentence, I echoed the sentiments he must have felt.

"Holmes, that lady is no true Scotswoman! What is more, though it grieves me to say so, I would wager a year's half-pay she is no relation whatever to The McRea of McRea."

"You seem a little warm, Watson, upon the subject of your own forebears' ancestral homeland. Still, I cannot blame you. Such airs as Mrs. Cabpleasure's become a trifle ridiculous when worn at second-hand. But how to fathom the secret of the umbrella?"

Going to the window, I was just in time to see the white bird on the hat of our late visitor disappearing inside a four-wheeler. A chocolate-coloured omnibus of the Baker Street and Waterloo line rattled past through deepening dusk. The outside passengers of the omnibus, all twelve of them, had their umbrellas raised against a rawer, colder fall of rain. Seeing only a forest of umbrellas, I turned from the window in despair.

"Holmes, what will you do?"

"Well, the hour is a little late to pursue an obvious line of enquiry in Hatton Garden. Mr. James Cabpleasure, with his glossy moustache and his much-prized umbrella, must wait until tomorrow."

Accordingly, with no premonition of the thunderbolt in store, I accompanied my friend to Happiness Villa, The Arbour, Highgate, at twenty minutes past eight on the following morning.

It was pitch dark when we took breakfast by gaslight. But the rain had ceased, and the sky cleared into quiet, shivering cold. By the time a hansom set us down before Mr. and Mrs. Cabpleasure's house, there was enough grey light so that we could see the outlines of our surroundings.

The house was a large one. Set some thirty yards back from the road, behind a waist-high stone wall, it was built of stucco in the Gothic style, with sham battlements and also a sham turret. Even the front door was set inside a panelled entry beyond an open Gothic arch. Though the entry lay in darkness, two windows glowed yellow on the floor above.

Sherlock Holmes, in his Inverness cape and ear-flapped travelling-cap, looked eagerly around him.

"Ha!" said he, placing his hand on the waist-high wall along the road. "Semi-circle of carriage-drive, I see, entering the ground through a gate in the wall there," and he nodded towards a point some distance ahead of us on the pavement. "The carriage-drive passes the front door, with one narrow branch towards a tradesmen's entrance, and returns to the road through a second gate in the wall —here beside us. Hullo, look there!"

"Is anything wrong?"

"Look ahead, Watson! There, by the far gate in the wall! That can't be Inspector Lestrade? By Jove, it *is* Lestrade!"

A wiry little bulldog of a man, in a hard hat and a

plaid greatcoat, was already hurrying towards us along the pavement. Behind him I could see the helmets of at least two police-constables, like twins with their blue bulk and heavy moustaches.

"Don't tell me, Lestrade," cried Holmes, "that Mrs. Cabpleasure also paid a visit to Scotland Yard?"

"If she did, Mr. Holmes, she went to the right shop," said Lestrade, with much complacence. "Hallo, Dr. Watson! It must be fifteen years and a bit since I first met you, but Mr. Holmes here is still the theorist and I'm still the practical man."

"Quick, Lestrade!" said Holmes. "The lady must have told you much the same story as she told us. When did she call upon you?"

"Yesterday morning. We're quick movers at Scotland Yard. We spent the rest of the day investigating this Mr. James Cabpleasure."

"Indeed? What did you discover?"

"Well, everybody thinks highly of the gentleman, and seems to like him. Outside office hours he is a hard reader, almost a bookworm, and his wife don't like that. But he's a great mimic, they say, and got quite a sense of humour."

"Yes, I fancied he must have a sense of humor."

"You've met him, Mr. Holmes?"

"No, but I have met his wife."

"Anyway, I met him last night. Paid a visit to take his measure. Oh, only on a pretext! Nothing to put him on his guard, of course."

"No, of course not," said Holmes, with a groan. "Tell me, Lestrade: have you not discovered that this gentleman has a reputation for complete honesty?"

"Yes, that's what makes it so suspicious," said Lestrade, with a cunning look. "By George, Mr. Holmes! I'm bound to admit I don't much like his lady, but she's got a very clear head. By George! I'll clap the darbies on that gentleman before you can say Jack Robinson!"

"My dear Lestrade! You will clap the handcuffs on him for what offence?"

"Why, because—stop!" cried Lestrade. "Hallo! You, there! Stand where you are!"

We had advanced to meet Lestrade until we were all half-way between the two gates in the low boundary wall. Now Lestrade had dashed past us towards the gate near which we had been standing at the beginning. There, as though conjured from the raw morning murk, was a portly and florid-faced gentleman, rather nervous-looking, in a grey top hat and a handsome grey greatcoat.

"I must ask you, sir," cried Lestrade, with more dignity as he noted the newcomer's costly dress, "to state your name, and give some account of yourself."

The portly newcomer, even more nervous, cleared his throat.

"Certainly," said he. "My name is Harold Mortimer Brown, and I am Mr. Cabpleasure's partner in the firm of Cabpleasure & Brown. I dismissed my hansom a short way down the road. I—er—live in South London."

"You live in South London," said Lestrade, "yet you have come all the way to the heights of North London? Why?"

"My dear Mr. Mortimer Brown," interposed Holmes, with a suavity which clearly brought relief to the florid-faced man, "you must forgive a certain impulsiveness on the part of my old friend Inspector Lestrade, who is from Scotland Yard. My name is Sherlock Holmes, and I shall be deeply indebted to you if you will be good enough to answer only one question. Did your partner really steal—"

"Stop!" Lestrade exclaimed again.

This time he whipped round to look at the far gate. A milk-wagon, its large and laden cans of milk clanking to the clop of the horse's hoofs, went jolting through that gate and up the curve of the gravelled drive towards the house in stucco Gothic.

Lestrade quivered like the little bulldog he was.

"That milk-wagon will bear watching," cried he. "Anyway, let's hope it won't obstruct our view of the front door."

Fortunately, it did not obstruct our view. The milk-man, whistling merrily, jumped down from the wagon and went into the entry to fill the small milk-jug which we later found was waiting for him outside the front door. But, no sooner had he disappeared under the Gothic arch of the entry, than all thought of the milk-wagon was driven from my mind.

"Mr. Holmes!" whispered Lestrade in a tense voice. "There he is!"

Clearly we heard the slam of the front door. Distinguished-looking in glossy hat and heavy greatcoat, there emerged into the drive a conspicuously moustached gentleman whom I deduced, correctly enough, to be Mr. James Cabpleasure on the way to his office.

"Mr. Holmes!" repeated Lestrade. "He hasn't got his umbrella!"

It was as though Lestrade's very thought winged through the grey bleakness into Mr. Cabpleasure's brain. Abruptly the diamond-broker halted in the drive. As though galvanized, he looked up at the sky. Uttering a wordless cry which I confess struck a chill into my heart, he rushed back into the house.

Again the front door slammed. A clearly astonished milkman, turning round to glance back, said something inaudible before he climbed to the seat of the wagon.

"I see it all," declared Lestrade, snapping his fingers. "They think they can deceive me, but they can't. Mr. Holmes, I must stop that milkman!"

"In heaven's name, why should you stop the milkman?"

"He and Mr. Cabpleasure were close to each other in that entry. I saw them! Mr. Cabpleasure could have passed the stolen diamonds to his confederate, the milkman."

"But, my dear Lestrade—"

The man from Scotland Yard would not listen. As the milk-wagon rumbled towards the gate by which we stood, he hurried forward and held up his hand in its path so that the driver, with a curse, was obliged to rein in even that slow-moving horse.

"I've seen you before," said Lestrade, in his bullying voice. "Look sharp, now; I'm a police-officer. Is your name not Hannibal Throgmorton, alias Felix Porteus?"

The milkman's long, clean-shaven face gaped in amazement.

"Me name's Alf Peters," he returned warmly, "and here's me roundsman card with me photograph on it and the blinking manager's signature to prove it! Who do you think I am, Governor—Cecil Rhodes?"

"You pull up your socks, my lad, or you'll find yourself in Queer Street. Get down from the wagon! Yes, that's it; get down!" Here Lestrade turned to the two police-constables who accompanied him. "Burton! Murdock! Search that milkman!"

Alf Peters' howl of protest was strangled as the constables seized him. Though lanky and only of middle height, Peters put up such a sporting fight that it was minutes before the constables could complete their search. They found nothing.

"Then the diamonds must be in one of those five-gallon milk-cans! We've no time for kid-glove methods. Pour out the milk on the ground!"

The language of the infuriated milkman, as this was done, cannot be called anything save improper.

"What, nothing there either?" demanded Lestrade. "Well, he may have swallowed the diamonds. Shall we take him to the nearest police-station?"

"Oh, crickey," screamed Alf Peters, "he ain't fit to be loose. He's off his blooming chump! Why don't he take a blooming axe and smash the blooming wagon?"

It was Holmes's strident, authoritative voice which restored order.

"Lestrade! Have the kindness to let Peters go. In the first place, he is unlikely to have swallowed twenty-six diamonds. In the second place, if Mr. Cabpleasure wished to give the diamonds to a fellow-conspirator, why did he not do so late on Tuesday night, when he held a secret conversation with someone at a ground-floor window? His whole behaviour, as described by his wife, becomes as irrational as his conduct with the umbrella. Unless—"

Sherlock Holmes had been standing in moody doubt, his head forward and his arms folded inside his cape. Now, glancing first towards the tradesmen's entrance and then towards the front of the house, he raised his head. Even his cold, emotionless nature could not repress the exclamation which rose to his lips. For a moment he remained motionless, his tall, lean figure outlined against a lightening sky.

"By Jove, Lestrade!" said he. "Mr. James Cabpleasure is rather a long time in returning with his umbrella."

"What's that, Mr. Holmes?"

"I might venture to utter a trifling prophecy. I might venture to say Mr. Cabpleasure has gone; that he has already vanished from the house."

"But he can't possibly have vanished from the house!" cried Lestrade.

"May I ask why not?"

"Because I stationed police-constables all round the house, in case he tried to give us the slip. Every door and window is watched! Not so much as a rat could have got out of that house without being seen, and can't get out now."

"Nevertheless, Lestrade, I must repeat my little prophecy. If you search the house, I think you will find that Mr. Cabpleasure has disappeared like a soapbubble."

Pausing only to put a police-whistle to his lips, Lestrade plunged towards the house. Alf Peters, the milkman, improved this opportunity to whip up his horse and clatter frantically away as though from the presence of a dangerous lunatic. Even Mr. Mortimer Brown, despite his venerable portliness and florid face, ran down the road with his hat clutched to his head, and without having answered whatever query my friend had wished to ask him.

"Hold your peace, Watson," said Holmes, in his imperious fashion. "No, no, I am not joking in what I say. You will find the matter extremely simple when you perceive the significance of one point."

"And what point is that?"

"The true reason why Mr. Cabpleasure cherishes his umbrella," said Sherlock Holmes.

Slowly the sky strengthened to such wintry brightness that the two gas-lit windows, which I have mentioned as glowing from an upper floor, were paled by the sun.

Ceaselessly the search went on, with far more police-constables than seemed necessary.

At the end of a full hour, during which Holmes had not moved, Lestrade rushed out of the house. His face wore a look of horror which I know was reflected in my own.

"It's true, Mr. Holmes! His hat, his greatcoat and his umbrella are lying just inside the front door. But—"

"Yes?"

"I'll take my oath that the villain's not hidden in the house, and yet they all swear he never left it either!"

"Who is in the house now?"

"Only his wife. Last night, after I spoke with him, it seems he gave the servants a night off. Almost drove 'em out of the house, his wife says, without a word of warning. They didn't much like it, some of 'em wondering where they should go, but they had no choice."

Holmes whistled.

"The wife!" said he. "By the way, how is it that through all this tumult we have neither seen nor heard Mrs. Gloria Cabpleasure? Is it possible that last night she was drugged? That she found herself growing irresistibly drowsy, and has only recently awakened?"

Lestrade fell back a step as though from the eye of a sorcerer.

"Mr. Holmes, why do you think it was that?"

"Because it could have been nothing else."

"Well, it's gospel truth. The lady is accustomed to drink a cup of hot meat-juice an hour before going to bed. That meat-juice last night was so doused with powdered opium that there are still traces in the cup." Lestrade's face darkened. "But the less I see of that lady, by George, the better I shall like it."

"At least she has made a good recovery, for I perceive her now at the window."

"Never mind her," said Lestrade. "Just tell me how that thieving diamond-broker vanished slap under our eyes!"

"Holmes," said I, "surely there is only one explanation.

Mr. Cabpleasure departed by some secret way or passage."

"There's no such thing," shouted Lestrade.

"I quite agree," said Holmes. "That is a modern house, Watson, or at least one built within the last twenty-odd years. Present-day builders, unlike their ancestors, seldom include a secret passage. But I cannot see, Lestrade, that there is any more I can do here."

"You can't leave now!"

"Not leave?"

"No! You may be a theorist and not practical, but I can't deny you've given me a bit of help once or twice in the past. If you can guess how a man vanished by a miracle, it's your duty as a citizen to tell me."

Holmes hesitated.

"Very well," said he. "There are reasons why I should prefer to be silent for the time being. But perhaps I may give you a hint. Had you thought of disguise?"

For a time Lestrade gripped his hat with both hands. Abruptly he turned round and looked up at the window where Mrs. Cabpleasure contemplated nothingness with a haughty superiority which it seemed nothing could shake.

"By George," whispered Lestrade. "When I was here last night, I never saw Mr. and Mrs. Cabpleasure together. That may account for the false moustache I found hidden in the hall. Only one person was in that house this morning, and one person is still there. That means—"

Now it was Holmes's turn to be taken aback.

"Lestrade, what has got into your head at this late date?"

"They can't deceive me. If Mr. Cabpleasure is the same person as Mrs. Cabpleasure, if he or she simply walked out of the house in man's clothes and then walked back in again—I see it all now!"

"Lestrade! Stop! Wait! "

"We have female searchers in these days," said Lestrade, dashing towards the house. "They'll soon prove whether it's a lady or a gentleman."

"Holmes," cried I, "can this monstrous theory possibly be true?"

"Nonsense, Watson."

"Then you must restrain Lestrade. My dear fellow," I expostulated presently, as Mrs. Cabpleasure disappeared from the window and a piercing female shriek indicated that Lestrade had imparted the intelligence of what he proposed to do, "this is unworthy of you. Whatever we may think of the lady's manners, especially in commanding you to be here in a sober condition, you must spare her the indignity of an enforced visit to the police-station!"

"Yet I am not at all sure," said he, thoughtfully, "that the lady would be greatly harmed by such an enforced visit. Indeed, it may serve to teach her a salutary lesson. Don't argue, Watson! I have an errand for you."

"But—"

"I must pursue certain lines of enquiry which may take all day. Meanwhile, since my address is readily accessible to anyone, I feel sure that the conscientious Mr. Mortimer Brown will send me a certain telegram. Therefore I would be grateful, Watson, if you would wait at our rooms and open the telegram should it arrive before my return."

Lestrade's mood must have been contagious. Otherwise I know not why I should have rushed back in such a hurry to Baker Street, shouting to the cab-driver that I would give him a guinea if he took me there in an hour.

But the anticipated telegram from Mr. Mortimer Brown found me discussing midday dinner, and added a fresh shock. It read:

"Regret my too-expeditious departure this morning. Must state openly I am, and have always been, only a nominal partner of Cabpleasure and Brown, whose assets belong entirely to Mr. James B. Cabpleasure. My telegraphed enquiry as to the twenty-six diamonds in the Cowles-Derningham purchase was caused by caution in making certain he had brought these diamonds safely home. If he took the diamonds, he had a perfect right to take them.—Harold Mortimer Brown."

Then James Cabpleasure was not a thief! But, if he had not meant to fly the law, I was at a loss to account for his behaviour. It was seven o'clock that night, and I heard Holmes's familiar tread on the stairs, when inspiration came to me.

"Pray enter," cried I, as the knob turned, "for I have found the only possible explanation at last!"

Flinging open the door, Holmes glanced quickly round, and his face fell.

"What, is there no visitor? Yet, perhaps I am premature; yes, premature. My dear Watson, I apologize. What were you saying?"

"If Mr. Cabpleasure had in fact vanished," said I, as he scanned the telegram, "it would have been the miracle Lestrade called it. But miracles do not happen in the nineteenth century. Holmes, our diamond-broker only seemed to vanish. He was there all the time, but we did not observe him."

"How so?"

"Because he had disguised himself as a police-constable."

Holmes, who was in the act of hanging up his cape and cloth cap on the hook behind the door, turned round with his dark brows drawn together.

"Continue!" said he.

"In this very room, Holmes, Mrs. Cabpleasure said that her husband's moustache made him resemble a constable. We know him to be a fine mimic, with a reprehensible sense of humour. To procure a fancy-dress policeman's uniform would have been easy. After the misdirection with which he walked from the house and walked back again, he then put on the uniform. In the half-light, with so many constables about, he went unobserved until he could escape."

"Excellent, Watson! It is only when I have been with Lestrade that I learn to value you. Very good indeed."

"I have found the solution?"

"It is not, I fear, quite good enough. Mrs. Cabpleasure also said, if you recall, that her husband was of medium height and had no more figure than a hop-pole, by which she meant he was thin or lanky. That this was a fact I proved today by many photographs of him in the drawing-room at Happiness Villa. He could not have simulated the height or the beef of a metropolitan policeman."

"But mine is the last possible explanation!"

"I think not. There is only one person who meets our requirements of height and figure, and that person—"

There was a loud clamour and jangle of the bell from below.

"Hark!" said Holmes. "It is the visitor, the step upon the stair, the touch of drama which I cannot resist! Who will open that door, Watson? Who will open the door?"

The door opened. Clad in evening clothes, with cape and collapsible hat, our visitor stood upon the threshold. I found myself looking incredulously at a long, clean-shaven, familiar face.

"Good evening, Mr. Alf Peters," said Holmes. "Or should I say—Mr. James Cabpleasure?"

Realization smote me like a blow, and I all but staggered.

"I must congratulate you," continued Holmes, with sternness. "Your impersonation of the persecuted milkman was admirably done. I recall a similar case at Riga in 1876, and it is faintly reminiscent of an impersonation by a Mr. James Windibank in '88; but certain features here are unique. The subject of removing a heavy moustache for changing a man's appearance, especially in making him look younger, is one to which I may devote a monograph. Instead of assuming a moustache for disguise, you took yours off."

When he was dressed in evening clothes, our visitor's face showed as mobile and highly intellectual, with dancing brown eyes which crinkled at the corners as though he might smile. But, far from smiling, he was desperately worried.

"Thank you," said he, in a pleasant and well-modulated voice. "You gave me a very bad moment, Mr. Holmes, when I sat on that milk-wagon outside my own house and I observed that suddenly you saw through my whole plan. Why did you refrain from unmasking me then?"

"I wished first to hear what you had to say for yourself, unembarrassed by the presence of Lestrade."

James Cabpleasure bit his lip.

"Afterwards," said Holmes, "it was not difficult to trace you through the Purity Milk Company, or to send you the judiciously worded telegram which has brought you here. A photograph of James Cabpleasure with moustache eliminated, shown to your employer, disclosed the fact that he was the same man as one Alfred Peters, who six months ago applied for a post with the milk company, and obtained two days' leave of absence for Tuesday and Wednesday.

"Yesterday, in this room, your wife informed us that on Tuesday you 'returned' from an unheard-of six months' absence in Amsterdam and Paris. That was suggestive. Taken together with your curious conduct as regards the umbrella—which you did not prize when you purchased it, but only when you had decided on your plan—and your incredible statement that the umbrella would be the death of you, it already suggested a hoax or imposture designed to deceive your wife."

"Sir, let me tell you——!"

"One moment. Shaving off your moustache, for six months you drove that milk-round; and I have no doubt you enjoyed it. On Tuesday you 'returned' as James Cabpleasure. I find that Messrs. Clarkfather, the wigmakers, supplied you with a real-hair duplicate of your lost moustache. In dark winter weather or by gas-light it would deceive your wife, since the lady takes small interest in you and we know you occupy separate rooms.

"Quite deliberately you acted in a violently suspicious manner. On Tuesday night you staged that sinister scene with a non-existent 'fellow-conspirator' outside a window, hoping to drive your wife into those vigorous measures which you believed she was certain to take.

"On Wednesday night the visit of Inspector Lestrade, who is perhaps not the most subtle of men, told you that you would have witnesses for your projected disappearance and that it was safe to go ahead. Dismissing the servants and drugging your wife, you left the house.

"This morning, hatless and without a greatcoat, you had the effrontery—don't smile, sir!—to drive the milk-wagon straight up to your house, where in the pitchdark entry you played the part of two men.

"Descending from the wagon, you disappeared into the entry as the milkman. Inside, already prepared, lay Mr. Cabpleasure's greatcoat, hat, and moustache. It required only eight seconds to put on hat and coat, and hastily to affix a moustache which on that occasion need be seen only briefly from a distance and in halflight.

"Out you walked as the elegant diamond-broker, *seemed* to remember your missing umbrella, and rushed back in again. It took but a moment to throw the trappings inside the front door, together with an umbrella already left there, and slam the front door from the outside. Again you reappeared as the milkman, completing the illusion that two men had passed each other.

"Though Inspector Lestrade honestly believes he saw two men, we all observed that the entry was far too dark for this to have been possible. But we must not too much blame Lestrade. When he stopped the milk-wagon and swore he had seen you before, it was no mere bullying. He really had seen you once before, though he could not remember where.

"I have said you had no fellow-conspirator; strictly speaking, this is true. Yet surely you must have shared the secret with your nominal partner, Mr. Mortimer Brown, who appeared this morning for the purpose of drawing away attention and preventing close scrutiny of the milkman. Unfortunately, his caution and apprehension rendered him useless. You made a bad mistake when you hid that false moustache in the hall. Still, the police might have found it when they searched you. This so-called miracle was possible because you very deliberately had accustomed your wife and her acquaintances to your worship of that umbrella. In reality, you cherished the umbrella because your plans could not have succeeded without it."

Sherlock Holmes, though he had been speaking curtly and without heat, seemed to rise up like a lean avenger.

"Now, Mr. James Cabpleasure!" said he. "I can per- haps understand why you were unhappy with your wife, and wished to leave her. But why could you not leave her openly, with a legal separation, and not this mummery of a disappearance into nowhere?"

Our guest's fair-complexioned face went red.

"So I should have," he burst out, "if Gloria had not been already married when she married me."

"I beg your pardon?"

Mr. Cabpleasure made a grimace, with a sudden vivid flash of personality, which showed what he might have accomplished as a comic actor.

"Oh, you can prove it easily enough! Since she longs to go back to her real husband—never mind who he is; it's an august name—I'm afraid Gloria wants to be rid of me, preferably by seeing me in gaol. But I can earn money, whereas the august personage is too lazy to try, and Gloria's prudence has become notorious."

"By Jove, Watson!" muttered Holmes. "This is not too surprising. It supplies the last link. Did I not say the lady insisted too much on her married name of Cabpleasure?"

"I am tired of her chilliness; I am tired of her superiority; and now, at forty-odd, I wish only to sit in peace and read. However, sir, let me acknowledge that it was a cad's trick if you insist."

"Come!" said Holmes. "I am not the official police, Mr. Cabpleasure—"

"My name is not even Cabpleasure. That was forced upon me by my uncle, who founded the business. My real name is Phillimore, James Phillimore. Well! I have put all my possessions into Gloria's name, except twenty-six costly and negotiable diamonds. I had hoped to found a new life as James Phillimore, free of a blasted silly name. But I have been defeated by a master strategist, so do what you like."

"No, no," said Holmes blandly. "Already you have made one bad blunder, though I was deplorably late in seeing it. When a milk-wagon is driven to the front door instead of to the tradesmen's entrance, the foundations of our social world are rocked. If I am to help you in forming this new life—"

"If you are to help me?" cried our visitor.

"Then you must not be betrayed by a real name of which someone is sure to be aware. From diplomatic necessity, until the day you die, Watson shall call the problem of your disappearance unsolved. Assume what other name you choose. But Mr. James Phillimore must never more be seen in this world!"

—:—

Among these unfinished tales is that of Mr. James Phillimore, who, stepping back into his own house to get his umbrella, was never more seen in this world.

FROM "THOR BRIDGE"

5

The Adventure of the Black Baronet

"Yes, Holmes, the autumn is a melancholy time. But you are in need of this holiday. After all, you should be interested in such a country type as that man we see from the window."

My friend Mr. Sherlock Holmes, closing the book in his hands, glanced languidly out of the window of our private sitting-room at the inn near East Grinstead.

"Pray be explicit, Watson," said he. "Do you refer to the cobbler or to the farmer?"

In the country road past the inn, I could see a man on the driver's seat of a market-cart, clearly a farmer. But otherwise there was only an elderly workman in corduroy trousers, plodding towards the cart with his head down.

"Surely a cobbler," observed Holmes, answering my thought rather than my words. "He is left-handed, I perceive."

"Holmes, you would have been accused of wizardry in another age from ours! Why the man should be a cobbler I cannot conceive, but a left-handed cobbler? You cannot have deduced it."

"My dear fellow, observe the marks across the corduroy trousers where the cobbler rests his lap stone. The left hand side, you will remark, is far more worn than the right. He used his left hand for hammering the leather. Would that all our problems were so simple!"

That year of 1889 had brought some significant successes to Sherlock Holmes, which had added further laurels to his already formidable reputation. But the strain of almost unremitting work had left its mark upon him, and I was sincerely relieved when he had fallen in with my proposal that we should exchange the October fogs of Baker Street for the rich autumnal beauty of the Sussex country-side.

My friend possessed a marked resilience, and the few days of relaxation had already put back the old nervous spring in his step and a touch of colour in his cheeks. Indeed, I welcomed even his occasional outbursts of impatience as a sign that his vigorous nature had shaken off the lassitude which had followed upon his last case.

Holmes had lit his pipe, and I had picked up my book when there came a knock on the door and the landlord entered.

"There be a gentleman to see you, Mr. Holmes, sir," he said in his soft Sussex burr, "and so hurried-like that up I must come without even taking off me apron. Ah! Here he is now."

A tall, fair-haired man, wearing a heavy ulster and a Scotch plaid swathed round his throat, rushed into the room, threw his Gladstone bag into the nearest corner, and, curtly dismissing the landlord, closed the door behind him. Then he nodded to us both.

"Ah, Gregson," said Holmes, "there must be something unusual in the wind to bring you so far afield!"

"What a case!" cried Inspector Tobias Gregson, sinking into the chair which I had pushed towards him. "Whew! What a case! As soon as we had the telegram at the Yard, I thought it would do no harm to have a word with you in Baker Street—unofficial, of course, Mr. Holmes. Then, when Mrs. Hudson gave me your address, I decided to come on down. It's less than thirty miles from here to the place in Kent where the murder was committed." He mopped at his forehead. "One of the oldest families in the county, they tell me. By heaven, just wait till the papers get hold of it!"

"My dear Holmes," I interposed, "you are here on a rest."

"Yes, yes, Watson," said my friend hurriedly, "but it will do no harm to hear the details. Well, Gregson?"

"I know no more than the bare facts given in this telegram from the county police. Colonel Jocelyn Dalcy, who was a guest of Sir Reginald Lavington at Lavington Court, has been stabbed to death in the banqueting-hall. The butler found him there at about ten-thirty this morning. He'd just died; blood still flowing."

Holmes put down his book on the table. "Suicide? Murder? What?" he asked.

"It couldn't be suicide; no weapon was discovered. But I've had a second telegram, and there's new evidence. It appears to implicate Sir Reginald Lavington himself. Colonel Dalcy was well known in sporting circles, but with none too good a reputation. This is crime in high life, Mr. Holmes, and there is no room for mistakes."

"Lavington—Lavington?" mused Holmes. "Surely, Watson, when we drove last week to visit the Bodiam Ruins, did we not pass through a village of that name? I seem to recall a house lying in a hollow."

I nodded. In my mind rose the memory of a moated manor-house, almost stifled amid yew trees, from which a sense of oppressiveness had seemed to weigh upon me.

"That's right, Mr. Holmes," agreed Gregson. "A house in a hollow. My guide-book says that at Lavington the past is more real than the present. Will you come with me?"

My friend leapt from his chair. "By all means," he cried. "No, Watson, not a word!"

The excellent establishment of Mr. John Hoath again supplied us with a carriage in which for two hours we were driven through the narrow, deep-rutted Sussex lanes. By the time that we had crossed the Kent border, the chill in the air made us glad of our rugs. We had turned off the main road, and were descending a steep lane when the coachman pointed with his whip at a moat-girdled house spread out below us in the grey dusk.

"Lavington Court," said he.

A few minutes later we had alighted from our carriage. As we crossed the causeway to the front door. I had a sombre impression of dead leaves on dark, sullen water and a great battlemented tower looming through the twilight. Holmes struck a match and stooped over the gravelled surface of the causeway.

"H'm, ha! Four sets of footprints. Hullo, what's this? The hoof-marks of a horse, and furiously ridden, to judge by their depth. Probably the first summons to the police. Well, Gregson, there's not much to be gained here. Let us hope that the scene of the crime may yield more interesting results."

As Holmes finished speaking, the door was opened. I must confess to reassurance at the sight of the stolid, and red-faced butler who ushered us into a stone-flagged hall, mellow and beautiful in the light of old-fashioned, many-branched candlesticks. At the far end a stairway led up to an oaken gallery on the floor above.

A thin, ginger-haired man, who had been warming his coat-tails before the fire, hurried towards us.

"Inspector Gregson?" he asked. "Thank the Lord you've come, sir!"

"I take it that you are Sergeant Bassett of the Kent County Constabulary?"

The ginger-haired man nodded. "That will do, Gillings. We'll ring when we need you. This is a dreadful business, sir, dreadful!" he went on, as the butler departed. "And now it's worse than ever. Here's a famous gambler stabbed when he was drinking a toast to his best racehorse, and Sir Reginald *claims* to have been absent at the time, and yet the knife—" The local detective broke off and looked at us. "Who are these gentlemen?"

"They are Mr. Sherlock Holmes and Dr. Watson. You may speak freely."

"Well, Mr. Holmes, I've heard of your clever reputation," remarked Sergeant Bassett doubtfully. "But there's not much mystery about this affair, and I hope the police will receive the credit."

"Gregson can tell you that I play the game for the game's sake," my friend replied. "Officially, I prefer not to appear in this case."

"Very fair, I'm sure, Mr. Holmes. Then, gentlemen, please to come this way."

He picked up a four-branched candlestick, and we

were following him across the hall when there came a most unexpected interruption.

I have had considerable experience of women in many parts of the world, but never have I beheld a more queenly presence than the woman now descending the stairs. As she paused with her hand on the banister, the candle-light falling warmly on her soft copper-coloured hair and her heavy-lidded green eyes, I gained an impression of a beauty once radiant but now pale under the stress of some dreadful event which she could not understand.

"I heard your name in the hall, Mr. Holmes," she cried. "I know very little, but of one thing I am certain. My husband is innocent! I beg that you will think of that first."

For a moment Holmes looked at her intently, as though that melodious voice had struck some chord in his memory.

"I will bear your suggestion in mind, Lady Lavington. But surely your marriage has deprived the stage of—"

"Then you recognize Margaret Montpensier?" For the first time a touch of colour came into her face. "Yes, that was when I first met Colonel Dalcy. But my husband had no reason for jealousy—!" She paused in consternation.

"How's this, my lady?" exclaimed Gregson. "Jealousy?" The two detectives exchanged glances.

"We hadn't got a motive before," muttered Bassett.

Lady Lavington, formerly that great actress Margaret Montpensier, had said what she had never intended to say. Holmes bowed gravely, and we followed the sergeant towards an arched door.

Though the room we entered was in complete darkness, I had a sense of height and size.

"There are no lights here except from this candlestick, gentlemen," came Bassett's voice. "Stand in the door for a moment, please."

As he moved forward, the reflection of four candle-flames followed him along the surface of a great refectory table, with its narrow side towards the door. At the far end the light flashed back from a tall silver goblet with a human hand lying motionless on either side. Bassett thrust forward the candelabrum.

"Look at this, Inspector Gregson!" he cried.

Seated at the head of the table, his cheek resting upon the surface, a man lay sprawled forward with his arms outflung on either side of the cup. Against a welter of blood and wine his fair hair shone under the candle-flames.

"His throat's been cut," snapped Bassett. "And here," he cried, darting to the wall, "*was* the dagger that did it!"

We hastened forward to where he was holding up his light against the old wainscotting. Amid a trophy of arms, two small metal hooks showed where some weapon had hung.

"How do you know that it was a dagger?" asked Gregson.

Bassett pointed to a slight scratch on the woodwork some six inches below. Holmes nodded approvingly.

"Good, Sergeant!" said he. "But you have other proof besides the scratch on the panelling?"

"Yes! Ask that butler, Gillings! It's an old hunting-dagger: hung there for years. Now look at the wound in Colonel Dalcy's throat."

Inured though I was to scenes of violence, I stepped back. Bassett, laying hold of that yellow hair which was tinged with grey at the temples, raised the dead man's head. Even in death it was an eagle face, with a great curving nose above a remorseless mouth.

"The dagger, yes," said Holmes. "But surely an odd direction for the blow? It appears to strike upwards from beneath."

The local detective smiled grimly. "Not so odd, Mr. Holmes, if the murderer struck when his victim raised that heavy cup to drink. Colonel Dalcy would have had to use both hands. We know already that he and Sir Reginald were drinking in here to the success of the colonel's horse at Leopardstown next week."

We all looked at the great wine-vessel, fully twelve inches high. It was of ancient silver, richly embossed and chased, girded below the lip with a circlet of garnets.

As it stood there amid the crimson stains and the scratches of finger-nails on that dreadful table-top, I noticed the twin silver figures carved like owls that decorated the tops of the handles on either side.

"The Luck of Lavington," said Bassett with a short laugh. "You can see those owls in the family arms. Well, it brought no luck to Colonel Dalcy. Somebody stabbed him when he raised it to drink."

"*Somebody?*" said a voice in the background.

Holmes had lifted the cup and, after examining it closely, was looking at the scratches and wine-stains which had seeped beneath it, when the shock of this interruption made us all turn towards the far end of the banqueting-hall.

A man was standing near the door. The light of a single taper which he had raised above his head illumined a pair of dark, brooding eyes that glowered at us from a face as black-browed and swarthy as that of some Andalusian gipsy. There was an impression of formidable strength in the spread of his shoulders, and in his bull neck above an old-fashioned black satin stock.

"How's this?" he challenged in a rumbling voice, advancing on us with silent steps. "Who are ye? A pretty state of affairs, Bassett, when ye drag a set of strangers into the house of your own landlord!"

"I would remind you, Sir Reginald, that a serious crime has been committed," replied the local detective sternly. "This is Inspector Gregson from London; and these gentlemen are Mr. Sherlock Holmes and Dr. Watson."

A shade of uneasiness seemed to flit across the dark face of the baronet as he looked at Holmes.

"I've heard of ye," he growled. His gaze moved towards the dead man. "Yes, Buck Dalcy's dead, and probably damned. I know his reputation now. Wine, horses, women —well, there have been Lavingtons like that. Mayhap, Mr. Holmes, ye have the wit to recognize a mischance when others talk of murder."

To my amazement Holmes seemed seriously to consider this monstrous statement. "Were it not for one circumstance, Sir Reginald," he said at length, "I should probably agree with you."

Gregson smiled sourly. "We're all aware of that circumstance. The missing knife—"

"I did not say that it was the knife."

"There was no need for you to say so, Mr. Holmes. Can a man cut his own throat by accident and afterwards conceal the weapon?"

Seizing the candelabrum from the sergeant, Gregson held it up to the trophy of arms which glittered against the dark panelling. His stern eyes met those of the baronet.

"Where is the dagger that hung here?" he demanded.

"I took it," said Sir Reginald.

"Oh, you did, did you? Why?"

"I've told Sergeant Bassett there. I was fishing this morning. I used that old blade to gut the pike; ay, as my fathers did before me."

"Then you have it?"

"No; must I tell the police a dozen times? I lost it from my creel. Mayhap at the river, or on my way home."

Gregson drew the sergeant to one side.

"I think there's little more we need," I heard him mutter. "His wife has given us the motive, and we have it from his own lips that he took the weapon. Sir Reginald Lavington," he said with authority, advancing upon the baronet, "I must ask you to accompany me to Maidstone Police Station. There you will be formally charged with—"

Holmes darted forward. "One moment, Gregson!" he cried. "You must really give us twenty-four hours to think this over. For your own sake I tell you that any good counsel would tear your case to pieces."

"I think not, Mr. Holmes; especially with her ladyship in the witness-box."

Sir Reginald started violently, while a livid pallor mottled the swarthiness of his features.

"I warn ye not to drag my wife into this! Whatever she's said, she can't testify against her husband!"

"We would not ask her to do so. It is sufficient that

she repeat what she has already stated in the presence of police witnesses. However, Mr. Holmes," Gregson added, "in return for one or two small favours you've done us in the past, I see no harm in—well! in delaying matters for a few more hours. As for you, Sir Reginald, should you attempt to leave this house, you will be arrested at once. Well, Mr. Holmes, what now?"

My friend had dropped to his knees, and by the light of a candle was peering closely at the horrible splashes of blood and wine which dabbled the oaken floor.

"Perhaps you would have the goodness, Watson, to pull that bell-rope," he said, as he scrambled to his feet. "A word with the butler, who discovered the body, would not come amiss before we seek accommodation at the village inn. Let us adjourn to the hall."

I think that each of us was glad to leave that black, vaulted room with its terrible occupant, and to find ourselves once more before the log fire blazing on the hearth. Lady Lavington, pale but beautiful in a gown of bronze velvet with a collar of Brussels lace, rose from a chair.

For a moment her eyes seemed to search each one of us with a mute, intense questioning, and then she had swept to her husband's side.

"In God's name, Margaret, what have ye been saying?" he demanded, the veins swelling in his thick neck. "Ye'll have me at the rope's end yet!"

"Whatever the sacrifice, I swear you shall not suffer! Surely it is better that—" She whispered a few agitated words in his ear.

"Never! Never!" retorted her husband fiercely. "What? You here, Gillings? Have you too been condemning your master?"

None of us had heard the butler's approach, but now he stepped into the circle of fire-light, with a troubled expression on his honest face.

"Heaven forbid, Sir Reginald!" Gillings replied warmly. "I told Sergeant Bassett only what I saw and heard. Colonel Dalcy called for a bottle of port. He was in the banqueting-hall. He—he said he wished to drink a toast with you from the Luck of Lavington, to the victory of his horse in the Leopardstown races next week. Since there was port in the decanter on the buffet, I poured it into the great cup. I remember how the colonel laughed as he dismissed me."

"He laughed, you say?" said Sherlock Holmes quickly. "When did you actually see Sir Reginald with the colonel?"

"I did not actually see him, sir. But the colonel said—"

"And laughed when he said it," interposed Holmes. "Perhaps Lady Lavington would tell us whether Colonel Dalcy was a frequent guest under this roof?"

It seemed to me that some swift emotion glowed for an instant in those wonderful green eyes.

"For some years past, a frequent guest," she said. "But my husband was not even in the house this morning! Has he not told you so already?"

"Excuse me, my lady," doggedly interrupted Sergeant Bassett. "Sir Reginald says he was at the river, but he admits he can't prove it."

"Quite so," said Holmes. "Well, Watson, there is nothing more to be done here tonight."

We found comfortable accommodation at the Three Owls in the village of Lavington. Holmes was moody and preoccupied. When I attempted to question him, he cut me short with the statement that he had nothing further to add until he had visited Maidstone on the morrow. I must confess that I could not understand my friend's attitude. It was evident that Sir Reginald Lavington was a dangerous man, and that our visit appeared to have made him more so but when I pointed out to Holmes that his duty lay at Lavington Court rather than in the county town of Maidstone, he replied merely with the incongruous observation that the Lavingtons were a historic family.

I passed a restless morning. The wild weather kept me indoors over a week-old newspaper, and it was not until four o'clock in the afternoon that Holmes burst into our private sitting-room. His cape was dripping and rain-sodden, but his eyes glittered and his cheeks were flushed with some intense inner excitement.

"Good heavens!" I said. "You look as though you have found the answer to our problem."

Before my friend could reply, there came a knock and the door of our sitting-room had swung open. Holmes rose from the chair into which he had just relapsed.

"Ah, Lady Lavington," said he, "we are honoured by your visit."

Though her features were heavily veiled, there was no mistaking that tall, gracious figure now hesitating on our threshold.

"I received your note, Mr. Holmes," she replied in a low voice, "and I came at once." Sinking into the chair which I had wheeled forward, she raised her veil and let her head rest back among the cushions. "I came at once," she repeated wearily.

The fire-light threw her face into strong relief, and, as I studied her features, still beautiful despite the almost waxen pallor and restless brilliance of her eyes, I discerned in them the shock of the event that had shattered the peace of her life and the privacy of her home. A sense of compassion prompted me to speak.

"You may have complete confidence in my friend Sherlock Holmes," I said gently. "This is indeed a painful time for you, Lady Lavington, but rest assured that everything will turn out for the best."

She thanked me with a glance. But, when I rose to leave them together, she held up her hand.

"I would much prefer that you stayed, Dr. Watson," she begged. "Your presence gives me confidence. Why have you sent for me, Mr. Holmes?"

My friend, sitting back, had closed his eyes. "Shall we say that you are here in your husband's interests?" he murmured. "You will not object if I ask you to elucidate a few small points which are still obscure to me?"

Lady Lavington rose to her feet.

"Mr. Holmes, this is unworthy," she said coldly. "You are trying to trick me into condemning my own husband! He is innocent, I tell you!"

"So I believe. Nevertheless, I pray that you will compose yourself and answer my questions. I understand that this Buck Dalcy has been an intimate friend of Sir Reginald for some years past."

Lady Lavington stared at him, and then began to laugh. She laughed most heartily, but with a note in her mirth that jarred on me as a medical man.

"Friend?" she cried at last. "Why, he was unworthy to black my husband's boots!"

"I am relieved to hear you say so. And yet it is fair to suppose that both men moved in the same circles during the London seasons, and, perhaps unknown to you, might have shared interests in common—possibly of a sporting nature? When did your husband first introduce Colonel Dalcy to you?"

"You are pitiably wrong in all your suppositions! I knew Colonel Dalcy for years before my marriage. It was I who introduced him to my husband. Buck Dalcy was a creature of society: ambitious, worldly, merciless, and yet with all the charm of his kind. What interest could such as he share in common with a rough but honourable man whose world begins and ends with the boundaries of his own ancestral lands?"

"A woman's love," said Holmes quietly.

Lady Lavington's eyes dilated. Then, dropping the veil over her face, she rushed from the room.

For a long time Holmes smoked in silence, his brows drawn down and his gaze fixed thoughtfully upon the fire. I knew from the expression on his face that he had reached some final decision. Then he drew from his pocket a crumpled sheet of paper.

"A while ago, Watson, you asked whether I had found the answer to our problem. In one sense, my dear fellow, I have. Listen closely to the vital evidence I shall read to you. It is from the records in the Maidstone County Registry."

"I am all attention."

"This is a little transcription which I have put into comprehensible English. It was originally written in the year 1485, when the House of Lancaster triumphed at last over the House of York.

"And it came to pass that on the field of Bosworth Sir

John Lavington did take prisoner two knights and a squire, and carried them with him to Lavington Court. For he would take no ransom from any who had raised banner for the House of York.

"*That night, after Sir John had supped, each was brought to the table and offered the Choice. One knight, he who was a kinsman of Sir John, drank from the Life and departed without ransom. And one knight and the squire drank from the Death. It was a deed most un-Christian, for they were unconfessed, and thereafter men spake far and wide of the Luck of Lavington.*"

For a while we sat in silence after the reading of this extraordinary document, while the wind lashed the rain against the windows and boomed in the ancient chimney.

"Holmes," I said at last, "I seem to sense something monstrous here. Yet what connection can there be between the murder of a profligate gambler and the violence that followed on a battle four hundred years ago? Only the room has remained the same."

"This, Watson, is the second most important thing that I have discovered."

"And the first?"

"We shall find it at Lavington Court. A black baronet, Watson! Might it not also suggest blackmail?"

"You mean that Sir Reginald was being blackmailed?"

My friend ignored the question. "I have promised to meet Gregson at the house. Would you care to accompany me?"

"What is in your mind? I have seldom seen you so grave."

"It is already growing dark," said Sherlock Holmes. "The dagger that killed Colonel Dalcy must do no further harm."

It was a wild, blustering evening. As we walked through the dusk to the old manor-house, the air was filled with the creaking of tree-branches and I felt the cold touch of a blown leaf against my cheek. Lavington Court was as shadowy as the hollow in which it lay; but, as Gillings opened the door to us, a gleam of light showed in the direction of the banqueting-hall.

"Inspector Gregson has been asking for you, sir," said the butler, helping us off with our wraps.

We hurried towards the light. Gregson, with a look of deep agitation, was pacing up and down beside the table. He glanced at the now-empty chair beyond the great cup.

"Thank God you've come, Mr. Holmes!" he burst out. "Sir Reginald was telling the truth. I didn't believe it, but he is innocent! Bassett has dug up two farmers who met him walking from the river at ten-thirty yesterday morning. Why couldn't he have said he met them?"

There was a singular light in Holmes's eyes as he looked at Gregson.

"There are such men," he said.

"Did you know this all the time?"

"I did not know of the witnesses, no. But I hoped that you would find a witness, since for other reasons I was convinced of his innocence."

"Then we're back where we started!"

"Hardly that. Had you thought, Gregson, of reconstructing this crime after the French fashion?"

"How do you mean?"

Holmes moved to the end of the table, which still bore the marks of the recent tragedy. "Let us suppose that I am Colonel Dalcy—a tall man, standing here at the head of the table. I am about to drink with someone, who means to stab me. I pick up the cup like this, and with both hands I lift it to my mouth. So! Gregson, we will suppose that you are the murderer. Stab me in the throat!"

"What the devil do you mean?"

"Grasp an imaginary dagger in your right hand. That's it! Don't hesitate, man; stab me in the throat!"

Gregson, as though half-hypnotised, took a step forward with his hand raised, and stopped.

"But it can't be done, Mr. Holmes! Not like this, anyway!"

"Why not?"

"The direction of the colonel's wound was straight upwards through the throat. Nobody could strike upwards from underneath, across the breadth of the table. It's impossible!"

My friend, who had been standing with his head back and the heavy cup lifted to his lips by both handles, now straightened up and offered it to the Scotland Yard man.

"Good!" said he. "Now, Gregson, imagine that *you* are Colonel Dalcy. I am the murderer. Take my place, and lift the Luck of Lavington."

"Very well. What next?"

"Do exactly what I did. But don't put the cup to your lips. That's it, Gregson; that's it! Mark well what I say: don't put it to your lips!"

The light flashed back from the great drinking-vessel as it tilted.

"No, man, no!" shouted Holmes suddenly. "Not another inch, if you value your life!"

Even as he spoke, there came a click and a metallic slither. A slim, sharp blade shot from the lower edge of the cup with the speed of a striking snake. Gregson sprang back with an oath, while the vessel, falling from his hands, crashed and jangled across the floor.

"My God!" I cried.

"My God!" echoed a voice which struck across my own.

Sir Reginald Lavington, his dark features now livid, was standing behind us with one hand partly raised as though to ward off a blow. Then, with a groan, he buried his face in his hands. We stared at each other in horror-struck silence.

"If you hadn't warned me, the blade would have been through my throat," said Gregson in a shaking voice.

"Our ancestors had a neat way of eliminating their enemies," observed Holmes, lifting the heavy cup and once more examining it closely. "With such a toy in the house, it is a dangerous thing for a guest to drink in his host's absence."

"Then this was only an appalling accident!" I exclaimed. "Dalcy was the innocent victim of a trap fashioned four centuries ago!"

"Observe the cunning of this mechanism, very much as I suspected yesterday afternoon——"

"Mr. Holmes," burst out the baronet, "I have never asked favour of any man in my life—"

"Perhaps it would be as well, Sir Reginald, if you left the explanation to me," interrupted Holmes quietly, his long, thin fingers moving over the chased surface of the cup. "The blade cannot strike unless the cup be lifted fully to the lips, when the full pressure of both hands is exerted on the handles. Then the handles themselves act as triggers for the spring-mechanism, to which the old blade is attached. You will perceive the minute slot just below the circlet of jewels and cleverly disguised by the carving."

There was awe in Gregson's face as he gazed down at the ancient vessel.

"Then you mean," he stated somberly, "that the person who drinks from the Luck of Lavington is a dead man?"

"By no means. I would draw your attention to the small silver owl-figures on the crest of the handles. If you look closely, you will see that the right-hand one turns on a pivot. I believe this to act in the same way as a safety-catch on a rifle. Unfortunately, these old mechanisms are apt to become unreliable with the passage of the centuries."

Gregson whistled.

"It was an accident, right enough!" he stated. "Your reference to a mischance, Sir Reginald, has proved to be a lucky shot in the dark. I suspected it all the time. But one moment! Why didn't we see the blade when we first saw the cup?"

"Let us suppose, Gregson," replied Holmes, "that there is some form of recoil-spring."

"But surely, Holmes," I cried, "there could be no such—"

"As you were about to say, Watson, there was no such description of the cup as I had hoped to find in the Maidstone County Registry. However, it did yield me the interesting document I read you."

"Well, well, Mr. Holmes, you can give me the historic details later," said Gregson, turning to the baronet. "In regard to this affair, Sir Reginald, you can think yourself lucky that there are some sharp men hereabouts. Your possession of this dangerous relic might have caused a serious miscarriage of justice. Either you must have the mechanism removed, or entrust it to Scotland Yard."

Sir Reginald Lavington, who had been biting his lip as though to suppress some overmastering emotion, looked dazedly from Holmes to Gregson.

"Right willingly," he said at length. "But the Luck of Lavington has been in our family for over four hundred years. If it passes beyond this door, then I feel it should go to Mr. Sherlock Holmes."

Holmes's eyes met those of the baronet.

"I will accept it as a memento of a very gallant man," my friend replied gravely.

As Holmes and I made our way up the steep lane in the wind-swept darkness, we turned at the brow of the hill and looked down on the old manor-house with its lights dimly reflected in the moat.

"I do feel, Holmes," said I, somewhat nettled, "that you owe me an explanation. When I tried to point to you an error in your case, you indicated plainly that you wished me to speak no further."

"What error, Watson?"

"Your explanation of how the cup worked. By the release of a powerful spring from a trigger controlled by the handles, it would have been quite easy to make the blade strike. But to push it back again, unless this were done by hand so that the blade could be caught again in the mechanism—that, my dear fellow, is quite a different thing."

For a moment Holmes did not reply. He stood gaunt and lonely, his gaze fixed on the ancient tower of Lavington.

"Surely it was apparent from the first," said he, "that no living murderer could have stabbed Dalcy, and that something was wrong with the appearance of the crime as we saw it?"

"You deduced this from the direction of the wound?"

"That, yes. But there were other facts equally indicative."

"Your behaviour suggested as much at the time! Yet I cannot see what facts."

"The scratches on the table, Watson! And the wine spilled on both table and floor."

"Pray be good enough to explain."

"Colonel Dalcy's finger-nails," replied Holmes, "had clawed at the table-top in his death-throes, and all the wine had been spilled. You remarked that? Good! Taking as a working hypothesis the theory that he was killed by a blade in the cup, what must follow? The blade would strike. Then——?"

"Then the cup would fall, spilling the wine. I grant that."

"But is it reasonable that the cup, in falling, should land upright on the table—as we found it? This was overwhelmingly unlikely. Further evidence made it impossible. I lifted the cup, if you recall, when I first examined it. Underneath it, covered by it, you saw——?"

"Scratches!" I interrupted. "Scratches and spilled wine!"

"Precisely. Dalcy would die soon, but not instantly. If the cup fell from his hands, are we to assume that it hung suspended in the air, and afterwards descended *over* the scratches and the wine? No, Watson. There was, as you pointed out, no recoil-mechanism. With Dalcy dead, some living hand picked up the cup from the floor. Some living hand pushed back the blade into the cup, and set it upright on the table."

A gust of rain blew out of the dreary sky, but my companion remained motionless.

"Holmes," said I, "according to the butler——"

"According to the butler? Yes?"

"Sir Reginald Lavington was drinking with the colonel. At least, Dalcy is reported to have said so."

"And, as he said so," commented Holmes, "gave so curious a laugh that Gillings could not forget it. Had the laugh an ulterior meaning, Watson? But I had better say no more, lest I make you an accessory after the fact like myself."

"You do me less than justice, Holmes, should I become accessory after the fact in a good cause!"

"In my judgement," said Sherlock Holmes, "one of the best of causes."

"Then you may rely on my silence."

"Be it so, Watson! Now consider the behaviour of Sir Reginald Lavington. For an innocent man, he acted very strangely."

"You mean that Sir Reginald—"

"Pray don't interrupt. Though he had witnesses that he had not been drinking with Dalcy, he would not produce them. He preferred to be arrested. Why should Dalcy, a man of such different character from his host, pay frequent visits to this house? What was Dalcy doing there? Interpret the meaning of Lavington's statement, 'I know his character *now!*' We saw the answers to these questions played out in deadly pantomime. To me it suggested the blackest of all crimes, blackmail."

"Sir Reginald," I exclaimed, "was guilty after all! He was a dangerous man, as I remarked—"

"A dangerous man, yes," agreed Holmes. "But you have seen his character. He might kill. But he would not kill and conceal."

"Conceal what?"

"Reflect again, Watson. Though we know that he was not drinking with Dalcy in the banqueting-hall, he might have returned from the river just in time to find Dalcy dead. That was when he thrust the blade back into the cup, and set it upright again. But guilt? No. His behaviour, his willingness to be arrested, can be understood only if he had been shielding someone else."

I followed my friend's gaze, which had never moved from the direction of Lavington Court.

"Holmes," I cried, "then who set the diabolical mechanism?"

"Think, Watson! Who was the only person who uttered that one word, 'jealousy'? Let us suppose a woman has erred before a marriage, but never after it. Let us suppose, moreover, that she believes her husband, a man of the old school, would not understand. She is at the mercy

of that most vicious of all parasites, a society blackmailer.
She is present when the blackmailer drinks a toast—by
his own choice—from the Luck of Lavington. But, since
she is obliged to slip away at the entrance of the butler,
the blackmailer laughed and died. Say no more, Watson.
Let the past sleep."

"As you wish. I am silent."

"It is a cardinal error, my dear fellow, to theorize
without data. And yet, when we first entered Lavington
Court yesterday evening, I had a glimpse of the truth."

"But what did you see?"

As we turned away towards our inn and the comfort-
ing light of a fire, Sherlock Holmes nodded over his
shoulder.

"I saw a pale, beautiful woman descend a staircase,
as once I had seen her on the stage. Have you forgotten
another ancient manor, and a hostess named Lady Mac-
beth?"

—:—

*Since . . . our visit to Devonshire, he had been
engaged in two affairs of the utmost importance
. . . the famous card scandal of the Nonpareil
Club . . . and the unfortunate Madame Montpensier.*

FROM "THE HOUND OF THE BASKERVILLES."

6

The Adventure of the Sealed Room

My wife had a slight cold, as my note-book records, when on that morning of April 12th, 1888, we were introduced in such dramatic fashion to one of the most singular problems in the annals of my friend Mr. Sherlock Holmes.

At this time, as I have elsewhere recorded, my medical practice was in the Paddington district. Being young and active, I was in the habit of arising betimes; and eight o'clock found me downstairs, distressing the maid by lighting the fire in the hall, when I was startled by a ring at the street-door.

A patient at this hour could have come on no trivial errand. And, when I had opened the door to the clear April sunlight, I was struck no less by the pallor and agitation than by the youth and beauty of the young lady who stood swaying on my humble threshold.

"Dr. Watson?" asked she, raising her veil.

"I am he, madam."

"Pray forgive this early intrusion. I have come to—I have come to—"

"Be good enough to step into the consulting-room," said I, leading the way with a vigorous step, and meanwhile studying the young lady closely. It is as well for a medical man to impress his patients by deducing their symptoms, and hence their ailments, before they have spoken at all.

"The weather is warm for this season of the year," I continued, when we reached the consulting-room, "yet

113

there is always the possibility of a chill, unless the room
be well sealed against draughts."

The effect of this remark was extraordinary. For a
moment my visitor stared at me with the grey eyes widen-
ing in her beautiful face.

"A sealed room!" she cried. "Oh, my God, a sealed
room!"

Her cry became a shriek which ran through the house,
and then she collapsed on the hearth-rug in a dead faint.

Horrified, I poured some water from a carafe, dashed
brandy into the water, and, after lifting my patient gently
into a chair, persuaded her to swallow it. Scarcely had
I done so when the noise of that cry brought my wife
downstairs and into the consulting-room.

"Good heavens, John, what in the world—?" And here
she broke off. "Why, it's Cora Murray!"

"You know the young lady, then?"

"Know her! I should think I do! I knew Cora Murray
in India. Her father and mine were friends for years; and
I wrote to her when you and I were married."

"You wrote to India?"

"No, no; she lives in England now. Cora is the very
closest friend of Eleanor Grand, who married that rather
crotchety Colonel Warburton. Cora lives with Colonel
and Mrs. Warburton at some address in Cambridge
Terrace."

As my wife finished speaking, our visitor opened her
eyes. My wife patted her hand.

"Gently, Cora," said she. "I was only telling my husband that you lived in Cambridge Terrace with Colonel
and Mrs. Warburton."

"No longer!" cried Miss Murray wildly. "Colonel
Warburton is dead, and his wife so horribly wounded
that she may be dying at this moment! When I saw them
lying there under that terrifying death-mask, I felt the
evil thing itself had driven Colonel Warburton mad. He
must have been mad! Why else should he have shot his
wife and then himself in a locked room? And yet I cannot
believe he would have done this dreadful action."

Grasping my wife's hand with both of hers, she looked up at me with pathetic appeal.

"Oh, Dr. Watson, I did so hope you would help! Is there nothing your friend Mr. Sherlock Holmes can do!"

You may well believe that my wife and I listened with amazement to this tale of domestic tragedy.

"But you tell me that Colonel Warburton is dead," I demurred gently.

"Yet the shadow remains on his name. Oh, is my errand so hopeless?"

"Nothing is ever hopeless, Cora," said my wife. "John, what shall you do?"

"Do?" cried I, glancing at my watch. "Why, a hansom-cab to Baker Street at once! We shall just catch Holmes before breakfast!"

As I had expected, Sherlock Holmes was moodily awaiting his breakfast, the room acrid with the tang of his first daily pipe, which was composed of left-over dottles from the day before. His Bohemian disposition saw nothing strange in Miss Murray's and my arrival at this early hour, though he was inclined to be querulous.

"The fact is, Holmes," said I, "that I was interrupted this morning—"

"Quite so, my dear fellow," said he, "as you were engaged in your usual practice of lighting the fire. Your left thumb proclaims as much." Then he caught sight of Miss Murray's grief-stricken countenance, and his harsh face softened.

"But I think," he added, "that you could both do with a little breakfast before we discuss the shock which this young lady so obviously has had."

And not a word would he permit us to speak until I had consumed some food, though Miss Murray could touch only a cup of coffee.

"H'm!" said Holmes, with a shade of disappointment on his face after our fair client had faltered out as much of her story as she had told me. "This is indeed a grievous tragedy, madam. But I cannot see what service I can render you. A certain Colonel Warburton goes mad; he

shoots first his wife and then himself. I presume there is
no doubt of these facts?"

Miss Murray groaned.

"Unhappily, none," replied she. "Though at first we
had hoped it might be the work of a burglar."

"You *hoped* it might be the work of a burglar?"

I was much annoyed by the acidity of Holmes's tone,
though I could not help divining its cause. Ever since,
in the previous month, he had been outwitted and beaten
by Mrs. Godfrey Norton, *née* Irene Adler, his attitude
towards the whole female sex had become more bitter
than ever.

"Really, Holmes," I protested with some asperity,
"Miss Murray meant only that the work of a burglar-
murderer would have saved Colonel Warburton's name
from the stigma of suicide. I hope you will not hold her
responsible for an unfortunate choice of words."

"An unfortunate choice of words, Watson, has hanged
a murderer ere this. Well, well, we shall not distress the
young lady! But is it possible, madam, for you to be explicit?"

To my surprise, a smile of singular wistfulness as well
as strength illuminated the pale face of our visitor.

"My father, Mr. Holmes, was Captain Murray of the
Sepoy Mutiny. You will see whether I can be explicit."

"Come, this is distinctly better!—Well?"

"Colonel Warburton and his wife," said she, "lived at
number Nine Cambridge Terrace. You will have seen
many such prosperous, solid houses in the Hyde Park
district. On either side of the front door, behind a small
strip of rock-garden, there is a room with two French
windows. Colonel Warburton and my dear Eleanor were
alone in the room to the left of the front door, called
the curio room. The time was just after dinner last night.
The door of that room was locked on the inside. Each of
the French windows was double-bolted on the inside
though the curtains remained undrawn. No other person
was there or hidden there; nor was there any other access
to the room. A pistol lay at the colonel's right hand. There
had been no tampering with any bolt or fastening; the

room was locked like a fortress. These things, Mr. Holmes, you may accept as facts."

And, as I am now able to testify, Miss Murray spoke the literal truth.

"Yes, distinctly this is more satisfactory!" said Holmes, rubbing his long, thin fingers together. "Was it Colonel Warburton's habit to bolt the door upon himself and his wife—in the curio room, you said?—each evening after dinner?"

A sudden perplexity showed in our visitor's face.

"Good heavens, no!" she answered. "I never thought of it."

"Still, I fear it cannot affect the issue. On the contrary, it strengthens the indications of madness."

Cora Murray's grey eyes were steady now.

"No one, Mr. Holmes, is better aware of it than I. If it had been Colonel Warburton's wish to destroy Eleanor and himself—well, can I deny he would have bolted the door?"

"If I may say so, madam," remarked Sherlock Holmes, "you are a young lady of uncommon good sense. Apart from his Indian curios, would you say that the colonel was a man of conventional habits?"

"Eminently so. And yet . . ."

"You would speak of feminine intuition?"

"Sir, what are your own boasted judgements but masculine intuition?"

"They are logic, madam! However, pray forgive my irascible temper of a morning."

Miss Murray bowed her head graciously.

"The household was roused by the two shots," she continued after a moment. "When we looked through the window, and saw those two crumpled figures lying on the floor and the light of the shaded lamps striking a cold blue glitter from the lapis-lazuli eyes of that horrible death-mask, I was seized with superstitious dread."

Holmes was lounging back in his arm-chair, his old mouse-coloured dressing-gown drawn about his shoulders, in a bored and discontented fashion.

"My dear Watson," said he, "you will find the cigars

in the coal-scuttle. Be good enough to pass me the box: that is, if Miss Murray has no objection to the smoke of a cigar?"

"The daughter of an Anglo-Indian, Mr. Holmes," said our fair visitor, "would scarcely object to that." She hesitated, biting her lip.

"Indeed, when Major Earnshaw and Captain Lasher and I burst into that locked room, my most distinct memory is the smell of Colonel Warburton's cigar."

This casual remark was followed by a moment of intense silence. Sherlock Holmes had sprung to his feet, the cigar-box in his hand, and was staring down at Miss Murray.

"I would not distress you, madam, but are you quite sure of what you say?"

"Mr. Sherlock Holmes," retorted the lady, "I am not in the habit of meaningless speech. I remember even the incongruous thought flashing through my mind that incense would have been more suitable than cigar-smoke in a room glimmering with brasswork and wooden idols and rose-coloured lamps."

For a moment Holmes stood motionless before the fire.

"It is possible that there may be a hundred and forty-first sort," he observed thoughtfully. "At the same time, Miss Murray, I should like to hear a little more of what happened. For example, you mentioned a Major Earnshaw and a Captain Lasher. Were these gentlemen also guests at the house?"

"Major Earnshaw has been a guest for some time, yes. But Captain Lasher"—was it my fancy, or did a blush tinge Cora Murray's face at the mention of the captain's name?—"Captain Lasher merely paid a brief call. He is Colonel Warburton's nephew, his only relative, in fact, and is—is much younger than Major Earnshaw."

"But your account of last night, madam?"

Cora Murray paused for a time as though marshalling her thoughts, and then began to speak in a low but intense voice.

"Eleanor Warburton was my best friend in India. She is an exceptionally beautiful woman, and I am not being unkind when I say we were all surprised when she consented to become the wife of Colonel Warburton. He was a soldier of distinguished reputation and strong character; but not, I should judge, an easy man with whom to share one's domestic life. He was inclined to be fussy and short-tempered, especially about his large collection of Indian antiquities.

"Please understand that I liked George well enough, else I should not be here now. And, though their life was not without its quarrels—in fact, there was a quarrel last night—there was nothing, I swear, to account for this present horror!

"When they left India, I accompanied them to the house in Cambridge Terrace. There we lived almost as though we were at a hill-station in India, even to the white-clad figure of Chundra Lal, George's native butler, in a house full of strange gods and perhaps strange influences too.

"Last night, after dinner, Eleanor demanded to speak with her husband. They retired to the curio room, while Major Earnshaw and I were sitting in a little study called the den."

"One moment," interposed Sherlock Holmes, who had made a note on his shirt-cuff. "A while ago you stated that the house had two rooms facing the front garden, one of these being Colonel Warburton's curio room. Was the other front room this den?"

"No; the other front room is the dining-room. The den lies behind it, and the two do not communicate. Major Earnshaw was holding forth rather wearisomely when Jack hurried in. Jack. . . ."

"A welcome arrival?" interposed Holmes. "I take it you refer to Captain Lasher?"

Our visitor raised her frank, clear eyes.

"A very welcome arrival," she smiled. Then her face clouded. "He told us that on his way through the hall, he had heard the sounds of a quarrel between his uncle and Eleanor. Poor Jack, how annoyed he was. 'Here I've come all the way from Kensington to see the old man,' he cried, 'and now I daren't interrupt them. What keeps them quarrelling all the time?'

"I protested that he was doing them an injustice.

" 'Well, I hate rows,' he replied, 'and I do feel, if only for uncle's sake, that Eleanor might make more effort to get on with the family.'

" 'She is devoted to your uncle,' I said, 'and, as for yourself, it is only that she feels as we all do that you live your life too recklessly.'

"When Major Earnshaw suggested three-handed whist, at twopence a point, I'm afraid Jack wasn't very courteous. If he must be reckless, he said, he preferred to drink a glass of port in the dining-room. So Major Earnshaw and I settled down to a game of bezique."

"Did either you or Major Earnshaw leave the room after that?"

"Yes! As a matter of fact, the major did say something about fetching his snuff-box from upstairs." Under other circumstances I felt Cora Murray might have laughed. "He rushed out, fumbling in all his pockets, and swearing he couldn't settle to cards without his snuff.

"I sat there, Mr. Holmes, with the cards in my hand and as I waited in that silent room it seemed as though all the nameless fears of the night gathered slowly round me. I remembered the glitter in Eleanor's eyes at dinner. I remembered the brown face of Chundra Lal, the native butler, who has seemed to gloat ever since the death-mask was brought into the house. At that precise moment, Mr. Holmes, I heard the two revolver shots."

In her agitation, Cora Murray had risen to her feet.

"Oh, please don't think I was mistaken! Don't think I was misled by some other noise, or that these were not the shots which killed George and . . ."

Drawing a deep breath, she sat down again.

"For a moment, I was absolutely petrified. Then I ran out into the hall and almost collided with Major Earnshaw. He was muttering some incoherent reply to my questions when Jack Lasher came out of the dining-room with the decanter of port in his hand. 'You'd better stay back, Cora,' Jack said to me; 'there may be a burglar about.'

"The two men ran across to the door of the curio room.

" 'Locked, curse it,' I remember Major Earnshaw crying out. 'Lend a hand, my lad, and we'll have this door down.'

" 'Look here, sir,' said Jack; 'you'd want siege-artillery against a door like that. Hold hard while I dash round and try the French windows.' As a result, all of us ran outside . . ."

"All of you?"

"Major Earnshaw, Jack Lasher, Chundra Lal, and myself. One glimpse through the nearest window showed us George and Eleanor Warburton lying face upwards against the red Brussels carpet. Blood was still flowing from a wound in Eleanor's breast."

"And then?"

"You may recall my saying that the front garden is a rock-garden?"

"I made a mental note of it."

"A rock-garden with gravel soil. Calling out to the others to guard the doors and make certain no burglar escaped, Jack picked up a huge stone and smashed a window. But there was no burglar, Mr. Holmes. A single glance had shown me that both French windows were still double-bolted on the inside. Immediately afterwards, before anyone had gone near the door, I went to it and found the door locked on the inside. You see, I think I *knew* there could be no burglar."

"You knew it?"

"It was George's fear for his collection," Miss Murray answered simply. "Even the fireplace in that room is bricked up. Chundra Lal looked inscrutably at the hard blue eyes of the death-mask on the wall, and Major Earnshaw's foot kicked the revolver lying near George's hand. 'Bad business, this,' said Major Earnshaw; 'we'd better send for a doctor.' That, I think, is all of my story."

For a time after she had finished speaking Holmes still stood motionless before the fire, his hand toying with the knife whose blade transfixed his unanswered correspondence to the middle of the wooden mantelshelf.

"H'm!" said he. "And the position now?"

"Poor Eleanor lies badly wounded in a nursing home in Bayswater. She may not even recover. George's body has been removed to the mortuary. Even when I left Cambridge Terrace this morning, with some wild hope of enlisting your aid through Dr. Watson, the police had arrived in the person of an Inspector MacDonald. But what can he do?"

"What, indeed?" echoed Holmes. But his deep-set eyes gleamed, and he lifted the knife and brought it down like a weapon against the envelopes. "Still—Inspector Mac! That is much better. I could not have endured Lestrade or Gregson this morning. If the young lady will forgive me while I don coat and hat, we shall just go round to Cambridge Terrace."

"Holmes," cried I in protest, "it would be monstrous to encourage false hopes in Miss Murray!"

My friend looked at me in his coldly imperious fashion.

"My dear Watson, I neither encourage hope nor do I discourage it. I examine evidence. *Voilà tout.*"

Yet I noticed that he slipped his lens into his pocket; and he was moodily thoughtful, biting at his lip, as a four-wheeler carried us through the streets.

Cambridge Terrace, on that sunny April morning, stretched silent and deserted. Behind the stone wall, and the narrow strip of rock-garden, lay the stone house with its white window-facings and green-painted front door. It gave me something of a shock to see, near the windows towards the left of the entrance, the white-dressed figure and turban of a native butler. Chundra Lal stood there as motionless as one of his own idols, looking at us; then he melted into the house through one of the French windows.

Sherlock Holmes, it was clear, had been similarly affected. I saw his shoulders stiffen under the frock-coat as he watched the retreating figure of the Indian servant. Though the window immediately to the left of the front door was intact, a gap in the rock-garden showed where a large stone had been prised out; and the other window, further to the left, had been smashed to bits. It was through this opening that the native butler, on silent feet, had moved inside.

Holmes whistled, but he did not speak until Cora Murray had left us.

"Tell me, Watson," said he. "You saw nothing strange or inconsistent in the narrative of Miss Murray?"

"Strange, horrible, yes!" I confessed. "But inconsistent? Surely not!"

"Yet you yourself have been the first to protest about it."

"My dear fellow, I have uttered not one word of protest this morning!"

"Not this morning, perhaps," said Sherlock Holmes. "Ah, Inspector Mac! We are met upon the occasion of another problem."

In the shattered window, stepping carefully over fallen shards of glass, appeared a freckled-faced, sandy-haired young man with the dogged stamp of the police-officer.

"Great Scott, Mr. Holmes, you don't call this a problem?" exclaimed Inspector MacDonald, raising his eyebrows. "Unless the question is why Colonel Warburton went mad?"

"Well, well!" said Holmes good-naturedly. "I presume you will allow us to enter?"

"Aye, and welcome!" retorted the young Scot.

We found ourselves in a lofty, narrow room which, though furnished with comfortable chairs, conveyed the impression of a barbaric museum. Mounted on an ebony cabinet facing the windows stood an extraordinary object: the effigy of a human face, brown and gilded, with two great eyes of some hard and glittering blue stone.

"Pretty little thing, isn't it?" grunted young Mac-Donald. "That's the death-mask that seems to affect 'em like a hieland spell. Major Earnshaw and Captain Lasher are in the den now, talking their heads off."

To my surprise Holmes scarcely glanced at the hideous object.

"I take it, Inspector Mac," said he, as he wandered

about the room peering into the glass cases and display cabinets, "you have already questioned all the inmates of this house?"

"Mon, I've done nothing else!" groaned Inspector MacDonald. "But what can they tell me? This room *was* locked up. The only man who committed a crime, in shooting himself and his wife, is dead. So far as the police are concerned, the case is closed. What now, Mr. Holmes?"

My friend had stooped suddenly.

"Hullo, what's this?" he cried, examining a small object which he had picked up off the floor.

"Merely the stub of Colonel Warburton's cigar which, as you see, burnt a hole in the carpet," replied Mac-Donald.

"Ah. Quite so."

Even as he spoke the door burst open and there entered a portly, elderly man whom I presumed to be Major Earnshaw. Behind him, accompanied by Cora Murray, her hand on his arm, came a tall young man with a bronzed, high-nosed face and a guardsman's moustache.

"I understand, sir, that you are Mr. Sherlock Holmes," began Major Earnshaw stiffly. "I must say at once that I cannot perceive the reason why Miss Murray should have called you into this private tragedy."

"Others might perceive the reason," replied Holmes quietly. "Did your uncle always smoke the same brand of cigar, Captain Lasher?"

"Yes, sir," replied the young man with a puzzled glance at Holmes. "There is the box on the side-table."

We all watched Sherlock Holmes in silence as he went across and picked up the box of cigars. For a moment, he peered at the contents and then, lifting the box to his nose, he sniffed deeply.

"Dutch," he said. "Miss Murray, you are quite right in your affirmation! Colonel Warburton was not mad."

Major Earnshaw uttered a loud snort, while the younger man, with better manners than his senior, attempted to hide his amusement by smoothing his moustache.

"Deuce knows we are all very relieved to have your

assurance, Mr. Holmes," said he. "Doubtless you deduce it from the colonel's taste in cigars."

"Partly," my friend answered gravely. "Dr. Watson can inform you that I have given some attention to the study of tobacco and that I have even ventured to embody my views in a small monograph listing 140 separate varieties of tobacco ash. Colonel Warburton's taste in cigars merely confirms the other evidence. Well, MacDonald?"

A frown had settled on the Scotland Yard man's face and his small, light-blue eyes peered at Holmes suspiciously from beneath his sandy eyebrows.

"Evidence? What are ye driving at, mon!" he cried suddenly. "Why, it's as plain as a pikestaff. The colonel and his wife are both shot in a room that is locked, bolted and barred from the inside. Do you deny it?"

"No."

"Then, let us stick to the facts, Mr. Holmes."

My friend had strolled across to the ebony cabinet and with his hands behind his back was now engaged in contemplating the hideous painted face that stared above his head.

"By all means," he replied. "What is your theory to account for the locked door, Inspector Mac?"

"That the colonel himself locked it for privacy."

"Quite so. A most suggestive circumstance."

"It is suggestive merely of the madness that drove Colonel Warburton to his dreadful deed," answered MacDonald.

"Come, Mr. Holmes," interposed young Lasher. "We all know your reputation for serving justice through your own clever methods and naturally we are as keen as mustard to clear poor uncle's name. But, devil take it, there is no way round the evidence and whether we like it or not we are forced to agree with the Inspector here that Colonel Warburton was the victim of his own insanity."

Holmes raised one long, thin hand.

"Colonel Warburton was the victim of a singularly cold-blooded murder," he stated quietly.

His words were followed by a tense silence as we all stared at each other.

"By God, sir, whom are you accusing?" roared Major Earnshaw. "I'll have you know that there are slander laws in this country."

"Well, well," said Holmes good-humoredly. "I will take you into my confidence, Major, by telling you that my case rests largely on all those broken portions of glass from the French window which, you will perceive, I have gathered up into the fireplace. When I return tomorrow morning to piece them together, I trust that I will then be able to prove my case to your satisfaction. By the way, Inspector Mac, I take it that you eat oysters?"

MacDonald's face reddened.

"Mr. Holmes, I have had aye a liking and a respect for ye," he said sharply. "But there are times when it is neither douce nor seemly in a man to—what the deil have oysters to do with it?"

"Merely that to eat them you would presumably take the oyster fork nearest to hand. To the trained observer, surely there would be something significant if you reached instead for the fork beside your neighbor's plate. I give you the thought for what it is worth."

For a long moment MacDonald stared intently at my friend.

"Aye, Mr. Holmes," he said at length. "Verra interesting. I should be glad of your suggestions."

"I would advise that you have the broken window boarded up," replied Holmes. "Apart from that, let nothing be touched until we all meet again tomorrow morning. Come, Watson, I see that it is already past one o'clock. A dish of *calamare alla siciliana* at Pelligrini's would not come amiss."

During the afternoon, I was busy upon my belated medical round and it was not until the early evening that I found myself once more in Baker Street. Mrs. Hudson opened the door to me and I had paused on the stairs to answer her enquiry whether I would be staying for dinner when a loud report rang through the house. Mrs. Hudson clutched at the banister.

"There, sir, he's at it again," she wailed. "Them dratted pistols. And not six months since he blew the points off the mantelpiece! In the interests of justice, Mr. Holmes said. Oh, Dr. Watson, sir, if you don't get up there quick, like as not it will be that expensive gasogene that will have gone this time."

Throwing the worthy woman a word of comfort, I raced up the stairs and threw open the door of our old sitting-room just as a second report rang out. Through a cloud of pungent black powder-smoke, I caught a glimpse of Sherlock Holmes. He was lounging back in his arm-chair, clad in a dressing-gown, with a cigar between his lips and a smoking revolver poised in his right hand.

"Ah, Watson," he said languidly.

"Good heavens, Holmes, this is really intolerable," I cried. "The place smells like a rifle range. If you care nothing for the damage, I beg of you to consider the effect on Mrs. Hudson's nerves and those of your clients." I threw wide the windows and was relieved to observe that the noisy stream of passing hansoms and carriages had apparently concealed the sound of the shots. "The atmosphere is most unhealthy," I added severely.

Holmes stretched up an arm and placed the revolver on the mantelpiece.

"Really Watson, I don't know what I would do without you," he remarked. "As I have had occasion to observe before, you have a certain genius for supplying the element of a touchstone to the higher workings of the trained mind."

"A touchstone that has, to my knowledge, broken the law three times in order to be of assistance to you," I replied a trifle bitterly.

"My dear fellow," said he, and there was that in his voice that banished all resentment and mollified my ruffled feelings.

"It is some time since I saw you smoking a cigar," I pronounced, as I threw myself into my old chair.

"It is a matter of mood, Watson. In this instance, I took the liberty of purloining one from the stock of the late Colonel Warburton." He broke off to glance at the clock on the mantelpiece. "H'm. We have an hour to spare," he concluded. "So let us exchange the problems of Man's manifold wickedness for the expression of that higher power that exists even in the worst of us. Watson, the Stradivarius. It is in the corner behind you."

It was nearly eight o'clock and I had just lit the gas when there came a knock on the door and Inspector Mac-Donald, his long, angular figure wrapped in a plaid overcoat, bustled into the room.

"I got your message, Mr. Holmes," he cried, "and everything has been carried out in accordance with your suggestions. There'll be a constable in the front garden at midnight. Don't worry about the French window; we can get in without rousing the house."

Holmes rubbed his thin fingers together.

"Excellent, excellent! You have a gift for promptly carrying out—eh—suggestions that will take you far," he said warmly. "Mrs. Hudson will serve us supper here and afterwards a pipe or two may help to fill in the time. I consider that it might be fatal to my plans should we take up our positions before midnight. Now, Mr. Mac, draw up your chair and try this shag. Watson can tell you that it has marked characteristics of its own."

The evening passed pleasantly enough. Sherlock Holmes, who was in his most genial mood, lent an attentive ear to the Scotland Yard man's account of a gang of French coiners whose operations were actually threatening the stability of the louis d'or, and thereafter proceeded to bemuse the Scotsman with a highly ingenious theory as to the effects of runic lore upon the development of the highland clans. It was the striking of midnight which brought us back at last to the grim realities of the night.

Holmes crossed to his desk and, in the pool of light cast by the green-shaded reading lamp, I caught the grave expression on his face as he opened a drawer and took out a life-preserver.

"Slip this into your pocket, Watson," said he. "I fancy that our man may be inclined to violence. Now, Mr. Mac, as Mrs. Hudson has probably been in bed an hour since, if you are ready we will step downstairs and hail the first hansom."

It was a clear starlit night, and a short drive through a network of small streets carried us across Edgeware Road. At a word from Holmes, the cabby pulled up at a corner and as we alighted I saw the long expanse of Cambridge Terrace stretching away before us in an empty desolation of lamplight and shadow. We hurried down the street and turned through the gate leading to our destination.

MacDonald nodded towards the planks which now blocked the shattered window.

"They're loose on one side," he whispered. "But move carefully."

There was a slight creaking and, an instant later, we had squeezed our way past the boards to find ourselves in the utter darkness of Colonel Warburton's curio room.

Holmes had produced a dark lantern from the pocket of his Inverness and following its faint beam we groped our way along the wall until we came to an alcove containing a couch.

"This will do," whispered my friend. "We might have found a worse roost and it is near enough to the fireplace for our purposes."

The night was singularly quiet and, as it turned out, our vigil a dreary one. Once, some belated revellers went by in a hansom, the sound of their singing and the clip-clop of the horse's hoofs gradually dying away towards Hyde Park and, an hour or so later, there came to us the deep rumbling gallop of a fire-engine tearing furiously along Edgeware Road with a clamour of bells and the sharp pistol-shot cracking of the driver's whip. Otherwise, the silence was unbroken save for the ticking of a grandfather clock at the other end of the room.

The atmosphere, which was heavy with the aromatic mustiness of an Oriental museum, began to weigh me down with an increasing lethargy until I had to concentrate all my faculties to keep myself from falling asleep.

I have referred to the utter darkness, but as my eyes grew accustomed to the conditions I became aware of a pale reflection of light from some distant street-lamp steal-ing through the unboarded French window and I was idly following its path when my gaze fell upon something that brought a chill to my senses. A face, faint and nebulous yet dreadful as the figment of a nightmare, was glaring down at me from the far end of that dim radiance. I must have started involuntarily, for I felt Holmes lean toward me.

"The mask," he whispered. "Our own trophy is likely to be less impressive but rather more dangerous."

Leaning back in my seat I tried to relax, but the sight of that grisly relic had turned my thoughts into a new field of conjecture. The sinister white-clad figure of Chundra Lal, Colonel Warburton's Indian servant, arose in my mind's eye and I attempted to recall the exact words used by Miss Murray in describing the effect of the death-mask upon the man. Perhaps even more than Holmes, I knew enough about India to realize that religious fanat-icism and a sense of sacrilege would not only justify any crime but inspire in the devotee a cunning of execution which might well baffle the preconceptions of our Western minds, however experienced in the ways of our fellow-men.

I was considering whether I should open the subject to my companions when my attention was arrested by the low creak of a door-hinge. There was not a moment to lose in warning Holmes that somebody was entering the room. But when I stretched out my hand it was only to find that my friend was no longer beside me.

There followed a period of complete stillness and then a stooping figure, its footsteps muffled by the carpet, whisked across the faint ray of light from the French window and vanished into the shadows immediately in front of me. I had a fleeting impression of a high-collared cape and the dull glitter of some long, thin object grasped in a half-raised hand. An instant later, there came a gleam of light in the fireplace, as though the shutter of a dark lantern had been slid back, and then a gentle tapping and tinkling.

I was rising to my feet when a smothered yell rang

through the room followed instantly by the sounds of a furious struggle.

"Watson! Watson!"

With a thrill of horror I recognized Holmes's voice in that half-choked cry, and plunging forward through the darkness, I hurled myself upon a writhing mass that loomed suddenly before me.

A grip like steel closed round my throat and as I raised my arm to force back the head of my dimly seen assailant he buried his teeth in my forearm like some savage hound. The man possessed the strength of a madman and it was not until MacDonald, having lit a gas-jet, sprang to our assistance that we succeeded in mastering his struggles. Holmes, his face strained and bloodless, leaned back against the wall, his hand clasping his shoulder where he had been hit with a heavy brass poker that now lay in the fireplace amid the splintered shards of window-glass which he had placed there on our previous visit.

"There's your man, MacDonald!" he gasped. "You can arrest him for the murder of Colonel Warburton and for the attempted murder of his wife."

MacDonald flung back our assailant's cape and for a moment I stared in silence before an exclamation of amazement broke from my lips. For, in that first glance, I had failed to recognize in those lowering features and vicious, baleful eyes the bronzed, handsome countenance of Captain Jack Lasher.

The first streaks of dawn were glimmering through the window when my friend and I found ourselves back in Baker Street.

I poured out two stiff brandy-and-sodas and handed one to Holmes. As he leaned back in his chair, the gas-light beside the mantelpiece threw his keen aquiline features into bold relief and I was glad to observe that a little colour was stealing into his face.

"Really, Watson, I owe you an apology," said he. "Captain Jack was a dangerous man. How is your arm where he savaged you?"

"A little painful," I admitted. "But nothing that iodine

and a bandage cannot repair. I am far more concerned about your shoulder, my dear fellow, for he gave you an ugly blow with that poker. You must allow me to look at it."

"Later, later, Watson. I assure you that it is nothing worse than a bruise," he replied, with a touch of impatience. "Well, I can confess now that there were moments tonight when I had the gravest doubts that our man would walk into the trap."

"Trap?"

"A baited trap, Watson, and had he not swallowed my dainty morsel it would have gone hard with us to bring Captain Lasher to book. I gambled on the fact that a murderer's fears will sometimes override his intelligence. And so it turned out."

"Frankly, I do not understand even now how you unravelled this case."

Holmes leant back in his chair and put his finger tips together.

"My dear fellow, there was no great difficulty in the problem. The facts were obvious enough but the delicacy of the matter lay in the need that the murderer himself should confirm them by some overt act. Circumstantial evidence is the bane of the trained reasoner."

"I have observed nothing."

"You observed everything but failed to reason. In the course of Miss Murray's narrative, she mentioned that the door of the curio room was locked and yet the window-curtains were not drawn, not drawn, mark you, Watson, in a ground-floor room overlooking the public street. A most unusual proceeding. You may recall that I interrupted Miss Murray to enquire as to Colonel Warburton's conventional habits.

"The circumstances suggested to my mind the possibility that Colonel Warburton might have been expecting a visitor and that the nature of that visit was such that either he or the caller preferred that it should occur privately by the French windows rather than the front door. This elderly soldier was recently married to a young and beautiful wife and I therefore discarded the idea of a vulgar assignation. If I was right in my theory, then the visitor must be a man whose private interview with Colonel Warburton would be resented by some other member of the household and hence the obvious step of joining the colonel via the French windows."

"But they were locked," I objected.

"Naturally. Miss Murray stated that Mrs. Warburton accompanied her husband to the curio room immediately after dinner and apparently a quarrel arose between them. It occurred to me that, if the colonel was expecting a visitor, then what more natural than he would leave the curtains undrawn so that his caller should observe that he was not alone. At first, of course, these were all mere conjectures that could possibly fit the facts."

"And the identity of this mysterious visitor?"

"Again, a conjecture, Watson. We knew that Mrs. Warburton disapproved of Captain Lasher, her husband's nephew. I give you these vagaries as they first occurred to me during the earlier part of Miss Murray's narrative. I could not have moved in the matter, had not the latter part of her story contained the one singular fact that changed the slightest of suspicions into the absolute certainty that we were in the presence of a cold-blooded and calculated murder."

"I must say that I cannot recall . . ."

"Yet you yourself underlined it, Watson, when you used the term 'intolerable.' "

"Great heavens, Holmes," I burst out. "Then, it was Miss Murray's remark about the smell of the colonel's cigar . . ."

"In a room in which two shots had just been fired! It would have reeked of black powder. I knew, then, that no shots had been fired within the curio room."

"But the reports were heard by the household."

"The shots were fired from *outside* through the closed windows. The murderer was an excellent marksman and therefore conceivably a military man. Here, at last, was something to work upon and, later on, I received confirmation from your own lips, Watson, when having lit one of the colonel's cigars I waited until I heard you below and then fired two shots from the same calibre revolver as that which killed Warburton."

"In any case, there should have been powder burns," I said thoughtfully.

"Not necessarily. The powder from a cartridge is a tricky element and the absence of burns proved nothing. The smell of the cigar was of far greater importance. I must add, however, that useful though your confirmation was, my visit to the house had already elucidated the whole case in my mind."

"You were startled at the appearance of the Indian servant," I rejoined, somewhat nettled at the trace of self-satisfaction which I discerned in his manner.

"No Watson, I was startled at the broken window through which he retreated."

"But Miss Murray had told us that Captain Lasher broke the window in order to enter the room."

"It is an unfortunate fact, Watson, that a woman will invariably omit from her narrative that exact precision of detail which is as essential to the trained observer as bricks and mortar to a builder. If you will recall, she stated that Captain Lasher ran out of the house, looked through the French window and then, picking up a stone from the rock-garden, smashed the glass and entered."

"Quite so."

"The reason that I started when I saw the Indian was because the man was retreating through the wreckage of the *far* French window, while that nearer to the front door remained unbroken. As we hurried forward to the house, I observed the gap in the rockery immediately under the first window where Lasher had picked up the stone. Why, then, should he run on to the second window and smash it, unless it was that the glass bore its own story? Hence my broad hint to MacDonald of the oyster and the nearest fork. The groundwork of my case was complete when I sniffed the contents of Colonel Warburton's cigar box. They were Dutch, among the weakest in aroma of all cigars."

"All this is now quite clear to me," I said. "But in telling the whole household of your plans to piece together the glass of the broken window it seems to me that you were risking the very evidence on which your case was based."

Holmes reached for the Persian slipper and began to fill his pipe with black shag.

"My dear Watson, it would have been virtually impossible for me to reconstruct those shattered panes to the degree that would prove the existence of two small bullet holes. No, it was a question of bluff, my dear fellow, a gambler's throw. Should somebody make an attempt to destroy still further those shards from the window, then that person was the murderer of Colonel Warburton. I showed my hand deliberately. The rest is known to you. Our man came, armed with a poker, having let himself in with the duplicate latch-key which we discovered in his cape pocket. I think there is nothing to add."

"But the reason, Holmes," I cried.

"We have not far to look, Watson. We are told that, until Colonel Warburton's marriage, Lasher was his only relative and therefore, we may assume, his heir. Mrs. Warburton, according to Miss Murray's statement, disapproved of the younger man on the grounds of his extravagant living. It is obvious from this that the wife's influence must represent a very real danger to the interests of Captain Jack.

"On the night in question, our man came openly to the house and, having spoken with Miss Murray and Major Earnshaw, retired ostensibly to drink a port in the dining-room. In fact, however, he merely passed through the dining-room window, which opens on the front garden, walked to the French windows of the curio room and there shot Colonel Warburton and his wife through the glass.

"It would require no more than a few seconds to rush back by the way that he had come, seize a decanter from the sideboard and hurry out into the hall. But he cut it fine, for you will recall that he appeared a moment or two after the others. To complete the illusion of Colonel Warburton's madness, it merely remained for him to eliminate the bullet holes by smashing the window and, on entering, drop the revolver by the hand of his victim."

"And if Mrs. Warburton had not been there and he had been able to keep his rendezvous with his uncle, what then?" I asked.

"Ah, Watson, there we can only guess. But the fact that he came armed presupposes the worst. I have no doubt that when he comes to trial it will be found that Lasher was pressed for money and, as we have ample reason to know, he is a young man who would not shrink from taking his own measures to remove any obstacles that stood in the way of his needs. Well, my dear fellow, it is high time that you were on your way home. Pray, convey my apologies to your wife for any small interruption I may have caused in the tranquillity of your *ménage*."

"But your shoulder, Holmes," I expostulated. "I must apply some liniment before you retire for a few hours' rest."

"Tut, Watson," my friend replied. "You should have learned by now that the mind is the master of the body. I have a small problem on hand concerning a solution of potash and so if you would have the goodness to hand me that pipette—"

—:—

There were only two [cases] which I was the means of introducing to his notice, that of Mr. Hatherley's thumb and that of Colonel Warburton's madness.

FROM "THE ENGINEER'S THUMB"

7

The Adventure of
Foulkes Rath

"This is a most curious affair," I said, dropping *The Times* on the floor. "Indeed, I am surprised that the family have not already consulted you."

My friend Sherlock Holmes turned away from the window and threw himself into his arm-chair.

"I take it that you refer to the murder at Foulkes Rath," he said languidly. "If so, this might interest you, Watson. It arrived before breakfast."

He had drawn a buff-colored form from the pocket of his dressing-gown and now passed it across to me. The telegram, which bore the postmark of Forest Row, Sussex, ran as follows: "Having regard to Addleton affairs, propose to call on you at 10:15 precisely. Vincent."

Picking up *The Times* again, I ran my eye quickly down the column. "There is no mention of anybody named Vincent," I said.

"A fact of no importance whatever," replied Holmes impatiently. "Let us assume, from the phraseology of the telegram, that he is a lawyer of the old school employed by the Addleton family. As I observe, Watson, that we have a few minutes in hand, pray refresh my memory by running over the salient points from the account in this morning's paper, while omitting all irrelevant observations from their correspondent."

Holmes, having filled his clay pipe with shag from the Persian slipper, leaned back in his chair and contemplated the ceiling through a cloud of pungent blue smoke.

"The tragedy occurred at Foulkes Rath," I began, "an

ancient Sussex manor-house near Forest Row on Ashdown Forest. The curious name of the house is derived
from the circumstance that there is an old burial
ground—"

"Keep to the facts, Watson."

"The property was owned by Colonel Matthias Addleton," I continued rather stiffly. "Squire Addleton, as
he was known, was the local Justice of the Peace and the
richest landowner in the district. The household at
Foulkes Rath consisted of the squire, his nephew Percy
Longton, the butler Morstead and four indoor servants.
In addition, there is an outside staff consisting of the
lodge-keeper, a groom and several gamekeepers who
occupy cottages on the boundaries of the estate. Last night,
Squire Addleton and his nephew dined at their usual hour
of eight o'clock and after dinner the squire sent for his
horse and was absent for about an hour. On his return,
shortly before ten, he took a glass of port with his
nephew in the hall. The two men appear to have been
quarrelling, for the butler has stated that, on entering
with the port, he remarked that the squire was flushed
and brusque in his manner."

"And the nephew, Longton I think you said his name
was?" Holmes interrupted.

"According to the butler, he did not see Longton's
face as the young man walked to the window and stood
there looking out into the night while the butler was in
the room. On retiring, however, the butler caught the
sounds of their voices in a furious altercation. Shortly after
midnight, the household was roused by a loud cry apparently from the hall and, on rushing down in their night-
clothes, they were horrified to discover Squire Addleton
lying senseless in a pool of blood with his head split open.
Standing beside the body of the dying man was Mr. Percy
Longton, clad in a dressing-gown and grasping in his
hand a blood-stained axe, a mediaeval executioner's axe,
Holmes, which had been torn down from a trophy of arms
above the fireplace. Longton was so dazed with horror
that he could scarcely assist in lifting the injured man's
head and staunching the loss of blood. However, even as

Morstead bent over him, the squire raising himself on his elbows gasped out in a dreadful whisper, 'It—was— Long—tom! It—was—Long—!' and sank back dead in the butler's arms. The local police were summoned and, on the evidence of the quarrel between the two men, the discovery of the nephew standing over the body and finally the accusing words of the dying man himself, Mr. Percy Longton has been arrested for the murder of Squire Addleton. I see that there is a note in the late-news column that the accused man, who has never ceased to protest his innocence, has been removed to Lewes. These would appear to be the principal facts, Holmes."

For a while my friend smoked in silence.

"What explanation did Longton offer for the quarrel?" he asked at length.

"It is stated here that he voluntarily informed the police that he and his uncle came to high words on the subject of the latter's sale of Chudford Farm which Longton considered a further and unnecessary reduction of the estate."

"Further?"

"It appears that Squire Addleton has sold other holdings over the last two years," I replied, throwing the paper on the couch. "I must say, Holmes, that I have seldom read a case in which the culprit is more clearly defined."

"Ugly, Watson, very ugly," my friend agreed. "Indeed, presuming the facts to be as stated, I cannot conceive why this Mr. Vincent should propose to waste my time. But here, unless I am much mistaken, is our man upon the staircase."

There came a knock on the door and Mrs. Hudson ushered in our visitor.

Mr. Vincent was a small, elderly man with a long, pale, mournful face framed in a pair of side-whiskers. For a moment, he stood hesitating while he peered at us short-sightedly through his *pince-nez* which were attached by a black ribbon to the lapel of his rather dingy frock-coat. "This is too bad, Mr. Holmes!" he cried shrilly. "I assumed that my telegram would ensure privacy, sir, absolute privacy. My client's affairs—"

"This is my colleague Dr. Watson," interposed Sherlock Holmes, waving our visitor to the chair which I had drawn forward. "I assure you that his presence may be invaluable."

Mr. Vincent bobbed his head towards me and, depositing his hat and stick on the floor, sank into the cushions.

"Pray believe that I meant you no offence, Dr. Watson," he squeaked. "But this is a terrible morning, a terrible morning I say, for those who cherish goodwill for the Addletons of Foulkes Rath."

"Quite so," said Holmes. "I trust, however, that your early-morning walk to the station did something to restore your nerves. I find that exercise is in itself a sedative."

Our visitor started in his seat. "Really, sir," he cried, "I fail to see how you—"

"Tut, tut," Holmes interrupted impatiently. "A man who has driven to the station does not appear with a splash of fresh clay on his left gaiter and a similar smear across the ferrule of his stick. You walked through a rough country lane and, as the weather is dry, I should judge that your path took in a ford or water-crossing."

"Your reasoning is perfectly correct, sir," replied Mr. Vincent, with a most suspicious glance at Holmes over the top of his *pince-nez*. "My horse is at grass and not even a hack available at that hour in the village. I walked as you say, caught the milk train to London and here I am to enlist, nay, Mr. Holmes, to *demand,* your services for my unfortunate young client, Mr. Percy Longton."

Holmes lay back with closed eyes and his chin resting on his finger-tips. "I fear that there is nothing that I can do in the matter," he announced. "Dr. Watson has already put before me the principal facts, and they would appear to be quite damning. Who is in charge of the case?"

"I understand that the local police, in view of the gravity of the crime, appealed to Scotland Yard, who dispatched an Inspector Lestrade—dear me, Mr. Holmes, I fear that you have a painful twinge of rheumatics—an Inspector Lestrade to take charge. I should explain, perhaps," went on our visitor, "that I am the senior partner of Vincent, Peabody and Vincent, the legal practitioners of Forest Row to whom the Addletons have entrusted their interests for the past hundred years and more."

Leaning forward, Holmes picked up the paper and, tapping the place sharply with his finger, handed it without a word to the lawyer.

"The account is accurate enough," said the little man sadly, after running his eye down the column, "though it omits to state that the front door was unlocked despite the fact that the squire told Morstead the butler that he would lock it himself."

Holmes raised his eyebrows. "Unlocked, you say? H'm. Well, the probable explanation is that Squire Addleton forgot the matter in his quarrel with his nephew. However, there are one or two points which are not yet clear to me."

"Well, sir?"

"I take it that the murdered man was in his night-clothes?"

"No, he was fully dressed. Mr. Longton was in his night-clothes."

"I understand that after dinner the squire left the house for an hour or so. Was it his custom to take nocturnal rides?"

Mr. Vincent ceased to stroke his whiskers and shot a keen glance at Holmes. "Now that you mention it, such was not his custom," he shrilled. "But he returned safely and I cannot see—"

"Quite so," interposed Holmes. "Would you say that the squire was a wealthy man? Pray be precise in your reply."

"Matthias Addleton was a very wealthy man. He was, of course, the younger son and emigrated to Australia some forty years ago, that is to say in 1854. He returned in the seventies having amassed a large fortune in the Australian gold-fields and, his elder brother having died, he inherited the family property of Foulkes Rath. Alas, I cannot pretend that he was liked in the neighborhood, for he was a man of morose disposition and as unpopular with his neighbors as he was feared by our local ne'er-do-wells in his capacity as Justice of the Peace. A hard, bitter, brooding man."

"Was Mr. Percy Longton on good terms with his uncle?"

The lawyer hesitated. "I am afraid not," he said at length. "Mr. Percy, who was the son of the squire's late sister, has lived at Foulkes Rath since his childhood and, on the property passing to his uncle, he remained and managed the estate. He is, of course, the heir under an entailment which covers the house and a part of the land and, on more than one occasion, he has expressed deep resentment at his uncle's sales of certain farms and holdings which led, I fear, to bad blood between them. It was most unfortunate that his wife was absent last night, of all nights."

"His wife?"

"Yes, there is a Mrs. Longton, a charming, gracious young woman. She was staying with friends for the night at East Grinstead and is due back this morning." Mr. Vincent paused. "Poor little Mary," he ended quietly. "What a home-coming! The squire dead and her husband charged with murder."

"One final question," said Holmes. "What explanation does your client offer to account for the events of last night?"

"His story is a simple one, Mr. Holmes. He states that at dinner the squire informed him of his intention to sell Chudford Farm and when he remonstrated on the needlessness of the sale and the damage that it would do to the estate, his uncle turned on him roundly and high words ensued. Later, his uncle called for his horse and rode from the house without a word of explanation. Upon his return, the squire ordered a bottle of port and, as the quarrel threatened to grow from bad to worse, Mr. Percy bade his uncle good-night and retired to his room. However, his mind was too agitated for sleep and twice, according to his statement, he sat up in bed under the impression that he had caught the distant sound of his uncle's voice from the great hall."

"Why, then, did he not go to investigate?" interposed Holmes sharply.

"I put that very question to him. He replied that his uncle had been drinking heavily and therefore he assumed that he was raving to himself in the hall. The butler Morstead confirmed that this had occurred not infrequently in the past."

"Pray continue."

"The clock over the stables had just chimed midnight and he was drifting at last into slumber when in an instant he was brought back to full consciousness by a dreadful yell that rang through the great silent house. Springing out of bed, he pulled on his dressing-gown and, seizing a candle, ran downstairs to the hall, only to recoil before the terrible sight that met his eyes.

"The hearth and fireplace were spattered with blood, and sprawling in a great crimson pool, his arms raised above his head and his teeth grinning through his beard, lay Squire Addleton. Mr. Percy rushed forward and was bending over his uncle when his eyes fell upon an object that turned him sick and faint. Beside the body of the squire and horribly dappled with the blood of its victim lay an executioner's axe! He recognized it vaguely as forming a part of a trophy of arms that hung above the chimney-piece and without thinking what he was doing he had stooped and picked up the thing when Morstead accompanied by the terrified maidservants burst into the room. Such is the explanation of my unhappy client."

"Dear me," said Holmes.

For a long moment, the lawyer and I sat in silence, our eyes fixed upon my friend. His head had fallen back against the chair top, his eyes were closed and only a thin, quick spiral of smoke rising from his clay pipe hinted at the activity of the mind behind that impassive aquiline mask. A moment later, he had sprung to his feet.

"A breath of Ashdown air will certainly do you no harm, Watson," he said briskly. "Mr. Vincent, my friend and I are very much at your disposal."

It was mid-afternoon when we alighted from the train at the wayside station of Forest Row. Mr. Vincent had telegraphed our reservations at the Green Man, an old weald-stone inn which appeared to be the only building of any consequence in the little hamlet. The air was permeated with the scent of the woodlands clothing the low, rounded Sussex hills that hemmed us in on every side, and as I contemplated that green smiling landscape it seemed to me that the tragedy of Foulkes Rath took on a grimmer, darker shade through the very serenity of the pastoral surroundings amid which it had been enacted. Though it was evident that the worthy lawyer shared my feelings, Sherlock Holmes was completely absorbed in his own thoughts, and took no part in our conversation save for a remark that the station-master was unhappily married and had recently changed the position of his shaving-mirror.

Hiring a fly at the inn, we set out on the three-mile journey that lay between the village and the manor-house, and as our road wound its way up the wooded slopes of Pippinford Hill, we caught occasional glimpses of a sombre, heather-covered ridge where the edge of the great Ashdown moors loomed against the sky-line.

We had topped the hill and I was absorbed in the wonderful view of the moorland rolling away and away to the faint blue distances of the Sussex Downs when Mr. Vincent touched my arm and pointed ahead.

"Foulkes Rath," he said.

On a crest of the moor stood a gaunt, rambling house of grey stone flanked by a line of stables. A series of fields running from the very walls of the ancient mansion merged into a wilderness of yellow gorse and heather ending in a deep wooded valley from whence arose a pencil of smoke and the high distant droning of a steam-saw.

"The Ashdown Timber Mills," volunteered Mr. Vincent. "Those woods lie beyond the boundary of the estate and there is not another neighbour within three miles. But here we are, Mr. Holmes, and a sorry welcome it is to the manor-house of Foulkes Rath."

At the sound of our wheels upon the drive an elderly manservant had appeared at the beetle-browed Tudor doorway and now, on catching sight of our companion, he hurried forward with an exclamation of relief.

"Thank God you've come, sir," he cried. "Mrs. Longton—"

"She has returned?" interposed Mr. Vincent. "Poor lady, I will go to her at once."

"Sergeant Clare is here, sir, and—er—a person from the London police."

"Very well, Morstead."

"One moment," said Holmes. "Has your master's body been moved?"

"He has been laid in the gun-room, sir."

"I trust that nothing else has been disturbed?" Holmes demanded sharply.

The man's eyes turned slowly towards the dark arch of the doorway. "No, sir," he muttered. "It's all as it was!"

A small vestibule in which Morstead relieved us of our hats and sticks led us into the inner hall. It was a great stone-built chamber with a groiner roof and a line of narrow pointed windows emblazoned with stained-glass shields through which the sunlight, now waning towards evening, mottled the oaken floor with vivid patches of vert, gules and azure. A short, thin man who was busy writing at a desk glanced up at our entrance and sprang to his feet with a flush of indignation upon his sharp-featured countenance.

"How's this, Mr. Holmes," he cried. "There's no scope here for the exercise of your talents."

"I have no doubt that you are right, Lestrade," replied my friend carelessly. "Nevertheless, there have been occasions when—"

"—when luck has favoured the theorist, eh, Mr. Holmes? Ah, Dr. Watson. And might I enquire who this is, if the question may be forgiven in a police-officer?"

"This is Mr. Vincent, who is legal advisor to the Addleton family," I replied. "It was he who requested the services of Mr. Sherlock Holmes."

"Oh, he did, did he!" snapped Inspector Lestrade, with a baleful glance at the little lawyer. "Well, it's too late now for any of Mr. Holmes's fine theories. We have our man. Good day, gentlemen."

"Just a moment, Lestrade," said Holmes sternly. "You've made mistakes in the past, and it is not impossible that you may make them in the future. In this case, if you have the right man, and I must confess that up to now I believe that you have, then you have nothing to lose in my confirmation. On the other hand—"

"Ah, it's always 'on the other hand.' However—" Lestrade added grudgingly, "I do not see that you can do any harm. If you want to waste your own time, Mr. Holmes, that's your business. Yes, Dr. Watson, it's a nasty sight, isn't it?"

I had followed Sherlock Holmes to the fireplace at the far end of the room only to recoil before the spectacle that met my eyes. Across the oak floor stretched a great black stain of partly congealed blood while the hearth and fireplace and even the nearby wainscotting were hideously dappled with gouts and splashes of crimson.

Mr. Vincent, white to the lips, turned away and collapsed into a chair.

"Stand back, Watson," Holmes enjoined abruptly. "I take it, Lestrade, that there were no footprints on—" he gestured towards that dreadful floor.

"Just one, Mr. Holmes," replied Lestrade with a bitter smile, "and it fitted Mr. Percy Longton's bedroom-slipper."

"Ah, it would seem that you are learning. By the way, what of the accused man's dressing-gown?"

"Well, what of it?"

"The walls, Lestrade, the walls! Surely the blood-spattered front of Longton's robe goes far towards completing your case."

"Now that you mention it, the sleeves were blood-soaked."

"Tut, that is natural enough, considering that he helped to raise the dying man's head. There is little to be gained from the sleeves. You have the dressing-gown there?"

The Scotland Yard man rummaged in a Gladstone bag and drew out a grey woollen robe.

"This is it."

"H'm. Stains on the sleeves and hem. Not even a mark on the front. Curious but, alas, inconclusive. And this is the weapon?"

Lestrade had drawn from his bag a most fearsome object. It was a short-hafted axe made entirely of steel with a broad crescent-edge blade and a narrow neck.

"This is certainly a very ancient specimen," said Holmes, examining the blade through his lens. "Incidentally, where was the wound inflicted?"

"The whole top of Squire Addleton's skull was cleft like a rotten apple," answered Lestrade. "Indeed, it was a miracle that he regained consciousness even for a moment. An unfortunate miracle for Mr. Longton," he added.

"He named him, I understand."

"Well, he gasped out something about 'Longtom,' which was near enough to the mark for a dying man."

"Quite so. But whom have we here? No, madam, not a step nearer, I beg! This fireplace is no sight for a woman."

A slim, graceful girl, clad in the deepest mourning, had rushed into the room. Her dark eyes shone with almost fevered brilliance in the whiteness of her face and her hands were clasped before her in an agony of distress.

"Save him!" she cried wildly. "He is innocent, I swear it! Oh, Mr. Sherlock Holmes, save my husband!"

I do not think that any of us, even Lestrade, remained unmoved.

"I will do whatever lies in my power, madam," said Holmes gently. "Now tell me about your husband."

"He is the kindest of men."

"Quite so. But I mean physically. For instance, would you say that he was taller than Squire Addleton?"

Mrs. Longton looked at Holmes in amazement. "Good heavens, no," she cried. "Why, the squire was over six feet tall."

"Ah. Now, Mr. Vincent, perhaps you can inform me

when it was that Squire Addleton first began to sell portions of the estate?"

"The first sale occurred two years past, the second some six months ago," replied the lawyer hurriedly. "And now, Mr. Holmes, unless you require my presence, I propose to take Mrs. Longton back to the drawing-room."

My friend bowed. "We need not worry Mrs. Longton any further," said he. "But I would be glad of a word with the butler."

While we waited, Holmes strolled to the window and, with his hands behind his back and his chin sunk upon his breast, stared out over the empty landscape. Lestrade, who had returned to his desk, chewed the end of his pen and watched him curiously.

"Ah, Morstead," said Holmes, as the butler entered. "Doubtless you are anxious to do everything possible to assist Mr. Longton, and I wish you to understand that we are here with the same purpose."

The man looked nervously from Lestrade to Holmes.

"Come, now," my friend continued. "I am sure that you can help us. For instance, perhaps you can recall whether the squire received any letters by yesterday's post."

"There was a letter, sir, yes."

"Ah! Can you tell me more?"

"I'm afraid not, sir. It bore the local postmark and seemed a very ordinary cheap envelope such as they use hereabouts. But I was surprised—" the man hesitated for a moment.

"Yes, something surprised you. Something, perhaps, in the squire's manner?" asked Holmes quietly.

"Yes, sir, that's it. As soon as I gave it to him, he opened it and as he read there came a look in his face that made me glad to get out of the room. When I returned later, the squire had gone out and there were bits of burnt paper smouldering in the grate."

Holmes rubbed his hands together. "Your assistance is invaluable, Morstead," said he. "Now, think carefully. Six months ago, as you probably know, your master sold some land. You cannot, of course, recall a similar letter at about that time?"

"No, sir."

"Naturally not. Thank you, Morstead, I think that is all."

Something in his voice made me glance at Holmes and I was amazed at the change in him. His eyes gleamed with excitement and a touch of colour showed in his cheeks.

"Sit down, Watson," he cried. "Over there on the trestle." Then, whipping his lens from his pocket, he commenced his examination.

I watched him enthralled. The blood-stains, the fire-place, the mantelpiece, the very floor itself were subjected to a careful and methodical scrutiny as Holmes crawled about on his hands and knees, his long, thin nose within a few inches of the parquet and the lens in his hands catching an occasional sparkle from the light of the dying sun.

A Persian rug lay in the centre of the room and, on reaching the edge of this, I saw him stiffen suddenly.

"You should have observed this, Lestrade," he said softly. "There are faint traces of a foot-mark here."

"What of it, Mr. Holmes?" grinned Lestrade, with a wink at me. "Plenty of people have passed over that rug."

"But it has not rained for days. The boot which made this mark was slightly moist, and I need not tell you that there is something in this room which would easily account for that. Hullo, what have we here?"

Holmes had scraped something from the mat and was closely examining it through his lens. Lestrade and I joined him.

"Well, what is it?"

Without a word, Holmes passed him the lens and held out his hand.

"Dust," announced Lestrade, peering through the glass.

"Pine-wood dust," replied Holmes quietly. "The fine grain is unmistakable. You will note that I scraped it from the traces of the boot-mark."

"Really, Holmes," I cried. "I cannot see—"

My friend looked at me with a gleaming eye. "Come, Watson," said he, "we will stretch our legs as far as the stables."

In the cobbled yard, we came on a groom drawing water from a pump. I have remarked before that Holmes possessed a gift for putting the working classes at their ease and, after exchanging a few words, the man lost so much of his Sussex reserve that when my friend threw out the suggestion that it might be difficult to name which of the horses had been used by his master on the previous night, the information was instantly forthcoming.

"It was Ranger, sir," volunteered the groom. "Here in this stall. You'd like to see her hoofs? Well, why not. There you are, and you can scrape away with your knife to your heart's content and not a stone will you find."

Holmes, after closely examining a fragment of earth which he had taken from the horse's hoof, placed it carefully in an envelope and, pressing a half-sovereign into the groom's hand, strode out of the yard.

"Well, Watson, it only remains for us to collect our hats and sticks before returning to our inn," he announced briskly. "Ah, Lestrade," he continued, as the Scotland Yard man appeared in the front door. "I would draw your attention to the fireplace chair."

"But there is no fireplace chair."

"That is why I draw your attention to it. Come, Watson, there is nothing further to be learned here tonight."

The evening passed pleasantly enough, though I was somewhat irritated with Holmes who, while refusing to answer any of my questions on the grounds that they could be better answered on the morrow, encouraged our landlord to converse on local topics which could hold no interest whatever for strangers like ourselves.

When I awoke the next morning I was surprised to learn that my friend had breakfasted and gone out some two hours earlier. I was concluding my own breakfast when he strolled in, looking invigorated for his exercise in the open air.

"Where have you been?" I enquired.

"Following the example of the early bird, Watson," he chuckled. "If you have finished, then let us drive to Foulkes Rath and pick up Lestrade. There are times when he has his definite uses."

Half an hour later saw us once more at the old mansion. Lestrade, who greeted us rather surlily, stared at my companion in amazement.

"But why a walk on the moors, Mr. Holmes?" he snapped. "What bee has got into your bonnet this time?"

Holmes's face was very stern, as he turned away. "Very well," said he. "I had hoped to give you the undivided credit of capturing the murderer of Squire Addleton."

Lestrade caught my companion by the arm. "Man, are you serious?" he demanded. "But the evidence! Every single fact points clearly to—"

Sherlock Holmes raised his stick and pointed silently down the long slope of fields and heather to the distant wooded valley.

"There," he said quietly.

It was a walk that I will long remember. I am sure that Lestrade had no more idea than I had of what lay before us as we followed Holmes's tall, spare figure across the meadows and down the rough sheep track that led into the desolation of the moor. It was a mile or more before we reached the beginning of the valley and plunged down into the welcome shade of the pine woods through which the whirring of the steam-saw vibrated like the hum of some monstrous insect. The air grew redolent with the tang of burning wood and a few minutes later we found ourselves among the buildings and timber stacks of the Ashdown Timber Mills.

Holmes led the way without hesitation to a hut marked "Manager" and knocked sharply. There was a moment of waiting, and then the door was flung open.

I have seldom seen a more formidable figure than the man who stood upon the threshold. He was a giant in stature, with a breadth of shoulders that blocked the doorway and a matted tangle of red beard that hung down over his chest like the mane of a lion.

"What do you want here?" he growled.

"I presume that I have the pleasure of addressing Mr. Thomas Greerly?" asked Holmes politely.

The man remained silent while he bit off a cud of chewing-tobacco, his eyes roving over us in a cold, slow stare.

"What if you have?" he said at length.

"Long Tom to your friends, I think," said Holmes quietly. "Well, Mr. Thomas Greerly, it is no thanks to you that an innocent man is not called upon to pay the penalty for your own misdeeds."

For a moment the giant stood as though turned to stone and then, with the roar of a wild beast, he hurled himself on Holmes. I managed to sieze him round the waist and Holmes's hands were buried deep in that bristling tangle of beard, but it would have gone hard with us had not Lestrade clapped a pistol to the man's head. At the touch of the cold steel against his temples, he ceased to struggle and a moment later Holmes had snapped a pair of handcuffs upon his great knotted wrists.

From the glare in his eyes I thought that Greerly was about to attack us again, but suddenly he gave a rueful laugh and turned his bearded face towards my friend.

"I don't know who you are, mister," he said, "but it's a fair catch. So, if you'll tell me how you did it, I'll answer all your questions."

Lestrade stepped forward. "I must warn you—" he began, with the magnanimous fair play of British justice.

But our prisoner waved his words aside.

"Aye, I killed him," he growled. "I killed Bully Addleton and now that it has come I reckon that I'll swing with an easy heart. Is that plain enough for you? Well, come inside."

He led the way into the little office and threw himself into his chair while the rest of us accommodated ourselves as best we might.

"How did you find me, mister?" he demanded carelessly, raising his manacled hands to bite off a fresh cud of tobacco.

"Fortunately for an innocent man, I discerned certain traces of your presence," said Holmes in his sternest manner. "I admit that I believed Mr. Percy Longton to be guilty when first I was asked to look into the matter nor did I perceive any reason to alter my views when I reached the scene of the crime. It was not long, however, before I found myself faced with certain details which, though insignificant enough in themselves, threw a new and curious light on the whole affair. The frightful blow that killed Squire Addleton had spattered blood over the fireplace and even a part of the wall. Why, then, were there no stains down the front of the dressing-gown worn by the man who struck that blow? Here was something inconclusive and yet troublesome.

"Next, I observed that there was no chair in the vicinity of the fireplace where the murdered man had fallen. He had, therefore, been struck down when standing, not sitting, and yet as the blow cleft the top of his skull it had been delivered from the same level, if not from above. When I learned from Mrs. Longton that the squire was over six feet tall, I was left with no doubt whatever that a serious miscarriage of justice had been committed. But, if not Longton, then who was the real murderer?

"My enquiries brought to light that a letter had reached the squire that morning, that apparently he had burned it, and thereafter quarrelled with his nephew by proposing the sale of a farm. Squire Addleton was a wealthy man. Why, then, these periodic sales which had first commenced two years previously? The man was being heavily blackmailed."

"A lie, by God!" interrupted Greerly fiercely. "He was paying back what didn't belong to him, and that's the truth."

"On examining the room," my friend continued. "I found the faint traces of a boot-mark to which I drew your attention, Lestrade, and as the weather was dry I knew, of course, that the mark had been made after the crime. The man's boot was moist because he had stepped in the blood. My lens disclosed traces of some fine powder adhering to this boot-mark and on closer examination I recognized this powder to be pine sawdust. When I found, pressed into the dried earth in the hoofs of the squire's horse, a quantity of similar sawdust, I was able to form a fairly clear picture of the events which had occurred on the night of the crime.

"The squire, who had been subjected to the vehement protests of his nephew over the proposed sale of some valuable land, instantly mounted his horse after dinner and rode off into the darkness. Obviously, he intended to speak, perhaps appeal, to someone, and about midnight that someone comes. He is a man of lofty stature and of a strength sufficiently formidable to cleave a human skull in a single blow, and the soles of his boots are engrained with pine-dust. There is a quarrel between the two men, perhaps a refusal to pay, a threat and, in an instant, the taller man has torn a weapon from the wall and, burying it in his opponent's skull, rushes out into the night.

"Where, I asked myself, might one expect to find the ground impregnated with wood-dust? Surely in a saw-mill; and there down in the valley below the manor-house lay the Ashdown Timber Mills.

"It had occurred to me already that the clue to this terrible event might lie in the squire's earlier life, and therefore, following my usual practice, I spent an instructive evening gossiping with our landlord in course of which I elicited by an idle question that two years ago an Australian had been given the post of Manager at the Ashdown Timber Mills on the personal recommendation of Squire Addleton. When you came out of this hut early this morning, Greerly, to give your orders for the day's work, I was behind that timber shack. I saw you, and my case was complete."

The Australian, who had listened to Holmes's account with the closest attention, leaned back in his chair with a bitter smile.

"It's my bad luck they ever sent for you, mister," he said brazenly. "But I'm not the man to break a bargain, and so here's the little that you still need to know.

"It all began in the early seventies at the time of the great gold strike near Kalgoorlie. I had a younger brother who went into partnership with an Englishman whom we knew as Bully Addleton and, sure enough, they struck it rich. At that time the tracks to the goldfields were none too safe, for there were bushrangers at work. Well, only a week after my brother and Addleton hit the vein, the gold-stage to Kalgoorlie was held up and the guard and driver shot dead.

"On the false accusation of Bully Addleton and some trumped-up evidence, my unfortunate brother was seized and tried for the crime. The law was quick to act in those days and they hung him that night to the Bushranger's Tree. Addleton was left with the mine.

"I was away up the Blue Mountains, timber cutting, and two full years passed before I heard the truth of the matter from a digger who had it from a dying cook-boy who had been bribed to silence.

"Addleton had made his pile and gone back to the Old Country, and I hadn't the money to follow him. From that day I wandered from job to job, always saving and planning how to find my brother's murderer, aye murderer, may the devil roast him!

"It was nigh twenty years before I came alongside him and that one moment repaid all my waiting.

" 'Morning, Bully,' said I.

"His face went the colour of putty and the pipe dropped out of his mouth.

" 'Long Tom Greerly!' he gasped, and I thought the man was going to faint.

"Well, we had a talk and I made him get me this job. Then I began to bleed him bit by bit. No blackmail, mister, but restitution of a dead man's goods. Two days ago, I wrote to him again and that night he rode down here, cursing and swearing that I was driving him to ruin. I told him I'd give him until midnight to make his choice, pay or tell, and I'd call for his answer.

"He was waiting for me in the hall, mad with drink and fury, and swearing that I could go to the police or the devil for all he cared. Did I think that the word of a dirty Australian timber-jack would be accepted against that of the Lord of the Manor and Justice of the Peace? He was mad to have ever paid me a penny-piece.

" 'I'll serve you as thoroughly as I served your worthless brother!' he yelled. It was that which did it. Something seemed to snap in my brain and, tearing down the nearest weapon from the wall, I buried it in his snarling, grinning head.

"For a moment I stood looking down at him. 'From me and Jim,' I whispered. Then I turned and ran into the night. That's my story, mister, and now I'd take it kindly if we can go before my men get back."

Lestrade and his prisoner had reached the door when Holmes's voice halted them.

"I only wish to know," he said, "whether you are aware of the weapon with which you killed Squire Addleton?"

"I told you it was the nearest thing on the wall, some old axe or club."

"It was an executioner's axe," said Holmes drily.

The Australian made no reply, but as he followed Lestrade to the door it seemed to me that a singular smile lit up his rough, bearded face.

My friend and I walked back slowly through the woods and up the moor where Lestrade and the prisoner had already vanished in the direction of Foulkes Rath. Sherlock Holmes was moody and thoughtful and it was apparent to me that the reaction that generally followed the conclusion of a case was already upon him.

"It is curious," I observed, "that a man's hatred and ferocity should remain unabated after twenty years."

"My dear Watson," replied Holmes, "I would remind you of the old Sicilian adage that vengeance is the only dish that is best when eaten cold. But surely," he continued, shading his eyes with his hand, "the lady hurrying down our path is Mrs. Longton. Though I trust that I am not lacking in chivalry, nevertheless I am in no mood for the effusions of feminine gratitude and therefore, with your permission, we will take this by-path behind the gorse bushes. If we step out, we should be in time for the afternoon train to town.

"Corata is singing tonight at Covent Garden and, braced by our short holiday in the invigorating atmosphere of Ashdown Forest, I think that you will agree with me,

Watson, that we could desire no more pleasant home-coming than an hour or two spent amid the magic of *Manon Lescaut* followed by a cold supper at our rooms in Baker Street."

—:—

Here also I find an account of the Addleton tragedy.

FROM "THE GOLDEN PINCE-NEZ"

8

The Adventure of the Abbas Ruby

On glancing through my notes, I find it recorded that the night of November 10th saw the first heavy blizzard of the winter of 1886. The day had been dark and cold with a bitter, searching wind that moaned against the windows and, as the early dusk deepened into night, the street-lamps glimmering through the gloom of Baker Street disclosed the first flurries of snow and sleet swirling along the empty, glistening pavements.

Scarcely three weeks had passed since my friend Sherlock Holmes and I had returned from Dartmoor on the conclusion of that singular case, the details of which I have recorded elsewhere under the name of *The Hound of the Baskervilles* and, though several enquiries had been brought to my friend's notice since that time, none was of a nature to appeal to his love of the bizarre or to challenge that unique combination of logic and deduction which depended for its inspiration upon the intricacies of the problem which lay before it.

A merry fire was crackling in the grate and as I leaned back in my chair and let my eyes wander about the un-tidy cosiness of our sitting-room, I had to admit that the wildness of the night and the rattle of the sleet upon the window-panes served merely to increase my own sense of contentment. On the far side of the fire-place, Sherlock Holmes was curled up in his arm-chair, languidly turning over the pages of a black index-book marked "B" in which he had just completed certain entries under "Bask-erville" and giving vent to occasional chuckles and ejaculations as his eyes wandered over the names and notes covering every page of the volume. I had flung down *The Lancet* with some idea of encouraging my friend to touch upon one or two of the names which were strange to me when, beneath the sobbing of the wind, my ears caught the faint sound of the door-bell.

"You have a visitor," I said.

"Surely a client, Watson," Holmes replied, laying aside his book. "And on urgent business," he added, with a glance at the rattling window-panes. "These inclement nights are invariably the herald of—" His words were interrupted by a rush of feet on the staircase, the door was burst open, and our visitor stumbled into the room.

He was a short, stout man, wrapped up in a dripping mackintosh cape and wearing a bowler hat tied under his chin by a woollen muffler. Holmes had tilted the lamp-shade, so that the light shone towards the door and, for a moment, the man remained motionless, staring at us across the room while the moisture from his sodden garment dripped in dark stains upon the carpet. He would have been a comical figure, with his tubbiness and his fat face framed in its encircling muffler, were it not for the impression of helpless misery in the man's brown eyes and in the shaking hands with which he plucked at the absurd bow beneath his chin.

"Take off your coat and come to the fire," said Holmes kindly.

"I must indeed apologize, gentlemen, for my untoward intrusion," he began. "But I fear that circumstances have arisen which threaten—threaten—"

"Quick, Watson!"

But I was too late. There was a thud and a groan and there lay our visitor senseless upon the carpet.

Seizing some brandy from the sideboard, I ran to force it between his lips while Holmes, who had loosened the man's muffler, craned over my shoulder.

"What do you make of him, Watson?" he asked.

"He has had a severe shock," I replied. "From his appearance, he seems a comfortable, respectable person of the grocer class, and doubtless we will find out more about him when he has recovered."

"Tut, I think that we might venture a little further," my friend said thoughtfully. "When the butler from some wealthy household rushes on the spur of the moment through a snow-storm in order to fall senseless on my humble carpet, I am tempted to visualize some affair of greater moment than a broken till."

"My dear Holmes!"

"I would stake a guinea that there is a livery beneath that overcoat. Ah, did I not say so!"

"Even so, I do not see how you surmised it nor the wealthy household."

Holmes picked up the limp hands. "You will observe that the pads of both thumbs are darkened, Watson. In a man of sedentary type, I know of only one occupation that will account for this equality of discolouration. The man polishes silver with his thumbs."

"Surely, Holmes, a leather would be more usual," I protested.

"On ordinary silver, yes. Very fine silver is finished, however, with the thumbs, and hence my conjecture of a well-to-do household. As for his sudden departure, the man has rushed into the night in patent-leather pumps despite that it has been snowing since six o'clock. There, now, you are feeling better," he added kindly, as our visitor opened his eyes. "Dr. Watson and I will help you into this chair and after you have rested awhile doubtless you will tell us your troubles."

The man clapped his hands to his head.

"Rested awhile!" he cried wildly. "My God, sir, they must be after me already!"

"Who must be after you?"

"The police, Sir John, all of them! The Abbas Ruby has been stolen!" The words rose almost to a shriek. My friend leaned forward and placed his long, thin fingers on the other's wrist. On previous occasions I have noted Holmes's almost magnetic power for asserting a sense of peace and comfort over the minds of those in distress.

It was so in this case, and the wild, panic-stricken gleam faded slowly in the man's eyes.

"Come, now, give me the facts," Sherlock Holmes enjoined after a moment.

"My name is Andrew Joliffe," began our visitor more calmly, "and for the past two years I have been employed as butler to Sir John and Lady Doverton at Manchester Square."

"Sir John Doverton, the horticulturist?"

"Yes, sir. Indeed, there's them that say that his flowers, and especially his famous red camellias, mean more to Sir John than even the Abbas Ruby and all his other family treasures. I take it you know about the ruby, sir?"

"I know of its existence. But tell me in your own words."

"Well, it makes one frightened just to look at it. Like a big drop of blood it is, with a touch of devil's fire smouldering in its heart. In two years I had seen it only once, for Sir John keeps it in the safe in his bedroom, locked up like some deadly poisonous creature that shouldn't even know the light of day. Tonight, however, I saw it for the second time. It was just after dinner, when one of our guests, Captain Masterman, suggested to Sir John that he should show them the Abbas Ruby—"

"Their names," interposed Holmes languidly.

"Names, sir? Ah, you mean the guests. Well, there were Captain Masterman, who is her ladyship's brother, Lord and Lady Brackminster, Mrs. Dunbar, the Rt. Hon. William Radford, our Member of Parliament, and Mrs. Fitzsimmons-Leming."

Holmes scribbled a word on his cuff. "Pray continue," said he.

"I was serving coffee in the library when the captain made his suggestion and all the ladies began to clamour to see the gem. 'I would prefer to show you the red camellias in the conservatory,' says Sir John. 'The specimen that my wife is wearing in her gown is surely more beautiful than anything to be found in a jewel-box, as you can judge for yourselves.'

"'Then, let us judge for ourselves!' smiled Mr. Dunbar,

and Sir John went upstairs and brought down the jewel-case. As he opened it on the table and they all crowded round, her ladyship told me to light the lamps in the conservatory as they would be coming shortly to see the red camellias. But there were no red camellias."

"I fail to understand."

"They'd gone, sir! Gone, every single one of them," cried our visitor hoarsely. "When I entered the conservatory, I just stood there holding the lamp above my head and wondering if I was stark mad. There was the famous shrub, all right, but of the dozen great blossoms which I had admired on it this very afternoon there remained not so much as a petal."

Sherlock Holmes stretched out a long arm for his pipe.

"Dear, dear," said he. "This is most gratifying. But pray continue your interesting narrative."

"I ran back to the library to tell them. 'But it is impossible!' cried her ladyship. 'I saw the flowers myself when I plucked one for my dress just before dinner.' 'The man's been at the port!' said Sir John, and then, thrusting the jewel-case into the table drawer, he rushed for the conservatory with all the rest of them at his heels. But the camellias had gone."

"One moment," interrupted Holmes. "When were they seen last?"

"I saw them at four and as her ladyship picked one shortly before dinner, they were there about eight o'clock. But the flowers are of no matter, Mr. Holmes. It's the ruby!"

"Ah!"

Our visitor leaned forward in his chair.

"The library was empty for only a few minutes," he continued almost in a whisper. "But when Sir John, fair demented over the mystery of his flowers, returned and opened the drawer, the Abbas Ruby, together with its jewel-case, had vanished as completely as the red camellias."

For a moment we sat in silence broken only by the tinkle of burning embers falling in the grate.

"Joliffe," mused Holmes dreamily. "Andrew Joliffe. The Catterton diamond robbery, was it not?"

The man buried his face in his hands.

"I'm glad you know, sir," he muttered at last. "But as God is my judge I've kept straight since I came out three years ago. Captain Masterman was very good to me and got me this job with his brother-in-law, and from that day to this I've never let him down. I've been content to keep my wages, hoping that eventually I might save enough to buy my own cigar shop."

"Go on with your story."

"Well, sir, I was in the hall, having sent the stableboy for the police, when I caught Captain Masterman's voice through the half-opened door of the library. 'Damn it, John, I wanted to give a lame dog a chance,' said he, 'but I blame myself now that I did not tell you his past history. He must have slipped in here while everyone was in the conservatory and—' I waited for no more, sir, but telling Rogers, the footman, that if anybody wanted me then they would find me with Mr. Sherlock Holmes, I ran here through the snow, believing from all I've heard that you will not think it beneath you to save from injustice one who has already paid his debt to society. You are my only hope, sir, and—My God, I knew it!"

The door had flown open and a tall, fair-haired man, wrapped to the ears in a snow-powdered cape, strode into the room.

"Ah, Gregson, we were expecting you."

"No doubt, Mr. Holmes," replied Inspector Gregson drily. "Well, this is our man, and so we'll be getting along."

Our wretched client leaped to his feet. "But I'm innocent! I never touched it!" he wailed.

The police-agent smiled sourly and, drawing from his pocket a flat box, he shook it under his prisoner's nose.

"God save us, it's the jewel-case!" gasped Joliffe.

"There, he admits it! Where was it found, you say? It was found where you put it, my man, under your mattress."

Joliffe's face had turned the colour of ashes. "But I never touched it," he repeated dully.

"One moment, Gregson," interposed Holmes. "Am I to understand that you have the Abbas Ruby?"

"No," he replied, "the case was empty. But it cannot be far, and Sir John is offering a reward of five thousand pounds."

"May I see the case? Thank you. Dear me, what a sorry sight. The lock unbroken but the hinges smashed. Flesh-coloured velvet. But surely—"

Whipping out his lens, Holmes laid the jewel-case beneath the reading lamp and examined it closely. "Most interesting," he said at length. "By the way, Joliffe, was the ruby mounted?"

"It was set in a carved gold locket and chain. But, oh, Mr. Holmes—"

"Rest assured I will do my best for you. Well, Gregson, we will detain you no longer."

The Scotland Yard man snapped a pair of handcuffs on our unhappy visitor and a moment later the door had closed behind them.

For a while, Holmes smoked thoughtfully. He had pulled up his chair to the blaze and, with his chin cupped in his hands and his elbows resting on his knees, he stared broodingly into the fire while the ruddy light waxed and waned on his keen finely drawn features.

"Have you ever heard of the Nonpareil Club, Watson?" he asked suddenly.

"The name is unfamiliar to me," I confessed.

"It is the most exclusive gambling club in London," he continued. "The Members' List, which is privately printed, reads like Debrett with a spicing of the *Almanach de Gotha*. I have had my eye upon it for sometime past."

"Good heavens, Holmes, why?"

"Where there is wealth follows crime, Watson. It is the one fixed principle that has governed man's wickedness through all his history."

"But what has this club to do with the Abbas Ruby?" I asked.

"Perhaps, nothing. Or again, everything. Kindly hand

me down the Biographical Index marked 'M' from the shelf above the pipe-rack. Dear me, it is remarkable that one letter of the alphabet can embrace so many notorious names. You would find it profitable to study this list, Watson. But here is our man, I think. Mappins; Marston, the poisoner; Masterman. Captain the Honourable Bruce Masterman, born 1856, educated at—h'm! ha!—suspected of implication in the Hilliers Dearbon inheritance forgery; secretary of Nonpareil Club; member of—quite so." My friend flung the book on the couch. "Well, Watson, are you game for a nocturnal excursion?"

"By all means, Holmes. But where?"

"We will be guided by circumstances."

The wind had fallen and as we emerged into the white, silent streets, the distant chimes of Big Ben struck the hour of ten. Though we were well muffled, it was so bitterly cold that I welcomed the need of our brisk walk to Marylebone Road before we could hail a hansom.

"It will do no harm to call at Manchester Square," remarked Holmes, as we tucked the rug about us and jingled away through the snow-covered streets. A short drive brought us to our destination, and as we alighted before the portico of an imposing Georgian house, Holmes pointed to the ground.

"The guests have gone already," said he, "for you will observe that these wheel-marks were made after the snow ceased to fall."

The footman who had opened the door to us took our cards, and a moment later we were ushered across the hall into a handsome library where a tall, thin man with greying hair and a most melancholy countenance was warming his coat-tails before a blazing fire. As we entered, a woman, who was reclining on a chaise lounge, rose to her feet and turned to look at us.

Though the leading artist of our day has immortalized Lady Doverton, I venture to think that no portrait will ever do full justice to this imperious and beautiful woman as we saw her then, in a gown of white satin with a single scarlet flower flaming at her bodice and the golden glow of the candles shining on her pale, perfectly chiselled face and drawing sparkles of fire from the diamonds that crowned her rich auburn hair. Her companion advanced on us eagerly.

"Really, Mr. Sherlock Holmes, this is most gratifying!" he cried. "That you should face the inclemency of the night in order to fasten upon the perpetrator of this outrage speaks highly for your public spirit, sir! Most highly!"

Holmes bowed. "The Abbas Ruby is a famous stone, Sir John."

"Ah, the ruby. Yes, yes, of course," replied Sir John Doverton. "Most lamentable. Fortunately, there are buds. Your knowledge of flowers will tell you—" He broke off as his wife laid her fingers on his arm.

"As the matter is already in the hands of the police," she said haughtily, "I do not understand why we should be honoured by this visit from Mr. Sherlock Holmes."

"I shall take up very little of your time, Lady Doverton," replied my friend. "A few minutes in your conservatory should suffice."

"With what object, sir? What possible connection can there be between my husband's conservatory and the missing jewel?"

"It is that I wish to determine."

Lady Doverton smiled coldly. "In the meantime, the police will have arrested the thief."

"I think not."

"Absurd! The man who fled was a convicted jewel-robber. It is obvious."

"Perhaps too obvious, madam! Does it not strike you as somewhat singular that an ex-convict, though aware that his record was known already to your brother, should steal a famous stone from his own employer and then conveniently condemn himself by secreting the jewel-box under his mattress, where even Scotland Yard could be relied upon to search?"

Lady Doverton put a hand to her bosom. "I had not considered the matter in that light," she said.

"Naturally. But, dear me, what a beautiful blossom! I take it that this is the red camellia which you plucked this afternoon?"

"This evening, sir, just before dinner."

"Spes ultima gentis!" observed Sir John gloomily. "At least, until the next crop."

"Just so. It would interest me to see your conservatory."

We followed our guide along a short passage which, opening from the library, terminated in the glass door of a hothouse. While the famous horticulturist and I waited at the entrance, Holmes commenced a slow tour through the warm, stifling darkness, the lighted candle which he bore in his hand appearing and disappearing like some great glow-worm amid the weird shapes of cacti and curious tropical shrubs. Holding the light close to the camellia bush, he spent some time peering through his lens.

"The victims of a vandal's knife," groaned Sir John.

"No, they were snipped with a small pair of curved nail-scissors," Holmes remarked. "You will observe that there is no shredding on the stalks such as a knife would cause, and furthermore, the small cut on this leaf shows that the scissor-points overreached the stem of the flower. Well, I think that there is nothing more to be learned here."

We were retracing our steps when Holmes paused at a small window in the passage and, opening the catch, struck a match and craned over the sill.

"It overlooks a path used by the tradesmen," volunteered Sir John.

I leaned over my friend's shoulder. Below, the snow lay in a long, smooth drift from the house wall to the edge of a narrow pathway. Holmes said nothing but, as he turned away, I noticed that there was something of surprise, almost of chagrin, in his expression.

Lady Doverton was awaiting us in the library.

"I fear that your reputation is overrated, Mr. Holmes," she said, with a gleam of amusement in her fine blue eyes. "I expected you to return with all the missing flowers and perhaps even the Abbas Ruby itself!"

"At least, I have every hope of returning you the latter, madam," said Holmes coldly.

"A dangerous boast, Mr. Holmes."

"Others will tell you that boasting is not among my habits. And now, as Dr. Watson and I are already somewhat overdue at the Nonpareil Club—dear me, Lady Doverton, I fear that you have broken your fan—it only remains for me to express our regret for this intrusion and to wish you a very good night."

We had driven as far as Oxford Street when Holmes, who had sat in complete silence with his chin upon his breast, suddenly sprang to his feet, pushed up the trap and shouted an order to our driver.

"What a fool!" he cried, clapping a hand to his forehead, as our hansom turned in its tracks. "What mental abberation!"

"What then?"

"Watson, if I ever show signs of self-satisfaction, kindly whisper the word 'camellias' in my ear."

A few minutes later, we had alighted again before the portico of Sir John Doverton's mansion. "There is no need to disturb the household," muttered Holmes. "I imagine that this is the gate into the tradesmen's entrance."

My friend led the way swiftly along the path skirting the wall of the house until we found ourselves under a window which I recognized as the one opening from the passage. Then, throwing himself on his knees he commenced carefully to scoop away the snow with his bare hands. After a few moments, he straightened himself and I saw that he had cleared a large dark patch.

"Let us risk a match, Watson," he chuckled.

I lit one and there, on the black earth exposed by Holmes's burrowings in the snow-drift, lay a little reddish-brown heap of frozen flowers.

"The camellias!" I exclaimed. "My dear fellow, what does this mean?"

My friend's face was very stern as he rose to his feet.

"Villainy, Watson!" said he. "Clever, calculated villainy."

He picked up one of the dead flowers and stood for a while silently contemplating the dark, withered petals in the palm of his hand.

"It is as well for Andrew Joliffe that he reached Baker Street before Gregson reached him," he observed thoughtfully.

"Shall I raise the house?" I asked.

"Ever the man of action, Watson," he replied, with a dry chuckle. "No, my dear fellow, I think that we would be better employed in making our way quietly back to our hansom and then on to the purlieus of St. James's."

In the events of the evening, I had lost all sense of time, and it came as something of a shock when, as we wheeled from Piccadilly into St. James's Street and stopped before the door of an elegant, well-lighted house, I saw from the clock above Palace Yard that it was not far short of midnight.

"When its neighbours of clubland go to bed the Nonpareil Club comes into its own," remarked Holmes, ringing the bell. He scribbled a note on his calling-card and, handing it to the manservant at the door, he led the way into the hall.

As we followed the servant up a marble staircase to the floor above, I caught a glimpse of lofty and luxurious rooms in which small groups of men, clad in evening dress, were sitting about and reading papers or gathered round rosewood card-tables.

Our guide knocked at a door and a moment later we found ourselves in a small, comfortably furnished room hung with sporting prints and smelling strongly of cigar smoke. A tall, soldierly-looking man with a close-cropped moustache and thick auburn hair, who was lounging in a chair before the fireplace, made no attempt to rise at our entrance but, whirling Holmes's card between his fingers, surveyed us coldly through a pair of blue eyes that reminded me forcibly of Lady Doverton.

"You choose strange times to call, gentlemen," he said, with a trace of hostility in his voice. "It's cursed late."

"And getting later," my friend observed. "No, Captain Masterman, a chair is unnecessary. I prefer to stand."

"Stand, then. What do you want?"

"The Abbas Ruby," said Sherlock Holmes quietly.

I started and gripped my stick. There was a moment of silence while Masterman stared up at Holmes from the depth of his chair. Then throwing back his head, he laughed heartily.

"My dear sir, you must really excuse me!" he cried at length, his handsome face all a-grin. "But your demand is a little excessive. The Nonpareil Club does not number absconding servants among its members. You must seek elsewhere for Joliffe."

"I have already spoken with Joliffe."

"Ah, I see," he sneered. "Then you represent the interests of the butler?"

"No, I represent the interests of justice," replied Holmes sternly.

"Dear me, how very imposing. Well, Mr. Holmes, your demand was so worded that it is lucky for you that I have no witnesses or it would go hard with you in a court of law. A cool five thousand guineas' worth of slander, I should say. You'll find the door behind you."

Holmes strolled across to the fireplace and, drawing his watch from his pocket, compared it with the clock on the mantelpiece.

"It is now five minutes after midnight," he remarked. "You have until nine o'clock in the morning to return the jewel to me at Baker Street."

Masterman bounded from his chair.

"Now look here, damn you—" he snarled.

"It won't do, Captain Masterman, really it won't do. However, that you may realize that I am not bluffing, I will run over a few points for your edification. You knew Joliffe's past record and you got him the post with Sir John as a possible sinecure for the future."

"Prove it, you cursed busybody!"

"Later you needed money," continued Holmes imperturbably, "a great deal of money, to judge from the value of the Abbas Ruby. I have no doubt that an examination of your card losses would give us the figure. Thereupon you contrived, I regret to add with your sister's help, a scheme that was as cunning in its conception as it was merciless in its execution.

"From Lady Doverton you obtained precise details of the jewel-case containing the stone, and you caused a duplicate of this case to be constructed. The difficulty was to know when Sir John would withdraw the ruby from the safe, which he did but rarely. The coming dinner-party at which you were to be one of the guests suggested a very simple solution. Relying on the wholehearted support of the ladies, you would ask your brother-in-law to bring down the jewel. But how to ensure that he and the others would leave the room while the jewel was there? I fear that, here, we come upon the subtle traces of the feminine mind. There could be no surer way than to play upon Sir John's pride in his famous red camellias. It worked out exactly as you foresaw.

"When Joliffe returned with the news that the bush had been stripped, Sir John instantly thrust the jewel-case into the nearest receptacle and, followed by his guests, rushed to the conservatory. You slipped back, pocketed the case and, on the robbery being discovered, volunteered the perfectly true information that his wretched butler was a convicted jewel-thief. However, though cleverly planned and boldly executed, you made two cardinal errors.

"The first was that the duplicate jewel-case, which had been rather amateurishly smashed and then planted under the mattress of Joliffe's bed, probably some hours in advance, was lined in a pale velvet. My lens disclosed that this delicate surface contained not the slightest trace of rubbing such as invariably occurs from the mounting of a pendant jewel.

"The second error was fatal. Your sister stated that she had plucked the blossom in her gown immediately prior to dinner and, such being the case, the flowers must have been there at eight o'clock. I asked myself what I should do if I wished to dispose of a dozen blossoms as swiftly as possible. The answer was the nearest window, in this instance, the one in the passage.

"But the snow which lay in a deep drift below disclosed no traces whatever. This, I confess, caused me some perplexity until, as Dr. Watson can testify, the obvious solution dawned on me. I rushed back and proceeding very carefully to remove the snow-drift under the window, I came upon the remains of the missing camellias lying on the frozen earth. As they were too light to sink through the snow, they must have been flung there before the snow-fall commenced at six o'clock. Lady Doverton's story was therefore a fabrication and, in those withered flowers, lay the answer to the whole problem."

During my friend's exposition, I had watched the angry flush on Captain Masterman's face fade into an ugly pallor and now, as Holmes ceased, he crossed swiftly to a desk in the corner, an ominous glint in his eyes.

"I wouldn't," said Holmes pleasantly.

Masterman paused with his hand on the drawer.

"What are you going to do?" he rasped.

"Providing that the Abbas Ruby is returned to me before nine o'clock, I shall make no public exposure and doubtless Sir John Doverton will forbear further enquiries at my request. I am protecting his wife's name. Were it otherwise, you would feel the full weight of my hand upon you, Captain Masterman, for when I consider your inveiglement of your sister and your foul plot to ensnare an innocent man, I am hard put to it to recall a more blackguardly villain."

"But the scandal, curse you!" cried Masterman. "What of the scandal in the Nonpareil Club? I'm over my ears in card debts and if I give up the ruby—" he paused and shot us a swift furtive glance. "Look here, Holmes, what about a sporting proposition—?"

My friend turned towards the door.

"You have until nine o'clock," he said coldly. "Come, Watson."

The snow had begun to fall again as we waited in St. James's Street while the porter whistled for a cab.

"My dear fellow, I'm afraid that you must be very tired," Holmes remarked.

"On the contrary, I am always invigorated by your company," I answered.

"Well, you have deserved a few hours' rest. Our adventures are over for tonight"

But my friend spoke too soon. A belated hansom carried us to Baker Street, and I was in the act of opening the front door with my latch-key when our attention was arrested by the lamps of a carriage approaching swiftly from the direction of Marlebone Road. The vehicle, a closed four-wheeler, came to a halt a few yards down the street and, an instant later, the muffled figure of a woman hurried towards us. Though her features were hidden under a heavy veil, there was something vaguely familiar in her tall, graceful form and the queenly poise of her head as she stood face to face with us on the snow-covered pavement.

"I wish to speak with you, Mr. Holmes," she cried imperiously.

My friend raised his eyebrows. "Perhaps you would go ahead, Watson, and light the gas," he said quietly.

In the years of my association with the cases of my friend, Sherlock Holmes, I have seen many beautiful women cross our threshold. But I cannot recall one whose beauty surpassed that of the woman who now, with a deep rustle of skirts, entered our modest sitting-room.

She had thrown back her veil and the gas-light illumined with a pale radiance her perfect face and the brilliance of her long-lashed blue eyes which met and challenged Holmes's stern and uncompromising glance.

"I had not expected this late visit, Lady Doverton," he said austerely.

"I thought that you were omniscient, Mr. Holmes," she replied, with a faint mockery ringing in her voice. "But, perhaps you know nothing about women."

"I fail to see—"

"Must I remind you of your boast? The loss of the Abbas Ruby is a disaster, and I could not rest in my anxiety to know whether or not you have fulfilled your promise. Come, sir, admit that you have failed."

"On the contrary, I have succeeded."

Our visitor rose from her chair, her eyes glittering.

"This is an ill jest, Mr. Holmes," she cried haughtily.

I have remarked elsewhere that, despite his profound distrust of the opposite sex, it was my friend's nature to be chivalrous to women. But now, for the first time, as he faced Lady Doverton, I saw his face harden ominously in the presence of a woman.

"The hour is a trifle late for tiresome pretences, madam," said he. "I have visited the Nonpareil Club and taken some pains to explain to your brother both the manner in which he acquired the Abbas Ruby and the part which you—"

"My God!"

"—which you, I say, played in the matter. I beg that you will spare me my delusion that you played that part unwillingly."

For an instant the beautiful, imperious creature faced Holmes in the circle of lamplight, then, with a low moaning cry, she fell on her knees, her hands clutching at his coat. Holmes stooped and raised her swiftly.

"Kneel to your husband, Lady Doverton, and not to me," he said quietly. "Indeed, you have much to answer for."

"I swear to you—"

"Hush, I know all. Not a word shall pass my lips."

"You mean that you will not tell him?" she gasped.

"I see nothing to be gained thereby. Joliffe will be released in the morning, of course, and the affair of the Abbas Ruby brought to a close."

"God reward you for your mercy," she whispered brokenly. "I will do my best to make amends. But my unfortunate brother—his losses at cards—"

"Ah, yes, Captain Masterman. I do not think, Lady Doverton, that you have cause to worry too deeply over that gentleman. Captain Masterman's bankruptcy and the resultant scandal in the Nonpareil Club may have the result of starting him upon a more honourable path than that which he has pursued up to now. Indeed, once the scandal has become a thing of the past, Sir John might be persuaded to arrange a commission for him in some overseas military service. From what I have seen of that young man's enterprise and address, I have no doubt that he would do very well on the North-West frontier of India."

Evidently, I was more fatigued than I had supposed

by the events of the night, and I did not awake until nearly ten o'clock. When I entered our sitting-room, I found that Sherlock Holmes had already finished his breakfast and was lounging in front of the fire in his old red dressing-gown, his feet stretched out to the blaze and the air rancid with the smoke of his afterbreakfast pipe composed of the previous day's dottles. I rang for Mrs. Hudson and ordered a pot of coffee and some rashers and eggs.

"I'm glad that you're in time, Watson," he said, shooting an amused glance at me from beneath his drooping lids.

"Mrs. Hudson's capability to produce breakfast at any hour is not least among her virtues," I replied.

"Quite so. But I was not referring to your breakfast. I am expecting Sir John Doverton."

"In that case, Holmes, as it is a delicate affair, it would be better perhaps that I leave you alone."

Holmes waved me back to my seat.

"My dear fellow, I shall be glad of your presence. And here, I think, is our visitor a few minutes before his time."

There came a knock on the door and the tall, stooping figure of the well-known horticulturist entered the room.

"You have news for me, Mr. Holmes!" he cried impetuously. "Speak out, sir, speak out! I am all attention."

"Yes, I have news for you," Holmes replied with a slight smile.

Sir John darted forward.

"Then the camellias——" he began.

"Well, well. Perhaps we would be wise to forget the red camellias. I noticed a goodly crop of buds on the bush."

"I thank God that is true," said our visitor devoutly, "and I am glad to perceive, Mr. Holmes, that you place a higher value on the ascetic rarities of Nature than on the intrinsic treasures of man's handiwork. Nevertheless, there still remains the dreadful loss of the Abbas Ruby. Have you any hope of recovering the jewel?"

"There is every hope. But, before we discuss the matter any further, I beg that you will join me in a glass of port."

Sir John raised his eyebrows. "At this hour, Mr. Holmes?" he exclaimed. "Really, sir, I hardly think—"

"Come now," smiled Sherlock Holmes, filling three glasses at the sideboard and handing one to our visitor. "It is a chill morning and I can heartily recommend the rarity of this vintage."

With a slight frown of disapproval, Sir John Doverton lifted the glass to his lips. There was a moment of silence broken by a sudden startled cry. Our visitor, his face as white as the piece of linen which he had put to his mouth, stared wildly from Holmes to the flaming, flashing crystal which had fallen from his lips into his handkerchief.

"The Abbas Ruby!" he gasped.

Sherlock Holmes broke into a hearty laugh and clapped his hands together.

"Really you must forgive me!" he cried. "My friend Dr. Watson will tell you that I can never resist these somewhat dramatic touches. It is perhaps the Vernet blood in my veins."

Sir John Doverton gazed thunder-struck at the great jewel, smouldering and winking against its background of white linen.

"Good heavens, I can scarcely credit my own eyes," he said in a shaking voice. "But how on earth did you recover it?"

"Ah, there I must crave your indulgence. Suffice to say that your butler, Joliffe, who was a sorely wronged man, was released this morning and that the jewel is now returned safely to its rightful owner," replied Holmes kindly. "Here is the locket and chain from which I took the liberty of removing the stone in order that I might play my little trick upon you by concealing the ruby in your port wine. I beg that you will press the matter no further."

"It shall be as you wish, Mr. Holmes," said Sir John earnestly. "Indeed I have cause to place every confidence in your judgement. But what can I do to express—"

"Well, I am far from a rich man and I shall leave it to

you whether or not I have deserved your five thousand pounds reward."

"Many times over," cried John Doverton, drawing a cheque-book from his pocket "Furthermore, I shall send you a cutting from my red camellias."

Holmes bowed gravely.

"I shall place it in the special charge of Watson," he said. "By the way, Sir John, I will be glad if you would make out two separate cheques. One for £2500 in favour of Sherlock Holmes, and the other for a similar amount in favour of Andrew Joliffe. I fear that from this time forward you might find your former butler a trifle nervous in his domestic duties, and this sum of money should be ample to set him up in the cigar business, thus fulfilling the secret ambition of his life. Thank you, my dear sir. And now I think that for once we might really break our morning habits and, by partaking a glass of port, modestly celebrate the successful conclusion of the case of the Abbas Ruby."

—:—

Since . . . our visit to Devonshire, he had been engaged in two affairs of the utmost importance . . . the famous card scandal of the Nonpareil Club . . . and the unfortunate Madame Montpensier.

FROM "THE HOUND OF THE BASKERVILLES."

9

The Adventure of the
Dark Angels

"I am afraid, Watson, that the Nordic temperament offers little scope for the student of crime. It tends towards an altogether deplorable banality," remarked Holmes, as we turned from Oxford Street towards the less crowded pavements of Baker Street. It was a clear, crisp morning in May of 1901 and the uniforms of the lean, bronzed men who were flocking the streets on leave from the South African war struck a note of welcome gaiety against the sombre dresses of the women who were still in mourning for the death of the late Queen.

"I can remind you, Holmes, of a dozen instances among your own cases that disprove your assertion," I replied, noting with some satisfaction that our morning walk had brought a touch of colour to my friend's sallow cheeks.

"For instance?" he asked.

"Well, Dr. Grimesby Roylott of infamous memory. The use of a tame snake for the purpose of murder cannot be lightly dismissed as a banality."

"My dear fellow, your example proves my contention. From some fifty cases, we recall Dr. Roylott, 'Holy' Peters and one or two other merely for the reason that they employed an imaginative approach to crime which was startlingly at variance with the normal practice. Indeed, I am sometimes tempted to think that, just as Cuvier could reconstruct the complete animal from one bone, so the logical reasoner could tell from a nation's cooking the prevailing characteristics of the nation's criminals."

178

"I can observe no parallel," I laughed.

"Think it over, Watson. There, incidentally," he continued, gesturing with his stick towards a chocolate-coloured omnibus which, with a grinding of brakes and a merry jingle from the horses' harness, had drawn up on the opposite side, "you have a good example. It is one of the French omnibuses. Look at the driver, Watson, all fire and nerves and concentrated emotion as he argues with the petty officer on long leave from a naval shore station. It is the difference between the subtle and the positive, French sauce and English gravy. How could two such men approach crime from the same angle?"

"Be that as it may," I replied, "I fail to see how you can tell that the man in the check coat is a petty officer on long leave."

"Tut, Watson, when a man wearing a Crimea ribbon on his waistcoat, and therefore too old for active service, is shod in comparatively new naval boots, it is surely obvious that he has been recalled from retirement. His air of authority is above that of the ordinary sailor and yet his complexion is no more bronzed or wind-roughened than that of the bus-driver. The man is a naval petty officer attached to a shore station or training camp."

"And the long leave?"

"He is in civilian clothes and yet has not been discharged, for you will observe that he is filling his pipe from a plug of regulation naval twist which is unobtainable at tobacconists. But here we are at 221-B and in time, I trust, to catch the visitor who has called during our absence."

I surveyed the blank door of the house. "Really, Holmes!" I protested. "You go a little too far."

"Very seldom, Watson. The wheels of most public carriages are repainted at this time of the year and if you will bother to glance at the kerb you will perceive a long green mark where a wheel has scraped the edge and which was not there when we departed an hour ago. The cab was kept waiting for sometime, for the driver has twice knocked out the dottle from his pipe. We can but hope that the fare decided to await our return after dismissing the vehicle."

As we mounted the stairs, Mrs. Hudson appeared from the lower regions.

"There's been a visitor here nigh on an hour, Mr. Holmes," she stated. "She is waiting in your sitting-room, and that tired she looked, the poor pretty creature, that I took the liberty of bringing her a nice strong cup of tea."

"Thank you, Mrs. Hudson. You did very well."

My friend glanced at me and smiled but there was a gleam in his deep-set eyes. "The game's afoot, Watson," he said quietly.

Upon our entering the sitting-room, our visitor rose to meet us. She was a fair-haired young lady, still in her early twenties, slim and dainty, with a delicate complexion and large blue eyes that contained a hint of violet in their depths. She was plainly but neatly dressed in a fawn-coloured travelling-costume with a hat of the same colour relieved by a small mauve feather. I noted these details almost unconsciously for, as a medical man, my attention was arrested at once by the dark shadows lurking beneath her eyes and the quiver of her lips that betrayed an intensity of nervous tension perilously near the breaking-point.

With an apology for his absence, Holmes ushered her to a chair before the fireplace, and then sinking into his own surveyed her searchingly from beneath his heavy lids.

"I perceive that you are deeply troubled," he said kindly. "Rest assured that Dr. Watson and I are here to serve you, Miss . . ."

"My name is Daphne Ferrers," supplied our visitor. Then, leaning forward suddenly in her chair, she stared up into Holmes's face with a singular intentness. "Would you say that the heralds of death are dark angels?" she whispered.

Holmes shot me a swift glance.

"You have no objection to my pipe, I trust, Miss Ferrers," said he, stretching out an arm towards the mantelpiece. "Now, young lady, we have all to meet a Dark Angel eventually, but that is hardly an adequate reason for consulting two middle-aged gentlemen in Baker Street. You would do far better to tell me your story from the beginning."

"How foolish you must think me," cried Miss Ferrers, the pallor of her cheeks giving place to a faint but becoming blush. "And yet, when you have heard my story, when you have heard the very facts that are driving me slowly mad with fear, you may only laugh at me."

"Rest assured that I shall not."

Our visitor paused for a moment as though marshalling her thoughts, and then plunged forthwith into her strange narrative.

"You must know, then, that I am the daughter and only child of Josua Ferrers of Abbotstanding in Hampshire," she began. "My father's cousin is Sir Robert Norburton of Shoscombe Old Place, with whom you were acquainted some years ago, and it was on his recommendation that I have rushed to you at the climax of my troubles."

Holmes, who had been leaning back in his chair with his eyes closed, took his pipe from his mouth.

"Why, then, did you not come to me last night when you arrived in town instead of waiting until this morning?" he interposed.

Miss Ferrers started visibly.

"It was only when I dined with Sir Robert last night that he advised me to see you. But I do not understand, Mr. Holmes, how could you know . . ."

"Tut, young lady, it is simple enough. The right cuff and elbow of your jacket bear slight but unmistakable traces of sooty dust inseparable from a window-seat in a railway carriage. Your shoes, on the other hand, are perfectly cleaned and burnished to that high degree of polish that is characteristic of a good hotel."

"Do you not think, Holmes," I interrupted, "that we should listen without further ado to Miss Ferrers' story. Speaking as a medical man, it is high time that her troubles were lifted from her shoulders."

Our fair visitor thanked me prettily with a glance from her blue eyes.

"As you should know by now, Watson, I have my methods," said Holmes with some asperity. "However, Miss Ferrers, we are all attention. Pray continue."

"I should explain," she went on "that the earlier part of my father's life was spent in Sicily where he had inherited large interests in vineyards and olive groves. Following my mother's death, he seemed to tire of the country and, having amassed a considerable fortune, my father sold his interests and retired to England. For more than a year, we moved from county to county in search of a house that should suit my father's somewhat peculiar requirements before deciding at length on Abbotstanding near Beaulieu in the New Forest."

"One moment, Miss Ferrers. Pray enumerate these peculiar requirements."

"My father is of a singularly retiring disposition, Mr. Holmes. Above all else, he insisted on a sparsely populated locality, and an estate that should lie at some miles' distance from the nearest railway station. In Abbotstanding, an almost ruinous castellated mansion of great antiquity and once the hunting-lodge of the Abbots of Beaulieu, he found what he sought and, certain necessary repairs having been effected, we settled finally into our home. That, Mr. Holmes, was five years ago, and from that day to this we have lived under the shadow of a nameless, shapeless dread."

"If nameless and shapeless, then how were you aware of its existence?"

"Through the circumstances governing our lives. My father would permit no social contact with our few neighbours and even our household needs were supplied not from the nearest village but by carrier's van from Lyndhurst. The staff consists of the butler McKinney, a surly, morose man whom my father hired in Glasgow, and his wife and her sister who share the domestic work between them."

"And the outside staff?"

"There are none. The grounds were permitted to become a wilderness and the place is already overrun with vermin of all descriptions."

"I see nothing alarming in these circumstances, Miss Ferrers," remarked Holmes. "Indeed, if I lived in the country, I should probably create around me very similar conditions to discourage unprofitable intercourse with my neighbours. The household consists, then, of yourself and your father and the three servants?"

"The household, yes. But there is a cottage on the estate occupied by Mr. James Tonston who for many years managed our Sicilian vineyards before accompanying my father on his return to England. He acts as bailiff."

Holmes raised his eyebrows. "Indeed," said he. "An estate that is allowed to grow into a wilderness, no tenants and a bailiff. Surely a somewhat curious anomaly?"

"It is a nominal appointment only, Mr. Holmes. Mr. Tonston enjoys my father's confidence and occupies his position at Abbotstanding in recognition of the earlier years spent in his service in Sicily."

"Ah, quite so."

"My father himself seldom leaves the house and on the few occasions when he does he never goes beyond the confines of his own park walls. Where there is love and understanding and mutual interest, such a life might be tolerable. But, alas, such is not the case at Abbotstanding. My father's character, though God-fearing, is not of a type to encourage affection and, as time went on, his disposition, always severe and retiring, deepened into periods of gloomy, savage brooding when he would lock himself into his study for days on end. As you can imagine, Mr. Holmes, there was little of interest and less of happiness for a young woman isolated from friends of her own age, deprived of all social contacts and foredoomed to spend the best years of her life in the desolate magnificence of a half-ruinous mediaeval hunting-lodge. Our existence was one of absolute monotony and then, some five months ago, occurred an incident which, insignificant enough in itself, formed the first of that singular chain of events which have brought me to lay my problems before you.

"I was returning from an early-morning walk in the park and on entering the avenue leading from the lodge-gates to the house, I observed that there was something nailed to the bole of an oak tree. On closer examination I discovered the object to be an ordinary coloured print of the type used for illustrating Christmas carols or cheap books on religious art. But the theme of the picture was unusual, even arresting.

"It consisted of a night sky broken by a barren hilltop on the brow of which, in two separate groups of six and three, stood nine winged angels. As I stared at the picture, I was puzzled to explain the note of incongruity that jarred through my senses until, in an instant, I perceived the reason. It was the first time that I had beheld angels portrayed not in radiance but in robes of funeral darkness. Across the lower part of the print were scrawled the words 'six and three.' "

As our visitor paused, I glanced across at Sherlock Holmes. His brows were drawn down and his eyes closed, but I could tell from the quick spirals of smoke rising from his pipe that his interest had been deeply stirred.

"My first reaction," she went on, "was that it was a curious way for the carrier-man from Lyndhurst to deliver some new-fangled calendar and so, plucking it down, I took it in with me, and was on my way upstairs to my room when I met my father on the landing.

" 'This was on a tree in the avenue,' I said. 'I think McKinney should tell the Lyndhurst carrier to deliver at the tradesmen's entrance instead of pinning things in odd places. I prefer angels in white, don't you, Papa?"

"The words were hardly out of my mouth before he had snatched the print from me. For a moment, he stood speechless, glaring down at the piece of paper in his shaking hands while the colour ebbed from his face, leaving it drawn and livid.

" 'What is it, Papa?' I cried, clutching him by the arm.

" 'The Dark Angels,' he whispered. Then, with a gesture of horror, he shook off my hand and rushing into his study, locked and bolted the door behind him.

"From that day on, my father never left the house. His time was spent in reading and writing in his study or in long conferences with James Tonston whose gloomy and severe character is somewhat akin to his own. I saw him seldom save at meal-times and it would have been unbearable for me were it not for the fact that I had the friendship of one noble-hearted woman, Mrs. Nordham, the wife of the Beaulieu doctor, who perceiving the desolation of my life persisted in calling to see me two or three times a week despite my father's open hostility to what he considered an unwarranted intrusion.

"It was some weeks later, on February 11th, to be precise, that our manservant came to me just after breakfast with a most curious expression on his face.

" 'It's not the Lyndhurst carrier this time,' he announced sourly, 'and I don't like it, miss.'

" 'What is the matter, McKinney?'

" 'Ask the front door,' said he, and went away mumbling and stroking his beard.

"I hastened to the entrance and there, nailed to the front door, was a similar print to that which I had found on the oak tree in the avenue. And yet it was not exactly similar, for this time the angels were only six in number and the figure '6' was marked on the bottom of the page. I tore it down and was gazing at it with an inexplicable chill in my heart when a hand reached out and took it from my fingers. Turning round I found Mr. Tonston standing behind me. 'It is not for you, Miss Ferrers,' he said gravely, 'and for that you can thank your Maker.'

" 'But what does it mean?' I cried wildly. 'If there is danger to my father, then why does he not summon the police?'

" 'Because we do not need the police,' he replied. 'Believe me, your father and I are quite capable of dealing with the situation, my dear young lady.' And, turning on his heel, he vanished into the house. He must have taken the picture to my father, for he kept to his room for a week afterwards."

"One moment," interrupted Holmes. "Can you recall the exact date when you found the picture on the oak tree?"

"It was December 29th."

"And the second appeared on the front door on February 11th, you say. Thank you, Miss Ferrers. Pray proceed with your interesting narrative."

"One evening, it would be about a fortnight later," continued our client, "my father and I were sitting together at the dinner-table. It was a wild, tempestuous night with driving squalls of rain and a wind that sobbed and howled like a lost soul down the great yawning chimney-pieces of the ancient mansion. The meal was over and my father was moodily drinking his port by the light of the heavy candle-branches that illumined the dining-table when, raising his eyes to mine, he was seized with some reflection of the utter horror that was at that very instant freezing the blood in my veins. Immediately in front of me, and behind him, there was a window, the curtains of which were not fully drawn, leaving a space of rain-splashed glass that threw back a dim glow from the candlelight.

"Peering through this glass was a man's face.

"The lower part of his features was covered with his hand, but beneath the rim of a shapeless hat a pair of eyes, grinning and baleful, glared into my own.

"My father must have realized instinctively that the danger lay behind him for, seizing a heavy candelabrum from the table, in one movement he turned and flung it at the window.

"There was an appalling crash of glass, and I caught a glimpse of the curtains streaming like great crimson bat-wings in the wind that howled through the shattered casement. The flame of the remaining candles blew flat and dim, and then I must have fainted. When I came to myself, I was lying on my bed. The next day, my father made no reference to the incident and the window was repaired by a man from the village. And now, Mr. Holmes, my story draws to its close.

"On March 25th, exactly six weeks and three days ago, when my father and I took our places for breakfast, there upon the table lay the print of the demon angels, six and three. But this time there was no number scrawled across the lower portion."

"And your father?" asked Holmes very seriously.

"My father has resigned himself with the calm of a man who waits upon an inescapable destiny. For the first time for many years, he looked at me gently. 'It has come,' said he, 'and it is well.'

"I threw myself on my knees beside him, imploring him to call in the police, to put an end to this mystery that threw its chill shadow over our desolate lives. 'The shadow is nearly lifted, my child,' he replied.

"Then, after a moment's hesitation, he laid his hand upon my head.

" 'If anybody, any stranger, should communicate with you,' said he, 'say only that your father kept you always in ignorance of his affairs and that he bade you state that the name of the maker is in the butt of the gun. Remember those words and forget all else, if you value that happier, better life that will shortly commence for you.' With that he rose and left the room.

"Since that time, I have seen little of him and, at last, taking my courage in both hands, I wrote to Sir Robert that I was in deep trouble and wished to meet him. Then, inventing an excuse, I slipped away yesterday and came up to London where Sir Robert, having heard a little of the story from my lips, advised me to lay my problem frankly before you."

I have never seen my friend more grave. His brows were drawn down over his eyes and he shook his head despondently.

"It is kindest in the long run that I should be frank with you," he said at last. "You must plan a new life for yourself, preferably in London where you will quickly make new friends of your own age."

"But my father?"

Holmes rose to his feet.

"Dr. Watson and I will accompany you at once to Hampshire. If I cannot prevent, at least I may be able to avenge."

"Holmes!" I cried, horror-struck.

"It's no good, Watson," he said, laying his fingers gently on Miss Ferrers' shoulder. "It would be the basest treachery to this brave young lady to arouse hopes that I cannot share. It is better that we face the facts."

"The facts!" I replied. "Why, a man may have a foot in the grave and yet live."

Holmes looked at me curiously for a moment.

"True, Watson," he said thoughtfully. "But we must waste no further time. Unless my memory belies me, there is a train to Hampshire within the hour. A few necessities in a bag should meet the case."

I was hastily gathering my things together when Holmes came into my bedroom.

"It might be advisable to take your revolver," he said softly.

"Then there is danger?"

"Deadly danger, Watson." He smote his forehead with his hand. "My God, what irony. She has come just a day too late."

As we accompanied Miss Ferrers from the sitting-room, Holmes paused at the bookshelf to slip a slim calf-bound volume into the pocket of his Inverness cape and then, scribbling a telegram, he handed the form to Mrs. Hudson in the hallway. "Kindly see that it is dispatched immediately," said he.

A four-wheeler carried us to Waterloo, where we were just in time to catch a Bournemouth train stopping at Lyndhurst Road Station.

It was a melancholy journey. Sherlock Holmes leaned back in his corner seat, his ear-flapped travelling-cap drawn over his eyes and his long, thin fingers tapping restlessly on the window-ledge. I tried to engage our companion in conversation and to convey a little of the sympathy that I felt for her in this time of anxiety, but though her replies were gracious and kindly it was obvious that her mind was preoccupied with her own thoughts. I think that we were all glad when, some two hours later, we alighted at the little Hampshire station. As we reached the gates, a pleasant-faced woman hurried forward.

"Mr. Sherlock Holmes?" said she. "Thank heavens that the Beaulieu Post Office delivered your telegram in time. Daphne, my dear!"

"Mrs. Nordham! But—but I don't understand."

"Now, Miss Ferrers," said Holmes soothingly. "It would help us greatly if you will entrust yourself to your friend. Mrs. Nordham, I know that you will take good care of her. Come, Watson."

We hailed a fly in the station yard and, in a few moments, we were free from the hamlet and bowling along a desolate road that stretched away straight as a ribbon, rising and dipping and rising again over lonely expanses of heath broken here and there by clumps of holly and bounded in every direction by the dark out-spurs of a great forest. After some miles, on mounting a long hill, we saw below us a sheet of water and the grey, hoary ruins of Beaulieu Abbey, then the road plunged into the forest and some ten minutes later we wheeled beneath an arch of crumbling masonry into an avenue lined by noble oak trees whose interlocked branches met overhead in a gloomy twilight. Holmes pointed forward. "It is as I feared," he said bitterly. "We are too late."

Riding in the same direction as ourselves but far ahead of us down the avenue, I caught a glimpse of a police-constable on a bicycle.

The drive opened out into a wooded park with a gaunt, battlemented mansion set amid the broken terraces and parterres of that saddest of all spectacles, an old-world garden run to wilderness and bathed in the red glow of the setting sun. At some little distance from the house, a group of men were gathered beside a stunted cedar tree and at a word from Holmes, our driver pulled up and we hurried towards them across the turf.

The group was composed of the policeman, a gentleman with a small bag which I easily recognized and lastly a man in brown country tweeds with a pale, sunken face framed in mutton-chop whiskers. As we drew near, they turned towards us, and I could not repress an exclamation of horror at the spectacle that their movement disclosed to our eyes.

At the foot of the cedar tree lay the body of an elderly man. His arms were outstretched, the fingers gripping the grass and his beard thrust up at so grotesque an angle that his features were hidden from view. The bone gleamed in his gaping throat while the ground about his head was stained into one great crimson halo. The doctor stepped forward hurriedly.

"This is a shocking affair, Mr. Sherlock Holmes," he cried nervously. "My wife hastened to the station as soon as she received your wire. I trust that she was in time to meet Miss Ferrers?"

"Thank you, yes. Alas, that I could not myself have got here in time."

"It seems that you expected the tragedy, sir," observed the policeman suspiciously.

"I did, constable. Hence my presence."

"Well, I'd like to know . . ." Holmes tapped him on the arm and, leading him to one side, spoke a few words. When they rejoined us, there was a trace of relief in the man's worried face. "It shall be as you wish, sir," he said, "and you can rely on Mr. Tonston repeating his statement to you."

The man in tweeds turned his sunken face and pale grey eyes in our direction. "I don't see why I should," he said tartly. "You're the law, aren't you, Constable Kibble, and you've taken my statement already. I have nothing to add. You would be better employed in sending in your report of Mr. Ferrers' suicide."

"Suicide?" interposed Holmes sharply.

"Aye, what else? He's been glooming for weeks past, as all the household can testify, and now he's cut his throat from ear to ear."

"H'm." Holmes dropped on his knees beside the body. "And this is the weapon, of course. A horn-handled clasp-knife with a retractable blade. Italian, I perceive."

"How do you know that?"

"It has the mark of a Milanese bladesmith. But what is this? Dear me, what a curious object."

He rose to his feet and closely examined the thing which he had picked up from the grass. It was a short-barrelled rifle, cut off immediately behind the trigger by a hinged stock, so that the whole weapon folded into two parts. "It was lying by his head," observed the constable. "Seems that he was expecting trouble and took it with him for protection."

Holmes shook his head. "It has not been loaded," he said, "for you will observe that the grease is undisturbed in the breech. But what have we here? Perhaps, Watson, you would lend me your pencil and handkerchief."

"It's only the hole in the stock for the cleaning rod," rapped Mr. Tonston.

"I am aware of that. Tut, this is most curious."

"What then? You stuck the handkerchief wrapped round the pencil into the hole and now you've withdrawn it. There's nothing on the handkerchief, and yet you find it curious. What the devil did you expect?"

"Dust."

"Dust?"

"Precisely. Something has been hidden in the hole and hence the fact that the walls are clean. Normally there is always dust in the stock-holes of guns. But I should be glad to hear a few facts from you, Mr. Tonston, as I understand that you were the first to raise the alarm. It will save time if I hear them from your own lips instead of reading through your statement."

"Well, there's little enough to tell," said he. "An hour ago, I strolled out for a breath of air and caught sight of Mr. Ferrers standing under this tree. When I hailed him, he looked round and then, turning away, seemed to put his hand up to his throat. I saw him stagger and fall. When I ran up, he was lying as you see him now, with his throat gaping and the knife on the grass beside him. There was nothing I could do save send the man-servant for Dr. Nordham and the constable. That's all."

"Most illuminating. You were with Mr. Ferrers in Sicily, were you not?"

"I was."

"Well, gentlemen, I shall detain you no longer if you wish to return to the house. Watson, perhaps you would care to remain with me. And you too, Constable."

As the doctor and Tonston vanished through the parterres, Holmes was galvanized into activity. For a while, he circled the grass about the dead man on his hands and knees, like some lean, eager foxhound casting for its scent. Once he stooped and peered at the ground very closely, then rising to his feet, he whipped his lens from his pocket and proceeded to a searching examination of the trunk of the cedar. Suddenly he stiffened and at his gesture the constable and I hastened to his side. Holmes pointed with his finger as he handed the glass to the police-officer. "Examine the edge of that knot," he said quietly. "What do you see?"

"Looks to me like a hair, sir," replied Constable Kibble, gazing through the lens. "No, it's not a hair. It's a brown thread."

"Quite so. Perhaps you would kindly remove it and place it in this envelope. Now Watson, give me a hand up." Holmes scrambled into the fork of the tree and, supporting himself by the branches, peered about him, "Ha, what have we here!" he chuckled. "A fresh scrape on the trunk, traces of mud in the fork and another small thread from some coarse brownish material clinging to the bark where a man might lean his back. Quite a treasure-trove. I am about to jump down and I want you both to watch the exact place where I land. So!" He stepped to one side. "Now, what do you see?"

"Two small indentations."

"Precisely. The marks of my heels. Look wider."

"By Jingo!" cried the constable. "There are four, not two! They are identical."

"Save that the others are not quite so deep."

"The man was lighter!" I ejaculated.

"Bravo, Watson. Well, I think that we have seen all that we need."

The officer fixed Holmes with his earnest eyes. "Look here, sir," he said. "I'm clean out of my depth. What's all this mean?"

"Probably your sergeant's stripes, Constable Kibble. And now, let us join the others."

When we reached the house, the police-officer showed us into a long, sparsely furnished room with a groined roof. Doctor Nordham, who was writing at a table in the window, looked up at our entrance. "Well, Mr. Holmes?"

"You are preparing your report, I perceive," my friend remarked. "May I suggest that you pay particular regard that you do not convey a false impession?"

Dr. Nordham gazed stonily at Holmes. "I fail to understand you," said he. "Can you not be more explicit?"

"Very well. What are your views on the death of Mr. Josua Ferrers of Abbotstanding?"

"Tut, sir, there is no question of views. We have both visual and medical evidence that Josua Ferrers committed suicide by cutting his own throat."

"A remarkable man, this Mr. Ferres," Holmes observed, "who, not content with committing suicide by cutting his jugular vein, must continue to sever the rest of his neck with an ordinary clasp-knife until, in the words of Mr. Tonston here, he had cut his throat literally from ear to ear. I have always felt that, were I to commit murder, I should avoid errors of that kind."

My friend's words were followed by a moment of tense silence. Then Dr. Nordham rose abruptly to his feet, while Tonston, who had been leaning against the wall with his arms folded, lifted his eyes to Holmes's face.

"Murder is an ugly word, Mr. Sherlock Holmes," he said quietly.

"And an ugly deed. Though not, perhaps, to the *Mala Vita.*"

"What nonsense is this!"

"Tut, I was relying upon your knowledge of Sicily to fill in any small details that I may have overlooked. However, as you dismiss as nonsense the name of this terrible secret society, it will doubtless interest you to learn a few of the facts."

"Have a care, Mr. Holmes."

"To you, Dr. Nordham, and to Constable Kibble, there will appear to be gaps in my brief account." My friend continued. "But as these can be filled in later, I will address myself to you, Watson, as you were present during Miss Ferrers narrative.

"It was obvious from the first that her father was hiding

from some peril of so relentless a nature that even in the
depth of this deserted country-side he went in fear of his
life. As the man had come from Sicily, an island notorious
for the power and vindictiveness of its secret societies, the
most likely explanation was that either he had offended
some such organization or as a member he had trans-
gressed some vital rule. As he made no attempt to invoke
the police, I inclined to the latter supposition and this
became a certainty with the first appearance of the Dark
Angels. You will recall that they were nine in number,
Watson, and that the print, inscribed with the words 'six
and three,' was nailed to a tree in the avenue on December 29th.

"The next visitation took place on February 11th, exactly six weeks and three days from December 29th, but
this time the angels, six in number, were nailed to the
front door.

"On March 24th came the third and last appearance,
exactly six weeks after the second. The dreaded herald
of death, again nine in number, but now without inscrip-
tion, lay on the very platter of the master of Abbotstanding.

"As I listened to Miss Ferrers' voice and calculated the
dates rapidly in mind, I was dismayed by the discovery
that the final nine of the Dark Angels, assuming them to
represent the same period of time as the first, brought
the date to May 7th. Today!

"I knew then that I was too late. But, if I could not
save her father, I might avenge him and, with that object,
I attacked the problem from a different angle.

"The face at the window was typical, of course, of
perhaps the most barbarous trait in the vengeance of
secret societies, the desire to strike horror not only into
the victim himself but into his family. But the man had
been careful to cover his features with his hands, despite
the fact that he was looking not as Josua Ferrers but at
his daughter, thereby suggesting to my mind that he feared
recognition by Miss Ferrers as much as by her father.

"Next, it seemed to me that the cold, deadly approach
of the fatal prints from tree to door, from door to break-

fast-table, inferred an intimate knowledge of Josua Ferrers' circumscribed habits, possibly an unchallenged right to enter the house and thereby place the card on the table without the necessity for forced windows and smashed locks.

"From the first, certain features in Miss Ferrers' singular narrative stirred some vague chord in my memory, but it was not until your remark, Watson, about a foot in the open grave that a flood of light burst suddenly into my consciousness."

As Sherlock Holmes paused for a moment to draw something from his cape pocket, I glanced at the others. Though the old room was rapidly deepening into dusk, a sullen red light from the last rays of the sun glimmering through the window illumined the absorbed expressions of Dr. Nordham and the constable. Tonston stood in the shadows, his arms still folded across his chest and his pale, glittering eyes fixed immovably upon Holmes.

"It was to certain passages in this book, a fore-runner of Heckenthorn's *Secret Societies,* that my memory was recalled by Dr. Watson's words." My friend continued. "Here is what the author has to say on a certain secret society which was first introduced into Sicily some three centuries ago. 'This formidable organization,' he writes, 'aptly named the *Mala Vita,* communicates with its members through a variety of signs including Angels, Demons and the Winged Lion. The candidate for membership, if successful in his trials of initiation which frequently include that of murder, takes oath of fealty with one foot in an open grave. Punishment for infraction of the society's rules is relentless and, where death is the price, three separate warnings are given of the approaching doom, the second following six weeks and three days after the first, and the third six weeks after the second. Following the final warning, a further period of six weeks and three days are allowed to pass before the blow falls. Any member failing to carry out the punitive orders of the society becomes himself liable to the same punishment.' There follows a list of rules of the *Mala Vita,* together with the penalities for breaking them.

"That Josua Ferrers was a member of this dread society there can now be little doubt," Holmes added solemnly, as he closed the book. "What was his offense, we shall probably never know, and yet one may hazard a pretty shrewd guess. Article 16 is surely among the *Mala Vita's* most singular rules, for it states simply that the penalty for any member who discovers the identity of the Grand Master is death. I would remind you, Watson, that Ferrers laid emphatic instructions on his daughter that her answer to all enquiries must be that she knew nothing of his affairs, adding only that the name of the maker was in the butt of the gun. Not a gun, mark you, but *the* gun, which clearly indicated that the person receiving the message might be expected to recognize some specific weapon to which the words must refer. It is sufficient to add that the gun found beside the body of Josua Ferrers is unique to the members of the Sicilian secret societies.

"When he went to the assignation Ferrers carried the gun with him, not as a weapon but as a peace-offering valuable only for what it contained rolled up in the butt. Bearing in mind what we now know, I am in no doubt that it was a paper or document that named the Grand Master of the *Mala Vita* and which by some unhappy chance had fallen into his hands during his Sicilian membership. To destroy it was useless. He had seen the name and he was doomed. But, though his own life was already forfeited, he was playing for the life of his daughter. Ferrers can have had no idea of the actual identity of the assassin who had been selected for the work beyond the fact that the unknown must of necessity be a fellow-member.

"Concealed in the fork of the tree above the pre-arranged meeting place, the murderer lay in wait as a leopard waits for a sheep and, when his victim halted beneath him, he drew his knife and, leaping to the ground, seized him from behind and cut his throat. When he had searched Ferrers' body for the paper and eventually found it in the butt of the gun, his loathsome task was completed. He forgot, however, that in doing it he had left his heel-marks on the turf and two threads from his brown tweed coat on the rough bark of the tree."

As Sherlock Holmes ceased speaking, the silence of death fell on that darkening room. Then, stretching out one long, thin arm, he pointed silently at the shadowy figure of James Tonston.

"There stands the murderer of Josua Ferrers," he said in a quiet voice.

Tonston stepped forward, a smile upon his pale face.

"You are wrong," he said steadily. "The executioner of Josua Ferrers."

For a moment, he stood before us meeting our horrified stares with the serenity of one whose duty has been meritoriously fulfilled. Then, with a rattle of handcuffs, the constable leapt upon his man.

Tonston made no attempt to struggle, and with his hands manacled before him, he was accompanying his captor to the door when my friend's voice brought them to a halt.

"What have you done with it?" he demanded.

The prisoner looked at him silently.

"I ask," continued Holmes, "because if you have not destroyed it then it is best that I destroy it myself, and that unread."

"Rest assured that the paper is already destroyed," said James Tonston, "and that the *Mala Vita* preserves the secrets of the *Mala Vita*. In parting, take this word of warning to heart. It is that you know too much. Though your life may be an honoured one, Mr. Sherlock Holmes, it is most unlikely to be a long one." Then, with a cold smile in his grey eyes, he passed from the room.

It was an hour later and a full moon was rising when my friend and I, after parting from Dr. Nordham, turned our backs upon Abbotstanding, now gaunt and black against the night sky, and set out on foot towards Beaulieu village, where we planned to stay at the inn and take the morning train back to town.

I shall long remember that wonderful five miles' walk along a road all dappled with white fire and deepest shadow where the great trees met above our heads and the forest deer peered at us from the clumps of glistening bracken. Holmes walked with his chin upon his breast and it was not until we were descending the hill above the village that he broke his silence. It was little enough that he said then but for some reason his words have remained in my mind.

"You know me sufficiently well, Watson, to acquit me of all false sentiment," said he, "when I confess that there is an urge upon me tonight to walk for a while in the ruined cloisters of Beaulieu Abbey. It was the abode of men who lived and died at peace with themselves and with each other. We have seen much evil in our time, not least of which is the misuse of noble qualities such as loyalty, courage and determination for purposes that are in themselves ignoble. But the older I grow the more forcibly is it borne in upon me that just as these hills and moonlit woods have outlived the ruins that now lie before us, so too must our virtues which are sprung from God survive our vices which, like the Dark Angels, spring from man. Surely, Watson, this is the ultimate promise."

—:—

I am retained in this case of the Ferrers Documents.

FROM "THE PRIORY SCHOOL"

10

The Adventure of the
Two Women

I see from my note-book that it was late in September, 1886, shortly before my departure to Dartmoor with Sir Henry Baskerville, that my attention was first drawn to that curious affair, since termed "The Blackmailing Case," which threatened to involve one of the most revered names in England. Even at this late date, Sherlock Holmes has urged me to spare no pains to conceal the real identity of the personage concerned and, in my recital of the events, I shall certainly do my best to observe his wishes in this matter. Indeed, I am as sensitive as he is to the fact that, owing to the many cases in which we have been concerned over the years, we have been of necessity the depositaries of many strange confidences and secrets which, should they become known to the world, could only arouse scandal and amazement. Our honour is therefore deeply involved and I shall make very sure that no inadvertent word of mine shall point the finger of accusation at any one of those men and women, in high life or in low, who have poured out their troubles to us in our modest Baker Street chambers.

I recall that it was on a late September morning when I was first introduced to the adventure which forms the subject of this narrative. It was a grey, depressing day with a hint of early fog in the air and, having been summoned to a patient in Seaton Place, I was walking back to our lodgings when I became aware of a small street urchin slinking along at my heels. As he drew level I recognized the lad as one of the Baker Street irregulars,

as Holmes termed the group of grubby little boys whom
he employed on odd occasions to act as his eyes and
ears amid the purlieus of the London streets.

"Hullo, Billy," I said.

The lad returned no sign of recognition.

"Got a match, Guv'nor?" he demanded, exhibiting a
frayed cigarette-end. I gave him a box and, on handing
it back to me, he raised his eyes for an instant to my
face. "For God's sake, Doctor," he whispered swiftly,
"tell Mr. Holmes to watch out for Footman Boyce."
Then, with a surly nod, he slouched on his way.

I was not displeased to be the bearer of this cryptic
message to my friend, for it had been apparent to me for
some days past from his alternating moods of energy and
absorption and his deplorable consumption of tobacco
that Holmes was engaged upon a case. Contrary to his
usual practice, however, he had not invited me to share
his confidences, and I must confess that my sudden pre-
cipitation into the affair, irrespective of Holmes's wishes,
caused me no small satisfaction.

On entering our sitting-room, I found him lounging in
his arm-chair before the fireplace, still clad in his purple
dressing-gown, his grey, heavy-lidded eyes staring
thoughtfully at the ceiling through a haze of tobacco
smoke while one long, thin arm, dangling a letter between its finger-tips, hung down the side of his chair. An
envelope, embossed, I noticed, with a coronet, lay on the
floor.

"Ah, Watson," he said petulantly. "You are back
earlier than I expected."

"Perhaps it is as well for you, Holmes," I replied, a
trifle nettled at his tone, and proceeded to give the message with which I had been entrusted. Holmes raised his
eyebrows.

"This is most curious," said he. "What can Footman
Boyce have to do with the matter?"

"As I know nothing about it, I am hardly in a position
to answer your question," I remarked.

"Upon my soul, a distinct touch, Watson!" he replied,
with a dry chuckle. "If I have not taken you already into

my confidence, my dear fellow, it was not for any lack of faith in you. The affair is, however, of a most delicate nature and I preferred to feel my way a little before inviting your invaluable assistance."

"There is no need for you to explain further," I began warmly.

"Tut, Watson, I have reached a complete impasse. Possibly, it may prove one of those instances where an active mind may overreach, while a merely reflective one, functioning largely on the obvious—" he lapsed into a brooding silence for a moment, then springing to his feet, he strode over to the window.

"I am faced with one of the most dangerous cases of blackmail in all my experience," he cried. "I take it that you are familiar with the name of the Duke of Carringford?"

"You mean the late Under Secretary for Foreign Affairs?"

"Precisely."

"But he died some three years ago," I observed.

"Doubtless it will surprise you to learn, Watson, that I am aware of that fact," replied Holmes testily. "But to continue. A few days past I received a note from the duchess, his widow, couched in such urgent terms that I was constrained to comply with her request to call upon her at her house in Portland Place. I found her a woman of more than ordinary intelligence and what you would term beauty, but overwhelmed by the fearsome blow which, striking literally overnight, now threatens her with the complete social and financial destruction of herself and her daughter. And the irony of the situation is the more terrible because her destruction comes from no fault of her own."

"One moment," I interposed, picking up a newspaper from the couch. "There is a reference to the duchess in today's *Telegraph,* announcing the engagement of her daughter, Lady Mary Gladsdale, to Sir James Fortesque, the cabinet minister."

"Quite so. There lies the beautifully tempered point in this sword of Damocles." Holmes drew two sheets of paper, pinned together, from the pocket of his dressing-gown and tossed them across to me. "What do you make of those, Watson?" he said.

"One is a copy of a marriage certificate between Henry Corwyn Gladsdale, bachelor, and Françoise Pelletan, spinster, dated June 12th, 1848 and issued at Valence in France," I observed, glancing through the documents. "The other would appear to be the entry of the same marriage in the Valence church registry. Who was this Henry Gladsdale?"

"He became Duke of Carringford upon the death of his uncle in 1854," said Holmes grimly, "and five years later took to wife the Lady Constance Ellington, at present Duchess of Carringford."

"Then he was a widower."

To my surprise, Holmes drove his fist violently into the palm of his hand. "There is the diabolical cruelty of it, Watson," he cried. "We do not know! Indeed, the duchess is now told for the first time of this secret marriage made in her husband's youth when he was staying on the Continent. She is informed that his first wife is alive and ready if necessary to come forward, that her own marriage is bigamous, her position spurious, and the status of her child illegitimate."

"What, after thirty-eight years! This is monstrous, Holmes!"

"Add to that, Watson, that ignorance is not innocence in the eyes of society or the law. As to the lapse of time, it is claimed that the French wife, after her husband's sudden disappearance, did not associate Mr. Henry Gladsdale with the Duke of Carringford. Nevertheless, it is unlikely that I would engage in an affair of this nature were it not for the introduction of a more sinister element."

"I noticed that in speaking of the first wife coming forward you used the term 'if necessary.' So it is blackmail and doubtless for a large sum of money."

"We are moving in deeper waters, Watson. No money is demanded. The price of silence lies in the duchess' delivery of certain copies of state papers now lying in a sealed box in the strong-room of Lloyds Bank in Oxford Street."

"Preposterous, Holmes!"

"Not so preposterous. Remember that the late duke was Under Secretary for Foreign Affairs and that it is not unknown for great servants of the Crown to preserve copies of papers and memoranda when the originals themselves are safely lodged in the custody of the State. There are many reasons why a man in the duke's position might keep copies of certain documents which, innocent enough at the time, may become under the changing circumstances of later years matters of utmost gravity if viewed by a foreign, and perhaps unfriendly, government. This unhappy lady is faced with the choice of an act of treason to her country as a price for this marriage certificate or a public exposure followed by the ruination of one of the most revered names in England and the destruction of two innocent women, one of them on the eve of her marriage. And the devil of it is, Watson, that I am powerless to help them."

"Have you seen the originals of these Valence documents?"

"The duchess has seen them and they appear to be perfectly genuine, nor can she doubt her husband's signature."

"It might be a forgery."

"True, but I have already ascertained from Valence that there was a woman of that name living there in 1848, that she married an Englishman and later moved to some other locality."

"But surely, Holmes, a provincial Frenchwoman, if driven to blackmail by the desertion of her husband, would demand money," I protested. "What possible use could she have for copies of state papers?"

"Ah! There you put your finger on it, Watson, and hence my presence in the case. Have you ever heard of Edith von Lammerain?"

"I cannot recall the name."

"She is a remarkable woman," he continued musingly. "Her father was some sort of petty officer in the Russian

Black Sea Fleet and her mother kept a tavern in Odessa. By the time that she was twenty, she had fled her home and established herself in Budapest where, overnight, she gained notoriety as the cause of a sabre duel in which both combatants were slain. Later, she married an elderly Prussian Junker who, having borne away his bride to his country estate, upped and died most conveniently within three months from eating a surfeit of turtle-doves stuffed with chestnuts. They must have been interesting, those chestnuts!

"You will take my word for it," he went on, "that for the past year or so the most brilliant functions of the Season, be it London, Paris or Berlin, would be considered incomplete without her presence. If ever a woman was made by Nature for the profession of her choice, then that woman is Edith von Lammerain."

"You mean that she is a spy?"

"Tut, she is as much above a spy as I above the ordinary police-detective. I would put it that I have long suspected her of moving in the highest circles of political intrigue. This, then, is the woman, as clever as she is ambitious and merciless, who, armed with the papers of this secret marriage, now threatens to ruin the Duchess of Carringford and her daughter unless she consents to an act of treason, the results of which may be incalculable in their damage to England." Holmes paused to knock out his pipe into the nearest tea-cup. "And I remain here useless, Watson, useless and helpless to shield an innocent woman who in her agony has turned to me for guidance and protection," he ended savagely.

"It is indeed a most infamous business," I said. "But, if Billy's message refers to it, then there is a footman involved."

"Well, I confess that I am deeply puzzled by that message," Holmes replied, staring down thoughtfully at the stream of hansoms and carriages passing beneath our window. "Incidentally, the gentleman known as Footman Boyce is not a lackey, my dear Watson, though he takes his nickname, I believe, from the circumstance that he commenced his career as a man-servant. He is in fact the leader of the second most dangerous gang of slashers and racing-touts in London. I doubt that he bears me much goodwill, for it was largely owing to my efforts that he received two years on that Rockmorton horse-doping affair. But blackmail is out of his line and I cannot see—" Holmes broke off sharply and craning his neck peered down into the street. "By Jove, it is the man himself!" he ejaculated. "And coming here, unless I am much mistaken. Perhaps it would be as well, Watson, if you concealed yourself behind the bedroom door," he added with a chuckle as, crossing to the fireplace, he threw himself into his chair. "Mr. Footman Boyce is not among those whose conversational eloquence is encouraged by the presence of a witness."

There came a jangle from the bell below and as I slipped into the bedroom I caught the creak of heavy steps upon the stairs followed by a knock and Holmes's summons to enter.

Through the crack in the door I had a glimpse of a stout man with a red, good-natured face and bushy whiskers, clad in a check overcoat and sporting a brown bowler hat, gloves and a heavy malacca cane. I had expected a type far different from this vulgar, comfortable person whose appearance was more in keeping with a country yeoman until, as he stared at Holmes from the threshold of our sitting-room, I had a good view of his eyes. They were round as two glittering beads, very bright and hard, with that dreadful suggestion of stillness that belongs to the eyes of venomous reptiles.

"We must have a word, Mr. Holmes," he said in a shrill voice curiously at variance with that portly body. "Really, we must have a word. May I take a seat?"

"I would prefer that we both stand," came my friend's stern reply.

"Well, well." The man turned his great red face slowly round the room. "You're very snug here, very comfortable and snug and lacking nothing, I'll be bound, in the way of home cooking by that respectable woman who opened the door to me. Why deprive her of a good lodger, Mr. Sherlock Holmes?"

"I am not contemplating a change of address."

"Ah, but there are others who might contemplate it for you. 'Let be,' says I, 'Mr. Holmes is a nice-looking gent.' 'Maybe' says others, 'if his nose wasn't a little too long for the rest of his features, so that it is forever sticking itself into affairs that are no concern of his.' "

"You interest me profoundly. By the way, Boyce, you must have received pressing orders to have brought you up from Brighton at a moment's notice."

The cherubic smile faded from the ruffian's face. "How the devil do you know where I've come from!" he shrilled.

"Tut, man, today's Southern Cup racing-programme is peeping out of your pocket. However, as I am a trifle fastidious in my choice of company, kindly come to the point and put a close to this interview."

Boyce's lips curled back suddenly like the grin of some ill-conditioned dog.

"I'll put a close to something more than that, you nosey-parking busybody, if you get up to anymore of your flash tricks," he snarled. "Keep out of Madame's business or—" he paused significantly, his beady little eyes fixed immovably upon my friend's face—"or you'll be sorry you were ever born, Mr. Sherlock Holmes," he concluded softly.

Holmes chuckled and rubbed his hands.

"This is really most satisfactory," said he. "So you come from Madame von Lammerain?"

"Dear me, what indiscretion!" cried Boyce, his left hand sliding stealthily to his malacca cane. "I had hoped that you would take a word of warning, but instead you make free with the names of other folk. And so—" in an instant he had whipped off the hollow body of the stick, leaving in his other hand the grip and the long, evil razor-blade that was attached to it "—and so, Mr. Sherlock Holmes, I must make good my words."

"To which I trust, Watson, that you have paid the attention they deserve," remarked Holmes.

"Certainly!" I replied loudly.

Footman Boyce stopped in his tracks and then, as I emerged from the bedroom armed with a heavy brass candlestick, he leapt for the sitting-room door. On the threshold, he turned for a moment toward us, his little eyes flaming evilly in his great crimson face while a flood of foul imprecations poured from his lips.

"That will do!" interrupted Holmes sternly. "Incidentally, Boyce, I have wondered more than once how you murdered Madgern, the trainer. No razor was found on you at the time. Now, I know.

The ruddiness faded slowly from the man's features leaving them the colour of dirty putty.

"My God, Mr. Holmes, surely you don't think—only a little joke, sir, among old friends—!" Then, springing through the door, he slammed it behind him and went clattering wildly down the stairs.

My friend laughed heartily. "Well, well. We are hardly likely to be bothered any further by Mr. Footman Boyce," said he. "Nevertheless, the fellow's visit has done me a good turn."

"In what way?"

"It is the first ray of light in my darkness, Watson. What have they to fear from my investigations unless there is something to be discovered? But get your hat and coat and we will call together on this unhappy Duchess of Carringford."

Our visit was a brief one and yet I will long recall the memory of that courageous and still beautiful woman who, through no fault of her own, now stood face to face with the most terrible calamity that fate could have devised. The widow of a great statesman, the bearer of a name revered throughout the country, the mother of a young and lovely girl on the eve of her wedding to a public man and then, overnight, this dreadful discovery of a secret, the publication of which must destroy irrevocably the very fabric of her life and being. Here was enough to justify the extremes of human emotion. Instead, when my friend and I were ushered into the drawing-room of Carringford House in Portland Place, the lady who rose to meet us was as distinguished for the grace of her manner as for the beauty of her complexion and her delicate, serene features. It was only in the dark stains beneath her

eyelids and the too brilliant lustre of her hazel-tinted eyes
that one sensed the dreadful tensity that was eating its
way through her heart.

"You have news for me, Mr. Holmes?" she said calmly
enough, but I noticed that one of her long, slim hands
flew to her bosom. "The truth cannot be worse than this
suspense, so I beg that you will be frank with me."

Holmes bowed. "I have no news as yet, Your Grace,"
he said gently. "I am here to ask you one question and
to make one request."

The duchess sank into a chair and, picking up a fan,
fixed her fevered brilliant eyes upon my friend's face.

"And these are?"

"The question is one which can be forgiven from a
stranger only under the stress of the present circumstances," said Holmes. "You were married for thirty
years to the late duke. Was he a man of honourable
conduct in his sense of private responsibility as distinct
from his moral code? I will ask Your Grace to be very
frank with me in your reply."

"Mr. Holmes, during the years of our marriage, we
had our quarrels and our disagreements, but never once
did I know my husband to stoop to an unworthy action
or lower the standard which he had set himself in life.
His career in politics was not made the more easy by a
sense of honour that would not descend to the artifices
of compromise. He was a man whose character was nobler
than his position."

"You have told me all that I wished to know," answered Holmes. "Though I do not indulge in emotions
of the heart, I am not among those who consider that love
makes blind. With a mind of any intelligence, the effect
should be the exact opposite, for it must promote the
most privileged knowledge of the other's character. Your
Grace, we are face to face with necessity and time is not
on our side." Holmes leaned forward earnestly. "I must
see the original documents of this alleged marriage in
Valence."

"It is hopeless, Mr. Holmes!" cried the duchess. "This

dreadful woman will never let them out of her hands, save at her own infamous price."

"Then we must summon craft to our aid. You must send her a carefully worded letter, now, conveying the impression that you will be driven to comply with her demands if once you are convinced that the marriage documents are really genuine. Implore her to receive you privately at her house in St. James's Square at eleven o'clock tonight. Will you do this?"

"Anything, save what she asks."

"Good! Then one final point. It is essential that you find some pretext at exactly twenty minutes past eleven to draw her from the library containing the safe in which she keeps these documents."

"But she will take them with her."

"That is of no importance."

"How can you be sure that the safe is in the library?"

"I have a plan of the house, thanks to a small service once rendered to the firm who rented the property to Madame von Lammerain. Furthermore, I have seen it."

"You have seen it!"

"A window was broken mysteriously yesterday morning" smiled Holmes, "and the agents very promptly supplied a glazier. It had occurred to me that there might be advantages."

The Duchess leaned forward, her hand to her heaving breast. "What do you propose to do?" she demanded almost fiercely.

"That is a question in which I must use my own judgement, Your Grace," replied Holmes, springing to his feet. "If I fail, I will do so in a good cause."

We were making our adieux when the duchess laid her hand on my friend's arm.

"If you examine these terrible documents and convince yourself that they are genuine, will you remove them?" she asked.

There was a hint of concern under Holmes's austere manner as he looked at her. "No," he said quietly.

"You are right!" she cried. "I would not have them taken. A hideous wrong must be righted, whatever the cost to myself. It is only when I think of my daughter that all the courage goes from my heart."

"It is because I recognize that courage," said Holmes very gently, "that I warn you to prepare for the worst."

During the remainder of the day, my friend was in his most restless mood. He smoked incessantly until the atmosphere of our sitting-room was hardly bearable and, having exhausted all the daily newspapers, he threw the lot of them into the coal-scuttle and set himself to pacing up and down with his hands clasped behind his back and his thin, eager face thrust out before him. Then he came to the fireplace and, leaning his elbow on the mantelpiece, looked down at me as I lounged in my chair.

"Are you game to commit a serious breach of the law, Watson?" he asked.

"Most certainly, Holmes, in an honourable cause."

"It is hardly fair on you, my dear fellow," he cried, "for it will go hard with us if we are caught on that woman's premises."

"But what is the use?" I demurred. "We cannot conceal the truth."

"Admittedly. If this *is* the truth. I must see those original documents."

"Then there would appear to be no alternative," I observed.

"None that I can see," said he, thrusting his fingers into the Persian slipper and drawing out a handful of black shag which he proceeded to stuff untidily into his pipe. "Well, Watson, a lengthy sojourn in jail will enable me at least to catch up in my studies of Oriental plant poisons in the organic blood-stream and for you to bring yourself up to date on these inoculation theories of Louis Pasteur."

And there we left it, while the dusk deepeneed into night and Mrs. Hudson bustled in to poke the fire and light the gas jets.

It was at Holmes's suggestion that we dined out. "The corner table at Fratti's, I think," he chuckled, "and a bottle of Montrachet '67. If this should prove to be our last evening of respectability, at least let us be comfortable."

My watch showed me that it was after eleven o'clock when our hansom deposited us at the corner of Charles II Street. It was a moist, chill night with a hint of fog in the air that hung round the street-lamps in dim yellow haloes and glistened on the cape of the policeman who slowly passed us by, switching his bull's-eye lantern into the porticoes of the dark silent houses.

Entering St. James's Square, we had followed the pavement around to the western side when Holmes laid his hand upon my arm and pointed to a lighted window in the façade of the great house the reared above us.

"It is the light of the drawing-room," he murmured. "We have not a moment to lose."

With a swift glance along the empty pavement, he sprang for the top of the wall abutting the mansion and, pulling himself up by his hands, he dropped out of sight while I followed quickly at his heels. As far as I could judge through the darkness, we were standing in one of those dreary plots of grass and grimy struggling laurels that form the garden of the average "town house" and in consequence stood already on the wrong side of the law. Reminding myself that our purpose was, at least, an honourable one, I followed Holmes's figure along the flank of the house until he halted beneath a line of three tall windows. Then, in answer to his whisper, I lent him a back and in an instant he was crouching on the sill with his pale face outlined against the dark glass and his hands busy with the catch. A moment later, the window swung silently open, I had caught his outstretched fingers and, with a heave, I found myself in the room beside him.

"The library," Holmes breathed in my ear. "Keep behind the window-curtains."

Though we were enveloped in a darkness smelling faintly of calfskin and old leather, I was conscious of a sense of space about me. The silence was profound, save for the measured ticking of a grandfather clock in the depth of the room. Perhaps five minutes had dragged by when there came a sound from somewhere within the house followed by steps and a soft murmur of voices. A line of light gleamed for an instant beneath the edge of a door, vanished and, after a pause of some moments, slowly reappeared. I caught the sound of swift footfalls, the line of light grew brighter. Then the door was flung open and a woman, carrying a lamp in her hand, entered the room.

Though time tends to erase the sharp outline of past events, I recall as though it were but yesterday my first view of Edith von Lammerain.

Above the rays of an oil-lamp, I beheld an ivory-tinted face with dark, sombre eyes and a beautiful, scarlet, remorseless mouth. Her hair, piled high upon her head and of a raven blackness, was set with a spray of osprey plumes clasped with rubies and beneath her bare neck and shoulders a magnificent gown of black sequins flashed and shimmered against the darkness.

For a moment she stood as though listening and then, closing the door behind her, she swept down the great room, her tall, slim shadow trailing behind her and the lamp in her hand casting a dim, spectral glow along the book-lined walls.

I do not know whether it was the rustle of the curtain that reached her ears but, as Holmes stepped out into the room, she was round in an instant and, holding the lamp above her head so that the rays fell in our direction, she stood quite still and looked at us. There was not a trace of fear upon her ivory face, but only fury and venom in the dark eyes that glared at us across that great, silent chamber.

"Who are you?" she hissed. "What do you want?"

"Five minutes of your time, Madame von Lammerain," rejoined Holmes softly.

"So! You know my name. If you are not burglars, then what is it you seek? It would amuse me to hear before I raise the house."

Holmes pointed to her left hand. "I am here to examine those papers," said he, "and I warn you that I mean to do so. I beg that you will not make it necessary to prevent an outcry."

She thrust her hand behind her, her eyes blazing in her face.

"You ruffian!" she cried. "Now I understand! You are Her saintly Grace's hired burglar." Then, with a swift movement, she craned forward, the lamp out-held before her and, as she looked intently at my friend, I saw her expression of fury change into one of incredulity. A smile, as exultant as it was menacing, dawned slowly in her eyes.

"Mr. Sherlock Holmes!" she breathed.

There was a touch of mortification in Holmes's manner as he turned away and lit the candles on an ormolu side-table.

"The possibility of recognition had already occurred to me, madame," said he.

"This will earn you five years," she cried, with a flash of her white teeth.

"Perhaps. In that case, I must have my money's worth. The documents!"

"Do you imagine that you will accomplish anything by stealing them? I have copies and a dozen witnesses to their contents," she laughed throatily. "I had imagined you to be a clever man," she went on. "Instead, I find a fool, a bungler, a common thief!"

"We shall see." He held out his hand and, with a sneer and a shrug, she resigned the documents to him. "I rely on you, Watson," my friend remarked quietly, stepping across to the side-table, "to prevent any collusion between Madame von Lammerain and the bell-rope."

Beneath the glow of the candles, he read through the documents and then, holding them up against the light, he studied them intently, his lean, cadaverous profile cut in black silhouette against the luminous yellow parchment. Then he looked at me and my heart sank at the chagrin in his face.

"The watermark is English, Watson," he stated quietly. "But as paper of this make and quality was imported into France on a large scale fifty years ago, this does not help us. Alas, I fear the worst."

And I knew that he was thinking not of his own unenviable position but of the anxious, courageous woman in whose cause he had risked his own liberty.

Madame von Lammerain indulged in a little peal of laughter.

"Too much success has gone to your head, Mr. Holmes," she jeered. "But this time you have blundered, as you will find to your cost."

My friend had spread the papers immediately below the candle-flames and was bending over them again when I saw that a sudden change had taken place in his expression. The chagrin and annoyance that had clouded his face had gone, and in their place was a look of intense concentration. His long nose seemed almost to smell the paper as he stooped over it. When he straightened himself at last, I caught a gleam of excitement from his deep-set eyes.

"What do you make of this, Watson?" said he, as I hastened to his side. He pointed to the writing that inscribed the details on both documents.

"It is a very legible hand," I said.

"The ink, man, the ink!" he cried impatiently.

"Well, it is black ink," I remarked, leaning over his shoulder. "But I fear that there is little to help us in that. I can show you a dozen old letters from my father written in a similar medium."

Holmes chuckled and rubbed his hands together. "Excellent, Watson, excellent!" he cried. "Now, kindly examine the name and the signature of Henry Corwyn Gladsdale on the marriage certificate. And now, look at the entry of his name in the page from the Valence register."

"They appear to be perfectly in order, and the signature is the same in both cases."

"Quite so. But the ink?"

"There is a shade of blue in it. Yes, certainly it is ordinary blue-black indigo ink. What then?"

"Every word in both documents is written in black ink, with the exception of the bridegroom's name and signature. Does not this strike you as curious?"

"Curious, perhaps, but by no means inexplicable. Gladsdale was probably in the habit of using his own waistcoat-inkpot."

Holmes rushed to a writing-desk in the window and, after rummaging for an instant, returned with a quill and inkstand in his hand.

"Would you say that this is the same colour?" he asked, dipping the quill and making a mark or two on the edge of the document.

"It is identical," I confirmed.

"Quite so. And the ink in this pot is blue-black indigo."

Madame von Lammerain, who had been standing in the background darted suddenly for the bell-rope but, before she had time to pull it, Holmes's voice rang through the room.

"You have my word for it that if you touch that bell, you are ruined," he said sternly.

She paused with her hand upon the rope.

"What mockery is this!" she sneered. "Are you suggesting that Henry Gladsdale signed his marriage documents at my desk? Why, you fool, everybody uses ink of that description."

"Largely true. But these documents are dated June 12th, 1848."

"Well, what of that!"

"I fear that you have been guilty of a small error, Madame von Lammerain. The black ink that contains indigo was not invented until 1856."

There was something terrible in the beautiful face that glared at us across the circle of candlelight.

"You lie!" she hissed.

Holmes shrugged. "The veriest amateur chemist can prove it," said he, as he picked up the papers and placed them carefully in his cape pocket. "These are, of course, the perfectly genuine marriage documents of Françoise Pelletan," he continued. "But the real name of the bridegroom has been erased both in the certificate and in the page from the Valence church register and the name of Henry Corwyn Gladsdale substituted in its place. I have no doubt that, should the need arise, an examination under the microscope would show traces of the erasure.

The ink itself is, however, conclusive proof and represents but another example that it is on the small, easily committed error, rather than on any basic flaw in the conception, that most intricate plans crash to their ruin as the mighty vessel on the small but fatal point of rock. As for you, madame, when I consider the full implications of your scheme against a defenceless woman, I am hard put to it to recall a more cold-blooded ruthlessness."

"What are you to insult a woman!"

"In scheming to destroy another should she refuse you her husband's secret papers, you have surrendered the prerogatives of a woman," he replied bitterly.

She looked at us with an evil smile on her waxen face. "At least, you shall pay for it," she promised. "You have broken the law."

"True, and by all means pull the bell," said Sherlock Holmes. "My poor defence will be the provocation of forgery, attempted blackmail and—mark the word—espionage. Indeed, as a measure of tribute to your gifts, I shall allow you exactly one week in which to leave this country. After then, the authorities will be warned against you."

There was a moment of tense stillness, and then without a word Edith von Lammerain raised her white, shapely arm and pointed silently towards the door.

It was past eleven o'clock next morning and the breakfast things had not yet been cleared from the table. Sherlock Holmes, who had returned from an early excursion, had discarded his frock-coat for an old smoking-jacket, and now lounged in front of the fire cleaning the stems of his pipes with a long, thin bodkin that had originally come into his possession under circumstances with which I do not propose to harrow my readers.

"You have seen the duchess?" I enquired.

"I have, and put her in possession of all the facts. Purely as a precautionary measure, she is lodging the documents inscribed with her husband's forged signature, together with my statement of the case, in the hands of the family lawyers. But she has nothing more to fear from Edith von Lammerain."

"Owing to you, my dear fellow," I cried warmly.

"Well, well, Watson. The case was simple enough and the work its own reward."

I glanced at him keenly.

"You look a bit fine-drawn, Holmes," I remarked. "You should get away into the country for a few days."

"Later on, perhaps. But I cannot leave town until Madame has departed from these shores, for she is a person of singular address."

"That is a very fine pearl which you are wearing in your cravat. I do not remember seeing it before."

My friend picked up two letters from the mantelpiece and tossed them across to me. "They arrived while you were absent on your round," said he.

The one, which bore the address of Carringford House, ran thus:

"To your chivalry, to your courage, a woman owes her all, and such a debt is beyond reward. Let this pearl, the ancient symbol of Faith, be the token of the life that you have given back to me. I shall not forget."

The other, which had neither address nor signature, ran:

"We shall meet again, Mr. Sherlock Holmes. I shall not forget."

"It is all in the point of view," chuckled Holmes, "and I have yet to meet the two women who look from the same angle."

Then, throwing himself into his chair, he reached out lazily for his most obnoxious pipe.

—:—

At the present instant one of the most revered names in England is being besmirched by a blackmailer and only I can stop a disastrous scandal.

FROM "THE HOUND OF THE BASKERVILLES."

11

The Adventure of the Deptford Horror

I have remarked elsewhere that my friend Sherlock Holmes, like all great artists, lived for his art's sake and, save in the case of the Duke of Holderness, I have seldom known him claim any substantial reward. However powerful or wealthy the client, he would refuse to undertake any problem that lacked appeal to his sympathies, while he would devote his most intense energies to the affairs of some humble person whose case contained those singular and remarkable qualities which struck a responsive chord in his imagination.

On glancing through my notes for that memorable year '95, I find recorded the details of a case which may be taken as a typical instance of this disinterested and even altruistic attitude of mind which placed the rendering of a kindly service above that of material reward. I refer, of course, to the dreadful affair of the canaries and the soot-marks on the ceiling.

It was early in June that my friend completed his investigations into the sudden death of Cardinal Tosca, an enquiry which he had undertaken at the special request of the Pope. The case had demanded the most exacting work on Holmes's part and, as I had feared at the time, the aftermath had left him in a highly nervous and restless state that caused me some concern both as his friend and his medical adviser.

One rainy night towards the end of the same month, I persuaded him to dine with me at Frascatti's and thereafter we had gone on to the Café Royal for our coffee and liquors. As I had hoped, the bustle of the great room, with its red plush seats and stately palms bathed in the glow of numerous crystal chandeliers, drew him out of his introspective mood and as he leaned back on our sofa, his fingers playing with the stem of his glass, I noted with satisfaction a gleam of interest in those keen grey eyes as he studied the somewhat Bohemian clientele that thronged the tables and alcoves.

I was in the act of replying to some remark when Holmes nodded suddenly in the direction of the door.

"Lestrade," said he. "What can he be doing here?"

Glancing over my shoulder, I saw the lean, rat-faced figure of the Scotland Yard man standing in the entrance, his dark eyes roving slowly around the room.

"He may be seeking you," I remarked. "Probably on some urgent case."

"Hardly, Watson. His wet boots show that he has walked. If there was urgency, he would have taken a cab. But here he comes."

The police agent had caught sight of us and, at Holmes's gesture, he pushed his way through the throng and drew up a chair to the table.

"Only a routine check," said he, in reply to my friend's query. "But duty's duty, Mr. Holmes, and I can tell you that I've netted some strange fish before now in these respectable places. While you are comfortably dreaming up your theories in Baker Street, we poor devils at Scotland Yard are doing the practical work. No thanks to us from Popes and Kings but a bad hour on the Superintendent's carpet if we fail."

"Tut," smiled Holmes good-humouredly. "Your superiors must surely hold you in some esteem since I solved the Ronald Adair murder, the Bruce-Partington theft, the—"

"Quite so, quite so," interrupted Lestrade hurriedly. "And now," he added, with a heavy wink at me, "I have something for you."

"Ah!"

"Of course, a young woman who starts at shadows may be more in Dr. Watson's line."

"Really, Lestrade," I protested warmly, "I cannot approve your—"

"One moment, Watson. Let us hear the facts."

"Well, Mr. Holmes, they are absurd enough," continued Lestrade, "and I would not waste your time were it not that I have known you to do a kindness or two before now and your word of advice may in this instance prevent a young woman from acting foolishly. Now, here's the position.

"Down Deptford way, along the edge of the river, there are some of the worst slums in the East End of London but, right in the middle of them, you can still find some fine old houses which were once the homes of wealthy merchants centuries ago. One of these tumble-down mansions has been occupied by a family named Wilson for the past hundred years and more. I understand that they were originally in the China trade and when that went to the dogs a generation back, they got out in time and remained on in the old home. The recent household consisted of Horatio Wilson and his wife, with one son and a daughter, and Horatio's younger brother Theobold who had gone to live with them on his return from foreign parts.

"Some three years ago, the body of Horatio Wilson was hooked out of the river. He had been drowned and, as he was known to have been a hard-drinking man, it was generally accepted that he had missed his step in the fog and fallen into the water. A year later, his wife, who suffered from a weak heart, died from a heart attack. We know this to be the case, because the doctor made a very careful examination following the statements of a police-constable and a night-watchman employed on a Thames barge."

"Statements to what effect?" interposed Holmes.

"Well, there was talk of some noise rising apparently from the old Wilson house. But the nights are often foggy along Thames-side and the men were probably misled. The constable described the sound as a dreadful yell that froze the blood in his veins. If I had him in my division,

I'd teach him that such words should never pass the lips of an officer of the law."

"What time was this?"

"Ten o'clock at night, the hour of the old lady's death. It's merely a coincidence, for there is no doubt that she died of heart."

"Go on."

Lestrade consulted his note-book for a moment. "I've been digging up the facts," he continued. "On the night of May 17th last, the daughter went to a magic-lantern entertainment accompanied by a woman servant. On her return, she found her brother, Phineas Wilson, dead in his arm-chair. He had inherited a bad heart and insomnia from his mother. This time there were no rumours of shrieks and yells, but owing to the expression on the dead man's face, the local doctor called in the police-surgeon to assist in the examination. It was heart, all right, and our man confirmed that this can sometimes cause a distortion of the features that will convey an impression of stark terror."

"That is perfectly true," I remarked.

"Now, it seems that the daughter Janet has become so overwrought that, according to her uncle, she proposes to sell up the property and go abroad," went on Lestrade. "Her feelings are, I suppose, natural. Death has been busy with the Wilson family."

"And what of this uncle? Theobold, I think you said his name was."

"Well, I fancy that you will find him on your doorstep tomorrow morning. He came to me at the Yard in the hope that the official police could put his niece's fears at rest and persuade her to take a more reasonable view. As we are engaged on more important affairs than calming hysterical young women, I advised him to call on you."

"Indeed! Well, it is natural enough that he should resent the unnecessary loss of what is probably a snug corner."

"There is no resentment, Mr. Holmes. Wilson seems to be genuinely attached to his niece and concerned only for her future." Lestrade paused, while a grin spread over his foxy face. "He is not a very worldly person, is Mr. Theobold, and though I've met some queer trades in my time his beats the band. The man trains canaries."

"It is an established profession."

"Is it?" There was an irritating smugness in Lestrade's manner as he rose to his feet and reached for his hat. "It is quite evident that you do not suffer from insomnia, Mr. Holmes," said he, "or you would know that birds trained by Theobold Wilson are different from other canaries. Good night, gentlemen."

"What on earth does the fellow mean?" I asked, as the police-agent threaded his way towards the door.

"Merely that he knows something that we do not," replied Holmes drily. "But, as conjecture is as profitless as it is misleading to the analytical mind, let us wait until tomorrow. I can say, however, that I do not propose to waste my time over a matter that appears to fall more properly within the province of the local vicar."

To my friend's relief, the morning brought no visitor. But when, on my return from an urgent case to which I had been summoned shortly after lunch, I entered our sitting-room, I found that our spare chair was occupied by a bespectacled middle-aged man. As he rose to his feet, I observed that he was of an exceeding thinness and that his face, which was scholarly and even austere in expression, was seamed with countless wrinkles and of that dull parchment-yellow that comes from years under a tropic sun.

"Ah, Watson, you have arrived in time," said Holmes. "This is Mr. Theobold Wilson about whom Lestrade spoke to us last night."

Our visitor wrung my hand warmly. "Your name is, of course, well known to me, Dr. Watson," he cried. "Indeed, if Mr. Sherlock Holmes will pardon me for saying so, it is largely thanks to you that we are aware of his genius. As a medical man doubtless well versed in the handling of nervous cases, your presence should have a most beneficial effect upon my unhappy niece."

Holmes caught my eye resignedly. "I have promised Mr. Wilson to accompany him to Deptford, Watson," said he, "for it would seem that the young lady is determined to leave her home tomorrow. But I must repeat again, Mr. Wilson, that I fail to see in what way my presence can affect the matter."

"You are over-modest, Mr. Holmes. When I appealed to the official police, I had hoped that they might convince Janet that, terrible though our family losses have been in the past three years, nevertheless they lay in natural causes and that there is no reason why she should flee from her home. I had the impression," he added, with a chuckle, "that the inspector was somewhat chagrined at my ready acceptance of his own suggestion that I should invoke your assistance."

"I shall certainly remember my small debt to Lestrade," replied Holmes drily as he rose to his feet. "Perhaps, Watson, you would ask Mrs. Hudson to whistle a four-wheeler and Mr. Wilson can clarify certain points to my mind as we drive to Deptford."

It was one of those grey, brooding summer days when London is at its worst and, as we rattled over Blackfriars Bridge, I noted that wreaths of mist were rising from the river like the poisonous vapours of some hot jungle swamp. The more spacious streets of the West End had given place to the great commercial thoroughfares, resounding with the stamp and clatter of the dray-horses, and these in turn merged at last into a maze of dingy streets that, following the curve of the river, grew more and more wretched in their squalor the nearer we approached to that labyrinth of tidal basins and dark, evil-smelling lanes that were once the ancient cradle of England's sea trade and of an empire's wealth. I could see that Holmes was listless and bored to a point of irritation and I did my best, therefore, to engage our companion in conversation.

"I understand that you are an expert on canaries," I remarked.

Theobold Wilson's eyes, behind their powerful spectacles, lit with the glow of the enthusiast. "A mere student, sir, but with thirty years of practical research," he cried. "Can it be that you too—? No? A pity! The study, breeding and training of the *Fringilla Canaria* is a task worthy of a man's lifetime. You would not credit the ignorance, Dr. Watson, that prevails on this subject even in the most enlightened circles. When I read my paper on the 'Crossing of the Madeira and Canary Island Strains' to the British Ornithological Society I was appalled at the puerility of the ensuing questions."

"Inspector Lestrade hinted at some special characteristic in your training of these little songsters."

"Songsters, sir! A thrush is a songster. The *Fringilla* is the supreme ear of Nature, possessing an unique power of imitation which can be trained for the benefit and edification of the human race. But the inspector was correct," he went on more calmly, "in that I have put my birds to a special effect. They are trained to sing by night in artificial light."

"Surely a somewhat singular pursuit."

"I like to think that it is a kindly one. My birds are trained for the benefit of those who suffer from insomnia and I have clients in all parts of the country. Their tuneful song helps to while away the long night hours and the dousing of the lamplight terminates the concert."

"It seems to me that Lestrade was right," I observed. "Yours is indeed an unique profession."

During our conversation, Holmes, who had idly picked up our companion's heavy stick, had been examining it with some attention.

"I understand that you returned to England some three years ago," he observed.

"I did."

"From Cuba, I perceive."

Theobold Wilson started and for an instant I seemed to catch a gleam of something like wariness in the swift glance that he shot at Holmes.

"That is so," he said. "But how did you know?"

"Your stick is cut from Cuban ebony. There is no mistaking that greenish tint and the exceptionally high polish."

"It might have been bought in London since my return from, say, Africa."

"No, it has been yours for some years." Holmes lifted the stick to the carriage-window and tilted it so that the daylight shone upon the handle. "You will perceive," he went on, "that there is a slight but regular scraping that has worn through the polish along the left side of the handle just where the ring finger of a left-handed man would close upon the grip. Ebony is among the toughest of woods and it would require considerable time to cause such wear and a ring of some harder metal than gold. You are left-handed, Mr. Wilson, and wear a silver ring on your middle finger."

"Dear me, how simple. I thought for the moment that you had done something clever. As it happens, I was in the sugar trade in Cuba and brought my old stick back with me. But here we are at the house and, if you can put my silly niece's fears at rest as quickly as you can deduce my past, I shall be your debtor, Mr. Sherlock Holmes."

On descending from our four-wheeler, we found ourselves in a lane of mean, slatternly houses sloping, so far as I could judge from the yellow mist that was already creeping up the lower end, to the river's edge. At one side was a high wall of crumbling brickwork pierced by an iron gate through which we caught a glimpse of a substantial mansion lying in its own garden.

"The old house has known better days," said our companion, as we followed him through the gate and up the path. "It was built in the year that Peter the Great came to live in Scales Court whose ruined park can be seen from the upper windows."

Usually I am not unduly affected by my surroundings, but I must confess that I was aware of a feeling of depression at the melancholy spectacle that lay before us. The house, though of dignified and even imposing proportions, was faced with blotched, weather-stained plaster which had fallen away in places to disclose the ancient brickwork that lay beneath, while a tangled mass of ivy covering one wall had sent its long tendrils across the high-peaked roof to wreathe itself around the chimney-stacks.

The garden was an overgrown wilderness, and the air of the whole place reeked with the damp musty smell of the river.

Theobold Wilson led us through a small hall into a comfortably furnished drawing-room. A young woman with auburn hair and a freckled face, who was sorting through some papers at a writing-desk, sprang to her feet at our entrance.

"Here are Mr. Sherlock Holmes and Dr. Watson," announced our companion. "This is my niece Janet, whose interests you are here to protect against her own unreasonable conduct."

The young lady faced us bravely enough, though I noted a twitch and tremor of the lips that spoke of a high nervous tension. "I am leaving tomorrow, Uncle," she cried, "and nothing that these gentlemen can say will alter my decision. Here, there is only sorrow and fear—above all, fear!"

"Fear of what?"

The girl passed her hand over her eyes. "I—I cannot explain. I hate the shadows and the funny little noises."

"You have inherited both money and property, Janet," said Mr. Wilson earnestly. "Will you, because of shadows, desert the roof of your fathers? Be reasonable."

"We are here only to serve you, young lady," said Holmes with some gentleness, "and to try to put your fears at rest. It is often so in life that we injure our own best interests by precipitate action."

"You will laugh at a woman's intuitions, sir."

"By no means. They are often the signposts of Providence. Understand clearly that you will go or stay as you see fit. But perhaps, as I am here, it might relieve your mind to show me over the house."

"An admirable suggestion!" cried Theobold Wilson cheerily. "Come, Janet, we will soon dispose of your shadows and noises."

In a little procession, we trooped from one over-furnished room to another on the ground floor.

"I will take you to the bedrooms," said Miss Wilson, as we paused at last before the staircase.

"Are there no cellars in a house of this antiquity?"

"There is one cellar, Mr. Holmes, but it is little used save for the storage of wood and some of Uncle's old nest-boxes. This way, please."

It was a gloomy, stone-built chamber in which we found ourselves. A stack of wood was piled against one wall and a pot-bellied Dutch stove, its iron pipe running through the ceiling, filled the far corner. Through a glazed door reached by a line of steps and opening into the garden, a dim light filtered down upon the flagstones. Holmes sniffed the air keenly, and I was myself aware of an increased mustiness from the near-by river.

"Like most Thames-side houses, you must be plagued by rats," he remarked.

"We used to be. But, since Uncle came here, he has got rid of them."

"Quite so. Dear me," he continued, peering down at the floor, "what busy little fellows!"

Following his gaze, I saw that his attention had been drawn by a few garden ants scurrying across the floor from beneath the edge of the stove and up the steps leading to the garden door. "It is as well for us, Watson," he chuckled, pointing with his stick at the tiny particles with which they were encumbered, "that we are not under the necessity of lugging along our dinners thrice our own size. It is a lesson in patience." He lapsed into silence, staring thoughtfully at the floor. "A lesson," he repeated slowly.

Mr. Wilson's thin lips tightened. "What foolery is this," he exclaimed. "The ants are there because the servants would throw garbage in the stove to save themselves the trouble of going to the dustbin."

"And so you put a lock on the lid."

"We did. If you wish, I can fetch the key. No? Then, if you are finished, let me take you to the bedrooms."

"Perhaps I may see the room where your brother died," requested Holmes, as we reached the top floor.

"It is here," replied Miss Wilson, throwing open the door.

It was a large chamber furnished with some taste and even luxury and lit by two deeply recessed windows flanking another pot-bellied stove decorated with yellow tiles to harmonize with the tone of the room. A pair of bird-cages hung from the stove-pipe.

"Where does that side door lead?" asked my friend.

"It communicates with my room, which was formerly used by my mother," she answered.

For a few minutes, Holmes prowled around listlessly.

"I perceive that your brother was addicted to night reading," he remarked.

"Yes. He suffered from sleeplessness. But how—"

"Tut, the pile of the carpet on the right of the arm-chair is thick with traces of candle-wax. But hullo! What have we here?"

Holmes had halted near the window and was staring intently at the upper wall. Then, mounting the sill, he stretched out an arm and, touching the plaster lightly here and there, sniffed at his finger-tips. There was a puzzled frown on his face as he clambered down and commenced to circle slowly around the room, his eyes fixed upon the ceiling.

"Most singular," he muttered.

"Is anything wrong, Mr. Holmes?" faltered Miss Wilson.

"I am merely interested to account for these odd whorls and lines across the upper wall and plaster."

"It must be those dratted cockroaches dragging the dust all over the place," exclaimed Wilson apologetically. "I've told you before, Janet, that you would be better employed in supervising the servants' work. But what now, Mr. Holmes?"

My friend, who had crossed to the side door and glanced within, now closed it again and strolled across to the window.

"My visit has been a useless one," said he, "and, as I see that the fog is rising, I fear that we must take our leave. These are, I suppose, your famous canaries?" he added, pointing to the cages above the stove.

"A mere sample. But come this way."

Wilson led us along the passage and threw open a door.

"There!" said he.

Obviously it was his own bedroom and yet unlike any bedroom that I had entered in all my professional career. From floor to ceiling it was festooned with scores of cages and the little golden-coated singers within filled the air with their sweet warbling and trilling.

"Daylight or lamplight, it's all the same to them. Here, Carrie, Carrie!" he whistled a few liquid notes which I seemed to recognize. The bird took them up into a lovely cadence of song.

"A sky-lark!" I cried.

"Precisely. As I said before, the *Fringilla* if properly trained are the supreme imitators."

"I confess that I do not recognize that song," I remarked, as one of the birds broke into a low rising, whistle ending in a curious *tremolo*.

Mr. Wilson threw a towel over the cage. "It is the song of the tropic night-bird," he said shortly, "and, as I have the foolish pride to prefer my birds to sing the songs of the day while it is day, we will punish Peperino by putting him in darkness."

"I am surprised that you prefer an open fireplace here to a stove," observed Holmes. "There must be a considerable draught."

"I have not noticed one. Dear me, the fog is indeed increasing. I am afraid, Mr. Holmes, that you have a bad journey before you."

"Then we must be on our way."

As we descended the stairs and paused in the hall while Theobold Wilson fetched our hats, Sherlock Holmes leaned over towards our young companion.

"I would remind you, Miss Wilson, of what I said earlier about a woman's intuition," he said quietly. "There are occasions when the truth can be sensed more easily than it can be seen. Good-night."

A moment later, we were feeling our way down the garden path to where the lights of our waiting four-wheeler shone dimly through the rising fog.

My companion was sunk in thought as we rumbled westward through the mean streets whose squalor was the more aggressive under the garish light of the gas-lamps that flared and whistled outside the numerous public houses. The night promised to be a bad one and already, through the yellow vapour thickening and writhing above the pavements, the occasional wayfarer was nothing more than a vague hurrying shadow.

"I could have wished, my dear fellow," I remarked, "that you had been spared the need uselessly to waste your energies which are already sufficiently depleted."

"Well, well, Watson. I fancied that the affairs of the Wilson family would prove no concern of ours. And yet—" he sank back, absorbed for a moment in his own thoughts, "—and yet, it is wrong, wrong, all wrong!" I heard him mutter under his breath.

"I observed nothing of a sinister nature."

"Nor I. But every danger bell in my head is jangling its warning. Why a fireplace, Watson, why a fireplace? I take it that you noticed that the pipe from the cellar connected with the stoves in the other bedrooms?"

"In one bedroom."

"No. There was the same arrangement in the adjoining room where the mother died."

"I see nothing in this save an old-fashioned system of heating flues."

"And what of the marks on the ceiling?"

"You mean the whorls of dust."

"I mean the whorls of soot."

"Soot! Surely you are mistaken, Holmes."

"I touched them, smelt them, examined them. They were speckles and lines of wood-soot."

"Well, there is probably some perfectly natural explanation."

For a time, we sat in silence. Our cab had reached the beginnings of the City and I was gazing out of the window, my fingers drumming idly on the half-lowered pane, which was already befogged with moisture, when my thoughts were recalled by a sharp ejaculation from my companion. He was staring fixedly over my shoulder.

"The glass," he muttered.

Over the clouded surface there now lay an intricate

tracery of whorls and lines where my finger had wandered aimlessly.

Holmes clapped his hand to his brow and, throwing open the other window, he shouted an order to the cabby. The vehicle turned in its tracks and, with the driver lashing at his horse, we clattered away into the thickening gloom.

"Ah, Watson, Watson, true it is that none are so blind as those who will not see!" quoted Holmes bitterly, sinking back into his corner. "All the facts were there, staring me in the face, and yet logic failed to respond."

"What facts?"

"There are nine. Four alone should have sufficed. Here is a man from Cuba, who not only trains canaries in a singular manner but knows the call of tropical night-birds and keeps a fireplace in his bedroom. There is devilry here, Watson. Stop, cabby, stop!"

We were passing a junction of two busy thoroughfares, with the golden balls of a pawnship glimmering above a street-lamp. Holmes sprang out. But after a few minutes, he was back again and we recommenced our journey.

"It is fortunate that we are still in the City," he chuckled, "for I fancy that the East End pawnshops are unlikely to run to golf-clubs."

"Good heavens—!" I began, only to lapse into silence while I stared down at the heavy niblick which he had thrust into my hand. The first shadows of some vague and monstrous horror seemed to rise up and creep over my mind.

"We are too early," exclaimed Holmes, consulting his watch. "A sandwich and a glass of whisky at the first public house will not come amiss."

The clock on St. Nicholas Church was striking ten when we found ourselves once again in that evil-smelling garden. Through the mist, the dark gloom of the house was broken by a single feeble light in an upper window. "It is Miss Wilson's room," said Holmes. "Let us hope that this handful of gravel will rouse her without alarming the household."

An instant later, there came the sound of an opening window.

"Who is there?" demanded a tremulous voice.

"It is Sherlock Holmes," my friend called back softly. "I must speak with you at once, Miss Wilson. Is there a side door?"

"There is one in the wall to your left. But what has happened?"

"Pray descend immediately. Not a word to your uncle."

We felt our way along the wall and reached the door just as it opened to disclose Miss Wilson. She was in her dressing-gown, her hair tumbled about her shoulders and, as her startled eyes peered at us across the light of the candle in her hand, the shadows danced and trembled on the wall behind her.

"What is it, Mr. Holmes?" she gasped.

"All will be well, if you carry out my instructions," my friend replied quietly. "Where is your uncle?"

"He is in his room."

"Good. While Dr. Watson and I occupy your room, you will move into your late brother's bedchamber. If you value your life," he added solemnly, "you will not attempt to leave it."

"You frighten me!" she whimpered.

"Rest assured that we will take care of you. And now two final questions before you retire. Has your uncle visited you this evening?"

"Yes. He brought Peperino and put him with the other birds in the cage in my room. He said that as it was my last night at home I should have the best entertainment that he had the power to give me."

"Ha! Quite so. Your last night. Tell me, Miss Wilson, do you suffer at all from the same malady as your mother and brother?"

"A weak heart? I must confess it, yes."

"Well, we will accompany you quietly upstairs where you will retire to the adjoining room. Come, Watson."

Guided by the light of Janet Wilson's candle, we mounted silently to the floor above and thence into the bedchamber which Holmes had previously examined.

While we waited for our companion to collect her things from the adjoining room, Holmes strolled across and, lifting the edge of the cloths which now covered the two bird-cages, peered in at the tiny sleeping occupants.

"The evil of man is as inventive as it is immeasurable," said he, and I noticed that his face was very stern.

On Miss Wilson's return, having seen that she was safely ensconced for the night, I followed Holmes into the room which she had lately occupied. It was a small chamber but comfortably furnished and lit by a heavy silver oil-lamp. Immediately above a tiled Dutch stove there hung a cage containing three canaries which, momentarily ceasing their song, cocked their little golden heads at our approach.

"I think, Watson, that it would be as well to relax for half an hour," whispered Holmes as we sank into our chairs. "So kindly put out the light."

"But, my dear fellow, if there is any danger it would be an act of madness!" I protested.

"There is no danger in the darkness."

"Would it not be better," I said severely, "that you were frank with me? You have made it obvious that the birds are being put to some evil purpose, but what is this danger that exists only in the lamplight?"

"I have my own ideas on that matter, Watson, but it is better that we should wait and see. I would draw your attention, however, to the hinged lid of the stoke-hole on the top of the stove."

"It appears to be a perfectly normal fitting."

"Just so. But is there not some significance in the fact that the stoke-hole of an iron stove should be fitted with a tin lid?"

"Great heavens, Holmes!" I cried, as the light of understanding burst upon me. "You mean that this man Wilson has used the inter-connecting pipes from the stove in the cellar to those in the bedrooms to disseminate some deadly poison to wipe out his own kith and kin and thus obtain the property. It is for that reason that he has a fireplace in his own bedroom. I see it all."

"Well, you are not far wrong, Watson, though I fancy

that Master Theobold is rather more subtle than you suppose. He possesses the two qualities vital to the successful murderer—ruthlessness and imagination. But now, douse the light like a good fellow and for a while let us relax. If my reading of the problem is correct, our nerves may be tested to their limit before we see tomorrow's dawn."

I lay back in the darkness and drawing some comfort from the thought that ever since the affair with Colonel Sebastian Moran I had carried my revolver in my pocket, I sought in my mind for some explanation that would account for the warning contained in Holmes's words. But I must have been wearier than I had imagined. My thoughts grew more and more confused and finally I dozed off.

It was a touch upon my arm that awoke me. The lamp had been relit and my friend was bending over me, his long black shadow thrown upon the ceiling.

"Sorry to disturb you, Watson," he whispered. "But duty calls."

"What do you wish me to do?"

"Sit still and listen. Peperino is singing."

It was a vigil that I shall long remember. Holmes had tilted the lamp-shade, so that the light fell on the opposite wall broken by the window and the great tiled stove with its hanging bird-cage. The fog had thickened and the rays from the lamp, filtering through the window-glass, lost themselves in luminous clouds that swirled and boiled against the panes. My mind darkened by a premonition of evil, I would have found our surroundings melancholy enough without the eerie sound that was rising and falling from the canary cage. It was a kind of whistling beginning with a low, throaty warble and slowly ascending to a single chord that rang through the room like the note of a great wineglass, a sound so mesmeric in its repetition that almost imperceptibly the present seemed to melt away and my imagination to reach out beyond those fog-bound windows into the dark, lush depth of some exotic jungle. I had lost all count of time, and it was only the stillness following the sudden cessation of the bird's song that brought me back to reality. I glanced across the room and, in an instant, my heart gave one great throb and then seemed to stop beating altogether.

The lid of the stove was slowly rising.

My friends will agree that I am neither a nervous nor an impressionable man but I must confess that, as I sat there gripping the sides of my chair and glaring at the dreadful thing that was gradually clambering into view, my limbs momentarily refused their functions.

The lid had tilted back an inch or more and through the gap thus created a writhing mass of yellow, stick-like objects was clawing and scrabbling for a hold. And then, in a flash, it was out and standing motionless upon the surface of the stove.

Though I have always viewed with horror the bird-eating tarantulas of South America, they shrank into insignificance when compared with the loathsome creature that faced us now across that lamplit room. It was bigger in its spread than a large dinner-plate, with a hard, smooth, yellow body surrounded by legs that, rising high above it, conveyed a fearful impression that the thing was crouching for its spring. It was absolutely hairless save for tufts of stiff bristles around the leg-joints and, above the glint of its great poison mandibles, clusters of beady eyes shone in the light with a baleful red iridescence.

"Don't move, Watson," whispered Holmes, and there was a note of horror in his voice that I had never heard before.

The sound roused the creature for, in a single lightning bound, it sprang from the stove to the top of the bird-cage and, reaching the wall, whizzed round the room and over the ceiling with a dreadful febrile swiftness that the eye could scarcely follow.

Holmes flung himself forward like a man possessed.

"Kill it! Smash it!" he yelled hoarsely, raining blow after blow with his golf-club at the blurred shape racing across the walls.

Dust from broken plaster choked the air and a table crashed over as I flung myself to the ground when the great spider cleared the room in a single leap and turned at bay. Holmes bounded across me, swinging his club. "Keep where you are!" he shouted and even as his voice rang through the room, the thud ... thud ... thud of the blows was broken by a horrible squelching sound. For an instant, the creature hung there and then, slipping slowly down, it lay like a mess of smashed eggs with three thin, bony legs still twitching and plucking at the floor.

"Thank God that it missed you when it sprang!" I gasped, scrambling to my feet.

He made no reply and glancing up I caught a glimpse of his face reflected in a wall mirror. He looked pale and strained and there was a curious rigidity in his expression.

"I am afraid it's up to you, Watson," he said quietly. "It has a mate."

I spun round to be greeted by a spectacle that I shall remember for the rest of my days. Sherlock Holmes was standing perfectly still within two feet of the stove and on top of it, reared up on its back legs, its loathsome body shuddering for the spring, stood another monstrous spider.

I knew instinctively that any sudden movement would merely precipitate the creature's leap and so, carefully drawing my revolver from my pocket, I fired pointblank.

Through the powder-smoke, I saw the thing shrink into itself and then, toppling slowly backwards, it fell through the open lid of the stove. There was a rasping, slithering sound rapidly fading away into silence.

"It's fallen down the pipe," I cried, conscious that my hands were now shaking under a strong reaction. "Are you all right, Holmes?"

He looked at me and there was a singular light in his eye.

"Thanks to you, my dear fellow!" he said soberly. "If I had moved, then—but what is that?"

A door had slammed below and, an instant later, we caught the swift patter of feet upon the gravel path.

"After him!" cried Holmes, springing for the door. "Your shot warned him that the game was up. He must not escape!"

But fate decreed otherwise. Though we rushed down

the stairs and out into the fog, Theobold Wilson had too much start on us and the advantage of knowing the terrain. For a while, we followed the faint sound of his running footsteps down the empty lanes towards the river, but at length these died away in the distance.

"It is no good, Watson. We have lost our man," panted Holmes. "This is where the official police may be of use. But listen! Surely that was a cry?"

"I thought I heard something."

"Well, it is hopeless to look further in the fog. Let us return and comfort this poor girl with the assurance that her troubles are now at an end."

"They were nightmare creatures, Holmes," I exclaimed, as we retraced our steps towards the house, "and of some unknown species."

"I think not, Watson," said he. "It was the *Galeodes* spider, the horror of the Cuban forests. It is perhaps fortunate for the rest of the world that it is found nowhere else. The creature is nocturnal in its habits, and unless my memory belies me, it possesses the power actually to break the spine of smaller creatures with a single blow of its mandibles. You will recall that Miss Janet mentioned that the rats had vanished since her uncle's return. Doubtless Wilson brought the brutes back with him," he went on, "and then conceived the idea of training certain of his canaries to imitate the song of some Cuban nightbird upon which the *Galeodes* were accustomed to feed. The marks on the ceiling were caused, of course, by the soot adhering to the spiders' legs after they had scrambled up the flues. It is fortunate, perhaps, for the consulting detective that the duster of the average housemaid seldom strays beyond the height of a mantelpiece.

"Indeed, I can discover no excuse for my lamentable slowness in solving this case, for the facts were before me from the first, and the whole affair was elementary in its construction.

"And yet to give Theobold Wilson his dues, one must recognize his almost diabolical cleverness. Once these horrors were installed in the stove in the cellar, what more simple than to arrange two ordinary flues communicating with the bedrooms above? By hanging the cages over the stoves, the flues would themselves act as a magnifier to the birds' song and, guided by their predatory instinct, the creatures would invariably ascend whichever pipe led to it. Once Wilson had devised some means of luring them back again to their nest, they represented a comparatively safe way of getting rid of those who stood between himself and the property."

"Then its bite is deadly?" I interposed.

"To a person in weak health, probably so. But there lies the devilish cunning of the scheme, Watson. It was the sight of the thing rather than its bite, poisonous though it may be, on which he relied to kill his victim. Can you imagine the effect upon an elderly woman, and later upon her son, both suffering from insomnia and heart disease, when in the midst of a bird's seemingly innocent song this appalling spectacle arose from the top of the stove? We have sampled it ourselves, though we are healthy men. It killed them as surely as a bullet through their hearts."

"There is one thing I cannot understand, Holmes. Why did he appeal to Scotland Yard?"

"Because he is a man of iron nerve. His niece was instinctively frightened and, finding that she was adamant in her intention of leaving, he planned to kill her at once and by the same method.

"Once done, who should dare to point the finger of suspicion at Master Theobold? Had he not appealed to Scotland Yard and even invoked the aid of Mr. Sherlock Holmes himself to satisfy one and all? The girl had died of a heart attack like the others and her uncle would have been the recipient of general condolences.

"Remember the padlocked cover of the stove in the cellar and admire the cold nerve that offered to fetch the key. It was bluff, of course, for he would have discovered that he had 'lost' it. Had we persisted and forced that lock, I prefer not to think of what we would have found clinging round our collars."

Theobold Wilson was never heard of again. But it is perhaps suggestive that, some two days later, a man's body was fished out of the Thames. The corpse was mutilated beyond recognition, probably by a ship's propeller, and the police searched his pockets in vain for means of identification. They contained nothing, however, save for a small note-book filled with jottings on the brooding period of the *Fringilla Canaria*.

"It is the wise man who keeps bees," remarked Sherlock Holmes when he read the report. "You know where you are with them and at least they do not attempt to represent themselves as something that they are not."

—:—

In this memorable year '93, a curious and incongruous succession of cases had engaged his attention ranging from . . . the sudden death of Cardinal Tosca down to the arrest of Wilson the notorious canary-trainer* which removed a plague-spot from the East End of London.

FROM "BLACK PETER."

---

* In the Wilson case, Holmes did not actually arrest Wilson as Wilson was drowned. This was a typical Watson error in his hurried reference to the case in "Black Peter."

12

The Adventure of the
Red Widow

"Your conclusions are perfectly correct, my dear Watson," remarked my friend Sherlock Holmes. "Squalor and poverty are the natural matrix to crimes of violence."

"Precisely so," I agreed. "Indeed, I was just thinking—" I broke off to stare at him in amazement. "Good heavens, Holmes," I cried, "this is too much. How could you possibly know my innermost thoughts!"

My friend leaned back in his chair and, placing his finger-tips together, surveyed me from under his heavy, drooping eyelids.

"I would do better justice, perhaps, to my limited powers by refusing to answer your question," he said, with a dry chuckle. "You have a certain flair, Watson, for concealing your failure to perceive the obvious by the cavalier manner in which you invariably accept the explanation of a sequence of simple but logical reasoning."

"I do not see how logical reasoning can enable you to follow the course of my mental processes," I retorted, a trifle nettled by his superior manner.

"There was no great difficulty. I have been watching you for the last few minutes. The expression on your face was quite vacant until, as your eyes roved about the room, they fell on the bookcase and came to rest on Hugo's *Les Miserables* which made so deep an impression upon you when you read it last year. You became thoughtful, your eyes narrowed, it was obvious that your mind was drifting again into that tremendous dreadful saga of human suffering; at length your gaze lifted to the window with its aspect of snow-flakes and grey sky and bleak, frozen roofs, and then, moving slowly on to the mantelpiece, settled on the jack-knife with which I skewer my unanswered correspondence. The frown darkened on your face and unconsciously you shook your head despondently. It was an association of ideas. Hugo's terrible sub-third stage, the winter cold of poverty in the slums and, above the warm glow of our own modest fire, the bare knife-blade. Your expression deepened into one of sadness, the melancholy that comes with an understanding of cause and effect in the unchanging human tragedy. It was then that I ventured to agree with you."

"Well, I must confess that you followed my thoughts with extraordinary accuracy," I admitted. "A remarkable piece of reasoning, Holmes."

"Elementary, my dear Watson."

The year of 1887 was moving to its end. The iron grip of the great blizzards that commenced in the last week of December had closed on the land and beyond the windows of Holmes's lodgings in Baker Street lay a gloomy vista of grey, lowering sky and white-capped tiles dimly discernible through a curtain of snow-flakes.

Though it had been a memorable year for my friend, it had been of yet greater importance to me, for it was but two months since that Miss Mary Morston had paid me the signal honour of joining her destiny to mine. The change from my bachelor existence as a half-pay, ex-Army surgeon into the state of wedded bliss had not been accomplished without some uncalled-for and ironic comments from Sherlock Holmes but, as my wife and I could thank him for the fact that we had found each other, we could afford to accept his cynical attitude with tolerance and even understanding.

I had dropped in to our old lodgings on this afternoon, to be precise December 30th, to pass a few hours with my friend and enquire whether any new case of interest had come his way since my previous visit. I had found him pale and listless, his dressing-gown drawn round his shoulders and the room reeking with the smoke of his favorite black shag, through which the fire in the grate gleamed like a brazier in a fog.

"Nothing, save a few routine enquiries, Watson," he had replied in a voice shrill with complaint. "Creative art in crime seems to have become atrophied since I disposed of the late-lamented Bert Stevens." Then lapsing into silence, he curled himself up morosely in his arm-chair, and not another word passed between us until my thoughts were suddenly interrupted by the observation that commenced this narrative.

As I rose to go, he looked at me critically.

"I perceive, Watson," said he, "that you are already paying the price. The slovenly state of your left jawbone bears regrettable testimony that somebody has changed the position of your shaving-mirror. Furthermore, you are indulging in extravagances."

"You do me a gross injustice."

"What, at the winter price of fivepence a blossom! Your buttonhole tells me that you were sporting a flower not later than yesterday."

"This is the first time I have known you penurious, Holmes," I retorted with some bitterness.

He broke into a hearty laugh. "My dear fellow, you must forgive me!" he cried. "It is most unfair that I should penalize you because a surfeit of unexpended mental energy tends to play upon my nerves. But hullo, what's this!"

A heavy step was mounting the stairs. My friend waved me back into my chair.

"Stay a moment, Watson," said he. "It is Gregson, and the old game may be afoot once more."

"Gregson?"

"There is no mistaking that regulation tread. Too heavy for Lestrade's and yet known to Mrs. Hudson or she would accompany him. It is Gregson."

As he finished speaking, there came a knock on the door and a figure muffled to the ears in a heavy cape entered the room. Our visitor tossed his bowler on the nearest chair and unwinding the scarf wrapped around the lower part of his face, disclosed the flaxen hair and long, pale features of the Scotland Yard detective.

"Ah, Gregson," greeted Holmes, with a sly glance in my direction. "It must be urgent business that brings you out in this inclement weather. But throw off your cape, man, and come over to the fire."

The police-agent shook his head. "There is not a moment to lose," he replied, consulting a large silver turnip watch. "The train to Derbyshire leaves in half an hour and I have a hansom waiting below. Though the case should present no difficulties for an officer of my experience, nevertheless I shall be glad of your company."

"Something of interest?"

"Murder, Mr. Holmes," snapped Gregson curtly, "and a singular one at that, to judge from the telegram from the local police. It appears that Lord Jocelyn Cope, the Deputy-Lieutenant of the County, has been found butchered at Arnsworth Castle. The Yard is quite capable of solving crimes of this nature, but in view of the curious terms contained in the police telegram, it occurred to me that you might wish to accompany me. Will you come?"

Holmes leaned forward, emptied the Persian slipper into his tobacco pouch and sprang to his feet.

"Give me a moment to pack a clean collar and toothbrush," he cried. "I have a spare one for you, Watson. No, my dear fellow, not a word. Where would I be without your assistance? Scribble a note to your wife, and Mrs. Hudson will have it delivered. We should be back tomorrow. Now, Gregson, I'm your man and you can fill in the details during our journey."

The guard's flag was already waving as we rushed up the platform at St. Pancras and tore open the door of the first empty smoker. Holmes had brought three travelling-rugs with him and as the train roared its way through the fading winter daylight we made ourselves comfortable enough in our respective corners.

"Well, Gregson, I shall be interested to hear the details," remarked Holmes, his thin, eager face framed in the ear-flaps of his deer-stalker and a spiral of blue smoke rising from his pipe.

"I know nothing beyond what I have already told you."

"And yet you used the word 'singular' and referred to the telegram from the county police as 'curious.' Kindly explain."

"I used both terms for the same reason. The wire from the local inspector advised that the officer from Scotland Yard should read the *Derbyshire County Guide* and the *Gazeteer*. A most extraordinary suggestion!"

"I should say a wise one. What have you done about it?"

"The *Gazeteer* states merely that Lord Jocelyn Cope is a Deputy-Lieutenant and county magnate, married, childless and noted for his bequests to local archeological societies. As for the *Guide,* I have it here." He drew a pamphlet from his pocket and thumbed over the pages. "Here we are," he continued. "Arnsworth Castle. Built reign of Edward III. Fifteenth-century stained-glass window to celebrate Battle of Agincourt. Cope family penalized for suspected Catholic leaning by Royal Visitation, 1574. Museum open to public once a year. Contains large collection of martial and other relics including small guillotine built originally in Nimes during French Revolution for execution of a maternal ancestor of the present owner. Never used owing to escape of intended victim and later purchased as relic by family after Napoleonic Wars and brought to Arnsworth. Pshaw! That local inspector must be out of his senses, Mr. Holmes. There is nothing to help us here."

"Let us reserve judgment. The man would not have made such a suggestion without reason. In the meantime, I would recommend to your attention the dusk now falling over the landscape. Every material object has become vague and indistinct and yet their solid existence remains, though almost hidden from our visual senses. There is much to be learned from the twilight."

"Quite so, Mr. Holmes," grinned Gregson, with a wink at me. "Very poetical, I am sure. Well, I'm for a short nap."

It was some three hours later that we alighted at a small wayside station. The snow had ceased and beyond the roofs of the hamlet the long desolate slopes of the Derbyshire moors, white and glistening under the light of a full moon, rolled away to the sky-line. A stocky, bow-legged man swathed in a shepherd's plaid hurried towards us along the platform.

"You're from Scotland Yard, I take it?" He greeted us brusquely. "I got your wire in reply to mine and I have a carriage waiting outside. Yes, I'm Inspector Dawlish," he added in response to Gregson's question. "But who are these gentlemen?"

"I considered that Mr. Sherlock Holmes's reputation—" began our companion.

"I've never heard of him," interposed the local man, looking at us with a gleam of hostility in his dark eyes. "This is a serious affair and there is no room for amateurs. But it is too cold to stand arguing here and, if London approves his presence, who am I to gainsay him? This way, if you please."

A closed carriage was standing before the station and a moment later we had swung out of the yard and were bowling swiftly but silently up the village high street.

"There'll be accommodation for you at the Queen's Head," grunted Inspector Dawlish. "But first to the castle."

"I shall be glad to hear the facts of this case," stated Gregson, "and the reason for the most irregular suggestion contained in your telegram."

"The facts are simple enough," replied the other, with a grim smile. "His lordship has been murdered and we know who did it."

"Ah!"

"Captain Jasper Lothian, the murdered man's cousin, has disappeared in a hurry. It's common knowledge hereabouts that the man's got a touch of the devil in him, a hard hand with a bottle, a horse or the nearest woman. It's come as a surprise to none of us that Captain Jasper should end by slaughtering his benefactor and the head of his house. Aye, head's a well-chosen word," he ended softly.

"If you've a clear case, then what's this nonsense about a guide-book?"

Inspector Dawlish leaned forward while his voice sank almost to a whisper. "You've read it?" he said. "Then it may interest you to know that Lord Jocelyn Cope was put to death in his own ancestral guillotine."

His words left us in a chilled silence.

"What motive can you suggest for that murder and for the barbarous method employed?" asked Sherlock Holmes at last.

"Probably a ferocious quarrel. Have I not told you already that Captain Jasper had a touch of the devil in him? But there's the castle, and a proper place it looks for deeds of violence and darkness."

We had turned off the country road to enter a gloomy avenue that climbed between banked snow-drifts up a barren moorland slope. On the crest loomed a great building, its walls and turrets stark and grey against the night sky. A few minutes later, our carriage rumbled under the arch of the outer bailey and halted in a courtyard.

At Inspector Dawlish's knock, a tall, stooping man in butler's livery opened the massive oaken door and, holding a candle above his head, peered out at us, the light shining on his weary red-rimmed eyes and ill-nourished beard.

"What, four of you!" he cried querulously. "It b'aint right her ladyship should be bothered thisways at such a time of grief to us all."

"That will do, Stephen. Where is her ladyship?"

The candle flame trembled. "Still with him," came the reply, and there was something like a sob in the old voice. "She hasn't moved. Still sitting there in the big chair and staring at him, as though she had fallen fast asleep with them wonderful eyes wide open."

"You've touched nothing, of course?"

"Nothing. It's all as it was."

"Then let us go first to the museum where the crime was committed," said Dawlish. "It is on the other side of the courtyard."

He was moving away towards a cleared path that ran across the cobble-stones when Holmes's hand closed upon his arm. "How is this!" he cried imperiously. "The museum is on the other side and yet you have allowed a carriage to drive across the courtyard and people to stampede over the ground like a herd of buffalo."

"What then?"

Holmes flung up his arms appealingly to the moon. "The snow, man, the snow! You have destroyed your best helpmate."

"But I tell you the murder was committed in the museum. What has the snow to do with it?"

Holmes gave vent to a most dismal groan and then we all followed the local detective across the yard to an arched door-way.

I have seen many a grim spectacle during my association with Sherlock Holmes, but I can recall none to surpass in horror the sight that met our eyes within that grey Gothic chamber. It was a small room with a groined roof lit by clusters of tapers in iron sconces. The walls were hung with trophies of armour and mediaeval weapons and edged by glass-topped cases crammed with ancient parchments, thumb-rings, pieces of carved stonework and yawning man-traps. These details I noticed at a glance and then my whole attention was riveted to the object that occupied a low dais in the centre of the room.

It was a guillotine, painted a faded red and, save for its smaller size, exactly similar to those that I had seen depicted in woodcuts of the French Revolution. Sprawling between the two uprights lay the body of a tall, thin man clad in a velvet smoking-jacket. His hands were tied behind him and a white cloth, hideously besmirched, concealed his head, or rather the place where his head had been.

The light of the tapers, gleaming on a blood-spattered steel blade buried in the lunette, reached beyond to touch as with a halo the red-gold hair of the woman who sat beside that dreadful headless form. Regardless of our approach, she remained motionless in her high carved chair, her features an ivory mask from which two dark and brilliant eyes stared into the shadows with the unwinking fixity of a basilisk. In an experience of women covering three continents, I have never beheld a colder nor a more perfect face than that of the chatelaine of Castle Arnsworth keeping vigil in that chamber of death.

Dawlish coughed.

"You had best retire, my lady," he said bluntly. "Rest assured that Inspector Gregson here and I will see that justice is done."

For the first time, she looked at us, and so uncertain was the light of the tapers that for an instant it seemed to me that some swift emotion more akin to mockery than grief gleamed and died in those wonderful eyes.

"Stephen is not with you?" she asked incongruously. "But, of course, he would be in the library. Faithful Stephen."

"I fear that his lordship's death—"

She rose abruptly, her bosom heaving and one hand gripping the skirt of her black lace gown.

"His damnation!" she hissed, and then, with a gesture of despair, she turned and glided slowly from the room.

As the door closed, Sherlock Holmes dropped on one knee beside the guillotine and, raising the blood-soaked cloth, peered down at the terrible object beneath. "Dear me," he said quietly. "A blow of this force must have sent the head rolling across the room."

"Probably."

"I fail to understand. Surely you know where you found it?"

"I didn't find it. There is no head."

For a long moment, Holmes remained on his knee, staring up silently at the speaker. "It seems to me that you are taking a great deal for granted," he said at length, scrambling to his feet. "Let me hear your ideas on this singular crime."

"It's plain enough. Sometime last night, the two men quarrelled and eventually came to blows. The younger overpowered the elder and then killed him by means of this instrument. The evidence that Lord Cope was still alive when placed in the guillotine is shown by the fact that Captain Lothian had to lash his hands. The crime was discovered this morning by the butler, Stephen, and a groom fetched me from the village whereupon I took the usual steps to identify the body of his lordship and listed the personal belongings found upon him. If you'd like to know how the murderer escaped, I can tell you that too. On the mare that's missing from the stable."

"Most instructive," observed Holmes. "As I understand your theory, the two men engaged in a ferocious combat, being careful not to disarrange any furniture or smash the glass cases that clutter up the room. Then, having disposed of his opponent, the murderer rides into the night, a suit-case under one arm and his victim's head under the other. A truly remarkable performance."

An angry flush suffused Dawlish's face. "It's easy enough to pick holes in other people's ideas, Mr. Sherlock Holmes," he sneered. "Perhaps you will give us your theory."

"I have none. I am awaiting my facts. By the way, when was your last snow-fall?"

"Yesterday afternoon."

"Then there is hope yet. But let us see if this room will yield us any information."

For some ten minutes, we stood and watched him, Gregson and I with interest and Dawlish with an ill-concealed look of contempt on his weather-beaten face, as Holmes crawled slowly about the room on his hands and knees muttering and mumbling to himself and looking like some gigantic dun-coloured insect. He had drawn his magnifying-glass from his cape pocket and I noticed that not only the floor but the contents of the occasional tables were subjected to the closest scrutiny. Then, rising to his feet, he stood wrapped in thought, his back to the candle-light and his gaunt shadow falling across the faded red guillotine.

"It won't do," he said suddenly. "The murder was premeditated."

"How do you know?"

"The cranking-handle is freshly oiled, and the victim was senseless. A single jerk would have loosed his hands."

"Then why were they tied?"

"Ah! There is no doubt, however, that the man was brought here unconscious with his hands already bound."

"You're wrong there!" interposed Dawlish loudly. "The design on the lashing proves that it is a sash from one of these window-curtains."

Holmes shook his head. "They are faded through exposure to daylight," said he, "and this is not. There can be little doubt that it comes from a door-curtain, of which there are none in this room. Well, there is little more to be learned here."

The two police-agents conferred together and Gregson turned to Holmes. "As it is after midnight," said he, "we had better retire to the village hostelry and tomorrow pursue our enquiries separately. I cannot but agree with Inspector Dawlish that while we are theorizing here the murderer may reach the coast."

"I wish to be clear on one point, Gregson. Am I officially employed on this case by the police?"

"Impossible, Mr. Holmes!"

"Quite so. Then I am free to use my own judgment. But give me five minutes in the courtyard and Doctor Watson and I will be with you."

The bitter cold smote upon us as I slowly followed the gleam of Holmes's dark lantern along the path that, banked with thick snow, led across the courtyard to the front door. "Fools!" he cried, stooping over the powdered surface. "Look at it, Watson! A regiment would have done less damage. Carriage-wheels in three places. And here's Dawlish's boots and a pair of hobnails, probably a groom. A woman now, and running. Of course, Lady Cope and the first alarm. Yes, certainly it is she. What was Stephen doing out here? There is no mistaking his square-toed shoes. Doubtless you observed them, Watson, when he opened the door to us. But what have we here?"

The lantern paused and then moved slowly onwards.

"Pumps. Pumps," he cried eagerly, "and coming from the front door. See, here he is again. Probably a tall man, from the size of his feet, and carrying some heavy object. The stride is shortened and the toes more clearly marked than the heels. A burdened man always tends to throw his weight forward. He returns! Ah, just so, just so! Well, I think that we have earned our beds." ·

My friend remained silent during our journey back to the village. But, as we separated from Inspector Dawlish at the door of the inn, he laid a hand on his shoulder.

"The man who has done this deed is tall and spare," said he. "He is about fifty years of age with a turned-in left foot and strongly addicted to Turkish cigarettes which he smokes from a holder."

"Captain Lothian!" grunted Dawlish. "I know nothing about feet or cigarette holders, but the rest of your description is accurate enough. But who told you his appearance?"

"I will set you a question in reply. Were the Copes ever a Catholic family?"

The local inspector glanced significantly at Gregson and tapped his forehead. "Catholic? Well, now that you mention it, I believe they were in the old times. But what on earth—!"

"Merely that I would recommend you to your own guide-book. Good night."

On the following morning, after dropping my friend and myself at the castle gate, the two police-officers drove off to pursue their enquiries further afield. Holmes watched their departure with a twinkle in his eye.

"I fear that I have done you injustice over the years, Watson," he commented somewhat enigmatically, as we turned away.

The elderly manservant opened the door to us and, as we followed him into the great hall, it was painfully obvious that the honest fellow was still deeply afflicted by his master's death.

"There is naught for you here," he cried shrilly. "My God, will you never leave us in peace?"

I have remarked previously on Holmes's gift for putting others at their ease, and by degrees the old man recovered his composure. "I take it that this is the Agincourt window," observed Holmes, staring up at a small but exquisitely coloured stained-glass casement through which the winter sunlight threw a pattern of brilliant colours on the ancient stone floor.

"It is, sir. Only two in all England."

"Doubtless you have served the family for many years," continued my friend gently.

"Served 'em? Aye, me and mine for nigh two centuries. Ours is the dust that lies upon their funeral palls.

"I fancy they have an interesting history."

"They have that, sir."

"I seem to have heard that this ill-omened guillotine was specially built for some ancestor of your late master?"

"Aye, the Marquis de Rennes. Built by his own tenants, the varmints, hated him, they did, simply because he kept up old customs."

"Indeed. What custom?"

"Something about women, sir. The book in the library don't explain exactly."

"*Le droit du seigneur,* perhaps."

"Well, I don't speak heathern, but I believe them was the very words."

"H'm. I should like to see this library."

The old man's eyes slid to the door at the end of the hall. "See the library?" he grumbled. "What do you want there? Nothing but old books, and her ladyship don't like —Oh, very well."

He led the way ungraciously into a long, low room lined to the ceiling with volumes and ending in a magnificent Gothic fireplace. Holmes, after strolling about listlessly, paused to light a cheroot.

"Well, Watson, I think that we'll be getting back," said he. "Thank you, Stephen. It is a fine room, though I am surprised to see Indian rugs."

"Indian!" protested the old man indignantly. "They're antique Persian."

"Surely Indian."

"Persian, I tell you! Them marks are inscriptions, as a gentleman like you should know. Can't see without your spy-glass? Well, use it then. Now, drat it, if he hasn't spilled his matches!"

As we rose to our feet after gathering up the scattered

vestas, I was puzzled to account for the sudden flush of excitement in Holmes's sallow cheeks.

"I was mistaken," said he. "They are Persian. Come, Watson, it is high time that we set out for the village and our train back to town."

A few minutes later, we had left the castle. But to my surprise, on emerging from the outer bailey, Holmes led the way swiftly along a lane leading to the stables.

"You intend to enquire about the missing horse," I suggested.

"The horse? My dear fellow, I have no doubt that it is safely concealed in one of the home farms, while Gregson rushes all over the county. This is what I am looking for."

He entered the first loose box and returned with his arms full of straw. "Another bundle for you, Watson, and it should be enough for our purpose."

"But what is our purpose?"

"Principally to reach the front door without being observed," he chuckled, as he shouldered his burden.

Having retraced our footsteps, Holmes laid his finger on his lips and, cautiously opening the great door, slipped into a near-by closet, full of capes and sticks, where he proceeded to throw both our bundles on the floor.

"It should be safe enough," he whispered, "for it is stone-built. Ah! These two mackintoshes will assist admirably. I have no doubt," he added, as he struck a match and dropped it into the pile, "that I shall have other occasions to use this modest stratagem."

As the flames spread through the straw and reached the mackintoshes, thick black wreaths of smoke poured from the cloak-room door into the hall of Arnsworth Castle, accompanied by a hissing and crackling from the burning rubber.

"Good heavens, Holmes," I gasped, the tears rolling down my face. "We shall be suffocated!"

His fingers closed on my arm.

"Wait," he muttered, and even as he spoke, there came a sudden rush of feet and a yell of horror.

"Fire!"

In that despairing wail, I recognized Stephen's voice.

"Fire!" he shrieked again, and we caught the clatter of his footsteps as he fled across the hall.

"Now!" whispered Holmes and, in an instant he was out of the cloak-room and running headlong for the library. The door was half open but, as we burst in, the man drumming with hysterical hands on the great fire-place did not even turn his head.

"Fire! The house is on fire!" he shrieked. "Oh, my poor master! My lord! My lord!"

Holmes's hand fell upon his shoulder. "A bucket of water in the cloak-room will meet the case," he said quietly. "It would be as well, however, if you would ask his lordship to join us."

The old man sprang at him, his eyes blazing and his fingers crooked like the talons of a vulture.

"A trick" he screamed. "I've betrayed him through your cursed tricks!"

"Take him, Watson," said Holmes, holding him at arms' length. "There, there. You're a faithful fellow."

"Faithful unto death," whispered a feeble voice.

I started back involuntarily. The edge of the ancient fireplace had swung open and in the dark aperture thus disclosed there stood a tall, thin man, so powdered with dust that for the moment I seemed to be staring not at a human being but at a spectre. He was about fifty years of age, gaunt and high-nosed, with a pair of sombre eyes that waxed and waned feverishly on a face that was the colour of grey paper.

"I fear that the dust is bothering you, Lord Cope," said Holmes very gently. "Would you not be better seated?"

The man tottered forward to drop heavily into an arm chair. "You are the police, of course," he gasped.

"No. I am a private investigator, but acting in the interests of justice."

A bitter smile parted Lord Cope's lips.

"Too late," said he.

"You are ill?"

"I am dying." Opening his fingers, he disclosed a small empty phial. "There is only a short time left to me."

"Is there nothing to be done, Watson?"

I laid my fingers upon the sick man's wrist. His face was already livid and the pulse low and feeble.

"Nothing, Holmes."

Lord Cope straightened himself painfully. "Perhaps you will indulge a last curiosity by telling me how you discovered the truth," said he. "You must be a man of some perception."

"I confess that at first there were difficulties," admitted Holmes, "though these discovered themselves later in the light of events. Obviously the whole key to the problem lay in a conjunction of two remarkable circumstances—the use of a guillotine and the disappearance of the murdered man's head.

"Who, I asked myself, would use so clumsy and rare an instrument, except one to whom it possessed some strong symbolic significance and, if this were the case, then it was logical to suppose that the clue to that significance must lie in its past history."

The nobleman nodded.

"His own people built it for Rennes," he muttered, "in return for the infamy that their womenfolk had suffered at his hands. But pray proceed, and quickly."

"So much for the first circumstance," continued Holmes, ticking off the points on his fingers. "The second threw a flood of light over the whole problem. This is not New Guinea. Why, then, should a murderer take his victim's head? The obvious answer was that he wished to conceal the dead man's true identity. By the way," he demanded sternly, "what have you done with Captain Lothian's head?"

"Stephen and I buried it at midnight in the family vault," came the feeble reply. "And that with all reverence."

"The rest was simple," went on Holmes. "As the body was easily identifiable as yours by the clothes and other personal belongings which were listed by the local inspector, it followed naturally that there could have been no point in concealing the head unless the murderer had also changed clothes with the dead man. That the change had been effected before death was shown by the blood-stains. The victim had been incapacitated in advance, probably drugged, for it was plain from certain facts already explained to my friend Watson that there had been no struggle and that he had been carried to the museum from another part of the castle. Assuming my reasoning to be correct, then the murdered man could not be Lord Jocelyn. But was there not another missing, his lordship's cousin and alleged murderer, Captain Jasper Lothian?"

"How could you give Dawlish a description of the wanted man?" I interposed.

"By looking at the body of the victim, Watson. The two men must have borne a general resemblance to each other or the deception would not have been feasible from the start. An ash tray in the museum contained a cigarette stub, Turkish, comparatively fresh and smoked from a holder. None but an addict would have smoked under the terrible circumstances that must have accompanied that insignificant stump. The foot-marks in the snow showed that someone had come from the main building carrying a burden and had returned without that burden. I think I have covered the principal points."

For a while, we sat in silence broken only by the moan of a rising wind at the windows and the short, sharp panting of the dying man's breath.

"I owe you no explanation," he said at last, "for it is to my Maker, who alone knows the innermost recesses of the human heart, that I must answer for my deed. Nevertheless, though my story is one of shame and guilt, I shall tell you enough to enlist perhaps your forbearance in granting me my final request.

"You must know, then, that following the scandal which brought his Army career to its close, my cousin Jasper Lothian has lived at Arnsworth. Though penniless and already notorious for his evil living, I welcomed him as a kinsman, affording him not only financial support but, what was perhaps more valuable, the social aegis of my position in the county.

"As I look back now on the years that passed, I blame myself for my own lack of principle in my failure to put an end to his extravagance, his drinking and gaming, and certain less honourable pursuits with which rumour already linked his name. I had thought him wild and injudicious. I was yet to learn that he was a creature so vile and utterly bereft of honour that he would tarnish the name of his own house.

"I had married a woman considerably younger than myself, a woman as remarkable for her beauty as for her romantic yet singular temperament which she had inherited from her Spanish forebears. It was the old story, and when at long last I awoke to the dreadful truth it was also to the knowledge that only one thing remained for me in life—vengeance. Vengeance against this man who had disgraced my name and abused the honour of my house.

"On the night in question, Lothian and I sat late over our wine in this very room. I had contrived to drug his port and before the effects of the narcotic could deaden his senses I told him of my discovery and that death alone could wipe out the score. He sneered back at me that in killing him I would merely put myself on the scaffold and expose my wife's shame to the world. When I explained my plan, the sneer was gone from his face and the terror of death was freezing in his black heart. The rest you know. As the drug deprived him of his senses, I changed clothes with him, bound his hands with a sash torn from the door-curtain and carried him across the courtyard to the museum, to the virgin guillotine which had been built for another's infamy.

"When it was over, I summoned Stephen and told him the truth. The old man never hesitated in his loyalty to his wretched master. Together we buried the head in the family vault and then, seizing a mare from the stable, he rode it across the moor to convey an impression of flight and finally left it concealed in a lonely farm owned by his sister. All that remained was for me to disappear.

"Arnsworth, like many mansions belonging to families that had been Catholic in the olden times, possessed a priest's hole. There I have lain concealed, emerging only at night into the library to lay my final instructions upon my faithful servant."

"Thereby confirming my suspicion as to your proximity," interposed Holmes, "by leaving no fewer than five smears of Turkish tobacco ash upon the rugs. But what was your ultimate intention?"

"In taking vengeance for the greatest wrong which one man can do to another, I had successfully protected our name from the shame of the scaffold. I could rely on Stephen's loyalty. As for my wife, though she knew the truth she could not betray me without announcing to the world her own infidelity. Life held nothing more for me. I determined therefore to allow myself a day or two in which to get my affairs in order and then to die by my own hand. I assure you that your discovery of my hiding-place has advanced the event by only an hour or so. I had left a letter for Stephen, begging him as his final devoir that he would bury my body secretly in the vaults of my ancestors.

"There, gentlemen, is my story. I am the last of the old line and it lies with you whether or not it shall go out in dishonour."

Sherlock Holmes laid a hand upon his.

"It is perhaps as well that it has been pointed out to us already that my friend Watson and I are here in an entirely private capacity," said he quietly. "I am about to summon Stephen, for I cannot help feeling that you would be more comfortable if he carried this chair into the priest's hole and closed the sliding panel after you."

We had to bend our heads to catch Lord Jocelyn's response.

"Then a higher tribunal will judge my crime," he whispered faintly, "and the tomb shall devour my secret. Farewell, and may a dying man's blessing rest upon you."

Our journey back to London was both chilly and depressing. With nightfall, the snow had recommenced and Holmes was in his least communicative mood, staring out of the window at the scattered lights of villages and farm-houses that periodically flitted past in the darkness.

"The old year is nodding to its fall," he remarked

suddenly, "and in the hearts of all these kindly, simple folk awaiting the midnight chimes dwells the perennial anticipation that what is to come will be better than what has been. Hope, however ingenuous and disproven by past experience, remains the one supreme panacea for all the knocks and bruises which life metes out to us." He leaned back and began to stuff his pipe with shag.

"Should you eventually write an account of this curious affair in Derbyshire," he went on, "I would suggest that a suitable title would be 'the Red Widow'."

"Knowing your unreasonable aversion to women, Holmes, I am surprised that you noticed the colour of her hair."

"I refer, Watson, to the popular sobriquet for a guillotine in the days of the French Revolution," he said severely.

The hour was late when, at last, we reached our old lodgings in Baker Street where Holmes, after poking up the fire, lost not a moment in donning his mouse-coloured dressing-gown.

"It is approaching midnight," I observed, "and as I would wish to be with my wife when this year of 1887 draws to its close, I must be on my way. Let me wish you a happy New Year, my dear fellow."

"I heartily reciprocate your good wishes, Watson," he replied. "Pray bear my greetings to your wife and my apologies for your temporary absence."

I had reached the deserted street and, pausing for a moment to raise my collar against the swirl of the snow-flakes, I was about to set out on my walk when my attention was arrested by the strains of a violin. Involuntarily, I raised my eyes to the window of our old sitting-room and there, sharply outlined against the lamplit blind, was the shadow of Sherlock Holmes. I could see that keen, hawk-like profile which I knew so well, the slight stoop of his shoulders as he bent over his fiddle, the rise and fall of the bow-tip. But surely this was no dreamy Italian air, no complicated improvisation of his own creation, that drifted down to me through the stillness of that bleak winter's night.

> Should auld acquaintance be forgot
> And never brought to min'?
> Should auld acquaintance be forgot
> And days o' auld lang syne.

A snow-flake must have drifted into my eyes for, as I turned away, the gas-lamps glimmering down the desolate expanse of Baker Street seemed strangely blurred.

My task is done. My note-books have been replaced in the black tin deed-box where they have been kept in recent years and, for the last time, I have dipped my pen in the ink-well.

Through the window that overlooks the modest lawn of our farm-house, I can see Sherlock Holmes strolling among his beehives. His hair is quite white, but his long, thin form is as wiry and energetic as ever, and there is a touch of healthy colour in his cheeks, placed there by Mother Nature and her clover-laden breezes that carry the scent of the sea amid these gentle Sussex Downs.

Our lives are drawing towards eventide and old faces and old scenes are gone forever. And yet, as I lean back in my chair and close my eyes, for a while the past rises up to obscure the present and I see before me the yellow fogs of Baker Street and I hear once more the voice of the best and wisest man whom I have ever known.

"Come, Watson, the game's afoot!"

—:—

In the case of the Darlington Substitution Scandal it was of use to me, and also in the Arnsworth Castle business.
　　　　　　　　FROM "A SCANDAL IN BOHEMIA"